MW01134700

Mark Tufo

Visit us at marktufo.com
http://www.facebook.com/pages/Mark-Tufo/133954330009843
http://zombiefallout.blogspot.com/
http://twitter.com/#!/ZombieFallout

Cover Art by Shaed Studios, shaedstudios.com

Dedications

I want to dedicate this book to my wife without whose encouragement this would have remained a file on my computer. She is the light that shines my path and for that I will be eternally grateful.

I also need to send out an honorable mention to my brother, no matter what he may say to the contrary the sickest thing you will read in this book came from his festering mind.

I would like to take a second to also add Mo Happy into my dedications. She has taken her considerable talent and helped to soften and polish the many rough edges that this book used to possess.

To all the brave men and women, that are currently on active duty or who have ever served in the armed forces, police or fire department! I salute you all my brothers and sisters in arms!

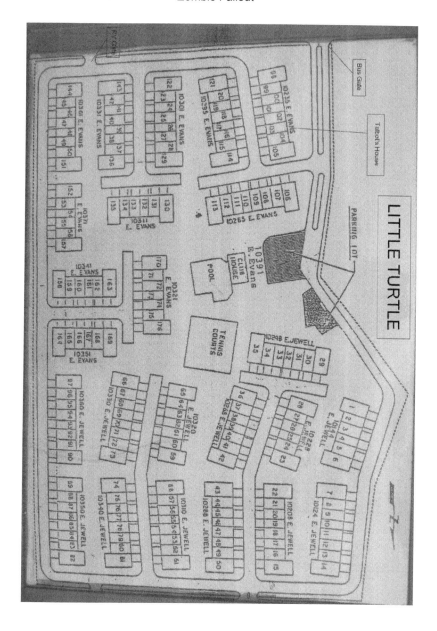

Prologue

Late Fall – 2010

Reuters – Estimates say that nearly three thousand people nationwide and fifteen thousand people worldwide have died of the H1N1 virus (otherwise known as Swine flu). Nearly eighty thousand cases have been confirmed in hospitals and clinics across the United States and the world, the World Health Organization reported. The influenza pandemic of 2010, while not nearly as prolific as the one that raged in 1918, still has citizens around the world in a near state of panic.

New York Post (Headlines October 31st) – Beware! Children Carry Germs! – Halloween Canceled!

New York Times – (Headlines November 3rd) – Swine flu claims latest victim – Vice President surrounded by family and friends at the end.

Boston Globe – (Headlines November 28th) – Swine Flu Vaccinations Coming!

Boston Herald – (Headlines December 6th) – Shots in Short Supply – Lines Long!

National Enquirer – (Headlines December 7th) – The Dead Walk!

There would be no more headlines.
It started in a lab at the CDC (Center for Disease Control). Virologists were so relieved to finally have an effective vaccination against the virulent swine flu. Pressure to come up with something quickly had come from the highest office in the land. In an attempt at speed, the virologists had made two mistakes. First they used a live

virus, and second, they didn't properly test for side effects. Within days, hundreds of thousands of vaccinations shipped across the U.S. and the world. People lined up for the shots like they were waiting in line for concert tickets. Fights broke out in drugstores as fearful throngs tried their best to get one of the limited shots. Within days the CDC knew something was wrong. Between four and seven hours of receiving the shot roughly 95 percent succumbed to the active H1N1 virus in the vaccination. More unfortunate than the death of the infected was the added side effect of reanimation. It would be a decade before scientists were able to ascertain how that happened. The panic that followed couldn't be measured. Loved ones did what loved ones always do. They tried to comfort their kids or their spouses or their siblings, but what came back was not human, not even remotely. Those people that survived their first encounter with these monstrosities usually did not come through unscathed. If bitten they had fewer than twenty-four hours of humanity left; the clock was ticking. During the first few hysteria ridden days of The Coming as it has become known, many thought the virus was airborne. Luckily that was not the case or nobody would have survived. It was a dark time in human history; we may never be able to pull ourselves out of the ashes.

CHAPTER 1 – Dec 8th, Denver, CO – 7:02 p.m.

 **Journal Entry - 1**

This wasn't supposed to be how it began...dammit! I had just turned the shower on and was preparing to scrub the dirt and grime away that I had amassed during the day on-the-job. I worked for the highway department fixing potholes. At one time in my life I was what you would consider a white-collar worker. I was a Human Resources Generalist for a Fortune 500 company. To put it delicately, I made bank. And then President Bush saw fit to end my salad days. Was it really his fault? I don't know, but he was an easy scapegoat. After the unemployment benefits petered out and still with no hot prospects, I took a city job. It was dirty, backbreaking work and I made less than when I was collecting unemployment, go figure. I made more sitting on my ass playing the Wii. But at least it was honest work. Never once in the three months that I had been working there did I wake up in the middle of the night in a cold sweat and stress out about having not filled in a hole on Havana Avenue. There were benefits to blue-collar work, lack of stress being one of them.

But I digress. So there I was, sticking my hand into the shower to see if it was the right temperature. I had even begun to spread some body wash on myself in preparation for the invigorating feeling of being clean. (Yeah BODYWASH, you got a problem with that?) I have two pet peeves in life. Well shit, if I'm being honest I probably have about seventeen but who's counting? In particular two come to mind, and I'll explain. The first is being dirty. I just hate feeling dirt and grime around my neck. I hate the way my shirt collar will stick just a little bit. It irritates the living crap out of me. The second pet peeve is feeling dried soap on my body. I don't know if any of you have ever been to New Orleans. The water is 'soft' or 'hard,' I don't know which. I always get the two mixed up. Anyway, the water just won't wash the soap off of you, so you walk around all day with this invisible film on you. Everything's sticky. Your clothes stick to your body, shit, your own body sticks to you. Just bend your arm, you can barely straighten it back up. So you walk around all day like a scarecrow with a stick up its ass. Yeah I know, I know!! My wife tells me all the time I have problems! Shit, where was I? Yeah, so there I am about to hop in the shower when I hear my wife scream this bloodcurdling shriek. Now you've got to know my wife, she wouldn't scream if I fell down the stairs and broke my arm. Hell, she'd probably call me a klutz and get me into the car for the ride to the emergency room, all the while calling the kids to tell them Dad hurt himself again. She's just not that into histrionics. So when I heard the scream I knew something bad was up. I stared longingly at the shower I was foregoing as I grabbed a towel and headed downstairs.

"What the fuck...." I yelled, but the rest of my expletive sentence died on my lips as I saw the terror in my 15-year-old son's face. Nothing scares Travis, not even me, and I'm a former Marine. Hell, just last week I watched him tear a phone book in half and not of some little town in Nebraska either. The kid was starting middle linebacker on his freshman team. And he was scaring the hell out of the starter on the JV team. The boy didn't care who was coming after him, or who he was going after. Well I guess that's a lie, they have to be living.

He never looked up when I came down the stairs. "Mom, lock the door!" he yelled. "LOCK IT!" he screamed again.

"I can't figure out the lock!" my wife yelled back.

I didn't know whether I should laugh or be worried. To be honest it was a funny scene. My wife frantically trying to lock the security door with no luck while my linebacker son, who normally towers over his mother, was cowering behind her. I couldn't see out the door from my vantage point. When the front door is open it blocks off the landing, so I rushed to push it closed, forcing my wife and son away from the security door. I had no sooner shut the heavy gauge steel front door when I heard the glass pane in the security door shatter. (We had to move to a townhome in a less than desirable neighborhood after I lost my job, and security was a big issue. We even had bars across all the lower windows, THANK GOD!

I was a millisecond away from opening the door and severely chewing the ass off some neighborhood punk who was going to cost me a hundred dollars to repair the glass.

"NO!" my wife and son yelled in unison. My wife slammed up against the door to reiterate her point.

"What the hell is going on?!" My adrenaline was pumping. My pet peeves were throbbing, all seventeen of them.

"Look out the peephole," my wife whispered.

I put my eye to the hole expecting to see some little shit gang-bangers out there tearing things up. What I saw was a tongue.

"I see a tongue! Some asshole is licking my peephole," I said, then I laughed a little bit. That sounded a little gross even to me.

My wife didn't see the humor, her face still hadn't regained her color and my son looked like he was starting to hyperventilate.

My wife told me to look out the window but she made no move to look with me. I'm not the brightest bulb on the string but even *I* knew at this point something was really messed up. I put on my best male bravado and stepped over to the window. I rolled up the shade and to this day I don't know how it happened but I simultaneously felt my stomach lurch into my throat and my balls fill in the abandoned spot my belly left behind. There had to have been at least a couple of dozen dead people milling about our communal lawn. Okay, so they weren't dead in the traditional way, they were still moving, but they were dead all the same.

My quasi-nightmare dream had come true. ZOMBIES were afoot. Now, I know this is a sick fantasy so bear with me. I had always wished for this. I had watched nearly every zombie movie, from the early Dawn of the Dead, with the slow shuffling brain eaters, to the newer 28 Days Later flicks with the fast, semi- intelligent brain eaters. Hell, I even liked the films that made fun of the style, like Shaun of the Dead and Boy Eats Girl. If it involved a zombie I was game.

Now back to the slightly insane part of my fantasy. I guess if you get right down to the guts of it, no pun intended, it would be a way to escape the responsibilities (and boredom) of everyday life. Forget the 9 to 5 grind, the mortgage and clothes shopping, it would just become all about survival of the fittest. I had been planning for this day for almost twenty-five years of my life. I know, pathetic, right? I had a gun safe full of multiple caliber rifles and pistols. I told my wife it was for hunting. I've never even BEEN hunting. Either she was REALLY gullible or she was just turning the other cheek. We all have our own crosses to bear. I'll be honest though, my fantasy involved more the slower, shuffling zombies than the ultra-fast Resident Evil kind. Like it or not, it appeared that IT had finally happened. I closed the blinds as fast as I could, hoping that I didn't attract any undue attention. My brain was in overdrive.

"Tracy! I yelled a little louder than I meant to. I wrestled with my emotions and tried to calm my flittering heart. "Turn on the TV please."

She was still in a little bit of shock. "Talbot (our family name), this is no time for ESPN," she responded waspishly.

"You know, I *would* like to know how the Giants did tonight, but I was hoping for the news," I answered sarcastically.

"Oh," was all she could muster as the thin film of terror began to peel away from her vision.

"Travis." He didn't move. "Travis!" I said a little louder.

He finally broke away from his mother's back, confusion and fear still warring for control over his features.

"Go look out the back window, if our deck is clear I want you to make sure the back gate is locked." Now before you go getting all out of sorts at me, our backyard is about as big as most people's master bathrooms. The kid would be perfectly safe as long as the gate was still closed and our yard hadn't yet been breached.

But still Travis looked at me with pleading eyes, not believing that his own father would put him back in harm's way.

"Oh for fuck's sake! I'll do it!" I sighed disgustedly. The relaxation on his face was clearly perceptible. I should take it easy on the kid, he was shaken up, and I was going to need his help before this was all over with. I peered out the back, through our vulnerable French doors. We hadn't been able to afford security bars for them yet. "Oh crap," I muttered, I could see the gate was open. 'Nothing to it but to do it right? If I die in a towel I'm gonna be pissed though.' I was able to tell in less than a heartbeat that our postage stamp sized back deck didn't have any unfriendlies on it. But what I wasn't able to discover from my present vantage point was if anything (or anyone) was on the other side of the gate. It was a full picket gate and did not afford me the luxury of seeing through to the other side. I opened one of the French doors and immediately wished I hadn't. The smell was beyond putrid; it smelled like sour milk mixed with a hint of steaming broccoli (which I hate) and a healthy dose of shit all stirred in for the fun of it.

The walking dead weren't in my backyard but they were close. If they came through the gate now, this was going to be a short novella. My towel caught on the next-to-useless excuse for a lock on the door. I didn't even stop to grab it. Somehow it seemed more noble to die naked like a savage than with a terry cloth towel around my waist. I moved as quickly as I dared, when it happened! I felt something warm and squishy give way under my right foot. My first thought was BRAINS but then the unmistakable smell of fresh dog shit wafted up to my nostrils. I had to vigorously defend against the revulsion that welled up in me. I so wanted to vomit but I pushed on. I was two steps away from the gate when I heard the telltale shuffling. Did the smell of the shit draw them or were they already close? I threw myself against the gate, quashing down my rising panic, frantically trying to drive the lock home.

You know when you see this crap in the movies, you are always like, "Oh come on, just lock the gate, how effen hard can it be?" Well I'll tell you. When your heart is going like a trip-hammer and your arms are shaking like you're on ground zero on the San Andreas Fault during The Big One, it's unbelievably hard. I felt an impact as something or somebody pushed against the gate from the other side. It wasn't a concerted effort, which was a good thing; I might have abandoned ship and headed screaming for the house. It was one good push that sent the gate about six inches my way. I pushed back so hard that I almost pushed the gate through the backstop, which obviously would have caused its own set of problems. I was able to drive the bolt home, but I didn't hang around long to revel in my victory.

"Talbot, get in here!" my wife bawled.

'MAN,' I said to myself, doesn't she realize I almost died out here? Yeah, I was being a little melodramatic but I think I had an appropriate excuse. I was about to ask her "what," when she pointed to the television. The picture was horrible. I knew I shouldn't have switched from cable to satellite. Why was I getting lost in the details when the situation was so serious? Maybe it was my way of coping, who knows. I tried to minor in psychology in college but couldn't stand it. The newscaster looked like she had been dragged out of bed to do the report. She probably had been.

"...By all accounts it appears the threat ('OH for God sake's lady! Call it like it is, a spade is a spade already') is overwhelming our ground troops! Estimates have it that nearly a third of our country is already in enemy hands and spreading fast. Do not let one of the infected scratch or bite you. In a matter of hours the virus will kill and then reanimate you. If you or someone you know becomes infected the only way to stop them is to destroy the brain. Do not approach them. Do not try to reason with them. The worst is yet to come," she continued. "It also seems the pathogen is airborne!" (My heart skipped!) "Even if someone were to die of means other than direct contact with the infected, they also will become reanimated within a few hours of their death."

"What does that mean?" my wife asked. I knew she knew the answer but she was dealing with her shock in the only manner she knew how…denial.

"It means we're in a lot of trouble," I answered solemnly.

"What the hell is that smell?" she snapped, as she also snapped out of her stupor. She was looking directly at the source of the stink. I wanted to blame it on the zombies but I had Henry's crap halfway up my ankle. Henry was our English bulldog and I loved him to death. Before this I would have even said his shit didn't stink, but I can now tell you that is a lie. Gotta love English bullies, the world was going to hell in a hurry and he hadn't even left the comfort of his dog bed yet to see what was happening.

My son Travis still seemed fogged over so I wanted to give him something to do to keep his mind and body occupied.

"Travis, go load the guns," I said.

"Which ones?" he countered.

My heart leaped when I realized he was rebounding. "All of them," was my reply. Just as quickly as my feeling of elation rose, the spirit of dread brought me crashing back. "Where's Justin?" I asked my wife. Justin is my middle child. He's 19 and had recently moved home after a brief stint living with his sister up in the town of Breckenridge.

He's a good kid with a huge heart. He doesn't always prioritize his life correctly, but then again how many teenagers do? I needed him here, not only because he's our kid and I wanted to make sure he was safe, but he's a hell of a shot and I needed the third man of our fire team present and accounted for. Preparing like I had been for the aforementioned zombie invasion entailed taking my two boys to the shooting range as often as possible. I made sure that they were well versed in the ins and outs of handling firearms correctly, no matter the caliber. They could shoot everything from my illegal (shhh) fully automatic M-16 to my small cannon (my 30 aught 6) to the various .22 caliber rifles and pistols I owned. I needed my flank men!

My wife's face dropped; the fear in her eyes made her forget the rancid excrement I was leaving on her carpet. The thump against the front door steeled her resolve. She moved back from the abyss she was heading toward.

"He's at work," she answered with a sob. Work was Wal-Mart, and it was exactly 3.7 miles from our house. I knew because on most days I drove his ass to and from. He didn't have his license yet, refer back to the part about his prioritizing skills.

"Travis, how's it coming with the guns?" I hollered up the stairs.

"Almost done, Dad," came his reply.

The front door shuddered again, but it wasn't going to give anytime soon. I slipped the dead bolt in place anyway. "I'm going to get some clothes on." I grabbed my wife's shoulders and swung her towards me so she was staring at me. "We're going to get him," I added reassuringly.

She nodded in agreement and muttered the same words she said on our wedding day as part of her vows: "Uh huh."

"Hon." I held her firm. "Get some food together." She looked at me questioningly. "We're going to get Justin and then, I hope, come back home. But I want to be prepared. Go get the boxes of MRE's." (The military had developed these Meals Ready to Eat; they taste like dirt but all the caloric intake one needs to fend off the undead. Or does the word 'undead' refer to vampires? Ok, ok, so the zombies would be the 'living' dead, is that better?) "Hon, you've got to come back from Traceyville." We sometimes joked when my wife had a blonde moment or just lapsed out of our reality into her own made up one. Life came back into her eyes, and just like that she was back. She had a mission: saving one of her offspring. Don't ever get between a mother and her young.

"I'm gonna get some clothes on and then we're going, okay?" I questioned.

I was a little worried about her but I didn't need to be; she was back and nothing was going to deter her…unless of course the damn lights went out. The TV announcer was now telling us we should stay in our homes. 'No screaming eagle shit!' I was about to tell her, when she was cut off in mid-sentence as the electricity failed. Tracy latched on to me. The sudden quiet was broken only by the occasional thumping on our front door. 'Those Girl Scouts are persistent,' kept flashing across my brain plate. Hey, nobody said I didn't go to Mikeyville occasionally.

"Dad?" Travis half-moaned from upstairs. I snapped back, if not for me then for him.

"I'm here bud, give me two seconds. I'm going to get some candles and a flashlight." I'd been meaning to get that circuit breaker fixed, but I wouldn't be going to Home Depot tonight.

"Umm, could you hurry?" he asked. I could hear the panic welling up in him.

There's something to be said about being a survivalist. Most people think we're nuts. Hell, *I* think that and I'm one of them. We're always preparing for what we think is an eventuality, Doomsday, the end of the world, invasions from another planet, when the odds say the worst that might happen is an errant tornado. But one thing about always preparing for the worst, is that, well, we're always prepared. 'Isn't that the Boy Scout motto?' I thought to myself. I hauled myself back from Mikeyville again and turned back to my troops.

"Travis, next to the left hand side of the gun safe, on the wall near the floor, you should see a small light. That's a flashlight, grab it and I'll be right up. I want to get your mother some light too."

"Got it!" he answered triumphantly. I could hear the tremor in his voice relax as I saw the beam of light cut a swath down the staircase.

I padded upstairs with my own candle. Tracy went to the basement to grab the grub. On the bed Travis had all the weapons laid out, locked and loaded. There was the M-16, then my 'elephant killer,' the 30 aught 6. Oh, stop your PETA protests, I already told you I don't hunt. I continued my visual inventory: Two shotguns, a .22 caliber rifle and a pistol, my .357 Magnum, my 9mm Glock and my .17 caliber lever action rifle. I had over a thousand rounds for each weapon and all I could think to myself was, 'I should have bought more.' Survivalism is addictive. You can never have too much ammo.

The front door thumped again. "BITCH!" I said as I grabbed the .357 off the bed. I ran downstairs and peeked through the spy hole, thankful that there was a full moon tonight, although was I? Was that the reason the dead were walking around? I didn't know. All I could see was the douche bag that was still licking my peephole, and that *still* sounded a little disturbing, even to me.

I held the Magnum up to the eye slot and pulled the trigger. The explosion was deafening in our quiet home. I looked through the now gaping hole in my front door. Sir Licks-A-Lot was dead for the second time around, and he was not going to be getting back up any time soon. He lay on his side on my front porch; the back of his head was just gone. The bullet had entered his mouth and had torn away most of his teeth and that god-awful tongue. There was some blood and a little gristle hanging out the back of his melon but that was it. His compadres did not even take note of his passing, but the noise sure got their attention. I hastily opened the front door and kicked Sir Licks' foot out of the way so I could shut the security door. Even though the glass pane was gone, the door would still afford some much needed protection against the zombies' unwelcome advances.

The noise of the gun might have the natives restless, but the sight of fresh meat stirred them into a frenzy. The shuffling turned into an ambling and the ambling turned into a slow trot, eh maybe more like a power walk. Okay, they weren't going to break any land speed records, but this wasn't the slow shuffle the visionary George R. Romero envisioned in his documentaries.

I had just kicked the zombie's dead... undead... redead? foot out of the way and shut the door, much more easily engaging the lock this time around, when the first of my uninvited guests slammed up against the metal casing; the bars were intact, but that did nothing to stop the impact of the foul odor that he gave off. I slammed the front door shut, and only then realized I had just killed my first zombie and I was buck naked.

CHAPTER 2
Journal Entry - 2

On hearing the shot, Travis had run halfway down the stairs, 12 gauge at the ready (bless his heart). "Everything all right Dad?"

"Everything's cool, finish packing up," came my measured response.

Tracy yelled from the bottom of the cellar stairs. "What's going on?"

I don't know why I didn't tell her the truth. "Accidental discharge," I answered.

"Be careful, that's what you said the night Nicole was conceived, and look how that turned out," she said plainly.

'Are you kidding me?' I thought. 'How does she remember these things? Yeah we were young when Nicole was born, and I might have been a little overeager in bed, but I'm sure I didn't say "accidental discharge" it was probably more like "uh..uh..uh.. aahhh."

I was still a little shaken from the killing. Sure it was a zombie, but at one time he was a normal air breathing, hamburger munching individual. I tried my best not to think of the person he had been, but more of the monster he had become. There would be time later to ruminate. Now, however was the time for action and Justin needed our help. I went upstairs. Travis had begun to bring the weapons and the ammo boxes downstairs. The fear was wiped off his face now that he had a purpose and protection. I grabbed the first shirt I got my hands on. It was an old Widespread Panic concert t-shirt, one of my favorites. I no sooner pulled it over my head and I froze. The feeling of the collar scraping and tugging against the dirt and dried soap on my neckline made me want to jump out of my skin. It was akin to someone dragging their fingernails down a chalkboard, with a megaphone for amplification. I almost couldn't move, I was a heartbeat and a half from saying 'FUCK IT!' and pulling the t-shirt off and hopping in the shower real quick, but I knew every second counted getting to Justin.

"Damn!" I bellowed as I pulled my arms through the sleeves, wincing every time the fabric scraped against me. If I had known what kind of shape Justin was in already, I would've just taken the shower.

As I was coming down the stairs Tracy looked up, holding her cell phone to her ear. "I can't get a hold of Nicole, the line is just busy," she stated. Nicole was our oldest child and by far and away my favorite daughter (and our only daughter). She now lived in the city of Lakewood (having lost her job in Breckenridge) with a man I hoped would eventually become part of the family, Brendon Van Hutchinson. Our family was quirky and he fit in just right. I was hoping that my wife would have been able to get through to Nicole. It would have been one less worry on my head. From where we lived, Lakewood was about eighteen miles away. I had no illusions that getting to Wal-Mart was going to be easy. Getting to Lakewood seemed a logistical nightmare.

"Hon, they live on the third floor and Brendon has a pistol and a shotgun, their place is much more defendable than ours," I said, not sure whether I was trying to make her or myself feel better. She nodded in agreement, but it didn't seem to make her feel any better. The crowd at the front of our house had swelled to about fifty. I wasn't going to sit at the window and get an accurate count. I would love to have a kegger with this many people, I'd make a fortune. Even *I* had to marvel sometimes at how my brain makes some of its connections.

"Dad, the car's packed," Travis made known.

"You got the food too?" I asked. He just looked at me in outraged disgust like any normal teenager would. "All right," I answered. "I was just making sure."

Henry had finally managed to pull himself off his bed. All the activity had aroused his curiosity level, which usually isn't all that high unless it involves a meaty bone treat.

Our townhome came with an enclosed two car garage. However, it was a detached garage, which was no big deal considering that it was on the far end of our backyard, which put it exactly ten feet away. There was still some moderate shuffling signs beyond the gate but it was nothing like the wholesale special going on in the front. I was tempted to climb on the gate and take a peek over but I couldn't see the upside to it. Henry had followed me out and he took a moment to sniff at his freshly disturbed pile, he then started sniffing my crap-covered foot. He was able to put two and two together pretty quickly. He snorted at me as if to say, 'Dad, how could you mess with my masterpiece?'

I slammed my fist up against the circuit breaker mounted to the wall of the garage. I think I hadn't fixed this yet because I always felt like Fonzi from Happy Days turning on the Jukebox. Power surged back on. Had I been more vigilant, I would have noticed that the entire complex had been in the dark and the lights coming on had more to do with Jed (who you'll meet later) than with my smooth moves. I went back in the house to shut the nonessentials off, including the now static-laced television, and headed back to the garage. I picked Henry up and placed him in the rear of my wife's Jeep Liberty with the ammo. He wasn't happy about sharing his bed; he snorted one more time before he laid down. My wife came out last, remembering to bring the eight-pack of PowerAde we had in the fridge. She stopped short at the garage door.

"Why are we taking my car?" she asked with a slight edge of attitude.

"It'll fit more stuff," I lied. Well, I mean not really, her car *is* bigger than my Jeep Wrangler, but that wasn't the only reason. I loved my car, I'd had it for a little over ten years and it was almost as cherry as the day it had rolled off the line, and I'd be damned if some brain eating, dead zombies were going to get their gooey parts all over it.

I hadn't convinced her with my half-truth; she still stood glaring at me from the doorway. "Plus Hon, mine is a stick, there's no way I can shoot and shift gears at the same time." Now that was an out and out lie, I can't tell you how many 4-wheel drive excursions I've gone on with my rifle hanging out the window. There were plenty of dead road signs to attest to my accuracy. I know she would have argued some more and eventually won, but the time it would have taken to shift everything over was precious moments more that it was going to take to get to Justin.

"Fine," she muttered. "I'll remember this." And I knew she would, she remembered stuff from when we were dating. If we were in the heat of a battle and she felt like she was in danger of losing, she would reach way back in time and pull one of those wonderful nuggets (sarcasm) out from nowhere and hurl it at me. I mean, at that point all you can do is just stare dumbfounded and say, 'Really? You're bringing that up *now*? How on God's green earth could I have known your aunt was a lesbian?'

And just like that, the tides of the battle would have shifted. I might not hear about the car until we were in a retirement home. But you can bet that if they were going to give me the better model wheelchair she was going to use this as ammunition to nix that.

She moved to push the garage door opener, when I half lunged to her. "Please don't do that," I pleaded.

"Oh right!" she answered. (God, it must be so awesome to just forget sometimes. But I wasn't going to say anything. I was already in hot water about the car.)

She got in to the shotgun seat, although Travis was already in the passenger seat behind her with the window rolled down and the shotgun hanging out, so I guess technically *he* was in the shotgun seat. I started the car before I hit the garage remote. Tracy rolled her window down.

I couldn't hold my tongue. "Really?" I asked as I

looked at her.

"What?" she replied. "It's stuffy in here, and you stink."

"Come back," I motioned dramatically. "Please come back from wherever you've gone. Both of you need to roll up your windows, at least until we get moving." I got another 'fine' out of Tracy, and Travis seemed a little pissed that I was taking his fun away.

The garage door rattled open. I couldn't see anything right away because of the disparity between the brightness in the garage and the gloom that was our back alleyway, but the thud that hit our rear end as I backed out was obvious. I was a breath away from opening my door and seeing what I had hit when my neighbor smeared up against my window. It's a good thing I had Henry shit on my foot. It masked what I let go of in my pants. My neighbor from across the alleyway was a decent person in a bull-dykeish way. Don't get me wrong, I liked her immensely, I just always felt like she was sizing me up for an arm wrestling competition and I would have put my money on her. She owned a Ford pick-up truck, and wore more plaid and wife beater t-shirts than your average trailer park resident. She sported a mullet, which hadn't been seen in these parts since 1984. She also owned more tools than I did and I ran a Handyman business on the side. You get the general picture.

The thing that pressed up against my car was no longer Jo(e?). She left a trail of pus and guts all across my side of the car, and slimy green pustules burst from her cheek. I swore a maggot crawled out, but by then I had had enough. I hit the accelerator hard enough to almost put my car through her garage door on the opposite side of the causeway. The thing that I had initially hit dragged itself over to my tool shelves and began to pull itself up. I wanted to get out of the car and kill those two but more zombies began to pile into both ends of the alleyway. I had no wish to see how many I could run over before the car stalled so I hit the remote and watched the garage door begin its slow descent, only then realizing that when we got home we were going to have two zombies in our garage to welcome us back. 'Great!' (sarcasm again.)

CHAPTER 3
Journal Entry - 3

I was able to get out of the alley before the majority of the zombies could begin to block us in. I winced when I sideswiped one, not because I had hit something but because I knew from the force of the impact I had just put a dent in my wife's car. I didn't even look over towards her, but the right side of my face was melting from the glare that was directed at it. There were fewer cars on the road than I would have expected for 8 o'clock on a Thursday night, but that was more than made up for by the sheer number of zombies. Most were just milling about looking for something or should I say 'somebody' to eat. Every few hundred feet or so there would be a cluster of ten or so tearing something apart. You and I both know what they were tearing apart but luckily my brain had enough protective competence to mask over that small insignificant fact.

"Oh Jesus," my wife muttered as we passed a small cluster, just ravaging some poor soul. I can tell you right now these variants on the traditional zombies weren't just interested in the brains of their victims. I saw one of the zombies look up from his 'meal' with what appeared to be a thigh muscle hanging out of its putrid maw. "I think I'm going to be sick," Tracy continued.

"Then roll down your window. Travis you too, if anything gets too close just shoot, just make sure it's dead first," I suggested. Travis looked at me questioningly. "You know what I mean," I clarified. "Just don't kill something that's still alive." Yeah, I made about as much sense as a Yankee's fan visiting Fenway Park.

Most of the cars that were on the road weren't moving; they had been abandoned. I had to keep my speed down to avoid the cars, the zombies, and the occasional victim-to-be.

"Shouldn't we help them?" my wife asked as she pulled her head back into the car, already looking better now that she'd emptied her stomach. I motioned that she had a little something on the side of her face. She lifted her hand to remove the offending detritus.

"Uh, other side," I explained. She missed again. I wiped my face again to show her where it was.

"Forget the damn puke!" she yelled. "Shouldn't we try to help?"

"No," I mumbled.

"What? Speak up, I can't hear your altruism," she retorted acerbically.

"Listen, if we stop we become vulnerable, and we don't know if the person we would be helping is infected. We can't take that chance, we have to look out for us," I argued. I'm not sure if my claim was good enough. Was that how I felt or was I just trying to cover up my cowardice?

Yeah, I was scared out of my mind that first day. Is it that easy for you to pass judgment? We're mostly in a standoff with the zombies now, but back in the beginning when panic reigned supreme the only thing that mattered to me was me and my family. God, I just hope not in that order.

I probably would have gotten another sarcasm-laden 'fine' from my wife if not for the thunder that tore through the car. Travis had decapitated a zombie that was approaching our right side while I had slowed to avoid a nasty five or six car pile-up. I don't think that he had nearly the feelings of dread I had when I had killed the zombie at our front door. To him this was not so far removed from playing Left 4 Dead on his Xbox 360.

"Got one Dad!" he yelled triumphantly, a gleam in his eye. I muttered my congratulations but all I could think of was some old phrase I had come across in one of my English classes: 'Take heed your actions lest ye become like the enemy ye seek to destroy.'

I didn't have much time to reflect on my misgivings as I turned into the Wal-Mart parking lot. It was worse than my worst fears of how this was going to play out. Cars were strewn across the parking lot. It looked like the longest happy hour in history had just finished and the patrons were all trying to get home at the same time. What was worse than the cars were the couple of hundred zombies strolling across the parking lot. I did a quick drive by the front of the store, and I could tell that an almost equal number were inside meandering about. Well, I bet tripe was going to be scarce. This did not bode well for Justin. I was in a quandary; I just didn't know what to do. I had to look for him, even if he had become one of those things, but I didn't even know how or where to begin. It's not like I could ask one of the zombies if they had seen a zombie that matched the description of my son. Luckily, Travis solved my problem with one simple question.

"Dad, why aren't the zombies attacking us?" Travis asked. I wasn't traveling much more than 5 miles an hour, fast enough to keep any of them from catching us but not fast enough to stop one from coming towards us. It was then that we took notice of a large congregation of zombies merely standing, all of them facing towards the store with their faces (or what remained of them) all upturned. They almost looked like they were worshipping, but what do zombies worship, is there a God of the Tasty Brain? Is their Eucharist a tiny slice of dried brain matter? I know! I know! It's sacrilegious but that's what I was thinking at the time. Even the remnants of the zombies that weren't already together in this impromptu meeting seemed to be heading in that direction. Some of the zombies that were recent accident victims from the carnage in the parking lot were dragging what remained of their former host body to the flock. Every once in a while I even noticed one or two of the zombies convulsing as if they were receiving HIS or ITS word.

"What in the fu…is going on here?" I asked nobody in particular. I had not so long ago promised my kids that I was going to do all in my power to cut the vulgarity out of my everyday vocabulary. As you can tell, I still have lapses but I think I deserved a pass on this one.

"Hey Dad!" I heard (barely). Somebody had shouted the words, but I couldn't for the life of me figure out where the voice was coming from. "Hey Dad!" I heard a little louder as we approached the large throng of zombies. As I made sure to skirt around the unholy gathering, I noticed activity on top of the Wal-Mart.

"Holy shit!" I yelled as I slammed on the brakes.

"What is it?" Tracy asked with alarm in her eyes. Travis was looking around hungrily for something to shoot, thinking that we were about to come under attack.

"Look on the roof!" I said incredulously.

Tracy leaned over my lap. "It's Justin!" she said with elation . I was also happy, but the gears in my head were still turning; how were we going to get him down from there?

At least we now knew what had the zombies so enthralled. Justin and a couple of his co-workers had escaped to the roof before it was too late. One of them had grabbed a couple of pellet guns and from the looks of all the empty beer cans on the ground somebody had the presence of mind to grab some cases of Keystone Light.

So let's make sure we're clear on this: Obviously the people that managed to get to the roof knew their lives were in danger. They had the presence of mind to climb to a safe haven and even to arm themselves as best they could. So far so good, but then one of the group decided that they might need some beverages to stave off thirst, still good. That person, fearing for his life, went to the beer section, which again is admirable, everyone knows beer is the nectar of the gods. But then he grabs Keystone Light? Are you kidding me? I'd rather eat the can than drink those contents.

My curiosity was now satisfied. The convulsions some of the zombies were experiencing were caused by pellet impacts. It wasn't enough to kill them by a long shot, but I will testify to this day that it definitely had the effect of pissing them off. Zombies by definition are murderous, but I'm telling you they now had a murderous intent to them. Did they want to exact revenge? Were they even still capable of such a sophisticated mind set? Of all the zombie movies I'd seen and all the zombie books I had read, only a small percentage dealt with zombies that had feelings. I did not want the zombies in MY nightmare to have feelings. Feelings ALWAYS complicated things. I'm a guy. Guys don't want to deal with feelings.

I got as far away from the multitude as I could while still hoping that Justin would be able to hear me. "Go to the other side of the store!" I yelled for all I was worth.

Justin just shrugged his shoulders, clearly not being able to understand me.

"Go to the other side of the store!" I screamed, my throat burning from the strain.

He shrugged again helplessly.

I made over-exaggerated motions for him to move to his right. He answered with an over-exaggerated nod, the light bulb clearly going off over his head. As he began to move off, a fair percentage of the gathered zombies also peeled off, heading in the same direction. Justin noticed this quirk too. He slowly walked back to his co-workers, and the zombies returned to the fold. I watched him hand his pellet gun off to a fat bear of a kid. The pellet gun looked no bigger than a Butterfinger in his hands, and I bet he wished it were the candy bar instead. Then Justin grabbed a beer and walked back towards the center of the roof, and out of the line of sight of his devoted followers.

"Why aren't they coming after us?" Tracy asked more surprised than anything.

I had been asking myself that same question. Sure, some of the zombies looked our way occasionally, especially the ones that were closest. But they couldn't have cared less if I got on my knees and poured A-1 on the top of my head, at least I think. I'm not willing to truth check that statement.

I thought carefully before I answered. "I think they're

pissed off." That was the only thing that seemed to make sense. Before Tracy could ask for clarification, I continued. "I mean, look at them," pointing towards the zombies, "obviously the people on the roof are potential food for them, but hell, we're a lot closer. I think that pellet gun is irritating them to no end."

"Can they be mad? Do they even have emotions?" Tracy asked.

"Umm Hon, you've known about the zombies for thirty seconds longer than I have. It's just a theory. Maybe they just can't smell us over the exhaust of the car. Let's just keep the windows rolled up in the meantime." This time no one argued.

I drove around to the side of the building where I had motioned Justin to meet us. He was peering over the edge when we pulled up.

I rolled down the window. "Justin, is there a way down?" I yelled. Almost instantly, two zombies began to shuffle our way. In life they most likely were twins, albeit not like the kind you see in the Doublemint commercials. Both were more than 200 pounds, wearing midriff shirts that showed off their expanding muffin tops. Whereas the sister on the left was wearing purple spandex, her twin on the right was adorned in the much classier Daisy Duke shorts. In life this would have been a vision hopefully never to behold, but now with their purple mottled flesh and fresh puss oozing out of every orifice I nearly gagged. You have to love Wal-Mart customers. I don't know if it was the noise or the smell of a meal that had them coming my way. My guess was the promise of food. These two didn't ever look like they passed up a chance at something to eat.

"Yeah, through the sprinkler room, but that's on the far side of the store," Justin answered.

"Travis, keep an eye on the double-fat twins over there," I said nervously. I tore my glance from the approaching horrors. It was like watching a train wreck in slow motion. "You won't be able to get out the front, if you went back downstairs could you go out an emergency exit?" I yelled.

"No, those things are in the stairwell leading up here. We can hear them banging against the door," was his reply.

"Any ladders up there?" I asked.

"No but there's a ladder section over by household goods," he answered helpfully, or so at least he thought.

"Yeah that's not going to work so much," I replied, remembering the hundred or so zombies still shopping for blue-light specials. We were at an impasse.

"Dad!" Justin yelled. Travis appended the point by blasting a round through the Mossberg. Muffin top one in the spandex went down in a heap, most of her belly liquefied by the impact of the pellets. Her sister screeched, I'm not even sure that's the right adjective. It was an inhuman sound. Something only dead, taut, rigor mortis induced vocal chords could produce. Travis almost dropped the shotgun out the window. Tracy and I could only stare in frightened bewilderment. But what came next stunned me even more. Daisy Dukes Girl didn't help her fallen sister up but she waited until the other one got up of her own accord. The wound was fatal, but fatality only applies to the living. I could see what I had at first thought were maggots roiling around in and about her guts, but at an inch or so long these weren't any ordinary maggots. They were worms of some sort. And I could tell from looking at the size of Spandex Girl, these weren't tapeworms.

Those things had to be the cause of whatever was going on here, but I wasn't a biologist. I stepped out of the Jeep with my M-16 and emptied a magazine into the two women. Most of my shots didn't even hit the desired target but I only needed one round in each of their heads for the job to be done. At fifteen shots a zombie we wouldn't make it through the night. I turned the selector lever on the M-16 from 'automatic' to 'single;' my hands looked like I suffered from a severe case of palsy.

"Dad!" Justin yelled again.

I couldn't tear my eyes off the two women I'd shot. Their fat was still jiggling from their impact with the ground, or was it the worms? I turned and puked. There wasn't much to it, I hadn't had a chance to eat dinner.

"Yeah?" I answered Justin as I stood back up dragging my sleeve across my mouth. The metallic, acidic taste in my mouth did little to contain the storm brewing in my stomach.

"There's a ladder in the docking bay," Justin responded eagerly. Thank God, I had something else to think about than this macabre scene behind me.

"Is it going to be tall enough?" I asked, looking into the car to see how everyone else was doing. Travis had pulled the shotgun into the car and rolled the window back up, but he still couldn't stop from looking at the carnage a mere ten feet from the car. Tracy had lit up a cigarette. Where she found it I have no clue. She HAD quit almost six months ago.

I didn't think now was the time to berate her for the infraction. If she had another one I would have taken it right there and then, and I had never smoked.

Justin shrugged in response to my question. "They use it for maintenance around the building, it should be," he replied without much conviction. It wasn't the definitive answer I was looking for but it was what I had.

"All right, you follow us on the roof and keep a look out."

Justin pulled back from the edge in response. I got back in the car, handing the empty magazine to Travis. "Could you please hand me a loaded magazine and reload this one?" I asked him, my hand a little more under control. Now I only looked like I had Jell-O for a wrist.

I know he was only trying to help, but when Travis said "Dad, you know you should take it easy on the ammo," I almost snapped. I'd probably still be there, chewing him a new one if I had ever gotten started.

I put the Jeep in gear, mumbled something to the

effect of smart-ass kid and left it at that. Tracy was hot boxing her cigarette. If there was a Guinness record for downing a smoke, she was sure challenging that mark. I drove the Jeep to the west side of the building and around to the back. When I got to the rear of the building I was relieved and apprehensive at the same time. Relieved because there were no zombies around but apprehensive for a couple of reasons. The first reason being that the dock was bathed in darkness. I couldn't see more than two feet into the store. I don't think zombies have the ability to lay a trap but if they did this was the perfect set-up. My other concern was the overturned semi; it looked as if it had been strategically placed to entirely block off the other entrance into the docks. That meant that by car, at least, there was only one way in and one way out. It was a narrow entrance, maybe twelve feet across. A six-foot high retaining wall ran along the parking lot directly opposite the building. Running on foot was always a choice but I'd witnessed firsthand the success rate of those on the ground.

CHAPTER 4
Journal Entry - 4

"Tracy, you stay in the car," I said as I got out.

"Yeah, that won't be a problem," she answered, dark circles forming under her eyes.

If I had a chance to get to a mirror I could probably witness the same thing happening to me. My life had only been turned upside down for less than an hour and I already felt like my soul was wrung out.

"Okay," I responded. "But I meant more in the driver's seat, with the car running." Was that degree of explanation needed? I don't know but I didn't want to leave anything to chance.

"Travis, you're going to have to come with me," I let him know. He didn't seem thrilled with the prospect at all, but he knew what he had to do.

His mother however let me know how she felt. "You can't!" she yelled.

Travis rushed to my defense. "Mom, Dad needs my help."

"He can do it on his own," she retorted. "You're my baby!"

"Hon…" I started.

"You shut up!" she spat fiercely. "Travis is my baby, he's my flesh and blood!"

"And who am I!" I yelled back.

"You're just some guy I met!" she shrilled.

I physically felt like someone had swung a hammer at my stomach and connected. The feeling was that intense. I was dumbfounded. I staggered back as if the blow had been physical and not metaphorical. Right now running into the midst of the zombies seemed like a viable proposition.

Tracy watched my eyes hollow out. "I'm, I'm sorry," she cried. She knew she had gone too far.

I turned and headed to the darkness of the truck bay. It mirrored my feelings exactly. Travis got out the car. Tracy motioned to him, but thought better of making any more comments. I heard the car door shut softly behind me; my back up was on the way. I hopped up onto the loading dock and turned to lend Travis a hand up. I turned on my small flashlight attached to my rifle (back to the whole 'survivalist' aspect). It couldn't penetrate more than twenty or so feet into the murkiness, but except for the occasional upturned box, it seemed we were alone. That was a vast relief because I knew if that shotgun went off Tracy would be up here in a flash, and our only means of a hasty escape would be unmanned. Shit, the dock was huge. I should have found out in what general direction I should be heading towards. I wanted to go outside and ask Justin, but the thought of yelling back and forth, and thus ringing the dinner bell for some unwelcome guests kept me inside. There was that, and I also had the sinking feeling that time was running out. Time felt oppressive, each second that ticked off added weight to the unseen burden I was carrying.

"Dad, sweep the light back to the right, I thought I saw a glint," Travis said.

I slowly panned the flashlight to the right. I did catch a flash of light. Unfortunately, it wasn't the glint of an aluminum ladder. It was a watch, and even from this distance I could tell it was expensive. 'Oh why couldn't this be a natural disaster,' I moaned to myself. I was surrounded by flat screen TVs and Xbox 360s and some dead dude's Rolex. That brought me back quick; attached to the watch was a three-quarter eaten employee of the store, probably a manager by the looks of the watch. As we stepped closer we could clearly see the small girl child that was chewing through his head.

'Well at least he won't be coming back,' I thought irrelevantly. The light struck her in the face and she looked up immediately. Malevolence creased her young features, almost as if to say 'I'll deal with you two after I'm finished here,' and then she turned back to the task at hand.

Travis and I stopped, and he raised the Mossberg. I pushed my hand down on the barrel and shook my head no. First off, she wasn't attacking us and I didn't want the noise to bring any others, and second the thought of killing a child - even a child that had nothing of humanity left in her - just didn't sit right. But that look, it was predatory. She knew what she was doing and she was enjoying it! God help us! God help us all!

We moved further down the bay, always aware of what was happening to our right, but the steady slurping of blood and the crunch of bone and cartilage stayed constant. We reached the far end of the bay before we came up on the ladder. It was a big ladder but I didn't think it was going to telescope out to the top of the roof, which I figured to be about thirty-five feet.

"All right Trav, I'm going to grab the ladder. You're going to have to cover us," I said as I slung my M-16 over my shoulder.

The ladder made a loud clanging noise as I pulled it off its hooks. The sound nearly made me drop it. My nerves were on edge and my senses were firing on all cylinders. Travis was tense and his senses appeared heightened, but he didn't seem any worse for the wear. We slowly made our way back towards the open bay we had come in through. When we were near where I thought the little girl was, I strained my ears to hear the telltale signs of a zombie eating. It was not a delicate affair. Nothing, I heard nothing. A cold chill, no scratch that, an arctic blast crept down my spine. I knew she was closing in, and somehow she was avoiding Travis' sweeps with the flashlight. And then I felt her cold touch against the back part of my leg. I tried to scream, I'm not proud of that, but what came out was more like a strangled gurgle. There was no way I was going to be able to drop the ladder and turn around quick enough to defend myself. I waited for the pain of gnashing teeth clamping down on my calf. I looked up to Travis hoping that he had heard my gurgle for help; maybe he already had a bead on her and I could be saved the fate of being dessert for some undead tweenie. But the gods were not aligned with me. Travis wasn't even looking my way. He had the light and the shotgun pointed off to our left where the little monster was now chewing her way through what was left of the manager's spinal column. I chanced a look behind me. What I saw would have blanched my face bone white, if not for the fact that blood was now flowing into my face. Relief and embarrassment commingled as I pulled the ladder's guide wire back up and wrapped it around one of the rungs.

"Dad, you all right back there?" Travis asked as his gun never wavered off the scene he was looking at.

"Ugh..." I started off brightly. "Yep." I wanted to add more, but a large chunk of self-loathing was stuck in my throat.

We were close to exiting when Tracy hit the horn. It wasn't a long blast, but it scared the crap out of me. This time I dropped the ladder, which rattled Travis. His gun fired, taking out a piece of meat still left on Mr. Department Manager who would never get the chance to realize his dream of mediocrity and middle management. Some of the shots peppered the little girl in the face. The pellets sank into the soft flesh of her face. Her left cheek sloughed off from the assault exposing tiny baby teeth stained red and encrusted with the gore of her meal. She rose to meet this new threat, and the sight left a lasting mark on me that still haunts most of my nights. In her right hand she dragged what appeared to be her dolly, a remnant from her past life. Did she just not have the mental capacity to let go of the dregs from her previous existence? Was there somewhere deep down in the nether-lands of her pillaged soul, some last hold out? I wanted to know.

Travis didn't. He blew her head off. Her small body, adorned in possibly her favorite blue dress, stood for perhaps a heartbeat longer before she crumpled to the floor atop her last meal, still clutching the doll. For all intents and purposes, if you took the blood away it looked like a happy embrace between a father and his daughter. I launched something from my stomach. What it was I'll never know because I was empty. It wouldn't have surprised me in the least if I had hacked up a kidney.

Travis looked a little green around the gills but he wasn't suffering the effects nearly as bad as I was. I stood back up, grabbed the ladder and headed out into the night. There was nothing more in there I EVER wanted to see again. I stepped down from the loading bay. The night seemed blindingly bright after the darkness we had just left, both literally and figuratively. Travis motioned with his gun to indicate what Tracy had beeped her horn about. Coming around the corner was a lone zombie. He was still a hundred yards away and didn't seem like a huge threat at the moment, but I was getting the sneaky suspicion this was not going to end well. Tracy was gesturing wildly in the car.

"I know, we see it too," I stage whispered to her. It amazed me that I was already starting to call them 'ITS' instead of 'THEMS.' "It" seemed such an impersonal word to describe what was once a human, but it was much easier this way.

I was extending the ladder out and preparing to stand it up when I heard a voice from above. No, unfortunately it wasn't THAT voice from above.

"Dad!" Justin said, a little more loudly than I would have hoped. I looked up to acknowledge him. "We're about to have some company," he finished.

"Yeah, we saw it," I replied as I struggled to get the ladder in position.

"Yeah, no," came his cryptic reply. "I mean there's about a dozen of them heading this way."

A sweat broke out on my forehead and it was only partially because of the exertion. "How much time?" I grunted. The ladder was in place and it was a good ten feet short from the top.

"A couple of minutes at the most," he riposted.

"Oh great! This just gets better and better!" was my response. Things just were not going as planned. And then I full out laughed. Maybe I was close to the edge, I don't know, but it was a laugh I could have lost myself in. Who the hell PLANS for this! I finished with my semi-hysterical outbreak, thankful for the relief it spawned.

"Dad? You all right?" Justin asked.

"I'm as good as I'm going to get," I retorted. "Get somebody, preferably two people to come and help you."

He looked at me quizzically.

"They are going to have to lower you over the edge and you're going to have to drop to the ladder."

"No fu..." he started. "I mean NO way, that's gotta be a twenty foot drop to the ladder, I'll never make it."

"It's twelve feet max," I told him. "You'll be fine."

"I don't know about this," He hedged.

"Justin, we don't have time to argue, you either get on the ladder within the next minute or so or we have to leave." I forced the issue.

I could see Justin mentally began to weigh his choices. I wasn't prepared to let him prioritize.

"Justin," I started. "So I know you have beer and a pellet gun plus you have a safe haven." I could see him nodding, he was thinking the same thing. Then I started with the negatives. "How much food do you have?" I asked.

"Food?" was his response.

"Yeah you know, the stuff you put in your mouth, chew and swallow," I answered. I was being on the dickish side but I didn't have time for diplomacy, the first zombie was within twenty yards and his teammates were now rounding the bend.

"Well Tommy has a box of ring dings and Bill has a power bar or two, and..." he reasoned.

'Are you kidding me?' I screamed in my brain. 'Calm down, breathe, count to ten, scratch that, better make it five.

One, two, three… .'

"Get some help now!" I demanded. "That FOOD won't last the night. As for your safe haven, do you have any blankets or tents or stoves or ANYTHING that will keep you warm?"

He just kept looking at me like I was nuts.

"Justin, you guys won't make it two nights up there; if you don't die of the elements, you'll die of dehydration in at most four days."

"We have beer!" he said triumphantly.

"How long is your 30-pack going to last you? Through the night maybe," I finished cynically.

"Dad, I've got to think about this, that's a huge drop," he responded.

"Okay fine, I'll give you until…" I pulled up my sleeve to look at my nonexistent watch. "NOW! Get your ass down here."

He still hesitated. If for a second I thought I could bridge the gap from the ladder to the roof, I would have done it, just so I could grab him by the ear and get him.

"Oh, shit," Justin moaned, as he moved to align himself with the ladder and begin down.

"Get your friends to help you!" I yelled up. He was finally doing what I wanted him to do, just not in the manner in which I wanted it done; isn't that about typical for teenagers.

"Um too late for that Dad," he added as his legs swung over the edge. "They just broke through the door."

I didn't need any more clarification than that. "Give me a second while I secure the ladder."

Justin let go of the roof just as I was attempting to secure the ladder's footholds. Somewhere in my semi-panicked mode I heard distant screams, and then it sounded like the world was blowing up. Justin fell and entirely missed the first two rungs. The ladder clanged and swayed violently as he caught himself on the third rung, his feet swinging wildly. He almost lost his tentative grip on the ladder when the Mossberg let go with a three-round burst, which was impressive considering it was a pump action shotgun. The closest zombie lay in a heap; what was left of him wouldn't feed a runway model. His backup, however, had swelled to around twenty, the first group was about sixty yards away and the second group had just come around the corner. We were about to have one humdinger of a get together. Justin was halfway down the ladder when I swung my attention back to him. I looked past him to notice the fat kid with the Butterfinger gun peering cautiously over the edge. I wanted to get Justin down and just plain haul ass out of here. But I couldn't do it.

"Wait till Justin gets off the ladder, then swing your legs down. We'll hold it steady," I yelled. Justin looked up to see who I was talking to.

"Tommy!" Justin yelled. "You can do it."

"They're up here Justin, they just killed Bill. I...I guess that means we won't have to come in to work tomorrow," Tommy said. His eyes had that hollowed out look I was growing to know so well.

Justin had finally hit terra firma.

"Justin, you've got thirty seconds to convince your fat friend to get his ass down here or we're leaving," I whispered harshly.

Tracy beeped the horn again.

I turned viciously. "Do you think that's helping?" I barked. She wanted out and so did I, but I wasn't leaving the big kid unless I had to, although I think we had passed that point a minute ago.

"Tommy!" Justin called. "Come on man, there's no time to figure it out, they're up there, let's go."

Bill's distant screams finally subsided, and I don't think it was because he got away. That steeled Tommy's resolve. He began to swing his huge bulk over the edge, still gripping the pellet gun. Images of the little girl clutching her doll welled up inside me.

"Let go of the pellet gun, Tommy!" I snapped, more

for me than him in all likelihood. "It isn't going to do you any good down here and you're going to need both hands to hold onto the ladder."

I didn't think anybody but the man of steel himself was going to be able to stop that bulk once it got in motion. The more I began to think it through the less I liked the idea. The odds were good that Justin and I were about to become human pancakes, sandwiched under the enormous bulk of Tommy. I was about to grab Justin and have him abandon his post, no sense in both of us dying in this vain attempt, when the ladder vibrated slightly. I looked up. Tommy had grabbed the first rung and was beginning his descent. 'Holy Crap' was all I could mutter. My amazement was short-lived however. The zombies that broke through the door on the roof were looking over the edge. I wanted to shout at them triumphantly that they had lost, 'no more dinner for you, nyah nyah nyah,' when the first of them simply walked off the roof, followed by a second and a third and then a half dozen. The snapping of multiple bones ricocheted off the Wal-Mart wall, sounding like small arms fire. It was deafening. It was sickening.

Tommy made it down the ladder and the three of us just stared at the horror that was unfolding in front of us. Most of the zombies had landed on legs that were now shattered beyond any use. Some had ended in a swan dive, never to rise again. The ones with the shattered legs and spinal columns started to pull themselves along with their arms or used their chins on the ground in a vain attempt to move. Whatever locomotion was available to them they used to try to get to us. It was like watching the 'Terminator.' Sadly, we were the Sarah Connors in this remake. Tracy's horn blared again. Travis had finished reloading and was firing again. Our reverie broken, we ran for the car.

"Get in!" I yelled, as if anyone needed the instruction.

Tracy scooted over so I could drive. Tommy's enormous bulk ended up on the hump seat in the back; he looked like a huge bowling ball, and my boys unhappily looked like two bowling pins pushed up against the windows.

"Sorry," Tommy said as he tried his best to reduce the crushing effect of his immensity.

We were staring down thirty or so advancing zombies and had fifteen or so mostly disabled zombies to our rear. Tommy extended his ring-ding glazed hand to me.

"I'm Tommy," he said with a beaming smile, mostly white teeth except for the chocolate stuck up on his gum line.

I sent my hand back, this wasn't the time but it was a conditioned response and besides I didn't see any reason to dispense with civility. "I'm Dad...I mean Mr. Tal...oh forget it, you can just call me Mike," I said.

"Mr. Tal, what's that smell?" Tommy said as he still gripped my hand. I pulled back and grunted.

"Dad stepped in Henry crap!" Travis smiled.

"Great, just great," I mumbled as I put the car in gear and gunned the engine.

I know Jeeps are tough, but how many bodies can I hit before I do irreparable damage? I'm sure the Chrysler Corporation never planned for this. I did my best to go around the edges of the oncoming horde, but with only twelve feet of width I only had so many options. Tracy ducked down under the dash as best she could. I could tell she was glaring at me in response to the damage I was about to inflict on her car. She'd have to wait, I could only deal with one deadly problem at a time.

Justin yelled, "Look out Dad, I think you're going to hit them!"

I honestly wanted to stop the car and thank Captain Obvious. If he hadn't forewarned me, I might just have gone and hit the zombies without ever realizing I was going to.

The impact was more jarring than I think any of us were prepared for. I didn't know a human body would have that much effect on a two-ton SUV. I guess it was because it was deadweight, and yes, even in my head I got the rim shot sound effect. By the time I'd plowed through the fourth or fifth zombie it looked like we had gone through a car wash designed by Stephen King. Pieces of bone, flesh and congealed blood littered the hood and the windshield. At some point in this zombie smash up derby I had the wherewithal to turn on the windshield wipers and the washers. Even *I* was impressed with myself until Tracy let the wind out of my sails; I saw her hand pulling back into the relative safety under the dashboard.

I was feeling good that we would make it out of the parking lot, but I didn't think Tracy's car was going to make it much further than that. The radiator was shot, and steam was pouring out of the front of the car. I could hear the serpentine belt whining as it was being shredded against some foreign object. The car was bucking wildly like we were on an unbroken horse. It felt like either the engine or the transmission was about to drop onto the ground. In all likelihood it was going to be both. But even at the blistering fifteen mph that I was making I was still putting distance between ourselves and the pack that followed. The car made it halfway home before it just plain died.

CHAPTER 5
Journal Entry - 5

Any semblance of a chance I thought I had of getting to Nicole's had vanished. After the damage from the second or third zombie hit, and with the addition of Tommy to our load, I didn't know how we would have fit her and Brendon in the car. But still my heart sank. Sure I'd saved one of my kids, but one was still out there. And to top it off I wasn't completely sure about the saving part. We were a good mile and a half away from sanctuary and there were still a bunch of zombies on the loose. I tried the ignition a couple of times with no success. I would have kept at it if it weren't for the fact that the sound would be attracting some undesirables and we had to leave. We could hear sirens and some small arms fire off in the distance, even some small explosions. Homemade bombs, I mused, I should have thought of that. I got out of the car quickly. Motioning everyone else to do the same, I opened the trunk to a yawning and stretching Henry.

"Damn it," I said in frustration.

We had more guns, food and ammo than we were going to be able to carry. Add that to the fact I would have to lug Henry because he couldn't walk more than two hundred yards before he would begin panting like a sex offender at a cheerleader convention. I know to everyone else he's just a dog, and right now it's survival of the fittest, but I would no sooner leave him to die than I would one of my kids. Tommy had finally gotten his immeasurable bulk out of the car to look in the trunk.

"What's the matter Mr. T?" he asked with a huge grin, the smile broadening when he noticed the boxes labeled MRE's.

I wanted to yell at him but he just seemed so damn

happy, so instead I answered him dejectedly. "Well Tommy, we just have too much stuff to carry plus the dog, and I have to figure out what to leave behind."

Leaving most of the ammo seemed the logical thing to do. It was by far the heaviest; no food meant starvation. We could leave the 2.5 gallon water jug too. I figured we'd still be able to get water through the pipes at least for a little while longer. So it was Henry, the firearms, whatever ammo we could carry in our pockets and the MRE's.

"Could you take the slings off the rifles, Mr. T?" Tommy said, his infectious grin never leaving his face.

I should have known how strong the kid was just by the way he caught his bulk on the ladder. I shook my head in disbelief as we walked away from the car. He had fashioned a couple of crude carrying devices with the slings. He had the three boxes of MRE's strapped to his back, off to his sides he hefted the four cases of ammo, and in his arms lay a slumbering Henry. He probably could have carried me too and not even have lost a step.

It would have been a beautiful fall night; the crispness in the air always harkened me back to my youth and the start of school. But the smell, the fetid odor of the dead and the living dead blended together to create one humongous wave of putrid stink. It pervaded everything. Only Tommy seemed to be immune as he walked on, seemingly unencumbered by the undead bouquet. The first mile or so went by unremarkably; we heard things (mostly screams) in the distance but never anything too close.

Things got radically difficult once we had about a half mile to go. I was asking Tommy for the tenth time if he wanted some help. He was telling me for the tenth time that he was fine, but he stopped short and the smile melted from his face. I followed his line of sight, and IF I had been smiling I would have stopped too. It didn't look like an ambush, it looked more like a convergence. The problem being, *we* were the attraction upon which they were converging. We were almost entirely surrounded. The only breaks in the zombie lines were caused by either natural occurrences like the fast running stream on our left, or the large block wall that surrounded the Isuzu dealership parking lot on our right. Otherwise this looked like a textbook besieging. We were outnumbered easily 50 to 1. Good thing they didn't know how to shoot.

"There's no way they pulled this off without some communication," I said out loud just to hear my thoughts manifest themselves.

"Mr. T, do you want me to put Henry down so I can shoot?" Tommy asked.

"Not yet Tommy, we're not going to stay and fight. Justin, I want you on my right side a step or two back. Travis, I want you on my left the same step or two behind me. Tracy, Tommy, you two stay close in behind us." Again with the superfluous directions, both of them were already close enough to tell if I was wearing boxers or briefs.

"Okay boys, we're not going to worry too much about what's coming behind and to the sides of us, we're going to concentrate our shots to the front and slightly to our left and right. Understood?" I asked, looking both of them in the eyes to make sure we were on the same page and to gauge their readiness.

They were both scared but they knew what had to be done. When the zombies were within fifty yards, I gave the signal. The signal involved me shooting. The frontline of the zombies crumpled under our withering fire, acrid smoke filled the air. Heads burst, limbs were blown apart, a river of thickening blood flowed in our direction, and hair fluttered down. But still they came, fearless, relentless but most disturbing of all, quietly. There was no battle cry, no gallant speeches, just the slow steady mindless march of the zombies. Kill or be killed, we fired on. The barrel of my M-16 shone a dull red. I knew I was moments away from making a deadly looking paperweight. We were making headway but it was much too slow. Our frontal assault was nearly complete, but to our sides and rear the zombies had halved their distance, some even closer than that. Our break towards freedom was close but not close enough. I slung my M-16 over my shoulder, the barrel grazing my cheek on the way. The smell of my burning flesh seemed to excite our opposition more.

I pulled out my 9 mm Glock and began to shoot zombies that had closed to within fifty feet. I motioned for the boys to keep shooting to the front. We had to have dropped half of them, most of those fatally, but the survivors still pressed in. I then noticed something strange; some of the zombies started to leave the fray. It was in ones and twos at first and then it was in fives and tens, and just like that we found ourselves alone in the road. The tattered remnants of what attacked us were now heading for new quarry. I watched as two men emerged from a small copse of trees about one hundred yards to our right. They started running for all they were worth towards a nearby golf course, the zombies in pursuit, not hot pursuit mind you, but definitely trailing them. Sweat was pouring off my body, "Sweatin' to the Zombies." It could be the next big workout fad. Maybe I'll run it by Richard Simmons. One of these days I was going to get a psych eval.

"Dad, what just happened?" Travis asked.

Justin was hopped up on beer and adrenaline. "We're just too bad assed for them!" he cheered just a little too loudly.

I thought about it for a second before I answered. "I think Justin has it mostly right; we weren't worth the losses, and they found an easier food source and went for it." But that still raised a lot more troubling questions than it answered. I would have to dwell on it eventually, but for right now I wanted to get out of this killing zone.

There was several questions I wanted answered, who was going to answer them was a different question all on its own. How had the zombies pulled off a coordinated attack? That the attack was coordinated I had no doubt, we had been completely surrounded. And why, when they were so close to taking us, did they stop? Because if they were scared, they never once betrayed their emotions. I looked like hell and I smelled worse. If I kept this up the zombies would think I was one of their own.

The remaining distance to the house was covered in a subdued silence. Even the gregarious Tommy was quiet. We knew how close we had come to feeling death's cold embrace. Henry slept on in Tommy's arms.

As we approached our town-home complex I had the boys once again spread out into flanking positions. Our complex was roughly ten square acres. It housed over three hundred units and was surrounded by an eight foot high stone and cement wall. There were four entrances, two on the northern side and two on the southern. The security of the complex was part of the reason we had moved here. The other was monetary; we couldn't afford anything better. The two northern entrance points had large, card activated chain-link fence gates. The two southern facing gates had nothing. That made no sense to me. Did the designers just hope that a criminal, upon seeing the northern gates, wouldn't try another avenue to gain entry? Although the residents would be up a creek if said criminal came this way first. I'd like to have said they were getting ready to install the gates but I'd lived here for almost two years and I hadn't seen hide nor hair of a construction crew.

A large RV had been toppled on its side, completely covering the first entrance. It was placed with entirely too much precision to have been an accident. There wasn't a gap on either side; this passageway was closed. We would have to walk another two hundred yards to the next opening. Hope surged. It appeared that a defense had been mounted at the Little Turtle housing community. As we got closer to the next entrance I saw a school bus, this one still on its wheels. The passenger side of the school bus covered most of the entrance. The only parts that were vulnerable to entry were towards the front end and underneath the bus itself. This would have been unsettling if we were dealing with a conventional enemy, but that bulk was going to stop ninety-nine percent of the zombies that attacked it. Smart bastard, whoever thought of that, I thought admiringly.

"Stop right there!" a voice shouted at us.

"I'm not in the mood for this crap!" I yelled in response.

The cocking, clicking and other sounds of multiple firearms being made ready got me in the mood in a hurry.

"What about now?" I heard the dry voice from within the bus ask.

The boys were confused. Sure, they had fought valiantly against the zombies, but once again we were outnumbered, and this time outgunned.

"Justin, Travis," I said as I turned, slowly. "Put your weapons on the ground, SLOWLY." I did the same.

"What business do you have here?" The raspy voice asked again.

I knew that voice. "Jed? Jed is that you?" Jed was a member on the Board of Directors for our HOA. I hate HOA's. Never before have I had so many people interested in my personal business. Jed had once written me up for putting my trash out at 5:30 at night when the bylaws said we couldn't put the trash out until 6:00 p.m. I couldn't even fathom how he caught me; he lived clear on the opposite side of the complex. I hated that man, but right now I wanted to kiss him.

"Yeah, it's Jed, who might you be?" came the terse reply.

"It's Mike, Mike Talbot, Unit 103."

Still no acknowledgment.

"You remember, we had that heated discussion about my trash going out early."

Heated discussion didn't even begin to describe how this event went down. I had called him every filthy name I could think of and I was a former Marine so you know I had a deep arsenal. I was eventually thrown out of the meeting, and not of my own accord. I was bodily removed. It's not one of my prouder moments in life, and I eventually sucked up my pride and went to his house to apologize. He had blanched when I showed up at his door, probably thinking I was going for round two. We weren't exactly friends after my mitigation but the hostility was gone, or at least buried under a few layers of civility.

He grunted. That was his acknowledgment. So maybe a few of those layers had been removed during this first night of death. "Are any of your lot bitten?" he asked.

"No," was all I could reply.

"Byron, move the bus," Jed commanded.

"Thank you Jed." Relief washed over me. My legs had nearly given out.

Again he grunted, but he loved this, he loved being in control. Right now that was fine with me. I could almost guarantee that he was the one who had orchestrated this defense.

As we were making our way through the small opening, I looked up to meet his eyes. Jed said offhandedly, "your daughter and her fiancée are here."

My wife and I both let out a cry of relief. A big shit-eating grin came across my face.

"Open that door!" I told Jed, pointing to the emergency hatch at the back of the bus. He looked at me questioningly. "I'm gonna come up there and give you a big kiss." I started pulling on the handle. Jed was throwing his weight into the other side thwarting my attempt at entry.

"Get your queer ass outta here Talbot!" Jed bellowed. "I ain't haven no pasty assed man kiss me."

I let go of the emergency handle. "Fine Jed, have it your way," I said as I was heading away. I noticed a small smile curve his lips. It was gone as quick as it had come.

"Talbot!" he yelled to my back.

I turned. "You having second thoughts about that kiss? The offer still stands," I answered coquettishly.

"Be at the clubhouse tomorrow at 7:00 a.m., and clean yourself up, ya smell like shit!" he voiced.

I waved. "Thank you Jed," came my solemn reply.

CHAPTER 6
Journal Entry - 6

Our weary band of travelers headed for the front door. Sir Licks-A-Lot and the rest of his merry gang were nowhere to be seen. Must have been one hell of a firefight, I thought. My greeting for Nicole was brief and intense. I think I would have sobbed with relief if I wasn't so exhausted. She gave her mother a huge hug and then bounded to me for the same; we embraced for a second before she pulled away, nose crinkled in disgust.

"I know I smell like crap, I know," I said before she could beat me to the punch. I wanted to go soak in a hot shower in the worst way. It almost hurt. But once Nicole got to talking, not much was going to divert her. We briefly recounted the highlights of our Wal-Mart rescue. I completely skipped over the little girl, trying my best to hide her in a remote fold in the darkest corners of my brain. It was my turn now to ask how Nicole and Brendon got here. I settled in and made myself comfortable. Even on a regular night Nicole would give me every detail of their journey, down to the minutiae of what color vest the cashier was wearing at the gas station.

I nodded to Brendon, he nodded in return, she had most likely already recounted the entire trip for him, and he had been there. He sat down heavily on the loveseat. Stress that had been etched on his face was only just now beginning to ease.

"So luckily," she began, "we were already on our way over. We wanted to get some of the boxes we have piled in your basement out to our new place…"

Travis interrupted from the kitchen. I could hear him open the refrigerator and then close it quickly, obviously not having found what he was looking for.

"I'm going to get drinks, does anybody want anything?" he yelled from the kitchen.

Everyone had a request, even Tommy. "Do you have any Yoo-Hoo?" he asked.

I shook my head. "We'll get some tomorrow if we can," I answered as I saw the disappointment on his face.

"Pepsi will be fine." Tommy's head was bowed.

"Coke alright?" Travis asked.

"I guess that'll have to do," came Tommy's reply.

I heard the back door and then the screen open and shut. I was listening to Nicole's account, when I abruptly jumped off the couch like my ass was on fire. My foot caught the edge of the coffee table as I went down screaming. Screaming not from the pain but for what laid in wait. My 'man-fridge' was located in the garage. At one time it had mostly been stocked with beer, but it had became a lot easier to just put all of our beverages in there, coke, juice, extra milk, whatever.

Tracy's face froze as she saw the sheer look of terror flit across my features.

"What's the matter?" she shrieked.

I scrambled to gain purchase.

I distantly heard Tommy. "Coke's fine, Mr. T!!" he bawled, reacting to my dread.

I was in a nightmare. I couldn't move fast enough, the ground was sucking me down. Gravity became a fiend. I weighed too much to move effectively. My feet were slipping and sliding on the area rug, but I finally gained purchase. Unfortunately, once I hit wood I had too much thrust and slammed into the wall as I turned left into the hallway. I heard more than felt the snap of impact as I dislocated my shoulder. The pain was blinding, the pain was clarifying. I was soaked in sweat running down the small hallway that connected the living room to the kitchen. By now everyone in the house was close on my heels, trying to discover my intentions. I made it to the kitchen. Now I had to make a hard left through the family room so I could finally make it out the back door. The gore on the soles of my sneakers made it nearly impossible to get traction on the linoleum. I moaned, a deep and mournful sound. Travis was half in the house holding the screen door open with his left hand, seeing my whole comedy of errors.

"Holy shit, Dad! You alright?"

"No swearing!" Tracy scolded him.

And now I did sob, some from the pain but mostly in relief at the sight of my son. "Zombies in the garage!" I mustered before my tunneling vision rapidly began to close.

"Holy shit!"

"I said no swearing!" I heard from a million miles away.

I awoke about ten minutes later, according to Nicole.

"Brendon set your shoulder back," Nicole said. Concern crisscrossed her face.

I sat up waiting for an explosion of pain to rip through me; I was grateful for the moderate throbbing that met me instead.

"Travis?" was all I could manage as I tried to break through the cobwebs that spidered through my thoughts.

"I'm fine, Dad," I heard from the other side of the kitchen counter.

Tommy had taken up nearly my entire field of view. "You alright, Mr. T? You know you still smell bad right?" Tommy said as he tried his best to put on a brave face.

"Help me up big guy." As I extended my hand out, he almost pulled that one out to match the left as he launched me to my feet. I swayed for a moment as my blood did its best to catch up with my movement.

Tracy was at the kitchen table, head in her hands, fresh tears staining the tablecloth.

"You alright Hon?" I asked as I stayed close to Tommy, using him as a balance beam.

"Just relieved." She looked up, I knew it was more than that, of course it was, but what was the point of pushing it.

"What are the chances that anybody grabbed the garage remote out of the car?" I looked at everybody, including Nicole and Brendon. I was that desperate. Everyone slowly shook their heads in negation.

I'll be right back," I said as I headed to the front door. "I just want to tell Jed to expect some noise."

I could hear shuffling in the garage but it was damn near impossible to ascertain their location. Who's to say that one of them wasn't right up at the door waiting for some unsuspecting person to stick their arm through. It would take me less than two seconds to open the door, grope wildly for the garage door wall switch, and then pull the door shut. But how long would it take a zombie in waiting to bite on my arm? I put on three sweaters, a heavy parka and a set of work gloves, so unless these zombies had fangs I should be able to do what needed to be done without becoming infected. My hope was the added bulk wouldn't burden me too much. I did not want to sacrifice speed.

"Dad, do you want me to go with you?" Nicole asked as I headed out the back door. "I could cover you with…with a gun," she added.

I looked down at her trembling hands. A palsy victim would have been appalled. "Um no, I think I might be safer if you stayed in the house."

She looked both hurt and relieved.

"I love you sweetie," I said as I pulled her close and kissed her forehead.

Justin came with me, standing right outside the closed back door, rifle not aimed yet but at the ready. Travis, Brendon and two guards from the bus gate who came to help finish off this mission, waited about ten feet to the side of the garage in the alleyway. I walked over to the garage entrance and took a couple of heavy breaths in preparation, listening one last time to see if I could make out the zombies' respective locations in the garage. I glanced over to the kitchen window. Tracy and Nicole were looking out, watching. Tommy's bulk in the background was unmistakable. The tension of this moment was lost on him, as I watched him playing with one of Travis' old toys. I looked again, and crossed the yard, passing Justin. Before he could ask the question that was on his mind, I walked back in the house. Nicole and Tracy both stared at me in confusion. I walked over to Tommy. "Hey buddy, whatcha got there?" I asked.

"A spaceship!" he said with a sparkle in his eyes.

"Where'd you get that spaceship?" I asked.

He seemed to like this new game. "It was on the floor of Mrs. T's car," he answered.

It must have been flung off the visor with all the impacts the car had been through.

"Do you think I can borrow your 'spaceship' for a minute?" I asked.

"Yeah no problem, I figure it's yours anyway, I found it in your car," he answered.

"Thanks buddy." I grabbed the garage remote and headed out the back gate to get rid of our unwanted guests.

The six of us were lined up in a row. We knew they weren't going to come out sprinting, but we were all poised as if that was exactly what was going to happen. This didn't 'feel' right. All the zombies we had killed so far had been a kill or be killed scenario and we hadn't *known* any of them. This just seemed like cold-blooded murder. I don't think a court in the land would convict me of killing a dead person though. This was much more personal, Jo(e), was, had been my neighbor. I had drank beers with her and talked sports and yeah, even women. (It had been a little strange to talk to a woman about what they found attractive in another woman.) I was staring down the gun sights of my M-16 about to kill someone that I considered more than an acquaintance. Goddamn it, I considered her a friend! That inconvenient truth wasn't going to make it any easier.

"Now remember," I said to everyone. "We wait until they come out of the garage before we start shooting." (I didn't want anyone putting a hole in my Jeep.)

Everyone nodded in agreement. Killing in the heat of battle was one thing, lying in wait and calculating death was a whole different story. The garage door rumbled up. We didn't have long to wait, both of the zombies had been lurking by the door. Whether they had heard us, or more than likely smelled me, it didn't matter. They walked out the door and into a hailstorm of fire and lead. The scene was a staccato burst of fire and shadow. The strobe light effect disoriented me. It made everything appear as if it was happening in slow motion. Jo(e)'s right arm was literally blown off. I watched in fascinated horror as the bits of bone and tendons flew in an arc, the wild flashing light highlighting their ascent and then rapid descent. And yet she still came forward. Merl, as I was to later learn his name, didn't make it a foot out of the garage before Justin had put a 30-06 round through his belfry. Merl's head swelled to twice its normal size trying to make accommodations for the bullet. When his noggin blew, it looked like someone had placed an M-80 in a watermelon. That was the simile I held onto, it allowed me to sleep at night.

And still Jo(e) kept coming. Travis seemed to have the stomach for this killing; his shotgun was slowly dissecting her, but the final blow hadn't landed yet. I hadn't even turned my safety off yet and still she came. I flinched every time the shotgun roared. Brendon walked up to Jo(e), a mere arm's length away, and shot her dead-on (no pun intended). The .380 round thankfully wasn't as blisteringly strong as Justin's round so we were all spared the sight of Jo(e)'s brain bucket scattering across the alley. Her head lashed back violently and her neck snapped loud enough to rival the Mossberg. She crumbled to a heap no more than five feet away from me.

"I'm sorry Jo(e)," I said to her collapsed form.

The two men from the gate produced some body bags and made short work of disposing of the bodies, I didn't stick around to compliment their efficiency. I walked into the garage solemnly, too distressed to even comment on the bird shot that peppered my passenger side quarter panel. This night just wouldn't end. It was 10:30 p.m. and I still hadn't had a shower.

CHAPTER 7 - December 9th 6:45am
Journal Entry - 7

I woke up with a start. I had to pry myself off the bed. It wasn't just that I was still bone-weary, which I was. I was stuck to the comforter I had plopped down onto the previous night, where I had immediately fallen asleep. I didn't even want to linger on what was keeping me so affixed to the quilt. I was trying to convince myself that I had fallen into a vat of cotton candy. That illusion, however tenuous, was broken when a bit of bone fell out of my hair. My eyes were adjusting to the vestiges of light that were seeping in from and around the drawn shades. Tracy was not here. I sat up with a start. 'What was going on?' Then it hit me! The putrid stink of death! They had made it past Jed's barriers and were now in the house! My gun was right next to me. I jumped up and out of the bed, anxious to see who, if anybody, could be saved. Fear gripped my chest in a vise. I could let air escape but I didn't have the capacity to let any in. I was on the verge of panicking. All that I held sacred in this world was in trouble, and my worthless ass had been sleeping. I could hear no sounds of disarray, but that did little to stem the rising tide of trepidation that threatened to dash me against the rocks of sanity. The living dead don't make much noise. I heard crunching! Bile involuntarily rose in my throat. I would choke on vomit long before I was able to help anyone. I flew down the stairs, turning the corner of the landing in one deft move. Henry greeted my heaving body, bone in his grinning mouth, short stubby tail wagging a mile a minute.

"Well, hey there, sleepyhead," my beautiful, beautiful wife said from the kitchen as she sipped on a cup of coffee. Dark rings circled her eyes, but I don't think I had ever beheld such a sight. I laid the rifle down, approaching my wife for a hug and kiss of reassurance.

"Oh hell no!" she said as her eyes lit up in alarm.

I stopped dead in my tracks, what was amiss?

"There's no way you're hugging me, smelling like that," she laughed. "Your stench is what made me wake up this early. Go take a shower, and if you can at least get to the point where you smell better than Henry, I'll think about kissing you."

Henry looked up to my wife with a hurt expression as if to say, 'Don't compare me to that guy, he stinks.' And then went back to the delightful chore of chewing on his steak bone. Relief poured, no GUSHED through my system, a wave of euphoria momentarily made me lightheaded. Thankfully I was already halfway back up the stairs. What the hell was going on with me? I was having *feelings*, I had sobbed and now I was swooning, a couple more days of this crap and I was going to need some Tampax.

I took a brief but intensely hot shower, hoping that I would be rewarded with a renewed and cleansed soul to go with my clean body. When I emerged from the steam and swept my hand over the mirror to wipe away the condensation, I noted that I looked a whole lot better than I felt. Last night's ordeal had aged me beyond my years. I looked to all concerned to be 43. I, however, felt to be about 63. No more time for reflection. I walked out of the steamy bathroom into the relative coolness of our bedroom. The reddish glow to my skin lit the way. I dressed quickly, delighting in the feel of my t-shirt NOT sticking to my neck, back or arms. I wanted to revel in the cleanliness a little longer but I was already running late for the town hall meeting. I grabbed my jacket from the hook at the bottom of the stairs and was about to head out.

Tracy yelled from the kitchen. "Do you want some breakfast before you go?"

"No time," I shouted as I turned back to get my rifle; it wouldn't do to go anywhere without it any more. The old

American Express ads moved into my hemisphere of thought. "Don't Leave Home Without It." 'Thanks, Karl Malden,' I murmured to myself.

"I made scones," Tracy teased.

I stopped short, lucky to not twist an ankle with the forces I used to turn around. "What kind?" I asked, hoping beyond hope. (Not the cranberry almond, not the cranberry almond, not the cranberry almond…) My fingers crossed like a third grader's.

"Blueberry."

"With glaze?" I asked, my voice tremulous.

She nodded.

"Yes!" I pumped my fist in the air. "I might be able to spare a minute or two," I said as I closed the front door.

"I thought so," she answered as she poured a glass of milk.

The meeting was being held in the complex's clubhouse. It was a sturdy looking structure, an 'A' frame that would probably look much more at home at some alpine setting than here in Aurora, Colorado. I showed up to the meeting twenty minutes late.

"Nice of you to show, Talbot," Jed said from the dais at the front of the committee room. Everyone present turned to see.

"Um, I got a little detained," I answered sheepishly.

"What is that on your mustache?" Jed said, straining to get a better look. "Is that blueberry?" he asked incredulously.

I licked it away furiously before he could confirm his suspicions.

"Where is everybody?" I asked trying to change the subject, only realizing too late that I had just made matters worse.

The room was usually standing room only, and that was if we were only going to discuss the mailbox placement. This seemed infinitely more important, and there were dozens of available chairs.

Jed let the blueberries go. His shoulders slumped. "This is all that's left," he answered.

I sat down with a thump into one of the many vacancies. "Oh dear God," I muttered.

Jed was a crotchety old fart but his community had been turned asunder and he was having a difficult time coming to grips with it. This was the fastidious man who scolded children for sledding on the snow-covered hills, fearing that they might tear up the grass underneath. And now his assembly was reduced in one night to a third of the mass it had been. It had been a shock to him, but the tough old badger was going to make sure the rest of us made it through the turmoil. I was impressed, considering he was prior army. I wouldn't have thought he had the intestinal fortitude for this. But he had already gone far above any of my expectations. While everyone had been running around like chickens without heads, he had the Northern gates shut, guarded and appropriated an RV from the Millers, who were here and still glowering. He had also somehow got hold of a bus to close off the last gate, all the while assembling a team to go house to house (not garage to garage) to dispatch the enemy. I was amazed, and that offer of a kiss was still valid if he ever decided he wanted it. I had done everything humanly possible to save my family; Jed had thought on a much broader scale.

The first part of the meeting had been a sounding of the bell ceremony for the Little Turtle fallen. I was thankful I had missed that. I had no wish to hear the names of the dead. They were just about to get to the meat of the meeting (sarcasm intended) when I showed up.

Jed continued. "I know it's going to be difficult to guard so much area." There was no reason for him to verbalize the reason; there were so few of us now. "We have to keep two people at each of the fenced gates at all times, and I'll take ideas on how to shore those up. They were never designed to stop a determined pedestrian. No need to worry about the southwest gate. The RV isn't going anywhere."

Old man Miller got up to protest. "You didn't say anything about turning it over on its side when you 'borrowed' it Jed," Gerald Miller sneered. "That was mine and the missus' vacation home!" he yelled as loud as his oxygen tank fueled lungs would allow.

Jed looked like he was about to blow a gasket. That was the same look that got me going and thrown out of the town meeting a few months earlier.

"Gerry, where exactly are you and the missus planning on going to vacation NOW?" Jed stated, placing the emphasis on 'now.'

"Well, we could have used it to escape to Florida," Gerry said dejectedly.

"Oh yeah," Jed stated sarcastically. "They didn't hand out ANY flu shots in the retirement capital of the world."

I had missed the news broadcasts that were still operational. They had decisive evidence that the flu vaccination was the culprit and not voodoo mysticism, as many of the more superstitious types (me) had reckoned. At this point though, what's the difference. A zombie's a zombie, I don't care how it got to the point of wanting to eat my brains, I just wanted to make sure that didn't happen. Gerry didn't make any more interjections. He pouted as best he could with an oxygen tube coming out of his nose.

"Okay, now that that matter is closed," Jed said, as he looked straight at Gerry. "I'd like at least four people at the bus gate. I'm worried about the clearance. The zombies that showed up last night showed no inkling that they even noticed there was a way in under the bus. I'd say let's flip the bus too."

Gerry loudly harrumphed.

"But I want it mobile in case we need to get it out of the way quickly, plus we're going to have cars coming and going all the time," Jed added, with a stern glance in Gerry's direction.

One of the residents, an older lady with white hair that I always saw walking her Corgi asked, "why don't we just seal it up and be done with it?"

I thought she answered haughtily for one that lived so close to the fringes of lower class society. Maybe her rich husband took off with a young floozy and only left her with that ankle biting little pecker Welsh Corgi.

"…Need to…" Jed had brought me back from my little inward detour. "Get supplies and food. And we might need it if we have to leave in a large group in a hurry," he continued. "Now I know nobody is going to like this part. I want to assemble teams of five to scour all the unoccupied townhomes. This is going to be a lot of work but we need to figure out where we are at. So grab all the food, gas, weapons, ammo, batteries, whatever you think we can use. Bring it here to the other smaller conference room and we'll go from there. Also look for a couple of larger stepladders. I want to use those as guard towers."

I stood up to ask a question. Jed didn't look happy about it.

"The floor recognizes Michael Talbot," Jed said, wiping his hand over his brow.

"Jed, fellow survivors," I started. Some winced at that, maybe because they hadn't thought of it that way or maybe they just didn't want to. "I've got a couple of questions."

"We figured that Talbot, or you wouldn't have gotten up," Jed sarcastically stated. I was going to take back my offer to kiss him if he kept this up.

"What's our stance on interlopers?" Jed had thought of everything but this issue. "I mean," I continued. "What are we going to do with…" I thought for a second, the word still didn't sound right when it came out of my mouth. "… refugees?" (This wasn't Grenada.)

Jed thought for a second. He didn't want to come to a snap decision. "I guess that's unavoidable," Jed stated to no one in particular. "On one hand it will ease up the load of responsibilities and burdens we will have to bear."

Miss White Hair with the canine ankle biter spoke

out. "Responsibilities? Burdens? Guard duty? I want no part of that," she said frostily.

'Wrong answer,' I thought.

Without missing a beat, Jed said, "Mrs. Deneaux, when will you be leaving then?"

Her face lost more color than her hair. Even her dog looked like he had been pistol-whipped. She didn't respond in any fashion. I took that to be she was agreeing to Jed's will.

"Back to the refugees," Jed said. I could tell that even he was having difficulty with that word. "Eventually it will become more and more problematic to house and feed them. We'd be all right for the first hundred or two until it began to tax our resources. But if we start taking people in we can't get to a point and then start turning them away. I mean we could, but I don't want to be that person that turns a family away because we're out of space. If we open the doors for one, we open it for all. We may get to the point where we will run out of empty homes and will have to open our own houses too."

"Oh for heaven's sake," Mrs. Deneaux interjected. "I will not open my doors to any strangers, especially if they're not the right color."

Mr. Hernandez stood up, angry as all get out. Even Tommy would have been able to tell where this was going.

"Sit down, Don," Jed said sympathetically to Mr. Hernandez. "Is it really worth arguing with her?"

Mrs. Deneaux glowered. This wasn't one of those touchy feely moments like in the movies, where Mrs. Deneaux reluctantly saw the errors of her ways and eventually accepted a black family into her home as they overcome all obstacles set in their way. She lived as a racist bigot bitch and she would probably die as a racist bigot bitch. C'est *LA VIE.* Mrs. Deneaux was happy Don hadn't said anything. She liked it a lot better when they stayed quiet and mowed the lawns.

I sucked in my breath as I watched Mr. Hernandez do

his best to control the rage that was threatening to boil over.

Jed didn't like Mrs. Deneaux any more than anyone else at the meeting. He was probably wondering if she had become this 'difficult' before or after her husband left her. Tension mounted, the pressure was palpable. That was of course until the nightmare began again. Where someone had dug out an old WWII siren, I don't know, all I know is when the siren went off I got to taste my scone a second time, and believe me it wasn't better this go around. Most everyone got up, unsure of what we should do next. Eyes invariably shifted to Jed.

"Just hold off until the siren stops and then we should hear some directions," he stated.

Just how many air raid sirens had this man lived through? The siren cut off as if it was placed under water. Then we heard, faintly at first and then with more vigor as the message passed on from sentry to sentry, "Zombies at the gate, zombies at the gate!"

"You idiots," Jed mumbled. "Which gate?"

As if in answer to his question, "Northwest and northeast gate, all hands!!"

Gerry, Mrs. Deneaux and a few of the older folks didn't move. Hell, I thought darkly, most of them already look like the walking dead, without the walking part. I wanted to pull Jed aside and tell him that we had already been infiltrated, but I somehow didn't think he'd find the humor in it.

I grabbed Jed's arm. "Do you want me to go get the boys?" It would delay my arrival by ten minutes but I'd be bringing more firepower with me.

"How many rounds you have for that fancy gun of yours?" he asked, looking down at my M-16.

"Four full clips, so a hundred and twenty rounds," I said as I began to shuffle my feet. Adrenaline had started to surge, I needed to direct this energy and quickly.

"Ants in your pants Talbot?" Jed mused. (When was the last time I'd heard that? When I was ten?) "Go to the gate and see how bad the threat is, they'll either come running when they hear the shots or I'll have a runner sent."

I was halfway out the door, when I turned. "Thanks Jed," I told him.

"For what?" came his grizzled reply.

"For a chance," I finished before dashing out the door.

I ran as fast as I could to the northern end of the complex. I knew this wasn't the proper approach. My slamming heart was going to make it difficult to steady my gun. There was no need for the rush. There were no more than twenty of them and half of them had been cut down before I got there. I saved my rounds. Well at least the question of what to do with refugees was answered. The zombies had been chasing a small family, a mother, father and two kids that didn't look much past two years old. As we let them past the barriers, relief was imprinted on the father's face. Fear and worry had corroded the mother's features. At one time she had been a very attractive lady, but the events of the past night had gnarled everything about her. I felt sorry for her and would have liked to have comforted her, but I was having a difficult time stretching the boundaries of my altruism; I only wanted to get home to my own family. I wasn't sure how much time I had left with my family and I didn't want to squander one precious moment.

CHAPTER 8
Journal Entry - 8

The next few days went by without too many problems. Our numbers swelled by a whopping twenty-one souls. We had hastily erected a six-foot high cinder block wall with mortar over the northeast gate. Some had argued to do the same on the other fenced gate but Jed had argued back, and rightfully so, if we needed to leave in a hurry, we would need a way to get out. Personally, I didn't think it was going to matter by that point, but I didn't want to argue about it. We strengthened the northwest gate by placing two minivans against it. They were parallel to the gate and parked rear hatch to rear hatch. They were close enough to the fence to scratch the paint but the previous owners weren't around to complain.

The bus gate was the most difficult of all to bulwark. Obviously we wanted to make it impregnable to the zombies but also mobile enough so that we could leave in an instant. It was our first new resident that came up with the idea. Alex Carbonara, a medium sized man in his thirties, had been a carpenter in his previous life and was used to finding ways to work around problems. We had mostly left him off the revolving guard duty because his wife had yet to snap out of her catatonic state. There was no way he could safely leave his children at his new home with a non-responsive spouse. So it was in this free time that he had first pondered and then drew the design for his 'movable wall.' It was a six, six and a half foot high by twenty-foot long wall built on wheels and placed on a track. It was ingenious. He placed studs every ten inches as opposed to the standard eighteen for added strength. Covered with drywall and with small wheels attached to the bottom, with some muscle power the gate could be retracted to either let someone in or out as the case might be.

We were as fearful of 'gangs' or desperate mobs as we were of the zombies. Normal humans would have an easy time breaching any of our defenses, so as much as we wanted to cut down on the number of sentries, we just didn't dare. Every hundred yards or so we had either a tall stepladder or a small sliding ladder set up against the wall. These were manned 24/7. I spent nearly six hours a day on guard duty. I didn't mind so much at the gates. The camaraderie heralded me back to my days in the Marines Corps. The time on the ladders, however, was excruciating. When I got off the ladder at the end of my shift, my feet and legs throbbed in pain for almost as long as I had been on it. When the opportunity to go on a supply run came, I jumped at it. A chance meeting with zombies seemed much better than the known pain of 'the ladders' (modern societies' newest form of torture). Thank God for Alex, he had already come up with a design for small gun towers to take the place of 'the ladders.'

The raid was set up specifically to search for food and batteries and that type of stuff, but when Alex came to us with his list of building materials, we promised to make sure to leave room in the van. Who knew what invaluable contraption he was going to come up with next?

Six of us went out in that van. Between all the guns and ammo we carried I didn't know how we were going to fit any food in here. Me, Justin, Travis, Brendon, Alex (he left his kids with Jed and his wife) and a slightly built man that barely looked like he could hold up his rifle; Spindler was his name. He said he had been a principal once upon a time in a town called Walpole or something like that. I didn't like him much but as long as he helped and didn't become a liability he was fine with me. Tracy and Nicole were not thrilled that we were heading out, but I assured them everything would be fine. We hadn't seen more than a dozen or so zombies in the last two days.

"Mike you've seen the news," Tracy pleaded.

And I had, that was all that was on. There were two television stations left and it was 'All News, All the Time.' It was horrendous. There was nothing else to report on except for zombies. Even the commentators seemed bored with the subject.

'Another mass killing in Ohio.' Yawn, big stretch, the newscaster would state. 'Film at eleven.' Stretch. Obviously the yawn and the stretch are figurative, but that was the implied tone. What wasn't implied, however, was that no matter how seemingly easy we had it at the moment, the worst of it wasn't over. The zombies were still out there and wherever they went havoc, death and destruction followed.

"Trace," I consoled. "Lowe's and Safeway are less than a half mile from here, we'll be loaded up and back within the hour." It ended up being a lot longer than an hour and incredibly more dangerous than I had said or figured. And like every Star Trek away team, we ended up losing a crew member.

We left by the minivan exit. It was on the side closest to our destination. Across from the gate on the other side of the road was a Jehovah's Witness freedom hall. I was wondering how many of the devout followers that went to this church were lucky enough to get one of the coveted 144,000 spots in the Promised Land this last week. When I reigned in my cynicism, I noticed someone standing at the far edge of the church parking lot. My heart beat a little faster. Why was somebody just standing there? Something didn't seem right. I told Alex, who was driving, to go into the church lot. He was not happy about any detours, he was thinking that Jed was most likely as good a baby-sitter as his near comatose wife. But when I pointed out what I was looking at he readily agreed. We were within twenty-five yards and still she didn't run away or amble towards us. We could tell it was a woman from the slight build and long hair, but beyond that we had no clue.

"Alex, get about twenty feet away and let's see what's going on," I said.

"This doesn't feel right, Mike," Alex said, echoing what we were all thinking.

As we got closer I could tell that in life, this woman had been downright beautiful. Even in death there was a certain majesty to her. Her long raven black hair hid the majority of sores on her face, but her uncovered arms showed the ravages of the disease she was carrying. I could see her arms rippling even though 'it' didn't move a muscle.

Justin had lined up his shot. "Dad do you want me to kill it?" he asked.

I knew deep down in my subconscious she was dangerous, as any beautiful woman was, and she *felt* worse, much worse. But I couldn't find it in my humanity to kill if we weren't in danger. She made no threatening move whatsoever, her eyes watching us warily, and that shook me because I knew there was more than some rudimentary intelligence going on. We sat there and just stared.

"Dad?" Justin asked again. He wanted this standoff done.

"Put the gun down. Alex, get us the fuck out of here," I said, never tearing my eyes from her.

I heard Spindler gasp, so I know he saw what I did. The zombie woman nodded once, as in 'thank you' for not killing her. I shuddered, but nobody else in the van was the wiser. Looking back just a few short weeks later, I wish I had let Justin shoot her.

When I got my composure back, I was able to rationalize the nod as stress induced or just perception problems. I knew better though, I'd wished Spindler hadn't seen it too. It would have made it a lot easier to brush this away if there hadn't been a corroborating witness.

"Alex, drive behind the Lowe's store," I said with a quaver in my voice. Luckily everyone else was too busy scanning the area to notice the octave change.

"Mike, you heard Jed, we need to get food first and then worry about the wood for the turrets," Alex bemoaned.

"Yeah, Jed would say that, the old geezer hasn't done

one shift on those god-awful things. I can barely sleep because of the pain in my legs."

Alex opened his mouth to say something but I cut him off. "Come on Alex, I know what I'm doing, how much food do you think we're going to fit in here anyway? Go to the back of the store, I can almost guarantee they'll have a big rig there, we'll fill it with all the supplies and food we'd need for a year."

"Mike, I don't know how to drive a rig," Alex pleaded.

"No sweat," I said as I put on my best bull-shitting smile. "I drove one back in my Marine Corps days."

He eyed me a little dubiously, if he had stared at me a little longer I would have cracked and just forgotten the whole damn plan.

My whole half-hour of driving a big rig had started as a dare from a fellow Marine friend of mine. We had been drinking all night at the base watering hole and had just started walking home to the barracks. We had passed the armory and a giant camouflaged truck sat in the parking lot.

"Betcha can't drive us home in that," my drinking buddy Chuck Blaylock dared.

"Can so," I blustered as I began to squeeze my way through the locked gate.

"What the fuck are ya doing?" Chuck asked, almost as if he had already forgotten what he had dared me about.

He had; unfortunately, my short-term memory wasn't as bad. I got up into the cab and turned over the ignition, which allowed the glow plugs to warm up. There was no need for keys, like all military vehicles there was no such thing as keys. It would do no good if in the heat of battle the driver was killed or blown apart and the keys disappeared with him. You get my point, right? So within half a minute of getting through the gate the truck roared to life. I lurched the truck forward.

"Crap, there's a bunch of gears," I mumbled. I was paying more attention to the shift box than I was the gate. I barely looked up as I crashed through it. The truck stalled, Chuck hopped into the cab from the passenger side.

"'Bout time," he said, and then he started snoring softly.

The barracks was only two streets over but I was so inebriated I had lost all sense of direction. When the eight trailing military police hummers had pulled us over, I was ten miles from home, had destroyed three cars and one guard shack. All in all, not a great ending to a great night. At my court-martial, the officer in charge of the proceedings, Colonel Laret, went easy on me. First off because the truck I was driving hadn't blown half the state away. Unbeknownst to us the truck was packed with C-4 explosive. I could have served life in prison at Leavenworth for that alone. When it was all said and done, I had lost two stripes (demoted from sergeant to lance corporal), three months' pay and one year of confinement to the barracks. Chuck lost a stripe just for getting in the cab. They also sent him to another duty station, Okinawa, Japan, so we couldn't be together to cause any more havoc. I was going to miss Chuck to no end, but this beat a life sentence at Leavenworth, and because of the hard labor, a life sentence at Leavenworth equated to seven years. So long story short, technically I *had* driven a big rig even if I had no recollection of it.

As it was, there were three trucks parked at Lowe's. Two were still mostly full, and the third looked as if it had just finished off-loading. That was going to be the one we wanted. We fanned out on the loading bay, thankful that this one was lit up like a spring day. The light was welcome, the sights however weren't. There had been a brief but intense fight here. Some zombies had re-died and so had a bunch of truckers and dock crew. They had fought with tire-irons, chains and even a floor tile stripper. Gore littered the floor. The only thing alive in here was the incessant buzzing of the flies. Curiously the flies, which I thought of as one of the nastiest creatures on the planet next to cockroaches, wanted nothing to do with the zombies. They covered the remains of the humans, but not a one alit on any of the zombies. Even flying cockroaches knew better. I was thankful that it was early December and not a hot sweltering day in August; the smell was already fetid. I couldn't begin to imagine what the smell would be like heated up to 98 degrees. I would have liked to have pulled the bodies out of the bay and onto the parking lot, but I didn't see the point. There were bound to be a lot more bodies in the store itself, and stopping to dispose of all of them would just be eating into precious time. I left Spindler to guard our rear echelon while the rest of us went forward to check out the store. When I swung open the large swinging doors I soon discovered the inside was much more malodorous than the airy bay. I motioned for the small party to retreat. Confusion and fear crossed their features. I calmed my tumbling stomach by pulling in great breaths of the air I had previously thought was fetid.

"We're going to need Vick's or something like that to put under our noses," I said, when I felt like I could finally speak without bits of discharge intermingling with my words.

We hunted for a couple of minutes, never finding the coveted Vick's. Travis discovered some cologne in one of the metal desks that lined every bay. We made some makeshift bandannas and soaked them in the cologne. So we went back to the swinging doors looking like the best smelling bandits this side of the Mississippi. The redolence of Eau de Death will haunt my olfactory nerves for the rest of my days. The one good thing about the swinging doors, besides being able to prop them open and get air, was that it had allowed the zombies to escape. In the long run that may have been bad, but for right now it was a welcome blessing. We did, however, do a thorough search of the entire store before we began our supply run, just in case there were undead lurkers still roaming about.

I had the unenviable task of finding the keys to the big rig. My biggest fear was that the drivers were all zombified and had just walked off, keys and all. The dockworkers were all dressed the same, blue jeans, light

colored shirts and blue smocks. All I needed to do was find
some fat men with jackets on. It's stereotypical but I was in a
hurry. After a few minutes of looking I was rewarded, or
more likely punished. I had found my quarry. There were two
men on the loading bay that fit the description. I was looking
for the one that was a little less decomposed than the other. I
flipped the first guy over. The left side of his face had been
removed. Jagged strips of flesh were all that remained. His
left eye had been chewed in half, like a bad Entenmann's
chocolate. Something had bitten into it and decided they
didn't like the flavor and had left it for someone else. My
stomach wasn't going to be right for a week after this.

'Stop looking at his face!' I silently screamed at
myself. This was much worse than the impersonality of
passing an accident on the side of the road. This was High
Def death brought to you in 1080dpi. 'What is wrong with
you?' Does that mean I'm in trouble when I refer to myself in
the third person, isn't that some form of psychosis? I think I
was trying to stall with myself. I'm a borderline germaphobe.
I didn't want to have to touch what was left of this person.
There's no telling what diseases he was carrying. If I had
been someone else I would have punched them and told them
to get moving. This internal dialogue was not getting my
family or me out of danger any quicker. That thought got me
moving, but when I plunged my hand into his pocket I was
compensated with the liquefication of Jared's (I had to name
him something, it somehow seemed easier than fat dead guy)
fat tissue. I pulled my hand out only to find it attached to a
two-foot long sinewy snot-like substance.

All the Clorox wipes in Lowe's weren't ever going to
make me feel clean again. I did, however, have the luck of
the Irish on my side. Clutched in my disgusting disease
riddled paw were keys, and hopefully not to some stupid
little Hyundai out front. I stiffly walked into the store and
found the cleaning supplies. I felt like I was on autopilot. I
was moving but no one was steering the ship. I dumped a
bottle of Pine-Sol on my arm. It smelled horrible, it burned

my skin, it was bliss. When I had emptied the bottle, I wiped off most of the gunk with clean-up towels, just a fancy name for paper towels. I then dug into the disinfectant wipes that promised to kill 99.9 percent of all germs and even some viruses. I could only hope that zombieism wasn't in that .1 percent. I began to come back from the obsessive-compulsive abyss. I didn't want to be THAT guy, the one that sits in a corner continuously rubbing at his now bleeding flesh with a small mountain of used wipes at his feet. It was close, but I felt like I had passed the worst of it. I went out to the truck that we were going to be using and tested the keys. They worked, which was a damn good thing because I'm not sure if I could have stuck my hand into any more glistening, decaying flesh again today. I walked back past Spindler, my face just a few shades lighter green than it had been.

"Wimp," he laughed. I think he thought he was being funny.

If I wasn't concentrating so hard on not puking I would have responded. I didn't even shake my head in disapproval. The vertigo would have been too much.

We were nearly completed at Lowe's. I was on my last haul dragging a pallet mover loaded with wood, nails, caulking and some other odds and ends when I saw Spindler toss his cigarette out the bay. His hands were shaking as he went to pick up his rifle.

"Useless," I muttered. Who the hell stands on guard duty against a deadly enemy and puts his rifle down. I would remember next time to bring someone else.

I heard the engine long before the useless Spindler gave the warning. I stopped pulling on the pallet jack and started racing over to the open bay, unslinging my gun on the way to assess the new threat. Spindler started to slide away. I knew it! I knew he'd be useless in a fight.

"Get your ass over here!" I said quietly but laced with menace. "Or I'll shoot you myself."

He sneered, but grudgingly did as I ordered. I could tell from the self-serving calculation on his face that he was trying to gauge which threat was worse, me or the incoming vehicle.

The Ford F-350 slowed to a stop about twenty-five feet from us. I couldn't see into the windows because of the way the sun was shining. Why the hell were visions of Snoopy and the Red Baron racing through my head? The seconds ticked by, I could HEAR Spindler sweating. The drops were cascading to the floor. It wasn't going to be long now, no matter how much he feared me, before he went running into the sunset.

"Why did you come on this raid?" I asked, not meaning to say anything out loud.

Spindler jumped at my words. "It's my van," was his response.

I looked at him, but when I realized he wasn't going to continue I prodded him further. "So?"

He licked his lips nervously before he continued. "I had a Cadillac once, I loved that car, it caught fire."

His choppy delivery was grating on my nerves. Again he didn't elaborate; this time I didn't care. I was saved from more 'conversation' when the passenger side door of the truck opened. My rifle wasn't at the ready but my grip intensified. Spindler began to bring his to the ready position. The foot that was stepping out, stopped suddenly. I grabbed Spindler's barrel and shoved it towards the ground. He got the message but that didn't mean he was happy with it. The cowboy boot covered foot once again began its descent to the pavement. The largest man I had ever seen in my life stepped out of that truck, not as in fat man from the Monty Python movie, 'The Life of Brian,' but rather of the Arnold Schwarzenegger variety from 'The Terminator.'

He would have looked intimidating even if he hadn't been carrying a Gatling gun. A Gatling gun? Who gets a Gatling gun? My brain asked in overdrive. It had to have weighed a couple hundred pounds, plus all the ammo, and he hefted it as if it were no more than a paint ball marker. If he opened fire we'd be dead before we could think about it.

While we were mesmerized by the gun, his friend stepped out of the crew cab door. He was a good-sized individual also, but compared with his steroid-induced partner he looked like Pee-Wee Herman. He carried a more traditional weapon, if you can consider a SAW a traditional weapon. A SAW is a 'light' machine gun, but at sixty-five pounds it's still no slouch to carry around. We were outgunned and nearly cut down when Spindler dropped his rifle. Lucky for us our two rivals weren't prone to panic, they both tensed but neither fired. The bigger man laughed. It was a mean laugh though. His watchful eyes never left mine. Obviously he was sizing up the only threat left to him.

"That's my store," he said matter-of-factly.

Why I let my smart ass mouth rumble sometimes I don't even know. My mother always said it was going to get me in trouble. "Do you mean literally or figuratively?" I wanted to laugh when I saw him thinking about my words. He hadn't a clue as to what I had just asked him.

"Umm, both," he said, realizing he may have just said something stupid.

I was laughing inside, but I knew if I gave a hint of that internal merriment away he would step over my blown-out brains to get into the store.

"Any chance we can share, big guy?" I asked, but I fathomed the sheer bulk of this guy let him get whatever he wanted.

"The name is Durgan," he bellowed. "Not 'big guy.'"

What the hell is his hang up? "Okay big…Durgan." Is that a first or a last name, I wondered. "There's plenty of store here for the both of us."

"You don't get it puny man, this is MY store!" The veins in his forehead threatened to burst as he yelled.

Damnit, where's a good zombie when you need one. It was then that I noticed the woman zombie we had seen at the church. She was standing a couple of hundred yards behind the men in the truck, seemingly watching this melodrama play out. I didn't have time to waste worrying about her now, I had bigger fish to fry at the moment. I heard liquid pattering to the ground next to me. What I thought was more sweat from Spindler turned out to be piss plunging from his bladder.

"See! Your little friend agrees with me." Durgan said, laughing his fake laugh again. "You have until the count of three to leave before I make you look like..." He turned to his friend and I heard him mumble, "what's that cheese with all the holes in it?"

"Swiss," came the stage-whisper reply. Now I know why the brain-eating zombies left these two idiots alone.

"Before I make you look like Swiss cheese!" Durgan shouted triumphantly.

I knew I had to act fast, we needed these supplies and we needed this truck. But my time was running short; I was not convinced that Durgan could count as high as three.

"One!" he screamed.

Who the hell was he yelling at, we were twenty feet away. Spindler took off like a shot, out the bay and away from Durgan.

"Pussy," I sputtered.

"TWO!" Durgan yelled even louder.

Fight or flight, fight or flight, flight or... I stared in amazement as I watched Steroid Freak Number Two try to brush away a speck on his shirt. The laser dot didn't move and then a second one joined the first. Durgan also had two on him but was slower to realize it.

"Durgan," Number Two groused. No response. "Durgan!" he bawled.

Durgan turned a little. "What, can't you see I'm a little busy right now," he growled.

"Look at my chest, man," Number Two nearly cried. "Look at yours!"

Both men were painted with two laser sniping dots on their chests. I wasn't sure where the help was coming from because none of our small party had laser scopes, but I wasn't about to look a gift horse in the mouth. I seized on the opportunity.

"I'm not going to give you until three, 'Big Guy,'" I said condescendingly.

He sneered in reaction to my words.

"Put the guns down now or you're dead," I warned softly.

Number Two reacted quicker than Spindler had. He was already halfway back in the truck.

"NOW!" I yelled. Durgan hitched his hand toward the trigger slightly, a murderous intent in his eyes. Finally he seemed to realize he wasn't going to win this Mexican standoff.

"This isn't over!" he bellowed in ferocity. So this is what a pissed off bear looked like. He never did put the gun down, but I wasn't going to push my luck as they both got back into the truck. "Debbie, drive!" I heard him yell even with the windows closed. It must have been deafening in that enclosed space. I was thankful they had left. I had no desire to detain them.

I let out a sigh of relief as I walked back into the bay to see who my allies were. Alex and Justin were as tense as I was and were just now shouldering their weapons. It was the mischievous grin of Travis, however, that had me laughing like a crazy man. In each of his hands he carried two laser leveling devices.

"Thanks for that," I said as I went over and clapped Travis on his back.

"No problem," he answered, but I could see the pride in his eyes.

"Where's Spindler?" Alex asked.

"He took off at the first sign of trouble," was my response.

"Spineless, worthless piece of s…." Alex kept saying but he was out of earshot as he was moving away to gather the last bit of his haul.

"All right guys," I said to Travis and Justin. "Let's finish up here, I can't imagine Durgan has many friends he could bring back with him but I don't want to find out."

"Right!" Justin was in complete agreement.

Travis nodded, still grinning. He placed the leveling devices in his pockets and went to help Alex and Brendon pull the load into the truck.

Finally we were ready to head for home. I pulled myself up into the cab of the big rig. Alex drove the van up alongside me. Travis was sitting with him, and Justin was with me.

"Are we going to look for Spindler?" Alex asked, looking up at me.

My first response wanted to be 'Fuck no!' But that didn't seem very humanitarian of me. Instead I came out with, "he knows where we're going, if he has balls enough to come back he'll meet us there."

"I guess we'll never see him again then," Alex laughed. "Little bandejo!"

I was starting to stress out a little, driving an 18-wheeler had seemed a whole lot easier when I was drunk. Staring at all the knobs and switches and 12-gear stick shift seemed terrifying at the moment. I couldn't tell everyone they had just wasted two hours of their time for nothing. Sweat broke out on my forehead.

Justin calmly looked over at me. "You don't know how to drive this thing do you?"

Captain Obvious strikes again. I ground the living shit out of first gear. It smelled like it did when I would blow up my toy models with firecrackers when I was 12; ahhhh, there's nothing like the smell of burned plastic in the morning! I was paraphrasing from Apocalypse Now. Okay, so I wasn't doing the movie any justice, but it was helping to calm my nerves. My brain works in mysterious ways. Just ask my wife, she'll tell you. The truck lurched forward five feet and stalled. I did the same routine three more times. I didn't have a true reference point but I figured this was what it felt like when those crazy cowboys hopped on one of those mechanical bucking broncos. I was hopping around that seat like I had eaten five cans of Mexican jumping beans. Justin was having a blast, I wasn't having nearly as much fun. I had only just gotten my stomach completely under control about fifteen minutes previously. Alex waited about fifty feet ahead of us. I wanted to wave him forward, my fear being that I might not be able to stop this behemoth once I got it going. On my fourth attempt I was finally able to get the truck into second. That probably had more to do with the fact that I had burned the first gear completely out rather than any newly attained skill. Thank God, Safeway was only five hundred yards away, as it was it took me all of ten minutes to get there. As there was no way I was going to back this thing into the rear dock, I pulled up to the front doors and did what I did best, I stalled it.

"Well, that was something special to behold," Alex said as he got out of the van smiling.

Sweat was pouring off me in sheets. Justin had broken a land speed record for carsickness. He puked as soon as he could scramble out of the cab.

"Not so funny now, is it?" I asked.

"Travis is riding home with you," Justin answered between heaves.

"Okay guys, you know the drill." I started. "Justin, you stay out here and keep watch. Blast the truck horn if you need us. Alex, Trav, you stay with me while we check this store out."

CHAPTER 9
Journal Entry - 9

Justin was wiping his face and getting ready to climb up on the truck hood to get a better vantage point as we entered the store. The smell was….antiseptic. I was in heaven for a second.

"Don't move!" came the voice from above, someone was using the store's P.A. system.

We stopped moving.

"We...we don't want any trouble," came the anxious voice. I don't know why *he* was so panicky, we were the ones being drawn down on, or so I thought. Who could possibly live in this day and age and not arm themselves. I should have known some pacifists would survive Armageddon.

"We don't want any trouble either," I responded, not knowing where to direct my voice so I found myself talking to the nearest speaker in the ceiling. "We just want to get some food and get back home."

"Home," the disembodied voice said with a whimsical lilt.

"Yeah, we live at the Little Turtle complex and we…" I began and didn't get a chance to finish.

"Little Turtle!" came the excited reply. "My aunt lives… lived there."

"That's great!" I was beginning to feel like we could connect.

"Yeah, yeah, Jane, Jane Deneaux," he added eagerly.

My hopes sank. If the nephew was a tenth like the aunt we were dead where we stood.

I'm not sure from what vantage point I was being watched but he must have seen my face fall at the mention of his aunt.

"Oh you must know her!" he said. "I know she's an uber-bitch but she's all the family I have now. If you put the guns down, we can talk."

"Umm…" I replied. "We're not having the best day today, I would feel much more comfortable if we held on to them. I will send these other two back outside and I will re-sling my gun, that's the best I can offer."

"That'll have to do," was his curt reply.

When Travis and Alex had gone back out and my weapon was back on my shoulder, a little man no more than 5'5" tall came out from behind the customer service desk. He wore coke bottle glasses, had a receding hairline that had probably earned him the nickname Five-Head. (I'll explain – it's like 'forehead' only his is so big it's a FIVE head. So it's not the funniest joke in the world, and it is at the expense of another, but you gotta admit it's still humorous). He had on penny-loafers, khaki pants, a shirt and a tie, and a Safeway smock that had his name, Store Manager Thad adhered to it.

"How you doing Thad?" as I extended my hand out.

"How…how did you know?" He quickly realized his mistake and blushed as he looked down at his nametag.

I couldn't believe this guy was still alive. A field mouse would most likely send him shrieking into the night. Bad example, *that* would probably send me shrieking into the night too.

"How many of you are there, Thad?" I asked as he finally closed the distance between us and took my proffered hand.

"Four." He winced; I may have gripped his hand a little too tightly. I was still a bundle of nerves.

"May I say something, sir?" he began.

"Mike," I answered.

"Mike?" he asked.

"Yeah, Mike Talbot's my name."

"Mike, please don't take this wrong." He looked a little embarrassed at what he was about to say, and he didn't want to offend me but he held true to his convictions. "You really do smell bad," he finished. I noted he had a distinctive not-oft used English accent buried in there somewhere.

"Yeah I get that a lot," I said as I put my non-offending arm around him.

He visibly relaxed. I told him about why we were here, and about the Little Turtle complex and that all of them were welcome. There was still plenty of room to be had.

Thad called out to the rest of his cohorts, who turned out to be two of his co-workers and one customer. From behind the aisle with the canned fruit came a woman in her late 50's. Sores covered most of her arms and she had some on her face. I gripped my rifle a little tighter thinking she might be one of the undead. When that didn't appear to be the case I wondered how she could possibly be developing a case of scurvy in a grocery store. She nodded in my general direction and headed back down the aisle picking at a sore at the bridge of her nose.

Thad whispered to me. "She's been doing that since this whole mess started, a sore no sooner closes up and she picks it open."

I shuddered in revulsion. The germaphobe in me was going to make sure that she wasn't in the same vehicle as me when we headed back.

From right behind me, where he had been waiting behind the shopping carts came a giant of a man carrying a tire iron. I would have thought it was Durgan but this man was a soft chocolate color. He unnerved me to the core; give me a zombie any day.

"Sure glad I didn't have to use this," he said as he smacked the iron into his open palm. Alex and Travis rushed in thinking it was a gunshot, it was that loud.

"Ah yeah, me too," I said honestly.

"That big fellow's name is O'Henry but we all call him Big Tiny, because…" Thad stated.

"I get it," I said looking straight into Big Tiny's sternum.

"B.T. for short," the big man said as he walked a little way past us to get a water out of one of the end cap coolers. I noticed he had a small smirk on his face, as if happy that his size had visibly flustered me like it did.

The last to show herself was the lone customer in the store when Thad had prudently locked the doors from the horrible nightmare that raged all around in the parking lot. Her name was Beth, and she was in her late 30's, early 40's, shoulder length auburn hair, green-hazel eyes, and a heart shaped face. She was attractive but there was something else about her; I had an overwhelming sense of déjà vu. I knew her somehow but I had never laid eyes on her before, at least not in this lifetime. Anyway, there was no time to solve mysteries. With four extra hands the loading of the truck went exceedingly smooth. I made sure that we also did a thorough raid on the pharmaceuticals. You never knew when you were going to need a Percocet or two, errr, I mean penicillin.

The truck was stuffed as full as it could get but the grocery store was still brimming with supplies. I would have liked to go unload this shipment and come back but it was already beginning to darken, and I had not the least desire to be out here any longer. We could come back tomorrow, zombies willing. I climbed back into the truck. Thad was in the process of getting in on the other side. When I stared ahead through the windshield, I felt like I had been punched in the gut. Standing not more than one hundred feet away was THE zombie woman and she was holding something. I was having a difficult time discerning what it was when she held it above her head.

"Oh Christ!" I opened my door and evacuated my guts.

Thad had just adjusted himself in the seat before he had looked. "Oh Dear Father in Heaven!"

More power to Thad, he didn't get nauseous, but then again he didn't know the person that head used to belong to.

"Dad!" Travis yelled, "That zombie has Spindler!"

I jumped down off the truck. I wanted to run up to her and scream 'What are you doing,' and 'Why are you following us?' My gaze kept returning to the head in her up stretched arm. Eyes rolled up so only the whites showed, tongue lolling out like a dog on a hot summer's day. Ragged flesh around the neck showed the numerous bite marks it had taken to separate the head from the body. There was at least six inches of blindingly white spine that hung down past the ropes of skin and vein. She dropped the head and even from this distance we heard the sound, mostly because I think all of us were holding our breaths. The skull cracked with an audible 'pop' and as luck would have it, Spindler's head, of course, rolled to a stop upside down, looking at us. I looked back up to her face, my mouth hanging open like a giant Venus flytrap. She nodded once and turned to walk back through the alleyway.

I shouted at her. "What does that mean?" not expecting any reply. "Is that what you're going to do to us?" And then it dawned on me. "Is that your brand of payback for us not killing you?"

She had been watching the exchange with Durgan. She had seen Spindler turn tail and run. I was scared all the way down to my meat and potatoes. This involved a much higher brain activity than 'Must Eat Brains.' She was displaying signs of justice, albeit a Thailand version, but a form of justice all the same. It took all of my control not to run to her and demand an answer. She had helped, of that I was sure. Spindler was a spineless little piece of shit but he wouldn't blindly run into a lone zombie. No, he was cornered, or more likely I thought, herded into a trap. The little pecker left me in the lurch and I had fully intended on busting his nose when I saw him back at Little Turtle, but I never would have wished on him what had happened. Big Tiny started to walk towards the end of the store to the alleyway that buttressed between the grocery store and a bar.

"B.T. I wouldn't do that," I told him.

"I know YOU wouldn't," he said condescendingly.

"Go ahead. But I'm sure she has friends. LOTS of friends," I said as nonchalantly as possible.

His step faltered a beat but he kept steadily onwards. Without turning back he asked, "How many friends do you think she has?" a minute quaver in his voice.

"At least a dozen or so. How many do you think you could kill with that tire iron before they overtake you?" I challenged.

His pace slowed but he didn't want to let up now that he was committed. I had to find him an out so he could save face, especially in front of the women.

"B.T., I'm sure you could take out the zombies, but it's getting dark and I want to get this truck home and unloaded before midnight," I temporized.

Even from seventy feet I could see the relaxation in his shoulders. "Yeah, you're right man, I am tired. Stupid zombies." He chucked his tire iron and turned to come back. The bar clanged and slid to the foot of the alleyway not more than five feet away from the woman zombie and a couple hundred of her closest friends. Evil oozed from the mouth of that darkness and I was happy to be leaving. As powerful as the déjà vu had been upon seeing Beth, so too was the feeling that we had just averted a major disaster. It would have been easier to use the whole parking lot to turn the truck around but I didn't want to be anywhere near the alleyway in case I stalled, which was a viable possibility. The truck ride home wasn't nearly as stomach-turning as my previous attempt. Either I was getting better or I was too distracted to care, although Thad was looking a little green, but that could have been from our encounter moments before. I waited by the bus gate, waiting for them to open it.

"Any zombies with you?" Jed's familiar voice rang out.

"Open this gate, old man, before I ram this truck through that stupid bus," I responded.

Jed waved the bus to move and the sliding wall retracted. Smiling a little, the old bastard was having a great time busting my balls. Great, just what I needed. And then the more I thought about it, I think he was right, but I wasn't going to let him know.

Damn it! I stalled the truck halfway through the entrance.

"Nice driving, Tex!" Jed shouted.

"Shut up you old fart!" I yelled, fresh sweat busting out on my forehead.

"Should I just put up a neon sign that says 'OPEN?'" he yelled back.

Now he was laughing and I was so flustered I flooded the damn engine. The guards were looking up and down the street, they were nervous. We hadn't had this large a breach since the night it all went down. I was finally able to get it started and all the way in. The bus almost slammed into my rear end in their haste to get the gate closed. I pulled the rig up to the clubhouse for the off-loading and I hopped down. Jed bustled over, beaming at our haul, including the four newcomers. However, he was a little put off when he noticed our returning party was one fewer than the departing one.

"Spindler?" he asked.

I shook my head subtly. There must have been something to the look in my eye because he didn't press the issue. I had other things on my mind to contend with, the strange zombie woman being at the forefront. I would wait for tonight to speculate on that though. I quickly gave Jed an account of our run-in with Durgan and then waved one of the Little Turtle women over, Joann Orefice. She was the unofficial official welcome wagon.

"Hey Joann, we've got four newbies," I began

"Three," Thad stated firmly.

I looked his way. My eyebrows arched up as if to say 'really?'

"Look," he said. "She might not be the nicest person in the world but she's family and she's all I've got left. Don't worry, I know where she lives." He headed off into the twilight.

From zombies to Mrs. Deneaux, I was weighing the choices.

"Three then," I finished.

Joann moved closer towards our small group. "Ohmigod." She stopped short. "What is that smell?"

"I'm leaving, I'm leaving," I said, this was preferable to an explanation. But before I left I had to ask one question. "Beth, have we ever met before?"

She said 'no' half a beat too quick. Great, now I would spend half the night in a fruitless attempt to try to figure out where I knew her from.

Joann smiled and the two women began to talk animatedly. When B.T. stepped from behind the tractor-trailer, Joann looked up with a worrisome expression across her face.

I laughed a little. "Don't worry, he's harmless," I yelled back as I added extra speed to my step to get the hell out of there.

I could hear Big Tiny growl behind me.

CHAPTER 10
Journal Entry - 10

I opened the front door to our home. Tommy was waiting by the door.

"Hey Tommy, how you doing bud?" I said, smiling at him. It was impossible not to, with his giant grin to match.

"Hey Mr. T, how you doing? Everything go all right?" he asked expectantly.

I had no wish to recap the horrific events of the day with Tommy, and he didn't need to know either way. This was all just small talk anyway. I knew what he was fishing for.

"Yeah not so bad, bud," I said as I pulled off my small rucksack. I thought for a second he was going to start dancing on his tippy-toes. That alone would have made the trip worthwhile.

"Hey Tommy, I found these while we were getting ready to leave," I said nonchalantly as I tossed him a Yoo-Hoo and a Butterfinger. In all reality it was the first two items I had sought out.

"Thanks Mr. T!" he said as he wrapped his arms around me. It was a hug of the innocent, something that was going to be sorely missed in this brave new reality.

"Please call me Mike, Tommy." I pleaded.

"Okay Mr. T," he answered as he took a bite of his Butterfinger right next to my ear.

The noise was loud enough to startle Henry, who had been sleeping on the couch. The same couch I wasn't allowed on if I even *looked* dirty.

I waited for Tommy to finish his Yoo-Hoo which he was gleefully slugging away on before I asked him a question that had been bothering me the better part of the day.

"Tommy," I said. He looked up. "Do you have family?"

The merriment in his eyes clouded over in distress with the swiftness of a storm at 14,000 feet. I was sorry I had asked. If I had known the pain I was going to put the boy through I would have left it alone.

"My parents are dead, Mr. T," he said solemnly.

With the finality and certainty with which he had answered I was wrongly under the impression that it had happened years ago in some tragic fashion, like a car accident or a building fire. I didn't press. I had all the answer I wanted even though it wasn't the right one.

But Tommy continued. "I sent a message and I haven't heard anything back."

I stared hard at him for a second straining to bring my thoughts back in focus, and then I let out a small whoosh through my teeth.

"Tommy that's all right," I said happily. "Cell phones are not working, they probably just didn't get your message."

I felt hopeful. I couldn't stand the thought of this big happy-go-lucky kid being depressed. That would be like the sun wearing a veil.   Tommy stared at me like I was going nuts.

"I don't have a cell phone, Mr. T. I kept losing them so Mom said to save my money."

I had a dozen questions I wanted to ask him but Tommy fixed all of his attention on his Butterfinger, as if to say in a passive aggressive manner that he was done discussing the matter. When I saw the sunshine come back into his eyes, I let it go. I walked into the kitchen, shaking my head a bit trying to get a grasp on the conversation Tommy and I had just had. I chalked up our miscommunication on intellectual lack. Mine, not his. I figured while I was heading this way I might as well get a kiss from Tracy.

"Get out of here," she begged. "I could smell you coming! You're going to make the food spoil." And then she flicked a noodle at me.

"Yeah it's all fun and games until someone loses an eye," I said dejectedly as I turned around to head upstairs and take a shower.

I took a shower hot enough to melt skin, well maybe only on a wax figurine, but it was still plenty hot. I toweled off and changed into some clothes that weren't going to need to be destroyed. I caught the aroma of dinner cooking and it smelled heavenly, but the pull of my bed was stronger. You know how people say that they were asleep before they hit the pillow? I never believed a word of it, at least until tonight when it happened to me. Right behind sleep came the nightmares. I dreamed of my daughter (not Nicole, of course it was the woman in the field). She was wearing the tattered blue dress from the little girl at Wal-Mart. She was running to greet me. I had been away but couldn't remember where I'd been. As she approached her mouth began to grow disproportionately to her size, and lined in the gigantic maw were razor sharp teeth. She kept getting closer. I wanted to scream but it was frozen in my throat. Spindler walked up beside me and asked, 'Do you want me to cut her head off?' I was shocked. He was holding a sword. I was nodding yes but mouthing 'No…she's my daughter.'

'Wimp,' he said as he walked away, twirling the blade in the air. I couldn't peel my eyes away as I watched the blade twist faster and faster catching and reflecting the sunlight. (Weren't we just inside?) The blade had ascended as far as it was going to go and began its long graceful descent. I shouted to Spindler, 'Get out of the way!'

I distracted him long enough for the blade to do its work. I watched his head roll on the floor, trying to ascertain how so sharp of an instrument could leave such a jagged edge. I looked up at my daughter, who was not my daughter. She was right in front of me. Her breath was noxious as she stood eye to eye with me, although I knew she was at least a half-foot shorter than I was. Her arms reached out to grab my hands. I was frozen. I accepted her cold embrace.

'Do you want to play?'

Nothing was frozen this time, I awoke screaming, but my distress was covered up by the sound of small arms fire.

Justin was halfway up the stairs when I got to the bedroom doorway.

"You get your brother and keep watch on the house," I said to Justin. "And tell Brendon to get his boots on, me and him are going out to see what's going on." Justin was about to say something and I had a gist of what it was going to be. "No," I shook my head. "You and Travis have had enough excitement for the day and I need to know your mom, sister and Tommy are safe."

That soothed him but it didn't appease him. Rifle fire was still chattering away, something was even more amiss than you would normally derive from gunfire at night. Nobody had sounded the alarm. Jed was going to have someone's ass for this lack of discipline. Then I heard a sound that was almost as nightmarish as the nightmare I had just woken from. It was undeniably the sound of a machine gun, something that none of us besides me had access to in this complex, and I was holding mine.

"Shit!" I yelled. "Everyone but Brendon upstairs. It's a raid! If anyone comes in this house without announcing themselves, you shoot first! You got that, boys? I'll lock up on the way out. No one is getting in without making a lot of noise."

Quasi-intelligent zombies were one issue to deal with, determined humans with weapons were another. The 'brrrrpppp' of the machineguns went off again. I could hear screaming and the sounds of confusion coming from the direction of the clubhouse. Well, it probably wouldn't be too difficult to tell where to look for stuff to raid, with that giant semi sitting out there. And then it hit me, I knew without a shadow of a doubt Durgan and his merry band of insane idiots were behind this. The machine gun I was hearing must be that menacing looking Gatling gun Durgan had been toting. Obviously it wasn't for show as I had hoped.

Brendon and I were halfway to the clubhouse when

we came across our first victim. I didn't know him well but he was at all the meetings, usually in the back, I think his name was Bob or Hank, Ted maybe. Oh, who gives a crap, his neck looked like it was cut with a machete. Whoever had done this was incredibly strong and had been trying to sneak in silently. 'Damn Durgan, I'm going to blow his head off,' I thought viciously.

As we crept in closer we could hear the moans of the wounded, some crying out for their moms. I knew from my previous combat tours that those would be the ones that wouldn't make it through the night.

Durgan's Gatling gun lit up the sky like a Christmas tree on 'roids, it was impossible not to find him. He was about forty feet away from me and looking in the other direction, so when I stepped out from behind my tree I didn't expect him to wheel on me with such precision. I watched in hyper-slow-motion as the barrels began their circular route. Bullets began to blaze, first into the grass next to the tree I had been hiding behind, and then into the tree Brendon was cuddling like it was his long lost lover. I heard the discernible sound of the tree snapping; it was coming down but for the life of me I couldn't remember how big it was and if it would crush me should it hit me. The only thing that saved me was my Marine Corps training; the moment I stepped from behind that tree I had started firing.

My bullets found their mark a moment before Durgan's had. It wasn't a head shot but it was just as effective. I had sheared his right leg off right above the knee. Blood gushed from the wound as he went down hard.

'The bigger they are the harder they fall.' Is there any chance I could get a CAT scan in this post apocalyptic world, FOCUS!' My introspection and celebration were short-lived as I felt the buzz of hot lead incredibly close to my head. Brendon began to pop off rounds with his .380 but with an effective range of about twenty-five feet, odds were we were in more trouble than our opposition. My clip was empty and I wasn't even sure of much more than our assailant's general direction. I pulled Brendon down behind the small fallen pine tree. The branches wouldn't do much to stop a bullet but it kept our positions concealed.

"Brendon, I only brought one magazine and it's gone," I told him. The look on his face was a Kodak moment.

Dejectedly he turned to me and said. "Yeah I popped off about five or six rounds, I've only got about four rounds left myself."

We could hear more screaming. Most of it was coming from the clubhouse, but the majority of it was coming from Durgan himself. The language he was using was making me blush. I wanted to take Brendon and back away so we could first off get out of harm's way and secondly to go get more ammo and preferably a better gun for him. I looked up just high enough to see over the trunk and was welcomed by an angry assault of hornets, well, more like MK-46 7.62 rounds but you get the general idea. One of Durgan's flunkies had us pinned.

I tried not to let my apprehension show in my voice. "Umm, I think moving out of here isn't going to be an option," I told Brendon.

"I kinda figured," he replied cynically.

We were pinned, low on ammo and the damn cavalry was nowhere in sight.

"Where the hell is Jed?" I asked of no one in particular.

"Oh, no!" Brendon said, as I watched his face fall.

"What? What's the matter?" I asked. Unless the zombies were taking this opportune time to attack, I couldn't understand what had him in such a funk. I then followed his line of sight.

"OH NO, you have got to be kidding me!" I yelled. I think I said something that more resembled Durgan's vernacular than my own, but it got lost in the translation.

Coming towards us was Tommy. He was advancing as stealthily as a 250-pound hulking kid can. Needless to say he sounded like a bull in a china shop during an earthquake with cowbells strapped to its back, am I making myself clear enough?

"Is that a…a bow and arrow?" I asked incredulously. I knew what it was, it just wasn't registering. We had been vacationing in Estes Park, oh man, had to have been ten years ago, back when Justin was the ripe old age of nine. We had gone into a sporting goods store and Justin had fallen in love with a kid's bow and arrow set. It was the type with the practice arrow tips. It was a safe 'toy' unless of course you played William Tell. When we got back to the cabin and Tracy saw what I had bought him she ripped me a new one. It sucked that I had to wipe two holes for a couple of weeks, but Justin was stoked. Was that too graphic? Sorry.

Anyway back to my backfill story, like any kid he played with it for a good two weeks before he became sick of it. I think there were two arrows left that weren't either broken or lost. I had put it up in the garage almost a decade ago and hadn't thought about it since. How Tommy found it and why he was coming to 'help' us was a different story.

I so desperately wanted to yell out to him to stop and go home, but I didn't want to bring undue attention to him either. But how the hell they didn't see him coming was beyond my comprehension. I was already mourning his passing in my head; I was going to miss the kid. He was like a ray of sunshine in an otherwise dark and desolate world. He got to within ten feet of our location. I was frantically gesturing for him to come and hide with us. I even rose a little to get him when the angry hornets came back. He just looked over at us and was smiling, Butterfinger mess spread all over his face. He then pulled the drawstring back so far on that little bow I thought it was going to snap in half. He let go, the arrow flew. I knew without a doubt in my mind that arrow was going to hit home. It was divine intervention, pure and simple. I heard the telltale thud of impact. Whoever that arrow had hit hadn't even had time to cry out in surprise.

"Hey Mr. T!" Tommy yelled, waving happily. "Do you think they have any Twinkies in there?" He gestured toward the clubhouse.

I stood up slowly, still half-crouching and waiting for someone else to pepper my location. When no one did I turned back to Tommy. I didn't know whether to kick his ass or kiss it. I know he wouldn't have understood either gesture. So I just held out my arms wide. He rushed forward for the offered hug and nearly toppled me over which would have completed the mission the raiders had attempted. I so wanted to yell at him, but that huge grin and the fact that he had saved our lives, well that factored into my decision not to.

"Yeah, there's Twinkies. Come on." I put my arm around him and led him past the worst of the carnage so we could rummage through the food.

Little Turtle residents were now scrambling in the aftermath to help the wounded or offer solace to the dying. I wasn't a medic or a priest, so I stayed with Tommy while the whirlwind of activity swirled around me.

Jed came in a few minutes later to assess the situation. "Good work Talbot," he said as he slapped me on the back. "I heard what you did. Most of these snot nosed 'hard asses,'" he sneered as he said that, "were running in the other direction. I'm glad you've got some mettle in you, we wouldn't have made it through the night, much less anything further."

I slightly nodded my head in acknowledgment. But then pointed to Tommy, who was gleefully stuffing two Twinkies in his face simultaneously, crumbs littered the floor at his feet. "He's the real hero, Jed, he took out a machine gunner with a bow and arrow."

"Holy cow!" Jed whooped. He shook Tommy's hand and was a little taken aback by the stickiness of the crème filled Twinkie center that cemented the shake. "You're a hero, boy," Jed finished as he wiped his hand on his pants.

"Fank you!" Tommy said, spitting blonde orts, smiling with his teeth all sugar coated and gummed up.

"Let's get you home Tommy. I'm sure Mrs. T is worried about you," I said.

"Youf toof,"he finished.

"Yeah probably a little worried about me too," I concluded.

Jed called out to us while we were leaving. "Emergency meeting in about an hour, I'd like to get this area cleaned up a little first."

I waved over my back letting him know I had heard, I wouldn't be sleeping much tonight anyway.

Tracy almost ripped the front door from its hinges when we came back up the walkway. Brendon had already come home to tell them where Tommy was and that we were all right.

"Are you crazy? What were you thinking? Are you hurt? Why didn't you just get your Yoo-Hoo? Where did you find that damned bow and arrow?" She was rapid firing questions so fast I couldn't even keep up.

Tommy's eyes at first furrowed and then began to water. It was safe to assume he wasn't liking Tracy berating him.

"Don't worry, kid," I said as an aside. "She'll peter out in a minute." It was funny watching this waif of a woman tongue-lash a person more than twice her size.

The glistening in Tommy's eyes broke Tracy's anguish. She immediately rushed forward, giving Tommy a big hug, getting swallowed up in his arms.

"What, no hug for me?" I asked dejectedly.

She pulled away from Tommy and directed the full force of her assault at me. "How could you? You're a grown man you should have known better. What were you thinking? Oh that's right, you weren't thinking at all, were you."

I was backpedaling as fast as I could to avoid the finger of doom she kept thrusting at me.

Tommy's words of encouragement did little to help me. "Don't worry Mr. T, she'll peter out in a minute!" he yelled as he began to dig into his pockets for another sugary snack.

When Tracy finally looked like she wasn't going to

thrust her finger through my sternum, I pulled Justin aside.

"Justin, how do you know Tommy?" I asked. There were questions that needed answering. Whether Justin was going to be able to answer them was a different story.

"He's just the retar…" He saw the scowl forming on my face, so he amended his words. "He's just the door greeter, and I mean, you already know he's a little slow."

"Yeah I figured that part out but there's something more to him too," I said.

Now it was Justin's turn to look perplexed. Good, now I wouldn't be alone.

"Did you go and get him when the zombies started attacking the Wal-Mart?" I asked

"Even if I had thought to, I didn't, Dad. My section, Gardening, is at the complete other end of the building. We barely made it as it was, and to be honest I don't think I've ever said more than hi to him. Although he gives me a damn sticker every time he sees me. He loves those stickers," Justin said with a smile. "And come to think of it Dad, Tommy was already on the roof when we got there, he's the one that unlocked it for us."

"Would he have access to the roof?" I asked.

Justin looked at me incredulously, "Dad I'm not even sure if he knew there was a roof."

There was more than meets the eye when it came to Tommy, and hopefully I'd have enough time to figure it out. I had a few minutes before Jed's emergency gathering and I just wanted to ask Tommy a thing or two. Tommy was in the midst of quaffing down some M&M's. (I didn't even remember liberating those from the store.)

"Hey Tommy, can I talk to you for a minute?" I asked.

He looked up and a bunch of the M&M's rolled to the floor. Tommy looked like he was having an internal battle with himself whether he should pick them up. Henry took care of the matter before it began to weigh too heavily on him. He pulled his gaze off Henry, maybe just a little miffed the dog had eaten his candy, but then Tommy gave Henry a big kiss on the forehead as an offering of apology for having had a bad thought. Henry in return licked his face, which Tommy delighted in, but personally I think the lick had more to do with the smattering of Twinkie all over Tommy's face.

"Tommy," I said again, hoping to reel back his attention.

"Hey Mr. T," Tommy answered. "Oh right! Yeah, you can talk to me for a minute."

I figured no sense in beating around the bush so I asked him straight out. "Tommy, how did you get on the Wal-Mart roof the other night?"

He was thinking hard. I almost believed I could hear the wheels creaking in his noggin. And then when he came out with the answer it was like it was no big deal, something he had been dealing with his entire life. "The Voice told me."

Goose bumps ran up and down my arms. "The voice?" I asked hoping for some elaboration.

"Yeah, you know, The Voice the one that tells you to do things," he explained, digging into his bag of candy, thrilled when he pulled out a blue M&M.

The way he said it gave me the impression that he thought everyone had a guiding voice.

"Did you hear this same voice earlier tonight when you came to help me and Brendon?"

"Oh yeah, I was going to get my Yoo-Hoo and I stopped with the refrigerator door open. Are you mad because I left the door open? I forgot about it once before. The Voice told me where to look for the bow and then the arrows and that I had to come help you quick 'cause you were in a lot of trouble." My mouth must have been hanging open because he just kept going. "So you're not mad about the fridge door being open?"

I snapped back to reality. "The door? No I'm not mad about the door. You saved my life, and Brendon's too. I don't care if a few Popsicles melt."

Tommy's expression became one of alarm. "Not the

Popsicles!" he said as he started to rise, I believe to go shut the fridge door.

I grabbed his arm. "Don't worry, Tommy. The Popsicles are in the freezer," I said, doing my best to calm his nerves.

His face relaxed. "Oh okay, I only left the fridge door open," he finished.

"Back to the voices," I started, realizing he was once again paying at least some attention to me as he dug around in the bag looking for some more blue M&M's.

"Voice," he muttered.

"Huh?" came my reply.

"You said 'voices,' there's only one, don't you know that?" he said, but not in a condescending way.

"Well I do now," I told him. Tommy just looked at me funny. I absolutely was intrigued, my 'need to know' meter was through the roof at this point. "Does the voice sound like God?" I asked conspiratorially.

"No," he answered as he shook his head. His eyebrows creased as if to say I was nuts.

"Jesus?"

He shook his head again.

"The archangel Michael?"

"Who?" he asked, a look of disfavor crossing his face as he pulled a green one out of the bag.

Well if that wasn't the voice then there was no real reason to explain who Michael was. "Tommy, who does the voice belong to?" I asked.

Tommy leaned in real close and whispered in my ear, making sure no one else heard.

I sat back in my chair hard when he told me. I was searching his face for any signs of deception or amusement. I found neither. The voice Tommy heard in his head belonged to Ryan Seacrest. 'Oh that's rich,' I thought to myself. I had just moments earlier been locked in a life-or-death gun battle and I now found myself on the verge of laughing hysterically. I knew the voice wasn't actually Ryan

Seacrest's, but that didn't stop Tommy from believing in it wholesale. Something was going on. I couldn't wait to see what Ryan had in store for Tommy next, as long as it didn't get the kid hurt. I gave him a big hug which he reciprocated in spades, and went to get something to eat before the meeting, shaking my head and muttering "Ryan fucking Seacrest" all the way to the kitchen.

CHAPTER 11
Journal Entry - 11

The mood at the meeting was, in a word, depressed. We had lost eight of our small community and none of them were Mrs. Deneaux, I thought sourly. There had been five raiders, four were killed, one wounded and subsequently captured. You guessed it, my old pal Durgan had lived.

"Okay," Jed began. "So now the question is, what do we do with the prisoner."

"Kill him! Shoot him! Put him outside the gates!" came an assortment of angry replies from the group.

Jed was trying his best to restore order, but the crowd (mob) wanted nothing to do with it. Eight of their own had been killed and they wanted good old-fashioned Western justice.

"Talbot, this is the second run-in you've had with this guy. What's your opinion?" Jed opted to turn the discussion over to me.

'Thanks so much, Jed, for dumping this mess on me,' I thought sourly as I stood up. "Jed, Durgan is dangerous and probably insane, but there isn't anywhere here that we could lock him up. Even if we did we would have to spread our already thin resources to guard him. I'm also not much for cold-blooded murder, so I guess I haven't solved anything," I sat down dejectedly.

Jed scowled at me as if to say 'Thanks for nothing.'

I shrugged. I wasn't getting paid the big bucks to make the difficult decisions.

"Well then, we're just going to have to set up a court system. I know that man killed our friends and neighbors, but I will not condone a lynch mob."

"What gives you the right? He killed my best friend!"

More than one resident yelled their agreement with Don Griffin, the man that had shouted out. "We know the outcome of the trial already, let's just skip the formalities." The yells of agreement were louder and contained more voices; it appeared to me that Jed was quickly losing ground and his tenuous hold on power.

I don't know why I stood again, part of me thinks it's because my whole life I've bucked the system. Society says go 'right' I go 'left.' I've always been a rebel even if only in my mind.

"LISTEN!" I shouted. I waited a few seconds for the murmurs to die down. "You know Jed and I don't always see eye to eye." That received some laughs, most people remembering an easier life when the biggest problem was the correct time to put out the trash. "But he's right - THIS TIME," I emphasized. "I would like nothing more than to kill Durgan but not like this, not in cold blood. Mr. Griffin?" I asked. "Could you, even now, as mad as you are, walk up to that man and kill him?" I didn't want him to have enough time to ponder the question. He was still pissed so I hastened on. "Of course you can't, you're not a murderer. I know it's cliché but do you want to step down to the level of that *man*?" I spat out the last word. It tasted funny on my tongue even as I was saying it. "Jed's right," I said with less vehemence. "We have to hold onto our civility or we just become a pack of rabid dogs." The crowd wasn't overly enthused with my speech but the dissension had died down and I think if put to a vote even Don Griffin would acquiesce.

Jed thanked me with a slight nod. "All right, we will meet tomorrow to discuss who will preside over the trial, who will defend the accused, who will prosecute and who will sit on the jury." There was still some grumbling in the audience but it didn't look like Jed was going to have his power usurped tonight. Jed continued. "Okay, now we have the more pressing concern of having to figure out how to defend against invaders. I honestly thought that zombies would be our only threat, for that I take full responsibility. I had the misconceived notion that any survivors would be thrilled at the prospect of joining our small society, not destroying it. If five armed men can cause this much destruction, we have to come up with another plan."

"How about putting their severed heads on pikes outside the gates," Griffin griped. Apparently he wasn't quite done. Jed did the best thing he could. He ignored the comment.

"Listen folks, I made a mistake," Jed said dejectedly. "We are going to have to be more vigilant, and more vigilance means more guards."

That did not sit well with the natives. "We already spend most of our day doing guard duty, what's the sense of living if all we're doing is defending against dying?" said one of the gentlemen I had seen around the complex walking his Bassett Hound during better times. There were other irritable words but Basset Hound man had pretty much hit the nail on the head.

Jed put his hands up in a placating manner before he began. "This is just temporary, I've already been talking to Alex and he has come up with plans for guard towers, and thanks to Talbot we now have the equipment and supplies to build them. They will be about fifteen feet tall, with a retractable ladder, armor plating and lights. Because of their height, the guards on duty will be able to cover a wider range. This will mean less guards in the foreseeable future. We have also had ideas about heightening the wall but materials are going to be a factor. So if anyone can think of something, I'm all ears."

I stood up again. I didn't get the same reproachable look from Jed I had received the first time. "I think I know what we can do, although I'm not all that thrilled about it. There's a National Guard armory about seven miles from here. Their entire enclosure is surrounded by Dannert wire. We could cut it down and place it here. It will be close but I think there will be enough."

For those of you who don't know what Dannert wire

is, picture it as beefed up barbed wire. This stuff is nasty. It literally has razors positioned on it every few inches. The team that was going to have to retrieve this stuff was most likely going to need blood infusions when the task was completed. Like a dumb ass, I had volunteered. Why didn't I listen to my drill instructor from boot camp? He told us flat out, 'Don't EVER volunteer for anything! If you're picked you go, but don't EVER volunteer your worthless lives!' Words to live by. Nice going Talbot.

"All right, now that we know I'm going, we're going to need a few more people, some to guard and most to help haul this stuff." Clearly these people had never been to boot camp, because I got more than enough volunteers without any serious cajoling. "A couple of things. Bring the heaviest gauge clothing you can. This stuff will slice through denim like a shark through water. I'm not kidding. Next, does anyone know how to drive a truck?" Thank God someone answered because just thinking about driving that behemoth again made my stomach turn.

"Excellent, excellent," Jed continued. "Tomorrow is going to be a very busy day. Alex will ask for volunteers to help build and erect eight towers. Three towers each on the West and East sides and one on each of the gated sides. We've got the folks going with Talbot, we'll need ten or so people for food distribution, and on a more lugubrious note…"

The guy next to me asked what in the hell 'lugubrious' meant. I had no clue, I was in remedial English in high school so I just shrugged.

"…We will need a burial detail for those of our family and friends that have fallen." I tuned back in to Jed's instructions.

Don Griffin immediately shot his hand up. "I'll go," he said sullenly. "He was my friend." The remainder of folks already not on one of the other work details raised their hands also.

"All right folks, let's let this night be done," Jed

finished.

Chairs squeaked, backs popped, soft sighs emanated from the crowd as the meeting came to an end. I walked up to Jed. He wasn't a spring chicken when this carnival ride began. He was looking every bit of his age and then some.

"You been getting any sleep Jed?" I opened with. He rubbed his eyes in response.

"Jed, you can't do it all. You can't be mayor and sheriff and a soldier, that's too much," I empathized.

"What, because of my age!" he shot back. He softened when he saw the look of semi-shock on my face. "I'm sorry Talbot, you've been an unexpected ally during this...this crisis. You're right, I am tired. I'm dead tired. No pun intended," he said as he pointed a bony finger at me. "I'm afraid."

I moved in to comfort him.

He shrugged me away. "Not for me you pansy, I always knew you Marines were a fruity lot." I laughed and so did he. The expression looked more natural on him than the scowl I had always thought was permanently fixed to his face. "Now if you're not going to get all soft on me, I'd like to continue."

"I'll try to keep my hands to myself," I assured him.

"I'm afraid for our little community we've got here. The TV reports say that humanity is on the brink of extinction."

"Oh, you know how the news exaggerates," I cut in trying to lighten the mood.

He wasn't having any of it. He continued joylessly, "There are other holdouts out there and eventually we'll find a way to get in touch with them. But right now we have to stay alive, and if it isn't against those soulless zombies, we also have to be on guard against humanity's worst offenders. So maybe the zombies don't have any clue what they're doing," (on an aside, I wanted to interject a differing opinion but wisely or not I kept it to myself) "but that animal Durgan, he is the epitome of evil. I saw him, he was laughing while he was killing folks. Laughing, Talbot!" he almost screamed. "It almost doesn't seem worth it, if that's what we're trying to save, let the damn zombies have the place."

Holy crap, I didn't think I'd ever hear Jed getting ready to throw in the towel, he must be a lot more tired than he looked.

"Jed I'd be inclined to agree with you," I said slowly.

He looked at me with his head slightly tilted as if to say 'Bah, you'd never agree with me.'

I pushed on." There have been days, even before all this atrocity came raining down that I wanted to just give up. But there are more important things in this world than just me. I trudge on because of my family and because of my friends, and most of all…" I paused for dramatic effect, "because of you." I raced in real quick and gave him a kiss on the cheek. "See you tomorrow Jed!" I yelled as I raced out of the meeting hall, something clattered close to my heels.

"Fucken fruit," Jed said softly, smiling as he wiped his cheek.

CHAPTER 12 - December 13th

Journal Entry - 12

I woke up early, dressed and got out of the house as quickly as I could. I had made up my mind last night I wasn't bringing the boys but I hadn't told them yet. This was going to bite me in the ass. I could already feel the teeth marks. The added stress of having to look out for their welfare weighed heavily on me and I was looking forward to not having that burden. Yeah, they were better under pressure than me, at least for this situation, and their aim was nearly equal to mine. The idea of zombies being real had not completely set in to my reality. Justin and Travis however, had not only grasped the implications of this corporeality, they were easily sliding into this new lifestyle. I take no small measure of responsibility for their transitional ease. My psychoses had to have spilled over. I'd been preparing for some form of Armageddon for the better part of three decades. And the other factor has to be the video games that are rife with otherworldly monsters, including but not limited to zombies. They'd been prepared and partially desensitized. I trusted them implicitly. I just couldn't handle the apprehensiveness of looking out for them. Besides, truth be told, if anything ever happened to one of the kids Tracy would kill me, and I'm not talking that ha, ha, figurative shit either.

So I left the house early, my breath leaving vapor trails behind. I carried enough ammo to almost be a hindrance, but it was a comforting weight all the same. Looking back on this day, I wish I had volunteered for the grave digging party. That would have been a clambake comparatively. The truck was already idling with the heat going, for which I was thankful. I was beginning to feel the bite of the cold through my thin gloves. I wasn't going to wear anything heavier that might hinder my access to the trigger. I walked up to the four people that were huddled by the front grille of the truck. I rightfully assumed they were the wire gathering team. I didn't 'know' any of them, even though I'd seen them around the complex in one fashion or another.

There was Jen, the 'feminine' partner in the pairing with Jo(e), the neighbor we had slaughtered coming out of my garage. (That nightmare still ranked in the top three). She wasn't nearly as outgoing as her former lover and I had never said more than pleasantries to her. I always thought it was a waste that she was a lesbian. Come to think of it, maybe that's why she avoided me. Maybe she had been able to pick up on my lascivious thoughts. She wasn't looking so good these days though. The deliberation she was giving the mourning process had aged her considerably. Her elfish features had diminished. If I'm being honest it's not so much that her looks weren't still there, it was more like her soul was hanging by a thread. The light behind her eyes had dulled leaving nothing more than two dimmed irises. The blackness that threatened to envelope them was not more than a heartbeat away.

Next was Carl, who nodded to me. He was an older guy, mid-fifties maybe, always in his garage working on his motorcycle with the door open whether it was 95 or negative 5 degrees out. He was quick with a wave and a smile, come to think of it I've probably waved to this guy a couple of hundred times in the months I've lived here and never once have I said hello. Strange. He had two pearl handled revolvers holstered to his belt. He looked like he knew how to use them but I would have hoped that he was carrying more firepower. Oh well, his call. Next was Ben, he was older than Carl, he was probably pushing 65 or 70, great. I was now dreading my decision to not bring the boys. I'd seen Ben around a few times. I don't think he went out too much.

He was always walking his Golden Retriever who looked older than him. I'm not sure which one of them went slower, neither one was in any great rush to get anywhere. I'm no Carl Lewis, but if we had to run for it I'm not sure Ben, or Carl for that matter, could outpace the zombies.

Last but not least, okay by sizing him up maybe he was least, was someone's nephew. He muttered something about an uncle or maybe elephant trunk, but I wasn't able to pick it up and I wasn't concerned enough to get clarification. His name was Tipper. I know! What kind of name is that? Tipper looked like a cokehead. He twitched more than Tom Arnold when Roseanne was yelling at him. I didn't trust any of them. Even though this was my idea, I now didn't want to go. I was more than half-tempted to turn around until Ben started to speak.

"Got the truck all warmed up for us," he drawled.

Everyone in our small party turned and deferred to me. I just wanted to go home and eat one of Tommy's Pop-Tarts. "Let's get going," I said instead. I inadvertently shivered, whether from the cold or someone walking over my grave; I wasn't sure but it seemed more the latter.

The truck rumbled by Don Griffin's small burial detail. They were headed out the Northern gate, shovels in hand and a small Cat backhoe trailing with a cart in tow. It wasn't until I actually saw the cart that the impact of what Don was doing hit. I hadn't thought about where the bodies would be buried although it seemed logical that they shouldn't be interred in the complex. There was a small field across the street well within the protective firing zone of the guards. Still I didn't think it was wise to leave without weapons, I mean who would go and bury the burial team if something happened to them? We swung out and away from the group, heading first east and then north. It would, in a normal world, be about a fifteen-minute drive with traffic and lights, though we now had neither of those to contend with. We had switched them out for zombies and bandits, a shitty exchange rate if you ask me. The drive was relatively uneventful, if not almost downright enjoyable. Ben knew how to handle the truck. Now if I could just get Tipper to shut up I might be able to think.

"Hey Mike," I winced. Tipper kept going. "Do you think we'll get to kill some zombies? Huh? I want to kill me some zombies. I was pretty messed up the night it went down, I mean I slept through the whole thing." He grinned sheepishly.

"My *friends* call me Mike," I said, lacing as much menace as I could through each word.

"Hey Mike, so how come there aren't any more zombies around? Huh? Where do you think they all went? Do you think they died? Or do you think they went somewhere else like Seattle? Huh?" Tipper kept at this pace for most of the ride until mercifully Jen spoke.

"Oh shut up, you little twit!" she yelled. "Decent people stop between questions so the person they are talking to has an opportunity to answer."

"Huh?" Tipper said tilting his head like a dog.

"But then I guess there's nothing to worry about, is there?" she continued mockingly.

Tipper finally shut up, maybe he was coming down. Now that I knew I had less of a chance of being interrupted I figured I might as well pass the time talking. I looked longingly over at Carl who was fast asleep and wished I were too. "I've been wondering the same thing, I mean, if these are 'traditional zombies.'"

Jen arched an eyebrow.

"I know, what the hell is a 'traditional zombie,'" I snorted. "Sorry, if these zombies are like the ones in stories then they are not going to die without a little assistance from us."

As I hefted up my rifle to show as an exclamation point, Jen's grip tightened on her own. Tipper had his back towards us, attempting to hide his habit. The telltale sniffing gave him away, that and his acerbic personality. Jen shook her head in disgust. I would have been amused if we weren't heading to a potential hot zone.

"More like a lukewarm zone," I said as I stepped off the truck and into the parking lot of what used to be Rocky Mountain National Guard Armory 17.

"Huh?" Jen asked quizzically as she shouldered on by.

"Uh, nothing, and let me know if I'm in your way," I said cheekily.

"I will," she responded without turning around.

'Someone's sense of humor had gotten up on the wrong side of the bed this morning,' I thought to myself.

Carl was rousing himself out of sleep, buttoning his pants back up and putting his jacket on before he stepped out. Ben was busy securing the truck, okay I thought, three out of four accounted for. Then I had a slight panic attack.

"Where's Twitchy?" I said louder than I meant to. In the cold still air of the morning it sounded like a shout.

Jen turned. "Who?" she asked

"Twitch...I mean Tipper," I clarified. The reply was quick and forthcoming but not the one I wanted.

"Look...arghhh, oh fuck!!!! Get it off!!!" Tipper screamed.

Jen and I both turned in horror. Carl was just coming down off the truck and gaped along with us. Tipper had walked up to the front door of the armory, which looked like it had been blasted off its hinges with a tank. Who knows, maybe it had been. But what was captivating our attention was the zombie attached to Tipper's head. Blood was streaming down the side of his face as he howled in a combination of terror and pain, the two of them staggering from side to side in a macabre dance. I brought my rifle up but I knew at this distance and their co-mingled movement I could not get a clean shot off. I never would have guessed if I hadn't seen it myself, but Carl was moving with all the speed and agility of a man half his age, unholstering his pistol as he went. Within moments he was within safe firing distance of Tipper and his new dance partner. The zombie paid no attention to Carl as the pistol was neatly placed against its head. If I thought my voice was loud, the Colt .45 shattered any of those illusions. The open entryway to the armory amplified the affect. The noise was deafening, but not to Tipper, his right ear went down with the zombie. Tipper was clutching at the gaping bloody hole where his ear used to be, screaming for all he was worth.

"Shut him up!" Ben was saying frantically. "He'll have half the zombie population here in a minute."

"Yeah, as opposed to that small cannon fire," I said sarcastically.

Jen was walking over to Tipper to try and console him, but Tipper was having none of it. He kept pushing her away. She had finally had enough.

"Either let me see the damn wound, or I'm going to have Carl finish you off!" Jen yelled.

Carl was busy wiping the gore off his gun and didn't notice that he had been involved in Jen's plan. But it was effective enough to shut Tipper up. He was sniffling and close to blubbering. I wanted to call him a baby and tell him to shut up, but when Jen finally calmed him down enough so she could examine the wound, I didn't say anything. I was too busy holding my bile down. The zombie had bitten the ear clean off but the ear had not come off without collateral damage. It had stayed mostly attached to his face when the zombie went down. The force had torn half of Tipper's cheek off. So not only was there the exposed ear hole but also the muscles that lined the side of his face. He looked worse than the poor bastard lying on the ground. Torn tissue sprayed blood as he swung his head from side to side in obvious agony. I thought the best thing we could do for him was to shoot him and put him out of our misery, I mean *his* misery.

"Ben!" Jen yelled. "Are there any rags in the truck?"

I didn't see the point and I let my opinion be known. "Move away Jen," I motioned with my rifle.

"Are you crazy!" she spat back.

"What good is a bandage," I said dismally. "He'll be

one of them in a few hours."

"You coward!" she screamed. "I can stop the bleeding, and I have some aspirin."

"And then?" I said lowering my rifle. I just didn't have the stomach for it.

Tipper was doing his best to hide his tall wiry frame behind Jen's petiteness, his misery forgotten for a moment under this much bigger threat. Ben was watching the stand-off when for the second time that day I thought my eardrums were going to burst. Jen stood stockstill as blood and gore from Tipper's demolished head sprayed all over her.

"WHAT THE FUCK DID YOU JUST DO?" she was screaming at me.

I was looking down at my rifle. 'I didn't do a damn thing, did I?'

Carl was walking into the armory. "He would have been one of them soon enough, I did what I had to do." And he offered no further explanation.

Jen still had not moved, at least not in a lateral direction. Even from this distance I could see her shivering, from either fear or rage. Ben hopped back up into the truck looking for a rag, but now for a different reason than before. He came down from the cab with a roll of paper towels. I grabbed his arm lightly before he passed by.

"Uh Ben, after you get her cleaned up could you stay out here on guard duty?"

He nodded sternly. I think Ben was doing his best to not let the situation affect him. If so, he was doing better than I was. I hastily passed Jen who was too intent on the gore running down her face to pay me any attention. I wanted to catch up with Carl before something else happened.

The blown apart doors were only the beginning of the destruction to the armory. The inside looked as if an F5 tornado had swept through. Um, maybe that isn't right, it was more like an F3. There was still SOME stuff lying around. Rows upon rows of empty racks that at one time contained M-16's were now empty. As I walked to the left I discovered even more foreboding news, the heavy stuff was gone too. You could see where there had been a few 50 caliber machine guns, about 10 SAW's (light machine guns) and two rocket launchers that were now missing. Just wonderful, there was a band of somebodies out there more heavily armed than an average battalion. Getting razor wire seemed like less of a priority; whoever had all this stuff wasn't going to be stopped by any glorified chicken wire.

"Hey Talbot," Carl beckoned. "Could you come over here and help me with these?"

I walked over to the armory repair station. Carl was rounding up about a dozen or so M-16's in various states of disrepair. I looked at him questioningly.

"We should be able to get at least a couple of these working, with all these parts," he answered me without even looking up.

Seemed like a worthwhile venture to me. I shouldered my weapon and grabbed a handful of rifles. There was loose ammo all over the place. Whoever had been here before us must have been in a hurry. Maybe they were leaving town. That would be awesome. They had spent enough time to clean out every working weapon and the vast majority of ammo, but it appeared as if some of the cartons had fallen and spilled out on the floor. They hadn't warranted those bullets important enough to pick up. There had to have been at least a few thousand rounds on the ground alone. God, how many did they take with them?

As I walked out into the brightness it took a moment for my eyes to adjust. Ben was just finishing getting most of the viscous material off Jen. They both looked more than a little green-tinged.

"Jen, when you're done here, could you go into the armory and start grabbing all the ammunition that's on the floor?" I asked. I'm not a psych major. I didn't know if I should approach her in a caring tone or a conciliatory one or any other damn method. I needed a job done and that's how I went about it.

"No," came her monosyballic reply.

I stopped short, one of the rifles threatening to fall out of my arms.

She started back up again. "I'm not going in there and I'm not staying out here. I'm getting back in the truck and lying down."

I wanted to throttle her. We were all a little thrown off by what had just happened but we had a mission to think about. That's what you get when you take civilians on a military endeavor.

"Jen, we have more to think about here than what just happened to Tipper. He messed up by running ahead and trying to be a hero. We have to get the remainder of this ammo and wire for the people back home," I almost pleaded. We were already one person short if Jen flaked out now, we'd be out here for hours longer than I had expected.

She turned to look at me, and fire flashed across her eyes. It was more likely sunlight reflecting off her sky blue irises, but the affect was staggering nonetheless. "See, that's where you're wrong Talbot! I don't have anyone at home! There's nothing for me there! I lost everything! I don't care whether we all live or die, I just don't care!"

"Then what the hell did you come out here for!" I yelled back. She flinched a little but nothing worth writing home about.

"Revenge! I thought I could exact some sort of pay back for what they did to Jo and to me! But I know that's useless now. They just don't care. No, it's even worse than that, they just don't know. They are mindless, one-track mind, killing and eating machines. They're almost as bad as MEN!" she shouted.

Wow, I guess there isn't going to be any hetero conversion there. Men and zombies were near enough equals in her mind. I didn't want anything more to do with Jen. She was a pulse away from going into shock and I had enough problems. I didn't bother answering her as I headed for the back of the truck.

A few seconds later, I heard the cab door shut as I exited the rear of the trailer. I hurried over to Ben.

"You have the keys?" I asked him apprehensively.

"Oh, you betcha," he replied.

"Any chance you could pick up the stray ammo?" I pleaded.

"I'd love to Talbot, but I've got a bad back, I couldn't bend over to save my life," he replied.

"Wonderful," I said scornfully. Ben looked a little taken aback. I had no desire to stroke his bruised feelings. "Keep guard then."

Carl had made a stack of rifles that he wanted to take with us. I guess I was the muscle. Carl had at least understood the necessity to grab all the strewn ammo and was down on his hands and knees pushing a large ammunition container in front of him as he filled it. Damn that thing was going to be heavy when he was done. I had grabbed another stack of weaponry when I heard Ben's shrill cry. I rushed out into the blinding light. Ben was pointing and trying to speak but I couldn't make it out yet. He was about as useless as Tipper, and as we all know, Tipper was dead.

"Zombies!" Ben finally vocalized. My sight was finally catching up. I saw a small contingent angling our way. The noise or the smell of meat must have garnered their attention, didn't matter which at this point. Jen sat up in the truck and locked the doors.

'What have I got myself into?' Ben was shaking so bad I thought his pants were going to fall off. Carl had followed me out when we heard Ben scream.

Thank God for Carl, of all the people here he was going to be my only true ally. He assessed the situation in a crack.

"Talbot, why don't you shut the gate. I'm going to finish gathering the bullets," he said and then turned and walked back into the armory.

"I love that guy," I said out loud.

There were six zombies heading towards us. If I

crawled backwards on my back to the gate I would still have had plenty of time to roll the gate closed. But zombies were zombies and they still scared the bejesus out of me. I jogged over to the gate and closed it. Then I wrapped the remnants of the remaining chain around the fence, just in case that by some grace of the devil they were able to figure out how to roll it back from where it came. We were effectively down three out of the five people we had started with, but I wasn't going home empty-handed. I went back into the tractor-trailer and grabbed the small ladder that we had placed in there so I could start the job. I cautiously approached the fence. The zombies didn't seem discernibly closer. I climbed the ladder and fished out the wire cutters that I had in my jacket. This was not going to be an easy task considering the thinness of the gloves I had put on for protection (or lack thereof). That and the fact that my goggles kept fogging up were making this a difficult venture. I had learned over the years that it is infinitely better to wear protection, no matter how cumbersome, rather than find ways to staunch the flow of blood from one's body.

Over the years as a handyman, a do-it-yourselfer and a general klutz, I had racked up more emergency room time than Tim the Tool Man Taylor. Please tell me you know who he was? Let's see, where do I start. I have broken a rib from installing an attic fan. I nearly cut off my index finger with a compound miter saw installing flooring. Put a drill bit through my thumb. Bruised my eyeball throwing a bunch of trash away at the dump when the errant cord from a toaster hit me. Cut a vein in my hand and sliced my head open while changing a light bulb. Sliced my leg open with a box cutter, you guessed it, while cutting a box. There are a least a dozen more instances over the years. I'm just listing the lowlights. So these days, most of the time I like to err on the side of caution. If there is some sort of safety gear for the task at hand, I want it. I'll take fogging up goggles over loss of sight any day. I was busy wiping said goggles for the third time and had already cut loose almost 50 feet of wire, when I felt the impact of the first zombie hitting the fence. My ladder shuddered, and my heart skipped a beat or two. I had almost forgotten about the persistent little buggers. Now Hector was looking up at me, arms outstretched, mouth agape. He was a heavyset Mexican man, small mustache, big belly. I'm not being racist. His name was Hector, it said as much on his name tag. That and he used to work at Tire Discount and he smelled as if he hadn't showered after five shifts at the physically demanding job. Flies were buzzing around him, but notably not on him. The flies seemed to be attracted to the sweet smell of decaying meat that emanated from his mouth but they were not enticed enough to get any closer. The oddest fact that struck me was not that a zombie was less than five feet from me, it was that flies were still around in early December. I wanted to put a round in Hector's bloated melon, if for nothing more than to get his putrid smelling ass away from me. But I had no inclination to see if the noise would attract more of his kind or anybody else's kind for that matter. So I kept cutting with the wire clippers, stepping down from my ladder to shift it over every five feet and climbing back up. And always Hector followed like a lovelorn puppy. Hector's friends had stayed at the gate to try their luck with Ben, who had only moved enough to get a better look at the zombies that wanted to eat him. For all intents and purposes it looked like a world-class staring competition.

On and on it went like this for another couple of hundred yards, Mr. Shuffles keeping consistent pace with my wire removal. My goggles had fogged for the umpteenth time, so this time I took my gloves off to get a better wipe down of the insistent miasma. After completing my job to a satisfactory level, I put my goggles back on and then began to pull my gloves on. The cold was having an adverse affect on me and I lost my grip on the second glove. As I reached over to try to grab the falling glove I compounded my troubles. The wire cutters that I had stowed in my jacket's breast pocket also fell as I leaned away from the ladder at an angle, and both items hit the ground and bounced, tumbling under the fence, they ended up at Hector's feet. I swear, if I didn't have bad luck I'd have no luck at all.

"Any chance you could hand those back to me?" I asked Hector. He only replied with a soft moan. "Yeah, I didn't think so."

I climbed down the ladder. His eyes never broke contact with mine. The glove and the cutters were less than six inches away on the other side of the fence. I could easily reach under and grab them, but if I somehow got hung up Hector would get his midmorning snack after all. Noise be damned, I was going to shoot him. I'd learned enough painful lessons over the years to not tempt fate. I began to un-sling my rifle, when Hector did something I was not expecting. He bent and recovered the glove and the cutters. With some motor skill difficulty he brought the glove to his nose and sniffed. Maybe he still smelled meat on them. He took a bite, ripping right through the thumb. He chewed for a moment and swallowed, then realized to his disappointment that it wasn't his desired nourishment, he dropped the glove. The wire cutters became Hector's next fascination. He started turning them over and over in his hands. He handled them like a newborn wearing mittens might, but I couldn't help thinking that this tool was somehow stirring some long forgotten memory in what used to pass as a human mind. His bluish-purple hands finally got the tool into a potentially usable fashion. He then began to thrust the cutters at the fence. I wasn't sure if what I was seeing was real or not. Was he trying to cut the fence? My mind whirled as the implications started setting in.

"Hey Carl, umm, could you come here for a minute?" I yelled over my shoulder. I was afraid that if I looked away for more than a fraction of a second, Hector would miraculously figure out how to use the cutters and make his way through the fence before I could turn back around.

"Talbot I'm a little busy," Carl shouted back. Seems there were more rounds than I had expected, Carl had been busy picking them up and loading them into the trailer.

"Yeah, still you might want to see this," I said determinedly, still not taking my eyes off Hector.

At one point the cutters made contact with the fence but Hector did not have the dexterity to close the pliers to do any damage. He moaned at that point, and I would have sworn it was because of frustration.

Carl was walking over, wiping the sweat from his brow with a bandanna. "Lost your pliers?" he said matter-of-factly.

"You know, you and my son, Captain Obvious, have a lot in common," I said dryly.

"Just shoot the bastard and get them back," he said as he began to turn around.

"Yeah I figured out that part all on my own, Dad," I said dryly. "Look at what he's doing."

Carl got closer. "Well I'll be damned, he's trying to cut the fence. Well ain't that a kick in the pants. Shoot him and get your pliers back."

"Still right about that, but don't you find that just a little freaken scary?" I asked him.

"What? Look at him, he can't even make the damn things close. He's not getting in here anytime soon," Carl pointed out.

"It's not whether he *can* operate the cutters, it's that he is trying at all. It's like he's remembering a lost skill or trying to attain a new one," I answered.

"So what?" Carl asked impatiently.

"So *what*?!" I retorted sharply. "If they have the ability to learn…"

The statement was left verbally unanswered but literally answered as we both turned to look when we heard the telltale twang of a chain link being cut. Hector appeared to be attempting to smile, but his rigor mortis locked lips would not upturn no matter how hard he tried. What was not difficult to see was the light of accomplishment in his dead flat black eyes.

"Well doesn't that beat all!" Carl said as he approached Hector. For the third time today I thought I was going to go deaf as Carl's Magnum went off.

Any excitement that Hector felt was short-lived as his head exploded. It happened so fast he never even dropped the cutters. Brain matter showered down hitting the hard ground. It sounded like the beginning of a sleet storm. An eye lazily rolled on the ground, finally coming to rest and perpetually looking to the heavens. Carl was halfway back to the truck when Hector's body finally slumped and partially rested up against the fence. I was beginning to feel a lot like Ben, I was having a hard time moving. A couple of the gate zombies started heading my way. It would be a minute or two before they got here but still I rushed to pry my pliers out of the cold dead hands of Hector. It would be ironic if he had one of those old NRA bumper stickers, although I didn't think it applied to hand tools. Was this the first sign of shock? How the hell would I know? I'm the one asking myself the questions. My lost glove was within retrieval distance. But it was covered in quickly freezing visceral. I was going to have to take my chances with frostbite and the Dannert wire, the germaphobe in me couldn't stomach the thought of putting that glove on again. I shakily climbed back on the ladder and began anew.

Carl had forced Ben back into action. Ben was using zip ties to bundle up the wire on the ground. This would make it easier to put into the truck and then to install once we got back to Little Turtle. Jen had yet to come out of the truck, hell as far as I knew she hadn't even peeked over the dashboard. Carl relieved me after he finished loading the rest of the ammo and any salvageable gun parts he could get his hands on. I was thankful for the opportunity to rest. My ungloved hand was frozen but what was worse were the multiple cuts on my hand. The pain was irksome, sure, but the frenzy it caused in the zombies, that was worse. Every time one of the fat globules of hemoglobin splashed to the frozen tundra the zombies would fall to the ground and tear up divots of sod to eat my offering. It was more than a little disturbing.

"Get your hand warmed up and then get rid of those things," Carl said with no more compunction than if he had asked me to take out the trash.

"What about the noise?" I asked with some dread. Killing zombies to save my ass was one thing, killing them like that made my blood run cold.

"What about it? Use your little pea shooter," he said pointing to my M-16. "It's a lot quieter than my Colts are, and we've been here for over an hour and we still only have five of the original six here."

I saw his point. It's just that I didn't want to.

"Besides," he continued, "we now have way more ammunition in your caliber than we do in mine."

Again I understood his damn point. I grabbed the keys from Ben and headed for the truck. Jen looked pissed that I was invading her space as I climbed into the cab to turn on the heater. I couldn't have cared less. Those that didn't pull their own weight were chattel and didn't deserve my consideration.

"Are we leaving now?" Jen asked hopefully.

I merely revved the engine a little more hoping the heat would kick on sooner rather than later.

"Are we leaving?" she asked again. This time she leaned over, grabbed the gearshift and shoved it into gear. The truck lurched forward and stalled. I was thrown forward and almost broke my damn nose on the steering column as I was already leaning forward trying to garner some heat. Both Carl and Ben were looking up at me, puzzlement on their features. I shrugged and over-exaggerated 'sorry' gesture.

I hissed at Jen, "You touch that shift box again and I'll break your fucking wrist!"

She pulled back as if I had slapped her.

"If you're so concerned about getting out of here quicker maybe you should be helping instead of hiding."

Defiance was on her face, but defeat was in her

features. She wanted to lash out but she didn't have the intrepidity to go through with it. She settled back into her uneasy crouch, this time however she sat with her back to me. My hands began to defreeze by small degrees. The pins and needles affect gave way to nails and tacks and then finally to spikes and stakes. The pain was more intense than I was expecting. I must have been close to frostbite. As the torture began to subside I looked around the cab; I knew I had seen a pair of work gloves. They were cheaply made and would do little to stop the bite of the razor wire but I hoped that it would at least keep some of the bitter sting of the cold away. I stayed a few minutes longer than I needed to, gathering my reserves to go deal with our unwanted transients.

"Damn it," I said as I shut off the truck. Jen jumped a bit but didn't turn around. My feet had no sooner hit the ground, when I heard the telltale sound of the lock being engaged. "Useless!" I said a little louder than I needed to.

I was having a difficult time empathizing with her. Here we were in the fight of our lives and she had just given up. The side of me that didn't want to kill, not even zombies, spoke up. 'How would you feel if Tracy had become a zombie?'

'Don't even think it!' My internal dialogue continued.

'Or one of your kids?'

'I'm telling you! Shut up!'

'Well?'

'Damn you! I'd probably want to curl up into a ball and die.' My masculine side finally iterated.

'Hmm.' My feminine side mocked.

'You can still kiss my ass.' I aimed my rifle and fired off 5 rounds, killing all of our nonhuman visitors. My feminine side had been stilled.

The ensuing quiet was only briefly interrupted by the twang of wire cutters severing through wire holders. Carl hadn't so much as turned to look as I had mowed down the noxious audience. My breathing had quickened as if from heavy exertion. Sweat formed and quickly began to freeze on my brow. I had yet to put the rifle down, gravity finally taking over and pushed the barrel towards the ground.

Ben, noticing my distress came over. "You all right Talbot?" he asked with concern.

It took a moment for me to acknowledge his presence. I turned towards him, my pupils dilated, my face as pale as the breath I exhaled.

"I could get real philosophical with that question, Ben." And that was my only answer to his inquiry as I went to the ladder to see if Carl needed any assistance. Ben scratched his head and began zip tying the coils again.

Not much was said as the three of us worked, I know at least for me I was thankful for the lack of speech. It was much nicer to be lost in the hard work. Carl and I switched off on climbing the ladder. My legs were burning from the strain of going up and down and I would have said something but Carl didn't so much as utter a heavy sigh and the guy was twenty years my senior. There was no way I was going to let him know I was hurting. Between my shifts on top I would help Ben coil and then pull the coil into the truck. We had a system and it was going well. I was thinking at this point we wouldn't have to spend the night. The remainder of the day was eerily quiet, no more zombies, no other people and not even any animals. I could understand why there were no people, either they were zombies, dead, or fled. The animals had most likely taken off too, please don't let there be zombie rabbits! But if the animals had fled because of the zombies, where were they? And as if my questions materialized into reality, I smelled them first. At first I had thought Carl had let one rip, but unless he had eaten rotten fish tacos the previous night, it couldn't be him. I must have turned a shade of green because Carl finally broke his vow of silence.

"What's a matter Talbot, you look like something's disagreeing with you? It's not all this hard work is it?" he asked, laughing a little at his own humor. I didn't have to answer him, I watched as his face took on the same hue as mine. "Oh sweet Jesus!" He magically produced a bandanna, as only people of his generation can, and began to tie it around his face to block at least some of the odor.

Ben had at this point just emerged from the back of the trailer. "Oh geez! What is that smell!" he yelled.

"Talbot, we've got fifty more yards of wire to go," Carl began. "Do we cut and run so to speak or stay and finish? But from that stench you know we're not dealing with some onesy and twosy lost zombies, that smells like the mother lode."

"Cut it," I said as I made the executive decision. "All this wire does no good if we can't get it there. I was wondering why there were no animals around here."

My last words fell to the grounds without an ear to pick them up. Carl had already ascended the ladder to this time cut the wire itself and not the holders.

"Look out below!" Carl yelled a moment too late.

The razor wire sliced past my face at an alarming rate, a couple inches more to the right and my facial features would have been neatly severed from their resting place. I looked up at Carl more in shock than anything.

He shrugged a bit and said, "Eh it didn't get you did it? Quit your belly aching."

I didn't know which was worse, the close call or the smell. I wanted to give Carl a little 'what for' but speaking meant that I would have to suck in more of the foul stench-laden air. I flipped him the finger and he laughed, so much for making a statement.

The armory sat on a lot by itself and afforded luxurious views on all sides. The closest homes were across Buckley Avenue and a small greenway lay between the street and the houses. All in all it was about 500 yards away, and it was from there the zombies began to spill forth. At first only a few ambled out, then half a dozen and almost within a blink of an eye there were hundreds. They stood in the greenway, some swaying like abhorrent stalks of corn. Their numbers swelled; standing room became a premium commodity as their numbers increased and still they didn't move. We lost precious time as the three of us just stood in awe wondering what kind of manifestation we were witnessing. Of course it was at this point that Jen decided to peek her head over the dashboard. The détente was broken by her shrill screams. Like the prince's kiss to Sleeping Beauty, the noise got the zombies moving and in turn so did we. We had about a hundred and fifty yards of wire that still needed to be loaded into the truck and I was a moment away from having to cut it loose when the zombies made it to the sidewalk. Again they stopped.

"What are they doing? Are they afraid of traffic?" I said aloud.

"Maybe they're looking for a crosswalk," Carl snorted.

Of us all he looked the least nonplussed, as if this were just some normal ordinary occurrence. We kept loading the wire, and I kept a wary eye on the zombies waiting for any indication they would make their move. It didn't happen.

Ben asked me what they were doing as we closed up the rear of the trailer. I wanted to scream at him, 'How the hell would I know, do I look like a fucking zombie expert you dumb hillbilly illiterate turd!!' Instead civility got the better of me, and I shrugged. "Hell if I know," I told him instead.

Jen's cacophonous voice assaulted all of our ears as soon as we entered the cab. She was somewhere between sobbing and screaming her desire to vacate the premises as soon as possible.

"Oh for the love of God girl, shut up!" Carl said evenly. His words had the desired effect, she shut up almost immediately, although she switched to an almost as bothersome half hiccup, half hushed sob. I think the screaming was better. This was the sound of the defeated.

The truck started on the very first turnover attempt. I was figuring that was good news. At least it wasn't going to be like those low budget horror slasher flicks, where the heroine either can't start her car or trips over a nonexistent tree root. Thank God for small favors.

The truck roared to life but we weren't moving. "Please don't tell me the transmission isn't working?" I gave voice to my concern.

Carl and Ben both turned to me in unison as if on some unseen telepathic command.

"What?" I asked, fear began to mount, a few more seconds of this and I might end up on the floor mat with Jen.

I don't to this day know how they did it but Ben and Carl, as if it was choreographed, simultaneously looked out the windshield at the same time. I followed the path of their gaze.

Realization dawned. "The gate? You want *me* to open the gate? Go through the damn thing," I half yelled. Jen bawled a little louder.

Ben spoke up verbally this time instead of any more unnatural synchronized motions. "I don't want to take the chance of puncturing the radiator or a tire or having the damn fence hang up underneath. 'Sides, they're all across the street."

I looked at Carl for some sympathy, but didn't find any.

"That's what you get for being younger," he quipped.

"Son of a bitch," I said as I opened the door and jumped down. Jen immediately reached up and locked the door.

I heard Carl mumble something to her as he undid the latch. The zombies weren't moving forward but every set of eyes turned to me as I walked towards the gate. I was deeply unnerved. I once had illusions of being a rock star but if this was what it felt like to have all eyes on you, then fame could find a different resting spot. There was jostling in the back as some of the zombies in the rear were trying to gain a better vantage point to see what was on the menu. Not one of them stepped into the street. It was if they were made of wood and the street flowed with lava. I could have most likely recited the Gettysburg address, done a little dance, possibly a crossword puzzle or two and even relieved my aching bladder before the fastest of the zombies could cover the distance to the gate. I swung open the gate and spun back toward the truck. I walked quickly, proud that I hadn't broken out into a panicked run but it was close. I hopped back up into the cab, thankful the door wasn't locked, and still nothing stirred, not even a mouse.

As the truck swung on to Buckley Avenue, the zombies' heads turned in harmony. As we passed, they began to step out onto the street. For the first quarter mile of our trip, zombies began piling out of every imaginable nook and cranny. There had to have been thousands of them as they ganged up behind us. It looked like the beginning of the world's slowest marathon.

Ben laughed as he said. "The dead sons of bitches aren't going to catch us!"

"Yeah at least for another seven miles," came my pensive reply.

Ben's smile dropped off his face; even the stoic Carl looked like he had eaten something that didn't sit well. Jen, however, was clueless.

"What….what's in seven miles?" came her quavering question.

"Home," I answered, as I looked in the side mirrors.

"Oh God," Jen groaned.

Except for the occasional gear grind the remainder of the journey home was unremarkable. Each of us in his or her own way was contemplating the reality which had just been driven home, no pun intended.

"Ben, stop," I said. No response. "Ben, stop this truck!" I yelled a little louder. How Ben was even concentrating on driving, I don't know, he was so far down deep in thought. Carl nudged him.

"What?" Ben asked, sounding a little irritable.

"Talbot wants you to stop the truck," Carl said, for

which I was grateful. I might have yelled it a little louder than was considered polite if I had to ask for a third time.

Ben shrugged. "Fine," he muttered. "But I ain't turnin' her off."

"Fine, fine," I said over the rumble of the engine. "What if we don't go back?"

Ben and Carl looked at me both with expressions of confusion on their face. I didn't bother to check Jen. I knew she still had her face buried in her hands.

"We saw those zombies," I went on to explain. "They're following us to see where we're going. If we don't go home they can't get to our loved ones."

Jen sobbed in response.

"Now hold on Talbot, I only saw a bunch of zombies milling about in a street. You can't for sure say they were following us," Ben said in reply.

Carl forged on. "And even if they were following us, and I said 'if,' what makes you think they can track us to our home. They're stupid brain-dead flesh eaters!" he yelled. It was the most expression I'd seen out of him all day. He might be trying his best to not look riled, but this development was getting under his feathers.

"You saw Hector and the pliers, they're not completely brain-dead," I said evenly.

Carl's face smoldered. Ben was looking from Carl to me in an attempt to garner some much needed information.

"Who's Hector and what does a pair of pliers got to do with anything?" Ben asked.

Carl began anew, but not in response to Ben. "That still doesn't make them Einstein wannabes, or Davy Crockett trail tracker wannabes for that matter." Carl was going to take some serious persuading.

"Listen Carl," I directed my dialogue towards him. Where Carl led, Ben would follow. "There's something different about these zombies."

Carl arched his eyebrow. "Different how? And what exactly does a zombie act like?"

I spent the next fifteen minutes relating everything I knew about zombies, learned from movies, books and comics. Sure, it was an imperfect argument, how could I possibly make an informed judgment about our fact-based reality when I was using fiction-based perceptions. The only hard facts I could give them were my observations of that woman zombie, the one that had killed Spindler. None of them had been there, my explanations fell on deaf ears.

Carl was of the mind to give me the benefit of the doubt, but I hadn't given him anything solid enough to leave what was left of his family and friends behind. Without Carl my words fell on the deaf ears of Ben. Jen was no one's ally.

"I'm sorry, Mike," Carl said. "The zombies, them I believe in. Hector was just an aberration, some legacy memory. The girl? I think she was a specter of an imagination in overdrive."

I was pissed. "Carl, I'll admit, I'm more scared than I've ever been in my whole life and I went to war. But I'm not a hysterical person. I did not imagine that girl showing me Spindler's head and nodding. I'm sure she was repaying a favor. That shows intelligence."

"You're 'pretty sure' Mike, but you're not absolutely sure," he fired back.

"Of course I'm not absolutely sure, how the hell could I be, they're zombies!" Anger filled my voice.

"Maybe they are following us and maybe they're not. I'm not about to give up the rest of my life on a hunch. And I'd rather be with my family if this is the end than traveling the highways waiting for this truck to run out of gas. Are you so ready to leave your family behind?" he finished.

Those words stung. "If it meant they'd be safe," I said, although without much conviction.

"Odds are Talbot, some group of flesh eaters are going to find our little haven sooner or later. I'd rather be there to help defend, than up by the Nebraska border," Carl finished with a softer tone.

I had nothing left to say. He was right and now I felt

crummy for arguing against him.

"We good now?" Ben asked. When Carl nodded in agreement, Ben put the truck back in gear. The small heave forward brought forth another small sob from Jen.

I could not help feeling like we were the Pied Pipers of Death as we rolled towards home. Instead of leading rats away, we were leading the zombies to their promised land. This was a funeral procession, of that I had no doubt, whatever Carl thought. The truck had no sooner pulled in to the complex when I hopped off, it was still rolling. I headed out to find Jed. It didn't take me long. He didn't usually wander too far off from the clubhouse. I was relieved to see the old fart.

"Welcome back Talbot," Jed said. I could tell he had some sort of jest to say but when he saw the look of consternation on my face he held his tongue.

"We've got to call an emergency meeting, Jed!" My voice was forced from the adrenaline.

"Now hold on Talbot, it's getting late and folks have been working hard all day. And that's not even including the ones that buried their kin, neighbors or friends. They need time to mourn," Jed finished.

"Jed, I'm not trying to be an ass or an alarmist, but if we don't have a meeting and real soon, we might be burying a lot more people. I don't necessarily want the whole population, just essential personnel," I said.

That got Jed going, he wasn't thrilled about it, but he would have an assembly together within the hour.

"Thanks Jed, and make sure Alex is one of those essentials," I told him.

"I'll try Talbot, but he looked exhausted," Jed added resignedly.

These are the stories that happened AFTER I left to go to the armory, you don't even want to know how pissed off I got when I found out.

CHAPTER 13

Justin woke as soon as he heard the front door open. He had always been a light sleeper, and now with the way things were it had only gotten worse. He came upstairs and watched as his father walked off towards the clubhouse in the predawn quiet. He thought about following him, but first off it wasn't much above five degrees out and he was in shorts and a tank top, and second, if his father wanted him along he would have come and gotten him. Justin's dad was a former Marine, a strong disciplinarian and an anal compulsive man. If he wanted something done, he was not afraid to tell any of his kids to 'get it done and get it done now.' Knowing his dad like he did, Justin always thought it was funny how his father always deferred to his mother. Dad was the boss of the kids and Mom was the boss of Dad. That was the hierarchy. For the most part Mike Talbot had mellowed with age, but when something got him riled, all hell broke loose, and it would take all of Tracy's calm demeanor to put the genie back in the bottle.

Justin turned back towards the kitchen to get a bottle of water when he noticed his father's Blackberry lying on the table next to the sofa. Back in the 'normal' days, his dad had the Blackberry almost surgically attached to his hip. To see the phone was to see the man. Nowadays the phone was not much better than a paperweight. Cell service was sketchy at best. It wasn't even worth carrying it. That was why Justin was puzzled when he saw a red light blinking, the telltale sign of a message waiting. This was intriguing to Justin. Sure they still had electricity, thanks to a network of generators. But television was for the most part nonexistent, except for some news, and they weren't broadcasting anything new. Telephones and cell phones were rapidly becoming instruments of the past. Justin was tempted to wake his mother and see if she would listen to the message, but if it was a spectral collection call and he woke her for that, there would be hell to pay. He decided to wait a few minutes for his dad to return. When it didn't look like that was going to happen right away, he figured he'd get some clothes on and track him down. Justin no sooner came up from the basement wearing more respectable seasonable clothing when he heard and then saw the tractor trailer head out the front gate. Without actually seeing his dad, he knew for a fact his father was on that truck.

"Damn it," he muttered. This meant it was going to be the better part of the day before he found out what the message was.....or from whom.

'What if it's Pops?' he thought. Pops was his grandfather from back East. Nobody had heard from any of the East Coast Talbots since the zombie plague had begun. All the kids loved Pops. Where Dad was hard and angular, Pops was soft and easygoing. Not one of the kids could ever remember Pops raising his voice, unless of course it was to tell everyone that dinner was ready.

Only Mike knew differently. Pops Talbot had also been a Marine. If anything, Mike at this age was infinitely calmer than his father had been. Mike remembered the days in his youth. If he had been caught doing any one of the myriad of things his father considered inappropriate, his hands would be bleeding from the task of digging holes and then filling them back in. The kids thought Pops was a saint and Mike had no wish to smash their illusions. He loved the old man more than the Man Code would allow him to say, but the fact remained, he knew another side of the old man the kids didn't.

Justin had never messed with his father's phone, first because of the privacy issue. Mike had striven to drive that into all of his offspring. Trust is a sacred institution, and once it is shattered it is nearly impossible to put back together with the same integrity again. And second, because Mike probably would have been able to tell Justin was trying to listen to his messages by the way Justin would have had to position himself with his ear next to his dad's hip pocket.

Mike also knew kids were curious by nature, if given the chance they would find all sorts of new and unusual ways to get into trouble. His goal had always been to remove as many opportunities as possible and, well, the rest will follow.

Justin didn't think it would be a big breach of trust if he just checked the call log, and if it was Pop's he could have his mom breach the code. Fumbling with the phone, Justin had a frozen moment of guilt and almost put the phone down, but his inquisitive mind wanted to know. What he saw disappointed him more than he thought possible. Something had been lost in the electronic netherworlds because the Blackberry screen only showed: "**u* **r* 7***2***5*"

'Oh, that's crap!' he thought. He had finally built up enough pluck to even look at the screen and his reward was gibberish. Justin didn't hesitate long, in for a dime, in for a dollar, so he pressed the voice mail button.

"......(Garble)....(static)...can't....(static)....want....(garble)...fell.....(dial tone)." 'End of message, to save message press 7, to delete, press 9'. Without even thinking, Justin pressed 9. 'Message deleted', came the officious voice. 'There are no new messages.' Justin broke out into a cold sweat when he realized what he had just done. 'Oh crap, the old man's gonna have my ass for this.' He was half tempted to erase the call log and further hide his evidence of tampering, but he couldn't do it.

The message may have been incomprehensible but the voice was not. It was his Uncle Paul, not by blood ties but maybe by something even stronger. His dad had known Uncle Paul for almost thirty years. They had grown up together in a small suburb outside of Boston. They had done everything together from playing football and baseball on the city and school teams to exploring an old Indian Burial ground aptly named Indian Hill. So when Paul's family moved away in their sophomore year of high school, they had vowed to remain friends forever. But things for teens happen at a different pace than the rest of the world. There are girls and Friday nights and football and countless other distractions to keep them occupied. Sometimes the two friends would go for months at a time without communicating, always able to pick up the easy flow of conversation as if only hours had passed. So it was almost not even a surprise when the two realized that unbeknownst to the other, they had both applied for the same college, the University of Massachusetts in Amherst. For four years they did not so much 'attend' the school as they did 'frequent' it. The two were much more interested in the social aspects of college rather than any educational benefits. When Paul went on the five-year degree program, the two parted ways again. Mike, under some heavy lobbying from his then girlfriend, Laurie, moved to Colorado. After a few months of the 'we are so grown up and in love' phase, Laurie and Mike's relationship soured by degrees until finally they broke up.

The break up affected Mike more than he had known. Booze was becoming more and more of a crutch to get through the lonely nights. After one intense drinking session and a 3:00 a.m. call to his friend, Paul flew out to Colorado. It had been eighteen months since they had seen each other but it might as well have been eighteen minutes. The deal was sealed. Mike packed up everything and drove back East to live with his friend Paul who now lived in New Hampshire. Mike knew without a shadow of a doubt that Paul had saved his life by flying out to Colorado, just as surely as Mike had saved Paul's by pulling him out of a burning car some years before. Living with Paul had begun Mike's healing, but still the booze beckoned. Five years with the love of his life suddenly over was not easily forgotten. Mike knew he had to make a radical change, so when he came home one night and told Paul he had enlisted in the Marines. Paul nodded in understanding but internally was conflicted, if anything the two of them were peaceniks or at worst apathetics. So again the brothers from a different mother went their separate ways. For five years Mike lived in dirt and battled foreign enemies. Whenever he could, he would contact his friend Paul, just so he could be reminded there was a world still out there where being shot at every day was not the norm. If anything, this separation strengthened their bond. It was during the Marines Corps days that Mike met, married and began a family with Tracy. Paul had also married and moved back to Massachusetts. So when Mike told Paul that he was bringing his family back to Massachusetts once his current tour was over, Paul had nearly giggled with glee, or at least as much as was acceptable by the Man Code. Mike was two months away from his discharge from the Marines when he received a disappointing call from Paul. Paul's marriage had acidified. The break up was imminent. Paul decided he needed the comfort of his family, who had in the meantime moved to North Carolina. Mike was understandably disheartened.

So for a couple of years Mike toiled at the family business in downtown Boston while Paul attempted what Humpty Dumpty had tried many years before. He began to put the pieces of his life back together. The two miscreants were able to get together a couple of times during this period and subsequently just tore the living crap out of their livers, reveling in the 'good old days.' It was after one of those lost weekends that Tracy announced to Mike that her father was terminally ill and she was moving back to her home state of Colorado with or without him. (Flash back to the part about who's the boss.) The house was on the market the next day. Within a week the U-Haul was packed and the Talbots were heading out West.

Mike and Paul kept in more communication than they had during their previous hiatuses, so Mike knew almost right away when Paul became serious with his on again-off again girlfriend Erin. Erin was good people. She saw some excellent qualities in Paul and knew this was the person she wanted to spend the rest of her life with. Paul, after already going through a nasty divorce, was not in so much of a rush. Erin, however, was skilled and patient in the ways of the heart. She didn't push Paul but she was wily enough to keep him on the hook. For three years they played this game of cat and mouse, Paul always thinking he was a word away from being able to break up and Erin believing she was a word away from getting his commitment. When Erin got the call one July evening that her mother had been rushed to a hospital for life threatening injuries sustained in an auto collision, she knew her place was with her family. They just so happened to live in Colorado. Paul knew the score. He either went with Erin and climbed a bunch of notches up the commitment ladder, or he walked away from a potentially beautiful union. This was not an easy decision for him. His first instinct had been to call Mike, who had been thrilled at the possibility that his lifelong friend might once again be within spitting distance. Mike did his best to temper the excitement in his voice during the phone conversation, but when they hung up he almost cackled with glee (see 'Man Code'). In Paul's mind he wasn't sure if he was ready for this. Being that close to Mike, while not the 'deciding' factor, was certainly a 'contributing' one. Bars beware! The dynamic duo was once again about to be reunited. Paul and Erin finally made the ultimate leap, got hitched and moved into their own house. Mike and Paul didn't get to see each other as often as they would hope, living only 9.98 miles away from each other, but they more than made up for it when they did.

Justin knew his dad loved Paul and Erin and that not knowing what had happened to his friends was weighing heavily upon him. Justin also knew the only thing keeping his dad from going to get Paul or find out his fate, was him. Well not just him, all the kids. Mike would not sacrifice the safety of his kids, not even for his 'brother' Paul. Justin decided there and then that if his father wouldn't go get Paul because of the kids, then the kids were going to have to do it themselves.

Justin went downstairs and not very carefully shook his younger brother to alertness. Travis came up from the depths of sleep quicker than Justin had expected. He was barely able to avoid the bat as it swung dangerously close to his rib cage. Mike had given every one in the family a firearm to protect themselves if needed, but they were all expressly forbidden from having the firearm within arm's length from where they slept. It was in the first seven seconds of being awakened that a person was not in complete control of their faculties, and Mike did not want any fatal accidents. Having other less lethal weapons at the ready was not discouraged; Mike had warned the family to wake somebody, including himself, from a safe distance. Justin in his haste and excitement had forgotten this rule and had almost paid dearly for it.

"What the hell Travis, you almost crushed my ribs!" Justin yelled, in the grips of an adrenaline rush from his decision and partly from the added stimulation of having avoided the bat.

"Huh?" Travis asked as he sat up rubbing the torpidity from his eyes.

"We're going to get Paul," Justin said, barely able to hide the enthusiasm in his voice.

"Huh?" Travis responded. Apparently the lingering effects of his siesta had not been shaken off.

"Paul called," Justin said.

That got Travis' attention. "Uncle Paul called?" he asked excitedly. 'Uncle Paul' had always been a favorite of Travis' because he was Paul's godson. Something Paul would never let him forget. "How? The phones don't even work!"

"I don't know how, he left a message on Dad's cell," Justin answered.

"When does Dad want to leave?" Travis asked as he got out of bed and began to dress for the undertaking.

"Dad doesn't know," Justin said as he involuntarily

lowered his eyes in guilt.

Travis stopped mid-way through putting his three-way tactical sling on as comprehension dawned on his face. "I don't know which will make Dad more pissed, the fact that you checked his phone or that you want to leave the complex," Travis told his brother.

Justin sagged in resignation.

"So when do we leave?" Travis asked nonchalantly as he began to place spare shells in his multitude of pockets.

Justin whooped with glee, and then caught himself and lowered his voice. "I want to leave now, but I want to get Brendon in on this."

"Can't," Travis said. "You wake Brendon, he wakes Nicole, Nicole gets Mom, we go nowhere."

"Shit, I hate it when you're right," Justin said. "But I wanted Brendon to drive his truck. If we take Dad's Jeep on top of everything else he'd probably just shoot us without ever asking questions."

"He won't shoot me," Travis said beaming. "I won't be driving."

Justin let a sickly smile ghost across his lips. Taking the Jeep was by far the worst offense of the many offenses he was about to commit.

Tommy came in a minute later, a trail of Kit-Kat crumbs marking his passage. "Whatcha you guys doing?" he asked, spraying peanut buttery goodness everywhere.

"Kit-Kats?" Travis asked. "We have Kit-Kats?"

"Weef did," Tommy said, spreading his chocolatey smile.

"Hey Tommy," Justin said. Concern laced his thoughts. It would not be easy getting out of the house quietly with Tommy asking all sorts of questions. "Did you just get up to get a snack?" He was hoping that Tommy was merely getting a little bite before going back to sleep. Tommy was famous for sleeping in, so much so that all of his shifts at Wal-Mart started no earlier than 1:00 p.m. For him to be up before the sunrise was an anomaly.

"Well I was sleeping good, right?" Tommy started. "I was dreaming about working at Wal-Mart before the deadheads came. You remember the time, Justin, when they were moving that huge pallet of Halloween candy and it tipped over."

Justin didn't remember, that incident happened six months before he had started, but he nodded anyway. His being there wasn't relevant to the story.

"I was happy no one was hurt but I was SO happy the candy got all smooshed. Joey the manager said I could have all that I could carry. Ended up I could carry a LOT." Tommy was smiling at his remembrance.

"Didn't Joe get in trouble for that? "Justin asked. "Something about having to return the damaged goods for inventory control."

Tommy's smile faded a bit at the memory of his friend getting in trouble, but slowly spread again as he said "Yeah but I sure could carry a lot!"

"That's a good dream Tommy," Justin said, trying to hurry Tommy along and hopefully back to bed.

Tommy wasn't having any of it. Justin would be more likely able to push over a non-sleeping cow than Tommy. Tommy began anew. Justin sighed.

"Hey Travis, why do you have your gun on?" Tommy asked. Alarm increased in the boys and just like that Tommy moved on, not waiting for a response. "So what I was telling you was not a dream, 'cause dreams are made up, and all of that stuff happened. I wish I had some more smashed mallow cups," Tommy's eyebrows furrowed. "But then Ryan Seacrest comes over while I'm carrying all my goodies away. He keeps following me saying I dropped a Kit-Kat. And I'm like, 'thanks Ryan, but there weren't any Kit-Kats on the pallet.' He keeps following me, and telling me about the Kit-Kat. He starts pulling on my arm and I start to drop stuff, so I was kinda getting a little upset." Tommy paused for dramatic effect. Justin's attention was peaked now. He had heard the conversation Tommy and his father had regarding Tommy's inner voice. Justin tore away from his inner dialogue as Tommy started up again.

"So now I have to pay attention because if I don't he'll make me drop everything. Joey said I can only have what I can carry and I don't want to miss out. So I turn and Ryan tells me that there's a Kit-Kat in the basement for me. Wait did he say that, or that I should go eat a Kit-Kat in the basement? Why would he tell me to eat a Kit-Kat in the basement? Wait, okay so I got the Kit-Kat upstairs, and then I came down here, but I started eating it upstairs, do you think that'll make Ryan mad?" Tommy looked ultra-concerned that he might be irking his spirit guide aka the host of the now defunct American Idol.

"I don't think he'll be mad, Tommy," Travis said earnestly.

"So I ate most of my Kit-Kat down in the basement!" Tommy said loudly, possibly trying to appease his spirit guide. "And then here were you guys, awake! Do you want to play Monopoly?" he asked hopefully.

"No Tommy, we can't play Monopoly right now," Justin answered.

"Oh, is it because you're going to get Paul?" Tommy asked as he licked some errant chocolate off his candy wrapper.

Justin swallowed loudly, his mouth having gone instantly dry. Travis' mouth hung slackly.

"Did you hear us talking?" Travis asked. Justin just shook his head; he knew better.

"Naw, that's spying. My mom said that's not polite. 'Sides, I couldn't hear you guys talking anyway, don't you know how crunchedy sounding Kit-Kats are in your head?"

"Tommy, are you gonna go back to bed?" Justin asked hopefully, already aware of the response.

"Can't," said Tommy matter-of-factly. "Ryan says I have to go with you."

Quarter inch goose bumps embossed up the entire length of Justin's spine.

"Are you going to tell Mrs. T?" Justin asked.

Tommy looked up to the ceiling as if trying to remember some missing facts. "Oh no, Ryan didn't say anything about her, but we should bring Oleyco's boyfriend." Tommy had become enamored with Nicole. He became flustered every time he thought of her. Because of this he could not remember her name. She was known as Oleyco most of the time, but sometimes she was Nickel, Coley, Colon, Coldstone and even once as Dime, no one was sure where that one originated from. Most likely Tommy had been thinking of 'Nickel' and Dime seemed like the next natural progression. Tommy never mentioned Brendon by name; everyone but Tommy noticed the slight.

Something or someone was intervening in the boys' plans, whether it was divine was yet to be determined. Brendon was out of bed, making an early morning bathroom delivery. Justin crept up the stairs, doing his best to avoid all the spots on the stairs that creaked. This was not an easy task. Tracy had been goading Mike for years to repair some of the worst offenders. Some of the creaks were as loud as a pistol shot, especially in the middle of the night. But Mike had staunchly held his ground. He had always thought of the creaks as his own alarm system. He had argued intensely that no intruder would ever be able to sneak up into the bedroom unsuspectingly. Tracy couldn't even begin to fathom the depths of Mike's survivalism and paranoia. Although as he would tell you, it's either one or the other, and he preferred to call it survivalism. Then he would add that if someone could get past the security bars, Henry and the 'stair alarm system' without garnering any attention, then they deserved to take some stuff. So, maybe using Henry in the equation wasn't a great example, but still.

Justin crossed from one side of the steps to the other, at one point climbing over one step completely to avoid a particularly nasty groan. He appeared to be playing some advanced three-dimensional version of hopscotch. He stopped at the top landing, directly facing his parents' bedroom.

There were four hot spots on the landing, the problem however was that not all were active at the same time. It was like playing Russian roulette with floorboards. There was no rhyme or reason to it. Justin had his suspicions that his dad somehow had the floor rigged. It wasn't out of the realm of possibilities. Justin's right foot came down tentatively. Nothing. He sighed in relief. Next he strategically placed his left foot as close to the banister as possible, more times than not this was a safe bet, but not today. CRAAACK – Justin froze, only the sweat on his forehead had the audacity to move. Nothing stirred, not even Henry. After a thirty-second pause in which Justin expected his mother to come bursting out of her bedroom, nothing happened. He took a quick left which marked his first successful completion down the gauntlet. The next part was going to be equally difficult. On the left of the hallway was his dad's office which was now Brendon and Nicole's room. Directly across from it was the bathroom. Justin noticed the light on underneath the bathroom door. If it was his sister, the jig was up before it ever got going. She would not be persuaded to not tell their mother. For the second time in two minutes, Justin found himself frozen. This time, however, it was with indecision. He needed to think of a valid reason for his being in the hallway at this time of the day if his sister came out of the bathroom. Somehow asking her if she wanted to play Monopoly at 6:30 in the morning didn't seem like a viable option. He then had the idea of getting Brendon awake, convinced and out of the bedroom before his sister returned. Not an acceptable alternative, she would surely go looking for Brendon if she came back and he wasn't in bed. They'd never get out in time unless of course she had fallen asleep on the john. Justin laughed a little at that picture, he couldn't for the life of him imagine his prim and proper sister falling asleep on the toilet.

It was the smell that got Justin moving. For a fearful second he thought that a zombie had broken in. When he realized that it only smelled LIKE something had died, and had not *actually* died, he sprang into motion. Without even looking, Justin quietly shut the office/bedroom door. His sister was lactose intolerant, and even if she had downed a whole cheesecake she was incapable of producing the noxious gas that oozed from beneath the closed bathroom door. Justin was now dead smack in the center of the hallway, between the bathroom and the bedroom. He didn't want to move for fear that Brendon would get back into the bedroom before Justin could intercept him. He was beginning to get woozy trying to hold his breath. Just when he began to lose his peripheral vision, Justin heard the toilet flush and the sink go on. He exhaled in bliss, only to be rewarded on the inhale with the full blast of pestiferous tang of Brendon's refuse as the door was opened. Brendon was momentarily stunned by the appearance of Justin at the doorway but quickly recovered.

"You might want to use a different bathroom," Brendon said quietly with a hint of a smile across his lips.

Justin was trying his best to breathe through his mouth, but the mere thought that he was now 'tasting' the essence of Brendon's offal did little to quell the queasiness that was building up in his stomach.

"Gotta talk to you," Justin rushed out on exhale, and pointed down the stairs. If Brendon in anyway delayed, Justin would have to go downstairs without him. Justin had promised himself that he would not take another gulp of air anywhere in the vicinity of the 'death zone.' Brendon nodded and followed Justin down. The floorboards had not had sufficient time to reset and both boys were able to make it all the way down without so much as a minor crackle. Justin took a few long pulls of fresh air, hoping to evacuate all the poison from his lungs. He felt almost immediately better.

"What were you eating, a rotten rhino?" Justin asked when he had sufficiently cleaned out his airways.

"Did you like that? I was working on that just for you. As a matter of fact I was going to come down and get you so you could get a whiff," Brendon laughed.

A greasy smile split Justin's lips. "Thanks man, I appreciate that," he said sarcastically.

"What's up?" Brendon asked more seriously. He could tell Justin had something to ask him but was hesitant to come out with it.

"All right, if I ask you something you have to promise if you say no, that you won't tell Nicole," Justin said tentatively.

Brendon had to think about this for a moment. If she were to somehow find out that he had important information and had withheld it from her that would not end well. Nicole was all of four foot eleven, but she was a veritable spitfire. Mountains would quake in the wake of her voluminous voice. What she lacked in size she MORE than made up in for in vocals. And to top it off she was quick to anger and so very slow to mellow. Those were not great ingredients if one were to perpetrate a lie. Brendon had learned the hard way.

"Justin, I don't know if I could do that," Brendon said in all seriousness. "You know how your sister gets."

Justin nodded in reluctant agreement. Of course he did, he'd had nineteen years of personal experience. Justin was secretly attempting to find a work around to this dilemma.

"How about this," Justin started. "What if I ask you something but you don't tell her until she wakes up?"

"Again, that depends," Brendon answered. "If it's important she'll be pissed that I didn't wake her to tell her."

"Damn it," Justin muttered.

"What's going on?" Brendon asked, curiosity starting to get the better of him.

"Damn it," Justin said for the second time. "Here goes nothing. I want to take Travis, Tommy and hopefully you to go get Paul."

"Your dad's best friend? Does your dad know? Of course not or we wouldn't be doing this whole covert conversation in the living room," Brendon said as he nervously wiped his forehead, even though sweat had not yet begun to form although it would soon. "What makes you think they'll even let us out of the gate?"

"My dad just left on the semi." 'I think,' Justin thought to himself. "I'll tell the guys at the gate that he wanted us to follow." 'And hopefully they won't ask where, cuz I have no clue,' he finished his inner dialog.

Brendon turned to walk back upstairs. Justin became anxious, fearful Brendon had made up his mind and not in the appropriate direction.

"I'm going to get my stuff," Brendon explained as he now began to play the advanced hopscotch game.

Justin was excited and worried at the same time. He ran downstairs to get the others and get out of the house before he changed his mind. This undertaking was of his design and if anything went wrong it would be his responsibility. This was a little bit more unnerving than making sure the shelves were correctly stocked for the frenetic holiday shoppers at Wal-Mart.

The boys had decided to take Brendon's Explorer, after some initial resistance. Brendon's truck had the habit of breaking down at the most inopportune times, but this fact still seemed like a better alternative than facing Mike Talbot if something should happen to his beloved Jeep. With nothing closing in and no elevated terror level, Brendon's truck, of course, clamored to life easily, just as the sun began to shine under an opaque sky. Brendon pulled up to the gate guard who was putting his hand out to halt them, although this was a useless gesture. It wasn't like Brendon could miss the five-ton yellow bus.

"Vere are you boys going?" Igor Drudarski, the guard, asked. Igor was a fifty something, fat Russian man who had emigrated over from the former Soviet Union some twenty years previously. He had not lost a hint of his former accent or his profound ability to drink vast quantities of vodka. The sour stench permeated through the truck as he looked over the boys and all the weapons they carried.

Tommy smiled back, greedily stuffing a blueberry Pop-Tart into his mouth.

"We have Pop-Tarts?" Travis asked softly.

"Weef did," Tommy smiled weakly back.

Justin leaned over Brendon a little and subsequently closer to the stink of Igor's breath. This morning was not working out well at all for his olfactory senses, which had just recently gotten over the assault at the bathroom.

"Mike Talbot asked us to follow him with some more fire power," Justin said, with a little more conviction in his voice than he felt.

"You are his boys, no?" Igor asked.

"That's right," Justin answered.

"He already had four people with him, what does he need you for?" Igor asked.

"Probably just guard duty," Travis threw in hastily. Justin silently thanked his brother.

Igor looked at all of them skeptically. "They left over fifteen minutes ago, you know how to get to the armory, yes?"

"Oh yeah," Justin responded, perhaps a little too eagerly.

Igor pulled his head out from the driver's side window, not convinced he was receiving the truth, but his main function was to keep people out, not in. He waved the bus driver to pull forward and out of the way.

Be safe, dah?" Igor yelled out. Brendon waved in response. The bus driver closed the gate, not waiting for Igor's hand signal.

"Which way do I go when I get to Havana?" Brendon asked Justin.

"Uh right," Justin told him, taking just a fraction of a second longer than appropriate to give the answer.

"You know the way right?" Brendon asked doubtfully.

"Uhhh, most of the way," Justin said meekly.

"Justin!" Brendon bellowed. "You are going to get us

all screwed, this is going to be an all risk and no reward venture! Your sister's going to kill me, not including what Mike's gonna do when he realizes I let you talk me into this harebrained scheme. It's not like we can ask somebody for directions. 'Hello Mr. Zombie, have you eaten any one lately named Paul Ginner? No? Then can you tell us how we might get there before you? What? You can't talk?'" Brendon was working himself up into a frenzy. He pulled into a now out-of-commission gas station so he could turn around.

"What are you doing?" Justin screamed in panic.

"We're going back before we get in any deeper over our heads," Brendon shot back.

Tommy had finished getting the final few crumbs out of his Pop-Tart bag when he spoke up. "I know the way."

Brendon and Justin turned to look at Tommy. There was not a hint on his features that he was speaking anything but the truth. Brendon sighed and got back on the road heading in the general direction of Paul's house.

Travis was busy looking in Tommy's knapsack for a wayward Pop-Tart. The quartet passed three cars on their way. All three were packed with people and provisions. All the people in those cars looked haunted, harried and in a rush. Not one of them so much as addressed the boys' presence with even a nod.

"They sure seem in a hurry," Travis said, putting into words what everyone was thinking. Well, maybe not Tommy. He had somehow pulled out another Pop-Tart from the bag Travis had previously checked. Travis added for Tommy's ears only, "Do you have a secret panel in there or something?" Tommy just smiled, strawberry goo plastered to his teeth.

"Need any help with that?" Travis asked. Tommy broke off half. Travis couldn't have been any happier than if he had won a shopping spree at Game Stop.

"You're gonna need it," Tommy said cryptically. Travis almost immediately lost all pleasure in the Pop-Tart.

Tommy led them unerringly to their destination.

When they were about to make their final left turn onto Paul's street, Tommy told them they "might want to park here." Brendon didn't question him at all as he pulled the car over and shut the engine off in the hopes of not attracting any undue attention.

"Prob'ly didn't want to do that just yet," Tommy said. When he didn't clarify, nobody asked for any further information, not knowing exactly what they would be trying to clarify.

As Brendon opened the door, the telltale redolence of the dead blasted through the car like an Arctic breeze through a windbreaker. What little flavor Travis' Pop-Tart had maintained had now embittered. The next few minutes were spent securing weaponry and stashing all extra ammo into as many free pockets as possible while still being able to move under the weight.

All fours boys slowly walked the twenty-five yards to the corner of Paul's street. The smell was intensifying. What was more disturbing was the incessant sounds of the dead. There was no talking, only the loitering shuffle. There was no laughter, only the constant sound of bodies maneuvering for position. There was no human sound, so to speak, there were the plaintive sounds only the dead can make.

Brendon peeked his head around the last privacy fence that marked the delineation between safety and demise. The other three waited expectantly a few feet behind. Paul lived at the end of a cul-de-sac, no more than a hundred yards long. What Brendon saw almost made him turn tail and run. It looked as if the world's most successful block party was raging. There had to have been at least three hundred lost souls wandering around; most looked as if they had a purpose. Some, however, looked lost and were somehow relieved to be among their own. Brendon, of course wouldn't swear to that, it was just a feeling he had perceived. He pulled his head back before any of those errant demons had a chance to spot him.

"Uh, I'm not so sure about this, guys," Brendon said

in hushed tones. "There have to be at least a couple hundred zombies. Most of them are clustered around one house. So we might be able to sneak by but I wouldn't want to bet our lives on it." Which of course they would be.

Justin asked. "Are they focused on the last house on the right, by any chance?"

"How did you...?" Brendon knew the answer before he finished. "That's Paul's, right?"

"Of course," Travis threw in sarcastically.

As if on cue the three boys looked to Tommy to see if he had any insight into their situation, but he merely smiled back. Their contemplation was interrupted by the sporadic firing of a small caliber pistol coming from the cul-de-sac. Travis ran up to the fence to hazard a look; Justin and Brendon followed. What they saw both lifted their spirits and simultaneously weighed heavy on their hearts. At the apex of the house was the distinctive outline of Paul's wife Erin. It appeared that she had knocked out the attic vent and was taking some ill-aimed shots at some of her besiegers. The boys were happy she was alive but saddened at the thought of the impossibility of a rescue attempt.

"So obviously a frontal assault is out of the question." Brendon stated the obvious.

Travis spoke up. "Let's go through the backyards on this side of the street, and see if we can spot a way in from that vantage point."

"It's not really the way we want to go," Justin said nervously.

"You know what I mean," Travis answered.

"That's going to put us about ten feet away from the nearest zombie," Brendon said. "Will they be able to smell us from that distance?"

"My dad asked the same thing when we went to get Justin. I think they can. But if they are focused on something it takes a lot to get their attention away from the first thing," Travis said optimistically.

"Let's hope your dad's right," Brendon added.

The brothers nodded in unison. Tommy was busy pulling wayward gobs of Pop-Tart off his shirt and popping them into his mouth.

"All right, let's fall back to the rear of these houses," Brendon said, taking charge. He didn't like the position at all.

The boys moved away from the zombie infestation to traverse behind the houses. Once they got to the house directly across from Paul's, they quickly climbed over the six-foot privacy fence. Brendon had thought that they might have to leave Tommy behind because of the fence, but he was surprisingly agile and seemed to have the least amount of problem getting over.

"Must be all the sugar," Brendon mumbled mirthfully to himself.

The boys moved to the front yard, still under concealment of the fence. The smell was unbearable. Even Tommy, who seemed immune to it, stopped eating.

"What's Paul's backyard like?" Brendon asked Travis.

"It's heavily sloped down and away from the house, but it won't do us any good," Travis answered.

Brendon cautiously looked over the fence. From his vantage point he could tell that the fence that led to Paul's backyard had been destroyed, most likely from the press of dead flesh against it. The fence hadn't stood a chance. "Yeah, it's as likely as not to have as many deaders in the back as in the front."

Over the preternatural quiet that enshrouded the neighborhood it was easy to hear Erin shout to Paul that she had seen someone over at the Henderson's house. Paul crowded Erin out of the small opening to take a look. Brendon had quickly jumped down before any zombies could see him, but apparently zombies suffered the same affliction that troubled dogs, they couldn't follow a pointed finger. And that was exactly what Erin was doing.

"I don't see anything," Paul said.

"He was right over there by the fence, you must have

scared him away," Erin answered.

"Yeah I'm sure it had nothing to do with the meat bags below," Paul responded sardonically.

Travis climbed up the fence when he realized the zombies weren't turning to investigate Erin's claims.

"See, there he is again!" Erin said excitedly. "Wait, that's not the same person."

"Travis?" Paul said softly, then a little louder "Travis, is that you? Wait don't answer! Just nod."

Travis nodded.

"Is your dad here?" Paul asked as hope surged in him. If anyone could get his wife and him out of this jam it would be Mike. The guy had a penchant for getting out of tight jams, the Marine Corps had only added to that legacy. When Travis shook his head no, Paul was dismayed. "How many of you are there?"

Travis held up four fingers. Paul couldn't imagine that Mike would send his boys alone to get him. He prayed that Mike hadn't died trying to save him.

"Where's your dad?" Paul asked. Travis shrugged his shoulders. There was only so much the boy could answer with body movements, but the fact that he didn't look too upset told Paul volumes.

"Any ideas?" Paul asked. Travis again shook his head no.

"I've got an idea," Brendon said from below. Travis held up one finger and mouthed 'Wait One'. Paul was left to ponder what this meant as Travis ducked back down off the fence.

"You three wait here. When the coast is clear get Paul and Erin and get back to the car," Brendon said as he began to move back towards where they had come from.

"Any chance you could be more specific?" Travis asked to Brendon's back, but he was already out of earshot of Travis' whisper.

A few moments later Travis got his answer. Brendon thought valor was highly overrated as he hesitantly walked out into the middle of the junction between Wheelspoke Avenue and Lacey Street. 'Couldn't it have been something a little more noble, like OK Corral Place and Okinawa Way?' he muttered to himself. At first, not one zombie took notice of the interloper. Brendon had aspirations that maybe he was somehow invisible to them. However, when he cleared his throat as if he wanted to reap attention in a loud auction house, he was rewarded beyond his wildest dreams. A zombie no more than twenty yards away turned to look at this newest nutrient food bag. The lone zombie started its hunt. Brendon felt like a fox about to be released. Although his body was moments away from bolting, his mind was holding steady. Pulling one whole zombie away from the fray was not the distraction Brendon was looking for. He aimed his gun in on the unaccompanied zombie and neatly removed the mass of its head from the rest of its offending body with a loud explosion. Most of the zombies were so tightly packed in around Paul's house that turning around was an industrious undertaking. It was only after a fair portion of the zombie crowd had peeled off to pursue this new quarry that the rest were able to swing into a position where they could see what the fuss was all about. In the rudimentary works that passed as thoughts in the zombies, the dinner bell had been sounded. 'Meat for me' would have been the vocalization of their thoughts if that were a possibility.

"Hey zombies! Dinnertime!" Brendon yelled in encouragement as he punctuated his point with some well-aimed shots.

A few zombies went down, a couple even stayed down, but it was the typical drop in the bucket. Brendon did not immediately turn and run as more and more zombies took note of his presence and began to come at him. He laid down shots almost on top of each other. If Travis hadn't known better, he would have thought Brendon had somehow obtained a fully automatic weapon with that rapid rate of fire. Brendon was holding his ground as best he could, only falling back a step or two when he should have been running as if hell itself were chasing him. In a few more seconds his window of escape would close but he was trying to get most, if not all, the zombies to come his way. Travis had knocked out a knothole in the fence and was just about to lay down some suppressive fire to help him, when Brendon finally understood he could not hold his ground anymore.

"That wasn't much of a plan," Travis said to Tommy. Tommy nodded in agreement.

Justin looked through the hole and noted that although it wasn't much of a plan, it had worked to near perfection. Travis and Justin could count on both their hands the remaining zombies. Of those that were left, Erin was doing her best to dispatch most of them. But unless the zombie's brains had somehow migrated to their feet, she wasn't doing much good. Most of the zombies that were left would now have a pronounceable limp, but they wouldn't be able to collect disability insurance any time soon. Travis, Justin and Tommy walked through the front gate, the Mossberg and the Winchester blazing hellfire. If the zombies were capable of any other thoughts besides 'meat,' they would have known to leave this place of re-death so they could salvage what remained of their ravaged bodies in order to attack at another time. The last zombie had fallen long before Travis and Justin stopped firing. It took Tommy's gentle hands on their shoulders and a couple of words to get their attention; they had been deep in the grip of battle fever.

"I found another Pop-Tart," Tommy said as he flashed the foil bag in front of Travis' eyes.

Justin turned to Tommy. "Were you whistling?"

Tommy grinned. "Yeah, it was the theme from The Good, The Bad and The Ugly."

Justin laughed. But the killing fog had not cleared from Travis' eyes. It took a giant bear hug from his godfather that threatened to cut off his oxygen supply to do the trick. Erin came out next; she was busy reloading her pistol.

"Holy shit boys, it's great to see you!" As Paul pulled Justin into the growing mass hug, Tommy stood to the side with his hands clasped behind his back, casually kicking his left foot into the ground. He looked like a puppy in a pet store window.

"I don't know who you are, kid, but get your ass over here," Paul said with a beaming smile, doing his best to stretch his arms across the three of them. Erin completed the circle on the far side.

"My name's Tommy," Tommy said happily with his face buried in Justin's back.

"Boys, I'd love to stay like this a while longer but I want to get the hell out of here," Paul said as he disentangled himself from the conglomeration. "So what's the plan?"

Justin and Travis merely looked at one another. Paul sensed their uneasiness.

Travis spoke first. "Well, you... um, kinda know as much of the plan as we do."

"Oh crap, we've got to get back in the house then," Paul said apprehensively.

"Paul, we can't. We've only got enough supplies for a day or two at most," Erin reminded him.

Paul's stress level was as stretched as high as it could be. Justin spoke before it snapped.

"Our truck is at the end of the street. Brendon should be back in a couple of minutes. As soon as he gets here we'll head back home."

Paul and Erin looked longingly back at their home, confident in the fact they would never see it again. "All right, let's get going," Paul said as he wrapped his arm around his wife.

A few moments later everyone was huddled around the car. Tommy was the sole occupant. The rest stayed outside in an uneasy silence. It seemed more prudent to be able to leave in a moment's notice rather than be imprisoned in the SUV. Only Tommy felt otherwise.

"Maybe we should get your car, Uncle Paul," Justin said. The waiting was plainly beginning to unnerve him.

"Not such a good idea," Paul answered. "I coasted

home on fumes the night before this all happened, I would have gone to your place before we got surrounded if I had thought to fill the damn tank. I just figured I'd have all the time in the world to do it." Just as Paul was done rebuking himself, a single shot rang out. It sounded distant. Everyone swung in the general direction of the sound.

"That was Brendon," Justin surged toward the noise.

"The captain is back!" Tommy yelled from the backseat.

Paul looked questioningly before Justin answered sheepishly. "Captain Obvious, you get it?"

"Oh," Paul forced a strained smile. He appreciated the humor, just not under the present circumstances.

Another solo shot rang out. This one was definitely closer, but still no sign of Brendon. Justin was about to speak but Paul saved him the trouble. "Yeah it does sound closer."

Time slowed to match the shuffle of a zombie. The group fervently waited for something, anything to happen. They were rewarded a few moments later with the compensation of a rapid three round burst.

"Shit, that was close," Travis said as he jumped a bit.

"*You* swear?" was all Paul could think to ask.

Travis grinned like he had been caught with his hand in the cookie jar. "Not in front of Dad."

"When we get to your place, I'll make sure I leave that part out," Paul said.

Brendon came sprinting around from the main street, still about two hundred yards away, but even from this distance they could tell he was drenched in sweat and laboring hard to keep up the pace. Three seconds later they could see the reason. Zombies were within spitting distance of his back. If he turned to shoot he'd never get the shot off. The boys flipped off their safeties, but at this distance there wasn't much they could do. Brendon was slowly pulling ahead of those closest to him, but zombies began spilling out of the yards along his path, facing him; they were trying to encircle him.

"Paul I'd like to get out of here *now*," Erin said stridently as the whites of her eyes began to expand in terror.

Travis and Justin didn't want to shoot the zombies between them and Brendon for fear they might hit Brendon. There was still room for Brendon to maneuver around but it was getting marginally narrower by the second. When Brendon was within a hundred yards the circle noosed shut; the time for inactivity was over. Tommy began to whistle his favorite Clint Eastwood theme again. Travis and Justin concentrated their fire to the left. Their theory was that they could open a hole without hitting their sister's fiancé. It was working, but more due to the fact that the forward-facing zombies had now taken notice of the new piles of warm meat directly behind them. The circle in front of Brendon broke down as those closest began to come towards their new prize. It was going to be a mad dash for who got to the car first. The cloudy day was lit up by the expended rounds. The smell of gunpowder would linger long after the battle was over. Brendon was now zigzagging around zombies; some were still interested in him and once or twice they got a hand on him. Most were disregarding him and were now focused on the main course instead of the entrée.

Paul opened the back door, weighing the myriad of possibilities laid out in front of him.

"Hey Tommy, you might want to get out of there," Paul said, feeling the possibility of escape was rapidly diminishing.

"I'm good," Tommy said matter-of-factly, blithely ignorant of what was going on around him.

Travis looked over his shoulder as he began to reload for the fourth time and saw Paul talking to Tommy. "What'd he say Uncle Paul?!" Travis screamed over the roar of Justin's shots.

Paul pulled his head from the inside the car door. "He says he's good," Paul answered although he looked thoroughly perplexed.

Travis knew Tommy's abilities and didn't doubt him

in the least as he yelled back to Paul, "Get Erin and get into the car!" Travis shouted as he drove his bolt home.

Paul slowly shook his head in response. "I think we should get back to the house."

Erin began turning in that direction, she wasn't going to need to be told twice.

Travis put the rifle up to his shoulder and fired a shot at a zombie ten feet away. "GET!" he fired again. "IN!" he fired again. "THE!" he fired again. "FUCKING!" he fired his last shot. "CAR!" he screamed as he fished more slugs out of his pants.

Paul was in shock but had the wherewithal to grab his wife and usher her into the car. "You sound more and more like your dad," Paul said dismayed as he pulled the door shut.

"Want a Snickers?" Tommy asked.

The car jumped. A zombie had run into the rear in an attempt to get to the boys. Brendon had dropped his pistol as he covered the last few yards, desperately trying to get his keys out of his pocket without slowing down. It was going to be close but the destructive fire of Justin and Travis had cleared a rapidly shrinking gap.

"Get in, brother," Justin told Travis.

Travis usually was not one to do as his brother told, but this seemed like a foolish time to keep up that tradition. He hopped in and scooted over to the middle of the front bench seat. Seconds later Justin slid in, pulling the door closed as the closest of the zombies smeared his decomposing hand on the passenger window.

Erin screamed in terror.

"Ah, just like old times," Travis said sarcastically.

Justin sometimes wondered how deep the depths of resolve went in his younger brother.

Brendon crossed in front of the car, for one heart-stopping beat all of his attention was on the set of keys that he fumbled in his hands. At one point he lost control of them. Everyone held their breaths as Brendon made a desperate bid to swipe them out of midair, and in a play worthy of a top ten mention on ESPN's Sports Center, he made contact and snatched life from the jaws of death. A moment later, Brendon plowed into the driver's seat, nearly snapping the key in the ignition with the brute force with which he drove it home. His chest heaving for air, Brendon turned the key but nothing happened.

"Told you about that," Tommy said from the backseat.

Brendon had some choice expletives but kept them to himself. The energy to issue them forth was more than he had right now. His heart was a trip-hammer as he began to fumble with the shift selector.

More to himself than anyone else in the car he said, "Sometimes the shifter doesn't go into park and the car won't start."

"Probably a good time to put it in park, don't you think?" Travis asked.

Brendon glared in his direction, but his girlfriend's little brother for once wasn't being sarcastic. Travis was looking out the windshield at the growing number of zombies. Fear creased his face. The sound of Justin's window exploding inwards masked the sound of the engine catching, so much so that Brendon was in danger of stripping out the starter as he held the key too far over for too long. A zombie reached in and clawed at Justin's face. Travis having realized what Brendon hadn't, slammed the car into gear. Brendon turned from the invading zombie as the car shot forward and threatened to stall. Brendon quickly realized what was happening and tried to put his foot through the floor. The car sagged at the over rush of gas, hesitated, sputtered and then shot out of the crush of zombies like a cat in a tub. A few unlucky zombies found out firsthand what it felt like to have three tons of Detroit steel run over your body, although they didn't seem to mind that, only that the 'meat' was getting away.

The zombie in Justin's window had its arm wrapped around the seat belt. It tried for a few feet to keep up but then it allowed itself to be dragged, its concentration fully fixated on the food within reach. Its arms swung wildly within the car as it tried to pull its body up and closer so its gnashing teeth could do their job, the fetor of its moldering breath rivaled even that of its undead flesh. Justin screamed in surprise as a hand closed around his cheek, trying to seek purchase or perhaps just trying to pull a bit off for a snack. Paul, reaching over Tommy, was desperately attempting to unravel the seatbelt from the zombie. Justin was flailing around like a drowning victim. Erin moved into Paul's vacated spot and placed one hand on Justin trying to calm him down. He didn't, at least until her other hand passed in front of his eyes, the one with the gun. Paul pulled back as Erin lined up her shot. Everyone in the car was a little hesitant after her not so successful display of shooting skills earlier. This bullet, though, hit home, dead center in the zombie's forehead. Its head whipped back and then forward from the backlash but it looked more like he was questioning 'Why?' as his slumped body fell from the car like a discarded McDonald's bag.

The zombies retreated quickly from view. It took a few moments for Justin's overloaded senses to regain equilibrium from the deafening shot and the acrid blast of smoke that had inundated his nose. But when his senses did clear the outcome was less than satisfactory.

As the ringing began to subside within his ears, Justin bowed his head to try to regain the precious breaths he had lost. At first he was uncertain what he was looking at as large crimson droplets splashed on his blue jean covered thigh. It was when he attempted to wipe his cheek clean that true terror infiltrated his heart. His fingers were covered in blood, his own.

"Oh, Jesus, no!" Justin wailed.

Paul looked out the back window thinking the zombies were somehow keeping up with the speeding get-away car. Justin buried his head in his hands. Travis made an attempt to discover what was the matter with his brother, but was shrugged off. Brendon slowed and then finally let the truck come to a rest (with the engine idling) to discover the problem. Justin was too far lost in his own thoughts to do more than show the offending blood to the rest of the occupants.

"Were you bitten?" Travis asked.

Justin shook his head 'no.'

"That's good then, right?" Travis asked, hoping someone would answer in the affirmative. "In most zombie movies you have to be bitten to be infected."

Nobody knew the answer. How could they? This wasn't a movie, and zombies weren't supposed to be real, right? Even Tommy looked concerned. Travis hoped it was because he was out of Snicker's bars. Nobody said anything. As Brendon accelerated the truck, nobody knew what to say anyway. Travis put his arm around Justin. It was a rare display of brotherly love. Justin was at first inclined to shrug it off but when he realized Travis was not going to relinquish his spot, Justin acquiesced.

As Brendon was racing closer to Little Turtle, he voiced his thoughts. "They're not going to let Justin in through the gate with that wound."

Travis instantly got upset. "We can't leave him outside!"

Justin didn't say anything. He had already resigned himself to his fate.

"I'm not saying we should leave him outside, Travis," Brendon said with a bit of attitude in his voice.

Justin and Brendon had become friends since Brendon had started dating his sister. He was offended that Travis would think he would abandon his friend this quickly.

"We could say he cut himself on the broken glass," Travis said hesitantly.

"Justin," Brendon said softly. Justin didn't respond. "Justin!" he said with a little more force. Brendon pulled over again. "Justin, look at me."

Justin reluctantly turned his head to face him.

Brendon inwardly winced when he saw the wound. A three-inch long slab of flesh had been raggedly pulled from Justin's cheek, and blood flowed freely from the laceration. If Brendon hadn't firsthand witnessed the attack, he would have assumed the wound to be caused by a bite. The notched pieces of sinew looked angry with swelling; Justin's eyes appeared to be sunken from the rapidly expanding swell from the damage. What was worse was the look of defeat in those same eyes. Brendon couldn't help but think that his friend was already turning. Better to leave him out here than take the possibility of him injuring someone else. Brendon definitely did not want to be the person that had to put a bullet between his eyes. All these thoughts raced through Brendon's mind, each one trying their best to gain a foothold and sway a decision in their favor. His lack of ability to think clearly under the circumstances may just have saved Justin's life.

Brendon at last spoke. "Yeah, there's no way the guards will mistake that for any type of cut." He swung his head to the back. "Hey Tommy, want to sit up front?"

Tommy was not his normal jovial self, and that as much as anything contributed to the downward spiral of morale in the truck. Erin had buried her head in Paul's shoulder and was crying softly. Tommy looked like he wanted to join her. Travis did not understand Brendon's motive to move Tommy and wanted to make sure he was one hundred percent clear on where he was going with this. Brendon saw the look of confusion on Travis' face and clarified.

"I want Tommy to sit upfront and for Justin to pretend he's asleep in the back, that's the only chance we've got of getting him back through the gate," Brendon elaborated.   "I'd just as soon hide him in the trunk if I had one but that isn't an alternative."

"What if he turns?" Travis asked.

"I'll take care of it," Brendon answered brusquely.

"I'm his brother, I should be the one to do it," Travis

said pointedly.

Justin began to open the passenger door as he spoke. "If it comes to it, I'll do it myself."

Tommy was busy coming around from the rear driver's side around the front of the truck as he met Justin. He gave Justin a huge hug which seemed to elevate Justin's spirits ever so slightly.

"That's not the hug of death, is it Tommy?" Justin asked.

"I've never hugged anyone to death," Tommy said seriously as he wiped a tear away from his cheek.

Justin's eyes were red rimmed and enshrouded in blackness. He looked like a trick-or-treater halfway made into his costume. Paul switched seats with Erin while they waited for Justin to get back in the truck, placing himself between Justin and his wife.

Within minutes the truck was about ready to make the final turn onto Evans Avenue.

"Everyone ready?" Brendon asked as he exhaled loudly.

Paul stiffened slightly as Justin laid his head on his shoulder. Justin noticed the rebuff but he couldn't blame his uncle. He was sure he'd do the same thing if the circumstances were reversed. As they pulled up to the gate Brendon put on his best award winning smile. It failed miserably.

"Boy, you look like you just had your balls stomped on by a golf player," the guard said. "Ain't that right Igor?" The guard said clearly amused with his pun.

Igor nodded and answered. "Da." But Igor wasn't paying so much attention to his partner. Igor's head was inside Brendon's truck looking around.

"Dere's much blood in here." Igor said, clearly not looking for an explanation, yet merely stating a fact. "Veren't you boys going to help your father?" Igor asked. Now he was clearly looking for answers. Nobody spoke at first until Paul began to brainstorm.

"They were, sir, but when they came across my wife and I in trouble, that Mike fellow rescued us and then told these fine young men to take us home."

Igor was not convinced. "What happened to the window?" he asked brusquely as he brushed shattered glass off the sill.

Travis spoke a little too soon and a little too loudly. "That was my fault sir, I shot at a zombie not realizing the window was still closed." Travis smiled weakly.

"Da glass is on the inside of the truck," Igor said, looking piercingly at Travis. Travis' smile weakened further. "Vat is wrong wit the other boy?" Igor asked, pointing to the rear seat.

"I'm fine!" Tommy beamed.

"Da, Not you," Igor answered firmly. Tommy frowned.

This time it was Brendon's turn to think quickly. "Sir, I'm just trying to get him home so he can sleep it off. We broke into Mr. Talbot's vodka last night and drank way too much."

Igor laughed, not convinced again that he was receiving even half of the truth, but he laughed any way at the thought of two young Americans trying to tame Russian water. "Da, he does look a little green around the gills, get him home and get him well," Igor said, his gaze boring directly into Brendon's eyes.

"Yes sir," Brendon answered as he drove into the complex.

Justin's sleeping act moved into the realm of reality as he had to have help to be removed from the truck. His steps were sluggish and weak. Paul supported one side as Travis supported the other. Brendon hustled up through the back gate to make sure the way was clear so they could get Justin into the house unimpeded. That didn't look like it was going to happen, at least not easily.

No sooner had Brendon opened the back gate than he was met by his girlfriend. The dangerous look of fire was in her eyes and her posture. A litany of lavish profanity was about to be issued forth until she caught sight of her brother being almost dragged into the yard. She didn't even acknowledge her uncle's presence, as all of her attention was focused on the ghostly image of her brother's face.

"Oh my God!" Nicole shrieked as she pushed by Brendon to wipe some of the sweat off of Justin's feverish brow. She quickly pulled her hand away. "He's burning up!" She turned back to face Brendon. "What did you do to him?"

Paul spoke up. "Now's not the time for accusations, Nicole. We need to get your brother into the house and get some antibiotics into him."

"Uncle Paul?" Nicole asked as she turned back and finally noticed him.

"Get your mother, Nicole," Paul said with force.

"Thank you," Brendon muttered under his breath.

"Don't worry kid, I did it for all of us. I've known Nicole long enough to realize 'shrill' was rapidly approaching," Paul said as they brought Justin through the back door.

The boys laid Justin down on Henry's favorite couch. Henry wouldn't mind, he was sleeping soundly upstairs on Mike's side of the bed. Tracy came downstairs awkwardly holding a rifle; it looked as much out of place in her hands as a cat holding an umbrella, but if there was trouble she wanted to be ready. She stopped short when she saw Paul and Erin, trying her best to assimilate this new information as quickly as possible. However, as soon as she saw Justin lying on the couch the rest was forgotten. In the meantime, Travis was going through the kitchen cabinets looking for any half-empty antibiotic bottles. Nicole and Tracy were famous for not finishing their medications. Within moments his effort was rewarded.

"Got 'em," he said triumphantly.

Tracy barely acknowledged his words as she pressed her hand to Justin's forehead.

"What's wrong with him?" Tracy exclaimed. "He's

so hot!" She turned her glare on Travis and Brendon. "Tell me right now what happened."

Justin's face was sallow and taking on hues of yellow and green. Brendon was hesitant to let his rifle down, feeling that he might need to use it at any moment. But how could he possibly tell Mrs. Talbot to get out of the way so he would have a clean shot.

"Nicole, go fill the tub with cold water. Travis, get all the ice and put it in the tub. And find me some antibiotics!" Tracy yelled.

Travis ran over and handed her the bottle of erythromycin, then headed back to the freezer, grabbed the ice and went to catch up with his sister. Anything to get away from the scene that was unfolding in front of him. Justin had a difficult time swallowing the pills his mother handed him. His tonsils had swelled to the point where they were almost making contact with each other.

Mike came back four hours later to find seven people including the dog crowded into the master bathroom. The bathroom was spacious for one but was never designed for that many people. Mike took little note of his best friend and wife when he was able to muster past the throng and see what everyone had their attention focused on. Justin was lying in the tub alternating between violent convulsive shivers and panting from the heat his body was throwing off. He groaned in despair and fell to his knees next to his son.

Tracy's Chapter - 14

"Mom!" Nicole yelled from the bottom of the stairs. "Everyone's gone!"

Tracy was irritated, last night was the first night in almost a week she had slept clean through. Between the nightmares and Mike's thrashing about, sleep had been as elusive as an eel in Jell-O. A couple of more hours of blessed sleep and she might almost feel human again. Best not to joke about that, she thought.

"Everyone?" she asked in alarm as she sat up in bed, head swimming in light-headedness. She had not been taking her vitamins as religiously as she had before 'the infection.'

Depression sometimes weighed heavily on her mind. What was the point of vitamins? They wouldn't protect against zombies. Guns, one of the things she loathed most in life, were now her only clear salvation. She had turned a blind eye when Mike had begun his slow, methodical collection of guns. She had her own vices, why should she deny him his. He didn't smoke, he didn't use drugs, he didn't run around with other women. He was a good man, maybe a card or two shy of a standard deck but you could always draw in the missing cards on the jokers. Guns! She had worried, A LOT, when he brought the boys shooting, but he was careful and respectful of the power and devastation these devices could inflict. The boys were taught in this manner also. What at first had seemed unnecessary was now paramount to their survival. Civilization and all of its trappings were gone. Darwinism was back. The infirm would die. The strong would survive.

"Everyone?" she asked again, much more softly as

she reined in her errant thoughts.

Nicole was now in the bedroom. "Even Tommy," she answered.

"Are you sure they're not out on a work detail or getting food or just walking the dog?" Tracy asked. The last question was answered when a loud snort came from the general vicinity of Tracy's feet.

"Henry, how do you get up on this bed, and without me knowing?" Tracy said as she reached down and patted his snout. Henry obediently rolled over onto his back, expecting and receiving a tummy rub.

"Mom, I went down to the clubhouse and then I went to the gate. They all left. Dad went to the armory and supposedly the boys went to help him but the guard thought they were full of shit."

"All right, give me a minute." Tracy said as she pulled the covers the rest of the way off, partially covering Henry. He didn't stir, apparently happy with his new covering. "What about the guns?" Tracy asked as she headed into the bathroom to put on pants.

"What about them?" Nicole asked, not having any idea where this conversation was heading.

"We're going to need some," Tracy yelled from the bathroom.

"Why? What for?" Nicole asked, alarm rising in her voice.

"We're going to look for the boys," Tracy said matter-of-factly, grabbing her sweater off the idly sitting exercise bike.

People don't cover their exercise equipment with clothing because it is an easy coat rack. They do it because it hides their guilt. Guilt for having spent so much money on a piece of equipment that now did what any 49-cent hanger could do. The guilt of not having lived up to one's own expectations, more like promises to oneself. Exercise equipment sent more people to therapists than any dysfunctional mother could hope to achieve.

"When we get back, Nicole, remind me to throw out this elliptical."

Nicole stared at her mother, believing that she had finally gone over the edge. The stress of the last few days had been great on everyone and obviously her mother had enough.

Tracy opened Mike's gun safe to find the cache had been nearly exhausted. All that remained was a 22-caliber pistol and rifle. Not that she had any clue to as to what type of guns they were. "How do we know if these are loaded?" Tracy asked Nicole as she picked up the pistol gingerly.

Nicole ducked. "Definitely not by pointing it at me."

"Oh yeah, sorry," Tracy answered sheepishly.

"Are you sure this is such a good idea Mom?"

"My boys are out there. I'm going to find them."

Nicole sighed and walked over to her mother to grab the rifle out of the safe. She proceeded to pretend to know how to load it as she placed it on the bed. Nicole spent the next few anxious minutes under the watchful eye of her mother looking for the nonexistent magazine well, not knowing that .22 rifles are barrel fed. Not wanting to appear ignorant, Nicole picked the weapon back up. "All loaded," she announced proudly. It wasn't.

"I didn't see you put any bullets in it," Tracy said, but she honestly had no clue. "What about this?" Tracy asked handing over the pistol.

Nicole had watched her boyfriend and her father shoot at least half a dozen times and they always pulled back on something on the top. So when she finally found the mechanism on the pistol that pulled back and then slammed home when her grip faltered, she proudly announced the pistol was also loaded. It wasn't. At this point Nicole didn't think they were headed out the gate and was hoping that her armory skills wouldn't be put to the test.

"Mom, we have no idea where they went and they have at least a fifteen minute head start," Nicole began pleading. Her mother might be stressed out to the max but

Nicole was to put it bluntly, scared shitless.

At 4'11" and maybe 90 pounds after a Thanksgiving dinner, Nicole's biggest defense had been a Marine dad that some thought might be unstable. Nicole had tortured many a potential threat with the words, 'My dad knows where you live.' For some reason Mike could not fathom, all of Nicole's friends and potential enemies were deathly afraid of him and he had not so much as said boo to any of them. This had all been a device of Nicole. She had made sure that everyone knew of a particular incident in Canada involving her father, several Mounties and a politician. Nicole couldn't have been any safer if everyone thought her father was Tony Soprano. When her brothers had gotten older they became a second layer of defense, and to top that off was Brendon. If all else failed she had a mouth that belied her diminutive size. To hear her scream one would think they were being besieged by a platoon of howler monkeys. Her dad, who had multiple drill instructors scream at him and shrug it off, shied away from his daughter when her ever-widening pie hole began to vibrate. But shorn of her bodyguards and with an impotent voice, zombies wouldn't care about screams. It would be more like the sound of a dinner bell to them. She would become what she truly was, Daddy's little princess. Strip away the abrasiveness of her attitude and there was just a scared young woman.

"I could use some cigarettes too," her mother announced.

"Let's go," Nicole agreed immediately. Addiction is a powerful motivator. Screw the zombies.

Henry looked up from his chair, watching the two women leave. He realized nobody was home and hoped that somebody would be home soon to put out his second breakfast. Tracy and Nicole walked out to the garage. It was when they entered that Nicole noticed the obvious. (Yes, you guessed it, Princess Obvious.)

"You're going to take Dad's car?" she asked tremulously.

"Well he did trash *my* car," Tracy answered, but not with much verve.

A few months back, Mike and Tracy had been at the grocery store picking out some Starbucks coffee. Mike was in heaven smelling the wonderful aromas of the different beans and spices.

'You know,' He began. 'If God told me I had to give up either beer or coffee, I honestly don't know what I'd do.'

Tracy had thought the dilemma was easily solved. 'Beer.'

Mike looked at her. 'All right then, God says coffee or cigarettes.'

Tracy now saw the point.

After they had filled up the backseat of Mike's Jeep and were heading out of the parking lot, Tracy had asked him, if God said this Jeep or me, how hard of a decision would that be for you.

Mike's answer came swiftly. 'Oh Hon, that wouldn't be hard.' But he hadn't elaborated and she more than half believed his non-verbalized implication.

"Any better ideas?" Tracy asked.

"Well, we do need cigarettes," Nicole smiled sickly. More than once in her rebellious youth she had wanted to 'borrow' her father's Jeep when she had snuck out of the house, but she was unruly, not insane. The Jeep had stayed safely tucked away in the garage.

Nicole cautiously climbed up into the passenger seat, half expecting some form of theft deterrent to activate. No matter how much she adjusted the seat and her posture she could not get comfortable; guilt was a difficult suit to wear. Her mother didn't seem to be wearing it any better than her. The Jeep started loudly in the confined space. If not for the seat belts strapped across their laps, they both might have jumped out. Tracy slowly placed the car in reverse.

"Um, Mom, you might want to open the garage door."

"Oh yeah, right," Tracy smiled weakly.

This expedition was getting off to a memorable start, cigarettes or no. Nicole wasn't sure about the wisdom of this crusade. The door rumbled open, Tracy jerkily popped the clutch, stalling the Jeep. "Oops,"she commented.

"Great," Nicole muttered under her breath. The next three attempts at reverse didn't go much better. Then there was first gear to contend with.

Tracy rolled up to the main gate, hopeful they would open it before she lost momentum and had to mess with first gear again.

Igor waved them to a halt.

"Dammit," Tracy and Nicole muttered at the same time and both for the same reason. Nicole had nearly got her nose broken on the dashboard as the Jeep bucked like a pissed off bronco.

"Vat's a matter vit you Talbots? You not like it here?" Igor asked.

"Igor, do you know where the boys went?" Tracy asked concernedly.

"They say to help their Da but I could tell they was full of it," he answered helpfully.

She wanted to yell at him for letting them go, but his job was who to let in, not out.

"They be all right, Missus Talbot, they were armed for bear," he finished when he saw the look of apprehension on her face. "You two should stay here and wait for them to return. It's too dangerous to go out there."

"Did you give the boys the same speech?!" Tracy lashed back.

Igor stepped back and motioned for the bus to move. He'd learned a lot of things since he had moved to the States. Women were not subservient like in Russia, and it was best not to stir a hornet's nest with a short stick. "Have a nice day." And he walked back towards the bus to get some heat.

Tracy stalled the Jeep twice more at the mouth of the gate. The bus driver seemed on the verge of panic. He was gesturing wildly for Tracy to get out of the entrance way.

"What the hell is he so worried about?" Tracy asked hotly, driving, or actually stalling Mike's Jeep was getting her flustered. "There isn't a zombie for miles!" She was wrong, very, very wrong, but they were definitely out of the line of sight. "Keep your damn shorts on!" Tracy yelled as she successfully ground through first and out of the way of the bus. "God, Mike always makes it look so easy."

"Mom, are you sure we should be out here?" Nicole couldn't put her finger on it but something didn't seem right. Her foreboding grew as Little Turtle diminished in the rearview mirror.

Tracy was too busy concentrating on shifting gears to notice anything. It was possible her difficulties with the clutch were stemming more from her subconscious than her foot to pedal interaction. "Huh, got it!" Tracy said triumphantly as she pulled away from the intersection of Havana and Evans with nary a rattle. Now, as she surveyed her surroundings in earnest she had to agree with Nicole. Maybe this hadn't been such a good idea. She had endangered her daughter and herself and for what, she hadn't a clue which way her boys had gone. Driving around without a purpose was tantamount to suicide. Sure, they were armed, but neither one of them had shot more than a half dozen bullets and none of those rounds had impacted with the desired targets.

Tracy felt exhausted from the stress of this brave new world, her husband gallivanting all over the place and now her boys were God knows where.

Tracy's head slumped over the steering wheel as she looked over at her daughter. "Nicole, I don't know what I'm doing or where I'm going. Mike will kill us if he finds out about this and not only because we took his Jeep."

Nicole had never seen her mom so defeated. She had to think of something fast or her mother might just shutdown completely. Nicole had lost her license to drive last year. Not that any patrolman would be stopping to check, but the fact remained that she could barely control an automatic transmission. A clutch was out of the question. The sense of foreboding that she was feeling had not diminished in the least. She had no wish to walk back to the complex.

"I sure could use a smoke," Nicole said, looking out the corner of her eye, hoping for some reaction besides despair from her mother.

Tracy picked her head up, anguish clearly visible on her taut features. There was also something else…resolve. She was a little bit more than pissed at herself that she should be able to pull out of her funk over a cigarette, but old habits don't die easily. They can be suppressed or even forgotten for a while but they can and will always rear their ugly heads at the most inopportune times. This, however, was an opportune time. Tracy wasn't sure if she was mad or grateful that Nicole knew which buttons to push with such precise precision, but after all, she had been practicing for the last eleven years.

Tracy put the truck in gear. "Sounds good to me. Contracting lung cancer is the least of my problems."

Nicole would have laughed if the thought wasn't so macabre. Somehow at this point lung cancer was the safer alternative. How the hell did that happen? They drove in silence for only a minute or so as Tracy pulled into the nearest service station a half-mile away. There were a couple of cars in the bays, but they were unattended. Tracy did a lazy figure eight through the parking lot looking for anything that might make this visit not worth their while. Besides spilled gas there were no imminent threats. The lights inside the convenience store were out and the opaque glass masked everything. Tracy parked in front of the store, the Jeep idling quietly. She and Nicole peered intently into the gloom looking for any movement.

"Keep the car running. I'll run in and grab a bunch of packs," Nicole said as she began to open the door.

"Wait a minute, I'm not letting you go in there!" Tracy yelled louder than she meant to.

"Mom, I'll be fine, I'm just gonna run in and run

out."

"No, if anyone should go in it should be me. I've already got two kids, God knows where. You stay here and I'll run in," Tracy said, convinced this was the correct maneuver. "If anything happens to me, you just take off,"she said as she began to open her door.

"Mom!" Nicole yelled.

Tracy slammed her door shut, convinced Nicole had seen something. She looked wildly around for the threat.

"Mom, I can't drive a stick, if something happens to you, I'll have to run. Have you seen me run?"

"Shit, you scared me," Tracy said. As Nicole's words settled in she realized the dilemma they were in. No matter which approach she took, she would be placing her daughter in danger.

"Let's go in together," Nicole interjected before the paralysis of fear took her mother over again.

Nicotine was a powerful drug. It had the power to overwhelm judgment. Tracy nodded weakly. They both opened their doors and stepped out. The cold air was redolent with the scent of spilled gasoline. The noxious fumes made breathing difficult but also had the benefit (or disadvantage) of masking the scent of death. They hurried to the entrance to get away from the overpoweringly strong smell. Had their sense of smell not been burned-out by the gas it would have been assaulted by the now all too familiar stink of death. It would be three breaths too late before they realized their error.

"God, I wish there were some lights on," Nicole said, a slight tremor in her voice.

Tracy had been first in and was silently glad that was the case. As her eyes adjusted to the gloom inside the store she could make out a pair of scrubs-clad legs sticking out from behind the counter. Those legs were not made for walking anymore. There was also a congealed pool of blood coming from the aisle closest to them. Tracy had no need whatsoever to see what had caused it. Sometimes ignorance *really* is bliss.

Tracy shot her hand out and grabbed Nicole's arm, steering her away from the offending aisle.

"Shhh…did you hear that?" Tracy stopped and listened intently.

Panic welled in them both and Nicole hadn't even heard a sound. They both stood stock-still as the seconds ticked by. Nicole's arm began to throb where her mother gripped it like a vise.

"Mom, let go," Nicole said in hushed tones. "There's nothing here."

A small scratching sound emanated from behind the cold drinks.

"It's probably just the refrigerator kicking on," Nicole said, more to convince herself than anything.

Tracy pointed to the un-lit lights overhead.

Nicole looked up and swallowed hard. "Yup, no power. I knew that."

"Shhh…" Tracy more motioned than vocalized.

Nicole was not one to let a word go unspoken and was about to ask another question when the sound repeated itself. It was rhythmic and faint. There was no menace implied from the sound. All the same Tracy was in no mood to hang around.

Tracy spun to face her daughter. "Let's just grab a bunch of smokes and some sodas for the boys and get the hell out of here."

"I'm with you on that, this place gives me the creeps and it's starting to smell worse than outside. Mom, any particular brand you want me to get?"

"Yeah, all you can carry. I've got a feeling it's going to be a longtime before Winston-Salem starts pumping more of these out, unless they start to market a brand for zombies. 'Hey, you're already dead, why not smoke?' she tried for a feeble joke.

"That's funny in a sick way," Nicole said with a stiff smile.

"Even if we don't smoke them, we'll be able to trade with them. In a couple of days they might as well be sticks of gold."

Nicole's eyes sparkled. "Gold? Huh."

"You know what I mean."

"I know exactly what you mean," Nicole said as she went over and grabbed one of the two half-sized shopping carts.

"Good call," Tracy said as she grabbed the lone remaining cart.

Both women were so busy 'shopping,' neither noticed when the door to the freezer section opened. In the shadows a lone figure stared out at them lustfully.

The image of meat, not the actual word, crossed what rudimentary intelligence the beast possessed. Forward it moved, always forward, always hungry, always in pursuit of its next meal. 'Life was easy' it would have thought if it had enough cognitive power to be self-aware. That was not the case though.

Nicole had finished filling her cart and had gone out to the Jeep to fill it with her first load of booty. She couldn't have been any happier if she had just found Davy Jones' locker. Her previous dread was long forgotten as she reentered the store. She stopped in her tracks, her smile frozen on her face as she watched in horror. An undead nightmare stalked her unwitting mother.

"Mom!" Nicole shrieked.

Tracy dropped the case of Pepsi. Cans shot out in all directions. As they ruptured, sticky liquid arced through the air. Tracy was about to yell at her daughter for scaring her but when she looked up and saw the sheer terror on her daughter's face, she knew something was terribly wrong.

Nicole was pointing wildly, her finger thrusting like a woodpecker. Words stuttered in her mouth. "Z-Z-Z…"

Tracy got the point. There weren't too many words that started with 'z' that could instill so much panic, unless of course a murderous zebra was loose in Denver and she was in the way of some succulent wild grass. Tracy spun around to face the threat. Her foot slipped on the newly spilled Pepsi. Her left leg shot out wildly as she plummeted to the ground. The expression on the zombie's face changed from happiness to confusion as it wondered where its meal had gone. It was a beat or two before its eyes tracked down and locked back on its prey.

Tracy had landed hard on her ass; the fall had not been broken in the least by the tiled floor. Tracy began to back-peddle as the zombie once again began its forward progress. Nicole couldn't get it out of her head that she wasn't watching a scary movie on cable; her mind was searching for an escape.

Tracy had pushed back as far as she could, her back colliding with the fridge doors. Her feet sought a purchase that still eluded her on the slick floor. Tracy looked up at her one-shoed pursuer. Shapely legs gave way to a slender waistline and then to what could only be described as porn star breasts. Tracy could barely see around that mounding cleavage to the face mostly hidden beyond. What Tracy saw pissed her off to know end.

"Allison?" Tracy asked indignantly.

Allison-thing slowed her pursuit, not stopping but definitely slowing, as if walking and processing this question were using up most of her operating system.

"Allison Pittman?" Tracy asked again.

The slender face that stared back at her looked confused. The long auburn hair that framed the green eyes was a little bedraggled but for the most part this might be the best looking zombie in the history of the genre, Tracy mused. "I would have hoped that your face got eaten, bitch!" Tracy yelled, as she was finally able to get her feet back under her with the help of the door handle behind her.

"Mom! What's going on?" Nicole moaned.

The Allison-thing had stopped, almost as if she had had a fatal operating error.

"This *thing*!" Tracy yelled, "is the bitch that almost

split up my marriage." She glared venomously at the curvaceous corpse.

Right before Mike was laid off from his job, he and Tracy had been having some marital difficulties, as most couples will during a marriage. These problems were exacerbated by the beauty of one conniving, manipulating bitch named Allison Pittman. Allison had become the 'shoulder' which Mike had leaned on. She listened intently, always saying the right thing, stroking his ego whenever it needed to be done. She was the perfect seductress. At first Mike hadn't noticed the subtle shift. They had been friends for almost three years and in that time they had told each other a myriad of private things. Mike could 'see' that Allison was one of the prettiest women he had ever laid eyes on. He was happily married and even if he wasn't, he had talked to Allison long enough to know that her idea of a good time was to devour some poor man's soul. Then when he was just a dried up husk of himself she would discard him like so much used trash. She was a modern day succubus. Still, she seemed to value their friendship. But when Allison had seen an opportunity, a chink in the marital armor of the Talbots, she did all in her powers to tear open an irreparable wound. It was like a disease with her. She was an unhappy person and wanted everyone else to wallow in her emotional mire. Even as she loathed herself for her actions, she reveled in the thought of bedding Mike and then throwing it in the face of that bitch wife of his.

Mike had finally come to his senses and seen the ruse for what it was. It was almost disastrously too late, but the light of recognition had dawned on him when he was at Allison's apartment. She had asked him if he would help her move some furniture from one room to the other. He had happily obliged, after all, that's what friends were for, even if his higher psyche smelled a rat. When he arrived there was a chilled bottle of wine on the table. Mike could see the shimmering candlelight emanating from Allison's bedroom down the hallway, but the coup de grace was the sheer negligee she was wearing. Mike had always known that she was a stunning looking woman, but this vision that greeted him at the door made him weak at the knees. Mike's mouth dropped open as panic welled up. He was at a crossroads in his life. Straight ahead lay his wife and kids. Sure, there was some cracked pavement and a pothole or two but it was a scenic, satisfying journey. All Mike could see if he took a hard right in his life with Allison was an 'under construction' sign: large orange traffic cones and glaring lit up warning signs that foretold of dangerous curves and hidden bumps that lined the street. That road could be fun for a mile or two. However, Mike was certain that it would end like so many roads he had seen Wile E. Coyote go down so many years before, with a huge sign in the middle of the road that told the driver 'The End Was Near.' That would be punctuated, of course, by a huge boulder lying just beyond it. All of this knowledge was too late for the Coyote because he had rocket skates on, but Mike had something that Wile E. didn't: foreknowledge.

Mike took one more look inside her apartment. Then, one long lingering look at the woman that stood before him. Later he would tell himself it was because he had wanted to be absolutely sure what Allison's intentions were. Then, without a word, he had turned and walked away. He knew if he had said something, anything, she would have had the perfect riposte and he would have caved. He would have stayed in the apartment and his life would have been irrevocably changed forever, and not for the better.

"Mike?" Allison had asked to his back. "What are you doing?" She had never been on this side of rejection and was not taking to the learning experience too kindly. "You're turning *this* down?" she yelled as she flaunted her body.

Even without the condescending tone Mike knew not to turn around. To do so might have turned him to salt like Lot's wife of Sodom and Gomorrah fame. Or worse yet, have him question what the hell he was doing.

"Go back to your wife!" she yelled. Her tremulous

voice reaching volumes that brought out her neighbors, the better to play out this drama.

"What are you, a *fag*?" she spat. Mike's face burned as he realized he now had an audience to this spectacle.

Relief flooded through him as he finally reached his car door but was quickly diminished as he realized he would have to turn around to get in. Even from this distance, Allison's beauty was unrivaled. The sheer hatred that etched her features only confirmed to Mike the wisdom of his decision. Mike's dick, however, was unstirred by the power of higher reasoning and screamed its own words of hate and discontent at him.

"Definitely not a fag," Mike said to himself as he made some adjustments to himself, started the Jeep and got the hell out of Dodge.

Allison's eyes burned holes into the back of Mike's head as he made his hasty retreat. Her apartment shook from the force she had applied to her door as she slammed it home. It was from that point forward that she had begun to formulate a plan to get Mike dismissed from his job. She had hoped for a scandal of epic proportions and was disappointed when she was only able to manage a 'job discontinuance.' She had felt nothing close to remorse when she came to his office that final morning, only something akin to a fulfilling satisfaction.

"Last day?" she had laughed from his office door, a smug smile on her face.

Mike was fairly certain of Allison's hand in this, but had no desire to give her any more satisfaction than she was already deriving from it.

"Yeah, it's time for a change, I've got some prospects back East that I'm looking forward to checking out."

It was all a lie, Mike was deeply scared about losing his job, but to see her smirk come off her face for just a fraction of a second made it all seem worthwhile. Mike continued to load his last box with his belongings. Allison was irate as she pushed off from his doorframe. Revenge, unfulfilled. She stalked off, looking for her next victim.

Mike had told Tracy everything about that day, except the part about his traitorous penis. The liabilities of that disclosure far outweighed the benefits. Tracy had on more than one occasion wanted to confront Allison and let her know what she thought of her. Unlike Mike, Tracy was completely convinced that Allison had engineered Mike's employment demise and had since wanted to exact revenge. Now the demon spawn stood before her, in all her deadly regal beauty.

"How does a zombie look so fucking good?" Tracy asked as she finally got to her feet.

"Mom?" Nicole was still bewildered, but finally took her mother's words to heart and looked at the monster in front of them.

Except for some unkempt hair and a grayish sheen to her skin tone, the zombie was a knock out. For a second or two Nicole wasn't sure if they were being confronted by a monster or just a starving civilian. All pretense of a peaceful outcome was shattered as the Allison-thing reengaged her one-track mind. Her mouth opened wide, revealing bits and chunks of her last conquest. Like the door of an ancient mausoleum creaking open, the stench of death issued forward. Nicole brought her pistol up to bear, her hand shaking wildly as she pulled the trigger. Nothing happened. Nicole waited impatiently for the terse spring of the recoil and the acrid smell of gunpowder. All that happened was her hand shook wildly from side to side and the acidic smell of decay flooded her senses.

"Shit!" Nicole yelled as she pulled the trigger again and again, but still nothing happened, not even the satisfactory slamming of the firing pin hitting home.

Tracy had not been stationary during this brief interlude; she had also brought her rifle to bear. The Allison-thing was so close that her mouth closed around the barrel of the rifle.

'Gonna be tough to miss from this distance,' Tracy

thought with a certain sense of satisfaction.

"This oughta take care of that shit-eating grin, BITCH!" Tracy yelled just as she pulled the trigger.

Yes, Allison-thing's grin did expand, but not because of any hot lead injection. Tracy realized the gun wasn't loaded. It was more useless than Viagra at a Promise Keeper's Convention. Allison-thing was held at bay as the muzzle of the weapon pressed against the back of her throat. Tracy wanted to scream in rage and frustration, in revenge unfulfilled. Meanwhile, Nicole picked up the closest object that she could find. Tracy reeled as the flying box of condoms narrowly missed hitting the side of her head.

"Really?! That's the best that you could do?" Tracy shouted.

"Sorry Mom. What are we gonna do?" Nicole shrieked, hysteria rising dangerously close to the surface.

"Go behind the register and see if there's a bat or a crowbar or something to hit her over the head with," Tracy said as she struggled with the Allison-thing.

The zombie still hadn't figured out that to get to the meat it would have to dislodge from the bitter metal stick. The barrel was coming dangerously close to pushing through the back of her slender neck.

"There's only a cane!" Nicole shouted from the register station.

"That'll have to do. Hurry, I don't know how much longer I can hold her back."

Tracy was struggling under the relentless assault. The Allison-thing would never stop. Tracy knew that even as her arms ached with the strain of holding the undead bitch away from her. Tracy was proud as her daughter conquered her rising tide of fear and approached the zombie, cane upraised. Nicole swung with all her might, but between the mass of the cane and the lack of muscle Nicole possessed, the blow did little more than irritate her mother's assailant. Again she raised the cane and struck. The zombie finally noticed that she was being attacked. It backed up, dislodging itself from the gun and turned her full attention on the small morsel of meat to her side. 'Succulent' was its vacant thought.

"Mom!" Nicole wailed as she dropped the cane and backed away.

Tracy's arms were burning from the exertion of holding the zombie at bay. As the Allison-thing came loose, Tracy's arms fell. The rifle in reality weighed only seven pounds, but right now it might as well have been seventy. She caught her breath as the zombie turned all of its attention to her daughter. Nicole was moving backwards, her eyes wild with fear. The look of sheer terror on her face got her mother moving.

"First my husband! Then me! And now you want my *daughter*?!" Tracy screamed. She turned the rifle around so she was holding the barrel. "Well, you can't have any of us! BITCH!" Tracy said, as she swung the beefy end of the stock with a strength and aim even Babe Ruth would have been proud of.

With contact came that disgusting sound that only a collapsing skull can make. Some compare it to the sound of a watermelon exploding after a three-story drop. In reality this isn't even close. It is a much more visceral concussion. The sound assails the senses with the ire of a screeching cat in the dead of night. It is as repellent as a horde of spiders crawling on your head or getting your sternum poked or watching people chew with their mouths open. You get the point. It is a sound that is not meant for human ears. The stock of the rifle nearly stuck in the caved-in cranium of the Allison-thing. As Tracy pulled the gun back she was greeted with an audible pop as the suction between bone, blood and wood separated. Allison-thing's head hung at an awkward angle. Her body stopped in midstride. It attempted to swivel its head to see its attacker but the bones in her delicate neck were in no better shape than her mashed in melon. Tracy heaved a cry of satisfaction and relief as the Allison-thing collapsed to the floor. Some violent twitching from her extremities kept Nicole and Tracy engrossed for a few long macabre moments. Tracy had more expletives she wanted to shout at her downed adversary but was fearful if she opened her mouth only the contents of her roiling stomach would issue forth. Finally the Allison-thing lay still.

Tracy grabbed Nicole's arm and pulled her through the exit. Not a word was said on the ride home, or ever again on the matter. Mike would learn of the cigarettes, eventually, but when he questioned his wife, the stern look on her face kept him from pressing the matter. He didn't see any reason to pry any further. Women were a complete and utter mystery to him but he knew enough about when to keep his mouth shut.

CHAPTER 15
Journal Entry - 13

It was not difficult to see the source of Justin's fever. The scarlet wound on his cheek screamed for attention. The sight of a thousand ravenous zombies could not compete with the fright one sick boy placed into me. If Paul hadn't been sitting on the toilet I would have used it for some dry heave practice. It was then I finally REALLY noticed my lifelong friend.

"Paul?" I asked. I had to blink and rub my eyes, how cliché is that?

"Hey buddy," Paul said, his voice strained. He was feeling extremely guilty for his part in this progressing drama.

Paul and Mike had talked occasionally, usually in drunken stupors, about what they should do in the event of a disaster. Now in Paul's defense, most of these scenarios involved terrorist attacks, not zombie infestations. But after much debate and loud obnoxious rants, it was agreed upon that Mike's house was easier to defend and had more supplies including armament. At the first sign of trouble, Paul was supposed to get his ass over to Mike's, but he had let indecision rule and that had threatened the lives of his nephews. He knew Mike would have a hard time ever forgiving him this transgression.

I was torn between figuring out why and how Paul was here and the health and welfare of my son.

Paul saw my distress and eased at least one burden. "We'll talk later, it's a long story," he said as he waved me away to the front of the crowd huddled around the bathtub.

Tracy didn't look up from Justin as she sought out my hand for comfort. Words didn't seem necessary. I could see the jagged groove of flesh missing from Justin's right cheek. His face had swollen to almost double its proportion. If it had been caused by a bee stung, it would have been hilarious. As much as his cheek stuck out, his eyes had sunken in. He looked more like a caricature of himself than the real article. Red lines of infection radiated out from the unsightly wound.

I would have already thought he was a zombie if not for the next few moments.

Justin's eyes gained a measure of focus as they found mine. His next words were strained and choked as he tried to force air over his tortured tonsils.

"I'm s...sorry Dad," he cried.

I took a big intake of air as I sobbed. My heart wanted to leap out of my chest. Paul stifled his own keening. Tracy didn't hold anything back as she let loose as only a grieving mother can. Her sobs racked her body; she released my hand in order to cover her face with both of hers.

In the back of my mind I heard Tommy speak, but I wasn't cognizant of any particular word he spoke.

"He didn't get bit," Tommy said.

I wanted to lash out. I wanted to smash things. I wanted to swear to the heavens for this hell thrust upon me. But what would it accomplish? It wouldn't make my son any better. It wouldn't restore order to the universe. I didn't know what had happened, but from the hangdog expressions on Travis and Brendon, it wasn't a difficult puzzle to put together. Paul, being Paul, had procrastinated his departure from his house until his window of opportunity had closed. My boys had somehow got the half-assed idea to go and save their uncle. I loved Paul with all my heart, but never would I have sacrificed one of my kids for him. I wanted to lay into Paul and scream 'How dare you!?' But the guilt that he had already placed on his own shoulders was more than I could ever hope to achieve, and again to what end? My son was infected with the deadly virus, and berating Paul would do nothing, absolutely nothing to save Justin. I felt hopeless, no, scratch that, for the first time in my life I felt impotent. Okay the second, there was that one time in college when Paul and I had bought some incredible sensamilian herb and for some reason I couldn't achieve the 'full vigor' of manhood with my girlfriend. But this was worse, much, much worse. I stroked Tracy's hair as tenderly as I could. She bristled from the contact. I told her I had a quick meeting at the clubhouse and I would be back soon. She never so much as looked up at me; I can't say I could blame her.

I looked at the crowd in the bathroom and demanded, "Keep his fever down, and Travis come get me right away if he gets worse. And whatever you do, don't *anyone* let word of this get out. They'll put him down like a mad dog." I ignored Tracy's flinch at my words; they were nothing but the truth. I hesitated for a moment, then knelt next to my waxen-faced son and tenderly kissed him on the brow. As I turned and left the room, my shoulders shook as I tried to restrain my own heart-wrenching sobs.

Ten minutes later, there were six people including myself present at the impromptu clubhouse meeting. Alex, who looked like he had no sooner hit the pillow when he got the call, Jed, and Tim Tinkle, (no, I did *not* make the name up). He was head of the new "Security Department." He was a good-looking guy, about 6'2", 185 pounds, in great shape. He had blue eyes that were striking next to his prematurely silver hair. But he had the look of someone who has had to constantly defend himself, and with that name he probably did. I had my doubts about Tinkle. He looked like he had a short fuse. Next, there was Wilbur Heathrow, an older, heavyset guy, with wide spaced eyes on a narrow face that gave him the look of a salamander. He was head of the Guards. I don't know what went on while I was gone, but it looked like there were a whole lot of new posts. Maybe the titles made these people feel more self-important or more likely made them feel like they were in control of the situation. It was my personal belief it did neither. Why did we need a head of Security and a Guard Warden. It was the same thing, like saying, ta-may-to, ta-mah-to, what's the difference? Whatever, if it made people feel all warm and fuzzy inside, then why not? And to round out the six, Carl had showed up.

When it looked like all the movers and shakers were present, I pulled away from Jed and asked for everybody to be seated. Tim Tinkle remained standing. "Gentlemen," I began. "I'm sorry to have taken you away from whatever you may have been doing." I looked at Alex especially, knowing he was way short on sleep.

He gave me a slight nod. "De nada," he said, acknowledging my apology.

"We've got some problems," I stated.

"Why are you wasting our time with the obvious, Michael?" Tinkle intoned self-importantly.

Why was this guy starting already? And I hated being called Michael, it always reminded me when I was young and in trouble.

"Um, okay," I looked questioningly at Tinkle. "What I wanted to finish saying…"

"Are you implying that I interrupted you? The mighty Michael Talbot?" Tinkle sneered.

"Uh, Ti… Tim, I'm not sure what's going on here. I'm just trying to pass on some information I think is vital to our safety and security," I put forth, doing my best to rein in my anger at this idiot.

"Are you saying I'm not doing my job right?!" Tinkle yammered, taking a step forward and thrusting his finger at me.

"What the hell, man, I didn't even know there *was* such a job until Jed told me five minutes ago. Listen, I'm not trying to get into a pissing contest with you." Ooops, wrong adjective, he blew like Vesuvius.

"What does that crack mean, Talbot? You making fun of me? You got a problem with me? I'm gonna kick your ass into Tuesday."

Which I thought was kinda hilarious, considering it *was* Tuesday, unless of course he meant next Tuesday and then it would suck. He was approaching fast, veins sticking out of all sorts of unnatural places.

"Tim, please," Jed stood up, trying to thwart the hostility.

Tim pushed him aside. Luckily Carl was able to grab him before Jed hit the deck. Tim swung with a roundhouse that a zombie would have been able to dodge. I dropped low and struck with all of my force into his solar plexus. The wind couldn't get out of his sails fast enough. I felt the force of the super-exhaled air as it traveled with velocity over my head. I was thankful he hadn't eaten any jalapenos for dinner. It might have melted my hair. He immediately doubled over, trying his best to gasp for the elusive air. I was a millisecond away from finishing him off with an uppercut when Jed finally righted himself.

"Enough you shitheads!" he yelled.

I felt like I was five. I pointed at Tinkle. "He started it!" I blustered.

Tinkle couldn't talk yet but he had the presence of mind to point at me and shake his head.

"I don't care!" Jed raged on. I didn't know the old coot had that much fire in him. "Tinkle, sit your ass down. Talbot, continue." Tim did as he was told, by small degrees he was able to retain more air, but luckily the firestorm had died down.

"Okay," I stated again. "Where was I before I was so rude…" Jed pointed a finger at me. "Um right, uh I think we're in for a bit of a mess."

"Mike," Alex said exasperatedly. "You know that I came here because you had something important for us. But if you woke me for that, I'll be the next one up there taking a swing."

"All right, sorry," I held my hands up. "I was just thrown off-track for a sec. We've all been wondering where the zombies are? Why aren't they attacking? Are they dying? Did they move on? Now I'm not saying this is fact, these are just my observations. I think these zombies are a little more advanced than we give them credit for."

Everyone stirred a bit except for Carl.

Wilbur spoke up. "This is ridiculous, they're brain-dead, flesh eating parasites. They have all the brainpower of Tim over there." Everyone laughed, even Tim.

I related the story about when we had gone to get Justin and how the zombies had just up and left us for easier prey. "Listen, I know it's just conjecture, I have as much knowledge about this as you guys. But I think the zombies know we're here."

"That's preposterous!" Wilbur yelled out. "They're not even self-aware."

"Since when do predators have to be self-aware, does a wolf KNOW it exists?" I shot back.

Wilbur withered a bit.

"I thought about this the entire way home from the armory after our encounter with the zombies." The news of the sighting of so many zombies had seemingly beat us back to Little Turtle "I think the zombies have exhausted the easier food supply."

Wilbur was like a pit bull; he just wouldn't give up. He must hang around a lot with Tinkle. "Those are our family and friends that you so casually call *food*." He clearly wanted to continue with his scathing diatribe, but the only place this was heading was another confrontation resulting in a punch to the abdomen and I'd probably lose my fist in his massive midsection.

"Wilbur." I said solemnly as I carefully interrupted his harangue. "I'm not trying to make light of the situation, I'm calling it like I'm seeing it. Those people the zombies have hunted down were the infirm or slow or those caught unawares. I think that the reason we have been so 'relatively' safe is because we are a much tougher prey."

Wilbur was about to unseat his great mass again.

"Hold on Wilbur, just let me finish. Lions go after gazelles and zebra and only occasionally water buffalo and even then only the smaller ones. But if desperate enough and hungry enough they will attack a full-grown elephant, I watched it on the Discovery Channel. I'm willing to bet the pickings have gotten real slim outside these walls and we're the next available source of food."

Wilbur finally got his bulk up. His chair sagged in relief. "Oh come on, are we really going to listen to this?" he said, addressing the rest of the gathering. "He's telling us zombies are smart and that they know we're here. He's drawing parallels between them and Wild Kingdom for goodness sake. Why are we wasting our time with this, or him for that matter. He's just pissed he's not in charge and this makes him feel more important."

I felt defeated, "I have no desire to be in charge of this three-ring circus."

"So you say!" Wilbur said fiercely

I ignored his barb and continued, "I was only trying to make sure we were prepared for what's coming. Jed, I'm going to pack my family up and get going. Those of you that want to are more than welcome to come along."

"Good riddance Talbot, we don't need your kind here anyway," Wilbur snorted. Tinkle nodded, agreeing.

Alex looked away. "I'd like to come, Mike, but it feels safe here."

"I understand Alex, you have to look out for your family. Good luck my friend," I said honestly.

"Now hold on," Carl said, standing up. I didn't know what his relationship to Wilbur was, but Wilbur immediately deferred to the older man. It was later that I learned Wilbur was Carl's son-in-law and Carl couldn't stand him. Wish I had known that then. "Now I'm not in total agreement with Talbot."

'Great,' I thought. 'Jump on the 'beat Talbot' bandwagon.'

"But those zombies *were* acting peculiar, and I've also been thinking a bit on what I witnessed. I won't stand here and pretend to know what's going on but if those things are coming and in the vast numbers that showed at the armory, we're in a world of hurt. Now I have no intention of leaving and I don't think Talbot should either." Wilbur was not pleased. "But I do think we should roust the populace, such as it is, and begin to buttress up some of our weaker points."

"Thanks Carl," I said earnestly.

"I didn't do it for you," Carl answered.

"I still love you man," I said smiling.

Jed finally spoke up. "You better be careful Carl, he seems to like older men."

Wilbur did not like being thwarted this close to the goal line but he respectfully kept quiet the remainder of the meeting.

With a newfound vigor and hope I pushed on. "Alex, you're the engineer, how much stress can those walls take?"

Alex looked confused. "I don't think I'm understanding the question Mike. More than likely the wall would stop a regular sized car traveling no more than 30 or 40 miles per hour. A full tractor trailer however would probably punch right through."

"No, no I'm talking much smaller, like zombie-sized," I said.

"I don't think the zombies possess super human strength, if that's what you mean," Alex said.

"I'm sorry Alex, I need to be clearer. I have a hundred things running around in my head and they're all fighting to come out at the same time. I'm talking about thousands of zombies all pressing up against the wall, could it hold?"

"Oh crap, I hadn't thought about that. I mean it's only cinder block and cement. There isn't any rebar in it at all. There are stanchions every twenty feet, those would hold because they're anchored but no, if you put it that way, the walls are extremely vulnerable, the zombies could push over entire sections with that much force."

Wilbur's fat face recoiled; it shouldn't have made me happy but it did.

Jed spoke. "Well, if the walls are not safe then none of the gates are either. I reckon they could push that RV out of the way a whole helluva lot easier than taking out the wall.'

"Now you're seeing my point," I said triumphantly.

I could almost see the gears in Alex's head churning. He quickly started reciting his grocery list of desired items to begin the fortification.

Jed wanted to talk a little more after the meeting broke up. I so wanted to. The thought of idly chitchatting small talk about zombies seemed unbelievably more desirable that returning to the horrendous reality that awaited me at home. But a father's responsibility is to his family in times of need, and I would not break that cycle. The cold air did little to invigorate me as I slowly marched home.

Justin was out of the tub and laid out on the futon in my office. Again it was a crowded venue. He looked worse huddled under the blankets. The best word I could use to describe him was diminished. Tracy was still diligently at his side.

"Everyone out," I choked.

Everyone seemed to be lost a little too deep in their own thoughts to even recognize that someone had spoke aloud.

I spoke a little louder. "Everyone out, NOW!" I punctuated my command by slamming my hand against the wall. That got their attention. Paul placed his hands on Erin's shoulders and helped her up. They were immediately followed out by Brendon, Travis and Tommy. Only Tracy and Nicole remained. Nicole was wrapped up in her mother's arms.

"I'm not leaving him," Tracy said matter-of-factly, never looking up at me. "You just want to shoot him," she said again in that assured tone.

I shook inside.

"Tracy," I said as I tried to wrap my arms around her, but she angrily shrugged me away.

"You can't shoot him," she pleaded, this time looking me directly in the eyes. MY heart crashed to the floor and was immediately stepped on by a hippo. I couldn't answer her. What words could possibly justify my actions in the next few minutes?

"Nicole, please get your mother to bed," I asked.

And for the first time in Nicole's life she did something I asked of her without putting up an argument. This was not when I wanted this new trend to start. I needed something or somebody to help me off this insane tilt-a-whirl. I could hear Tracy's sobs retreating in the hallway as I shut and locked the door to my office. Justin was blissfully ignorant of all the mad happenings going on around him. I pulled my Glock 9mm out of my shoulder harness. Tears immediately welled up in my eyes. I wanted to get this over in the worst way, even more so than when I was 11 and had to do an oral book report in front of my class. In those days I had crippling stage fright and would dread for weeks the coming of the fated day. That was nothing in comparison.

What could a few moments more with my son harm, as I sat down in my office chair five feet away. I sat and stared at his puffed face the entire night and into early dawn. I was playing back in my head all the fun and not so fun times we as the Talbot family had enjoyed and endured through the years. As the sun began its slow fateful journey across the horizon I was no closer to the final judgment than I had been when I kicked everyone out. I had long ago put the Glock on my desk, fearing I might accidentally shoot myself in the leg if I were to fall asleep and then jerk awake. As tired as I was though, sleep had eluded me.

Justin opened his eyes and looked over at me. Did he see his father or a tasty early morning treat? His face looked less swollen but his eyes appeared to be even further sunken. How was that possible? His mouth opened, long lines of filament thin spittle spread from roof to floor of his mouth. Without taking my eyes off him I reached out blindly to the Glock I had laid down hours earlier. Oh God, why hadn't I done this when his eyes were closed. He still so much looked like the son I had taught to throw a baseball so many years previous. Tears filled my eyes as my hand closed around the cold indifferent composite material of my Glock 26. His features became distorted in my glistened visage. That was for the best, I thought. I could tell he was sitting up. My hands shook. Some sort of noise emanated from him. It was more something I would expect to hear from a frog on a marshy wetland, on a hot summer night. Nothing human could make that sound. My heart caught in my throat. I was fearful of passing out from lack of oxygen. I wanted to turn the gun on myself rather than ever take the life of one of my own, and I would have deserved it. I had fundamentally failed. A father's primary mission after procreation, is protection. I HAD FAILED! The price for failure should be death, but if I killed myself I left this task to someone else while also putting everyone else at risk. I would only be compounding my errors on top of my cowardice. I was still in the midst of berating myself when Justin managed to croak out some words.

"I'm so hungry I could eat...."

My mind went into overdrive as I begged the gods that he wouldn't finish that sentence with 'brains.'

"... Mom's meat loaf," he concluded.

And then I rushed over and hugged him for all he was worth. Not even a desperate zombie would be prepared to eat Tracy's meat loaf. I wailed in his arms. I should have been the one comforting him but I found solace in his embrace. Tracy must have at some point in the night wandered back into the hallway because she flew into the room like a mom on a mission. How had she gotten through the lock? When she saw that her son was still alive and not chewing on his father's face she joined in the embrace. I still had the Glock in my hand, when I finally put it down, it felt dirty. I couldn't get rid of it quick enough. Within moments the room was once again filled to the brim, only this was a much more merry occasion. We probably could have restocked our water supply with the faucet works going on. I was wrung out when I finally disengaged myself from the fray. My face was puffed out like I had been stung by a hive of pissed off bees. Although that doesn't make any sense, I mean if a bee stings you then by nature he's pissed off right? Like I said, I was wrung out. I left the array of family and friends tending to Justin's needs. I staggered to my room and fell face first onto my pillow. I won't lie and say I fell asleep before I made contact. I was, however, unconscious before I was able to register the pain of drilling my nose into my ultrathin pillow.

CHAPTER 16
Journal Entry - 14

I awoke about ten hours later, more so because of the overwhelming thirst that had even permeated my dreams than from the loud incessant snoring next to me. Now don't get me wrong, after twenty-something years of marriage this wouldn't be the first time Tracy had sawed a log, but it was usually few and far between and usually related to a cold or allergy. This sounded like Paul Bunyan was going for the world record in tree felling. I reached out my hand to gently shake her when I was mildly surprised to make contact with fur. I couldn't figure out which amazed me more, the fact that a 65-pound dog that didn't stand more than a foot tall could somehow jump onto my king-size bed or that the impact of his landing hadn't woken me up. Henry sneezed in my face for my effort. Not the ideal way to be awoken and I let him know as I pinched his face gently. Henry again sneezed but I was already on the move. He bounded down off the bed next to me as I groped for the doorknob, doing my best not to wake Tracy. Henry's stub of a tail began to rapidly sway at the offer of a cookie. That is, if he stayed awake long enough to get downstairs with me to retrieve it. The house was quiet, not the preternatural quiet before a loud escalating disruption, but one of peace. It made for a nice change. Henry silently padded alongside me as I went down the stairs and to the kitchen, him for his cookie, me for a drink of water. Henry seemed nonplussed as I turned the kitchen light on to find Paul at the table working on what appeared to be his seventh or eighth beer. He startled the hell out of me. Henry was upset about how long it was taking to get his proffered biscuit.

Paul looked liked shit, but what was much more

disturbing was how fast he was going through my rapidly diminishing beer supply. Paul offered me one of my own beers. 'What the hell, it's mostly water,' I thought as I said my thanks and sat down at the table with him. Henry barked indignantly. Oops, I got up and got him his cookie; he was asleep before he finished it. Half the biscuit fell to the floor as his head drooped and his body followed suit.

"Too tired to eat, Henry?" I laughed. "That's a new low even for you." Paul took no notice. I sat back down with him.

"Dude, I am so sorry," he half sobbed. I wanted to simultaneously kick his ass, hug him, tell him everything was all right and tell him he was an idiot. If I could have somehow pulled all that off I would have. Instead I kept quiet, taking a long pull from my beer. He wasn't finished talking, and I wasn't finished listening.

"Man, I knew something was going on when I stopped for gas on the way home from work. I was just about to start pumping my gas when I saw what I thought was a homeless guy heading my way. All I could think was that this guy was 'effed' up, I mean he was staggering and even from twenty feet away he reeked. I was like 'hurry up and accept my credit card already.' I didn't want the guy to come up and ask for change. If his breath was anything like his body odor I would have puked. So the guy is still stumbling my way and the pump finally authorizes my card but I said 'screw it' and hopped into my car to get away from him. I didn't even care if the next guy to get gas used my card, that's how spooked this guy had me. I was so happy to be done with him, I figured as soon as I shut my door he would veer off and go bother someone else, but he didn't. He walked straight into my door. I was about to get out and give him a tongue-lashing but I...I couldn't get out of the car. This hobo bum, 120 pounds soaking wet, scared the crap out of me. Something wasn't right about him. He never asked for change, he just kept looking me in the eye. His mouth was moving but no words were coming out. And his...his skin, I couldn't tell if it was from the twilight or the crappy lighting at the gas station, but his skin looked blue and streaked with veins. His eyes looked like every capillary in them had burst at the same time. I couldn't get my keys in the ignition fast enough.

When I finally sped away he started walking the way I had gone, like he was going to follow me. I was still shaking when I got to the house. Erin was in the shower and I had time to collect my nerves and get some liquid courage (cognac) in me. By the time Erin had got out of the bathroom, dried off and changed, it all seemed like a bad nightmare that was rapidly diminishing from my memory. You know we don't have a television in the house." (I so wanted to stop him there and ask him how in the hell that was possible, hadn't he ever heard of ESPN? How do you not have a TV in this day and age, that's like a stone age man not having a cave. It's just not natural, but again this didn't seem the appropriate time to interject.) "So we didn't get any news reports. We were just sitting in the living room talking about the day and listening to one of my CD's, when I heard this thud." (I knew that thud.) "It wasn't at the front door, it was at the living room window. So I'm figuring it's some bird that smashed into the window, but how stupid does the bird have to be to smash into a shade drawn window? I guess that's why they call people bird-brained." He strained a small laugh through his teeth.

"It wasn't a bird though," I finished for him. The memory was traumatic for him and he was having difficulty relating it.

"No," he choked out. "It was the guy/thing from the gas station and he was holding what was left of Rebel." Rebel was Paul and Erin's beagle, about as mellow a dog as ever lived, quick to wag a tail and give a lick. I felt bad for his loss. "I could hear Erin screaming behind me as she was looking at the same thing I was. At first I wasn't sure what he was holding. It was just a jumble of fur, splintered bone and blood. It could have been anything, I guess," he sobbed.

After a few minutes he continued. "I had just let him out. He...he was adamant about going outside. I thought he really had to pee, so I let him out. Even with Erin screaming and the horror of what that thing was holding began to dawn on me I was still with it enough to notice there were about six or seven more *things* rummaging around in my yard. My blood was boiling, I wanted to go out and start swinging a bat at these people to get out of my yard, and then Gas Station Guy took a big sinewy bite out of Rebel's back, he was eating Reb like he was a corn on the cob." Paul stopped and sobbed for a moment, then gathered himself together to finish his story. "Dude I FUCKEN *heard* him crunching Reb's spine, he pulled strands of fluid away from Reb's back. My blood froze. I pulled the shade so hard I ripped it off its moorings. Gas Station Guy was looking right at me. Erin had gone to get her gun. She came running back into the living room waving the thing wildly around like the thing was on fire and she was trying to put it out. I turned to grab her gun hand before she put a bullet in my ass. She was sobbing about how she had to save Rebel. That train had already left the station minutes earlier. Dude, I couldn't think of what to do. I was shaking like a leaf in a gale. I turned off all the lights on the main floor and half dragged Erin upstairs. I was able to finally let her arm go when I realized in her haste she hadn't even put a clip in the damn thing. So for about half an hour we're up on our bed in the dark just holding each other. Every couple of minutes I start thinking to myself that we need to get out of here, we need to go be with Mike." At this point he looked up at me and gave me an anemic smile. "But dude, every time I thought of leaving, my next thought was of opening the door to the Gas Station Man. Staying at the house seemed like a much better and much easier thing to do," he admitted reluctantly. "After a while the thudding on the house got more and more frequent, it was to the point where the house was vibrating from the impacts. By the time the glass started breaking downstairs it was way too late to leave. I grabbed Erin and pulled the attic stairs down and that's where we've been since I called."

That was news to me. "You called?"

"Yeah I didn't think I got through, I must have tried a couple of hundred times. I was on my last bar of battery when it finally rang on your side."

"When?!" I asked incredulously.

"Damn, must have been yesterday morning," he answered.

"When I went to the armory," I finished more to myself than him.

"When…when I saw the boys across the street I thought the cavalry had shown up. When I realized you weren't with them I wanted them to leave, I really did. But I also wanted to live. I wanted to be able to protect Erin. You know how that is, right? Trying to protect a loved one I mean," he said as he looked up at me from his beer.

I nodded in agreement. I know that feeling all too well, and I also knew how it felt to feel as if you had failed. I couldn't blame my friend for wanting to get help. I was pissed my kids thought it would be a good idea to go and get him though. He stood up and swayed back a bit. He was looking for a hug, which I was all too willing to give. I told him I loved him and that he should go sleep it off, not so much because he was drunk but because I wanted him to stop drinking my damn beers. Paul felt absolved as he stumbled to the couch. A small smile spread across his lips as he pulled the blanket up to his chin and fell into a relaxed sleep uninterrupted by the interminable pounding of dead flesh against his abode.

I finished my beer and another three as I pondered what would happen when the zombies did break through our defenses. That they would break through was never in doubt as far as I was concerned. How I was going to be prepared for it was another matter. I had no desire to be trapped in my unfinished attic waiting to starve or freeze to death while a bunch of pus-mongers roamed freely through my house. I had a couple of ideas I wanted to immediately implement but the loud boisterous snoring of Henry reminded me that perhaps now wasn't the time to be doing home alterations. There was one thing I could do though as I went back upstairs and grabbed my jacket, flashlight, crowbar and rifle. It was kind of nice falling asleep fully dressed, it made getting ready a lot quicker proposition. The cold nearly snapped me out of my mild inebriation. What it actually did though was a much more pleasant sensation of awakening me fully while letting me keep my burgeoning buzz. Maybe there was an angle I could exploit here if the world ever returned to normal. "Drink Arctic Blast Beer, Be Fully Awake When You Say Something Inappropriate!" I could have a guy give a wide-eyed thumbs up as he grins to the camera after having received a slap from an attractive young lady. "Arctic Blast – When You Need To Know When You've Said Something Stupid! Remember Every Offending Remark! Every Hilarious Antic! Every I Love You Man!"

So, maybe the world wasn't ready for Arctic Blast Beer, a cold detonation with every twist top!

CHAPTER 17
Journal Entry - 15
I knew where I wanted to go, I just didn't know if it'd be worth it. It seemed like a considerable amount of preparation to walk a measly fifteen feet. Almost directly straight out from my front door in the middle of my lawn was a storm drain, I know what you're thinking, oh how convenient! Well it wasn't when I was throwing the football around with my boys, I had once had to go to my doctor because I had hyper-extended my knee on the damn thing. Who puts a storm drain on a lawn? I had never opened it or seen it opened in the time that I lived here. After some serious prying I was finally able to force the frost to yield its prize. The cover came up with a loud bang. I had a momentary glimmer of guilt and even stopped to look around and see if anyone had noticed my transgression. There would be no 9-1-1 call tonight. The top thudded to the side, the sound deadened by the frost in the air. I took out my flashlight and shone around in the hole for all the good it was going to do. If I had looked closer on the day that I tripped I would have realized it wasn't a storm drain, I guess I just always assumed, but we know about that idiom. It was an electrical conduit. That made much more sense being in the front lawn. The problem was that it was no more than twenty-four inches around and most of that space was taken up with, wait for it, wait…yup, you guessed it, electrical cabling. All right, so much for exit strategy Plan A. The more I looked down that hole the more trapped I felt. We weren't so much holding the zombies out as we were keeping ourselves in. Hell, we were like cattle all penned up awaiting our slaughter. I could not escape the truth of that phrase.

If I had not let the stupid higher reasoning overrule

my gut feelings I would have packed everyone up and left that night. Oh how I wish that was how it had played out.

I went back into the house, grabbed another beer and sat with Paul in the living room. He didn't say much as he was still asleep. I sat in the dark. I was in a brooding mood. Complacency meant death. My mind was feverishly coming up with and summarily dismissing possible escape plans. I had some viable ideas for defense and I would employ those later in the morning, but I could not for the life of me come up with a foolproof plan for evacuation WHEN the time came.

Tracy awoke me some hours later. I had fallen asleep in the chair still clutching my half drunken beer. I hadn't spilled any but I still hadn't finished it and with the thing now being body temperature warm and my mouth tasting like burnt cheese, that wasn't going to happen, party foul be damned!

Paul was in the kitchen getting a glass of water as I walked in and dumped the remains of my beer into the sink.

"I see nothing's changed since college," Paul said with a small laugh.

I wasn't awake enough to catch the barb.

Paul moved on. "So what's the plan for today?" he asked.

"Ass," I said to him. I had finally caught his meaning.

Now it was his turn to be lost. "Don't get me wrong buddy, I'm always up for a good time, but I'm not sure this is the right time," he answered.

At first I didn't garner his meaning. It was going to be a long day if we were always one sentence apart in our communications. I stopped for a second and thought about restarting the whole conversation. It just didn't seem like the prudent thing to do. I started on a whole new subject instead.

"Well, Alex is going to be using about every able bodied person he can find to begin setting up defenses."

Paul looked perplexed, so I explained everything that had happened the previous day with the assembly of zombies.

Paul didn't look overly concerned but he was a master of disguising his true feelings. That's why I never played poker with him. I had every intention of bringing Paul, the boys and myself to go help Alex, but first I was going to need a few hours to take care of some things at the house. My wife blanched at a few of my suggestions and made me alter a few of the more, well 'altering' ideas. First things first, I had Travis go scrounge me up a couple of ladders. I would have sent Justin too, except that he was still extremely weak from his ordeal. I needed a couple of ladders, lightweight and strong. Two of the longest that he could find should suit my purposes just fine. I grabbed some food supplies and extra water and placed them in my Jeep. I then got Brendon to follow me in his truck outside the complex. When we came back ten minutes later on foot, the guard looked like he wanted to ask us what we were doing, but he just shook his head and let us in. The next thing I did couldn't have been a bigger waste of a half hour of my life unless I had watched What Not To Wear on HGTV. I reinforced the gate in my backyard to the point where a charging rhino couldn't have busted through. I didn't nearly get the return on investment that I had hoped for. I'd like to think that I noticed a hole in my defenses but at this point I was much too busy patting myself on the back.

The next thing I did had my wife ranting throughout the house that I had completely lost my mind. I don't know, I thought it was one of the coolest ideas I had come up with. I was under the complete false sense of security that my house was now impregnable. Yeah right, but that is the ultimate beauty of being paranoid, I mean prepared, there's always something more you can do. Tracy was pissed that I was about to devalue our home. I honestly couldn't understand where she was coming from. First off I didn't think we would be retiring here and second, REALLY? Resale value? Who's gonna buy? I don't think there is a zombie family down the street looking for an extra bedroom. I could be wrong, as I usually am with Tracy, but I didn't think so. So I went ahead with my plan and in the midst of it I think Tracy went to the clubhouse to see if there was any rum for her coke.

I went halfway down the basement steps and looking up, I cut away most of the drywall above my head exposing the stairs that led to the second story. I then went back up the basement stairs and then onto the second floor risers. I cut away the carpet and pad. (It was old anyway, at least that's what I told Tracy as I tried to calm her.) With a five-pound hammer and crowbar I removed four treads and four risers effectively leaving a four-foot by three-foot wide gaping wound in the middle of the stairs. All the noise had brought Nicole out from her shower prematurely. Her face had a look of bewilderment on it as she looked down at me and then at what remained of the stairs.

"Does Mom know?" She asked with concern in her eyes. "You know she's going to kill you?" she answered when I didn't respond immediately.

Nicole was privy to some of my more insane (or inane) ideas. Mostly her mom was able to get me to rein in the horses before they roamed too far away from the stable but not always. There was that one time in Canada when the Royal Mounted Police were involved. It almost became an international incident, but that's ancient history, I was never charged.

"I know what I'm doing," I answered huffily, a little ticked that she had the audacity to rain on my parade.

Now that I looked at my handiwork, I realized that I did sort of forget that this was still a functioning household. I couldn't expect everyone to have to jump over this gap. If someone woke in the middle of the night and forgot, they'd find themselves in the basement in a heartbeat. I went and snagged my circular saw and proceeded to flatten out the stringers. Those are the supports that hold the tread and the risers. They go up and across in the same fashion as the stairs. They are basically the frame and the stairs are the shelving. So I just took the saw and cut off four triangles on each side, effectively making the stringers flat. The next thing I needed I didn't have. I sent Travis out on his second scavenging trip. I hoped to hell Tracy was having a difficult time finding some rum, if she came home now with this giant perforation on her stairs my only hope was going to be getting on the other side of the hole and hoping she wouldn't be able to bridge the gap. Thank God the boy beat his mother home. I would have taken him for ice cream if I had the time and there was any ice cream anywhere. He didn't find exactly what I requested but under such a short gun, beggars couldn't be choosers. What he brought was a piece of countertop from one of the abandoned units. It was about 6 feet by 2-1/2 feet. I trimmed a foot off the bottom, then turned it over so the Formica top was now on the bottom. Then I attached four 2-1/2 inch lengths of 2 inch by 2 inch wood slats onto the counter bottom so there would be some sort of foothold. Obviously this would never pass a home inspection but I honestly didn't think that was my biggest concern.

To finish off my wonderful contraption I anchored two large eyehooks on either side of the end of the countertop that would be facing the top of the stairs. I then anchored two equally large eyehooks at the top of the stairs, one as close to the wall as possible and the other as close to the railing as possible. The next thing was to tie it off. I needed to run rope from the 'new' stairs to the eye hooks at the top. I would like to say I knew how to tie these fancy quick release knots that would take a mere snap of the fingers to release but that wasn't the case. After my fourth granny knot on each side I figured prudence was the best course of action for the day. I got my fifth and last eyehook and made sure that I found a stud in the wall as I anchored it. I then took a length of rope and tied a utility knife to the eyehook. So if needed, one would only need to get the knife and cut both ends of the rope releasing the 'faux' stairs. Now that I was almost done there was only one thing left to do, try the stairs. The stairs seemed a lot sturdier 'in theory.'

"Hey Trav!" I yelled.

Travis came up from the basement where he and Tommy had been wrestling with Henry, who had gotten a whiff of Tommy's secret stash of Pop-Tarts and was hellbent on getting away with his prize.

"Yeah Dad?" Travis asked as he appeared at the bottom of the stairs.

He's young, if anything happens he'd heal faster. "Aw shit." I mumbled to myself. Guilt got the better of me. "I want you to stand there and get help if anything happens to me."

Travis looked at me like I was nuts until I pointed at my makeshift stair sled. This wouldn't be the first emergency room visit Travis had to make with his father. Travis even had the presence of mind to step off the landing and into the foyer in case I went tobogganing. I white-knuckled the handrail as I placed my first foot down on the makeshift tread. Not so bad, it was when I placed my second foot onto the 'stairs' that the swaying began. With the combination of being secured only by rope, and three inches of play on each side, I had successfully made the first in-home carnival ride. Travis laughed as my face turned the same shade as my knuckles. This was going to take some serious getting used to. Nicole had come to the top of the stairs just in time to view the festivities.

"Do you remember Canada?" she asked straight-faced, and again turned her back to finish whatever she had been doing. Her point was made. Tracy hadn't talked to me for over a month after that, this might even rival that momentous mark. As I reached the bottom rung of my contraption it slid over to the right. I had a death grip on the handrail, to the right I had a six-inch wide clear as day view of the basement stairs and they loomed ominously from this vantage point. This wasn't going to work. If someone had to walk up or down the stairs carrying anything that required the use of one hand this stairway was going to become a major spillway. I thought long and hard as I pondered my fall below, should I just put the thing back together? At that point I just might have. The problem, however, was that I had cut the stringer and for the life of me I couldn't figure out a way to put that back together again, at least not correctly. Humpty-Dumpty had nothing on me. There had to be a way to stabilize this moving nightmare. The whole point of this trapdoor was that it was a quick release mechanism. I designed it (Okay so 'design' might be a little strong) to keep unfriendlies downstairs if the need ever arose. This was not going to be worth it though if everybody alive was nursing broken bones.

I ended up attaching wood to both sides and after some serious pep talking to myself I braved another walk on the wild slide. Most of the play was gone so the swaying was kept to a minimum. At one point I even let go of the handrail; I was feeling a little saucy. Still, I didn't want anybody on this thing unless they were completely aware of their surroundings. My next bold move was to place duct tape over both light switches, the one at the foot and the head of the stairs, to keep them on twenty-four seven. This also wasn't going to win me any brownie points with the wife but at least I'd be able to see her coming when she went to push me down the stairs. I got Travis and quickly departed the scene of my crime. It would be for the best if I wasn't there when Tracy decided to kill me.

Work around the wall was frenetic to say the least. Whatever Jed and Alex had told the workforce to incite them had done its job all too well. Alex had decided that it would be wise to begin the project on the shorter gate sides. His reasoning being that the zombies would look for the natural openings. He had split up his workforce into two equal parts and sent them on their tasks. He was constantly driving from end to end to supervise the progress. The idea was simple enough to implement and ingenious in its design. The problem was materials. Ideally 1 inch thick metal plating (roughly 4 feet by 8 feet) attached to the wall, braced with train track thick metal support beams welded to another footer plate with 1 foot spikes driven into the ground was the optimum set up. The strengthening pylons were spaced 8 feet apart from each other. Alex had only enough of the metal plating and supports to alternate with the less strong wooden supports and only on the sides with the gates. The long walls that were on the west and east sides were all going to be supported by 1 inch thick plywood and 4 by 4's, still a formidable defense but not nearly as imposing looking as its metal cousins. Propping the RV was proving difficult; if even a modicum of pressure was applied the roof began to buckle. This troubled Alex but with time short and work to be done, this was a problem he would have to work out later.

The biggest concerns Alex fought with all day were the gates. They were by nature the weakest points of defense but because of pressure from the residents his hands were tied on how well he could bolster them, because whatever he put up to stop the zombies had to be able to be moved in a hurry in case of a mass exodus. What people weren't understanding was that by that point there would *be* no mass exodus. Just like the song says, 'Nobody gets out of here alive.' It was like the roach motel in theory, if the zombies get in, the people don't get out. But folks wanted to hold onto that hope, even as asinine as it was. They were putting themselves in MORE danger by being so pigheaded. That was why I was working so hard on my exit strategy.

CHAPTER 18
Journal Entry - 16

I found Alex up in the southeast corner. I had only known this man for a few days and I already considered him one of my closest friends. Funny how that happens. I've known some acquaintances my entire adult life and I wouldn't go to their weddings unless there was an open bar. Alex and his family had made such an impression on me he was rapidly climbing up the charts to those few who I would take a bullet for. Dramatic I know, but Marines think of these kinds of things.

"Hey Alex, how's it going?" I asked as I clapped my hand on his shoulder.

He turned to look, a scowl on his face. "Could be better, Talbot. I could have more laborers, more material and some engineers, other than that just peachy." Then his demeanor changed, a grin split his broad face. "Heard about your home decorating."

I was floored, I know news travels fast especially within a closed community but this is nuts. Then I discovered my culprit. Tommy meekly waved as he hefted the two hundred pound plating into place as if it weighed nothing more than its wooden counterpart.

Alex saw who I was looking at. "I wish I had fifty of him. The kid is strong as an ox."

I smiled back at Tommy as he held the plating in position with one hand while with the other he fiddled around in his pocket until he was rewarded with a Three-Musketeers bar.

"And he works for minimum wage," Alex laughed.

"Alex," I started in a serious tone. "That's part of the reason I came to find you." I spent the next few minutes telling him about my exit plan if everything went south. I also, to no avail, tried to get him to move closer to my house.

"I can't move," he bemoaned. "My wife finally feels safe. She has just stopped screaming in her sleep and she has some new friends that live around us. I know that they also provide a constant source of well-being for her. Mi amigo, I'm not even sure if what you have told me will work, although it's a start. Ladders you say? Sounds about as safe as your sledding stairs."

"Do you think these will work?" I asked pointing to the supports.

"For awhile," he answered solemnly.

"That's reassuring," I answered caustically.

He shrugged. "What can I tell you, the walls should be fine once the stanchions are up. It's the gates that are going to be the problem. Short of putting up a wall, I don't know." He shrugged again with the truth of what he left unsaid.

"That's all the more reason you should either move in with me or at least next to me," I told him.

Alex was no martyr. He had no desire to go down with the ship, his family meant everything to him. When it finally dawned on him that he was embarking on a doomed endeavor he wanted to rethink his choices.

"I will talk to Marta tonight." His sickly smile did not produce much confidence.

I placed my hand again on his shoulder. "Alex, you have to do more than talk to her. You have to convince her." His skin tone wasn't recuperating. "Listen, her friends are welcome to move too. We're only talking about a tenth of a mile away at most. This isn't a coast-to-coast thing."

My arguing wasn't winning him over. He saw the logic in what he needed to do. It was just convincing his better half about this. His wife had always been ruled by the heart and not the head. "All right, all right, I'll back off, for now. Just tell me where you need me and Travis to work."

Alex' shoulders slouched a bit in relaxation. He

would talk to his wife, just not at the moment.

The day was cold, the work was hard. It was uneventful except for the occasional hammer hit to thumb, and no they weren't all mine, I only did it twice. I was barely able to contain my tears the second time. The support beams had been completed on the two shorter gated sides and we had finished a good third of the east wall without anything too exceptional happening and just like that it changed. The alarm arose from the North gate. People began shouting. I hadn't heard any shooting yet so I figured things were still somewhat all right. Like every other looky loo, I left what I was doing mid-swing, probably a good thing. I think I was lined up for a third hit on my throbbing appendage and this time the tears would have spilled. This would have been considerable entertainment for Travis. I'm sure he thinks I don't have tear ducts. The makers of the Hallmark commercials would be happy to know that I do, but I'm not telling anyone. There was a group of sixty or seventy people at the gate by the time I got there. That was a good quarter of our population. I would've figured everyone would have been here but then it was nice to realize the gate guards and the tower guards hadn't left their posts, plus there were still a considerable number of folks who were just plain traumatized. Some so much so that they didn't even come out to get food, it had to be delivered. I meandered my way up to the front trying to figure out what was going on. There were no zombies or human invaders that I could see. I was wondering if someone had inadvertently hit the alarm. It wouldn't be the first time. Luckily this hadn't yet fallen under the boy who cried wolf syndrome, yet.

I had made it up to the front of the crowd and curled my fingers around the chain links. My fingers tightened as I saw what had aroused the natives. Standing in the field across from our little community was what I can only describe as the harbinger of doom. It was the symbol of everything that was wrong with the world right now. It was death incarnate. It was the four horsemen of the apocalypse all rolled into one package. It was the woman zombie that had killed Spindler. At one time she was some daddy's little girl, all pigtails and Sunday dresses. All sugar and spice and everything nice, all Barbie and Ken playhouse. Now she was the crux of all that was evil. She stood in that field two hundred yards away and still the closeness of her chilled my heart. Her tattered clothes swayed in a nonexistent breeze as if she created her own tempest of atrocity. The crowd which had been loud and alarmed grew as quiet as I had. The pall of impending doom disquieted us all. The only sounds were of clothes rustling together as each person tried their best to gain a better vantage. Some had seen enough. They peeled away, possibly to tell others that the boogieman was real and he was a she. The guard at the gate had half raised his weapon to take a shot but seemed to have frozen mid-decision. He looked like he wanted to leave with some of the others; I couldn't say I blamed him.

When the zombie pointed at us my breath caught in my lungs. I felt as if a frozen ice pick had been thrust into my chest. Cold blood radiated out from that phantom piercing. I had the distinct feeling she was pointing at me, but wouldn't all humans look the same to a zombie? I mean, I don't think I could tell one cow from another. They all taste delicious to me. I'm not saying that we were cattle, but to a zombie we are, right? I found myself slowly moving back and to the right, almost subconsciously. Sure, I had a history with that thing but that didn't mean I wanted a future. I mean at least with her, it, whatever. Even from this distance her outstretched arm with her straight as an arrow index finger followed my slow retreat. Un-fucking-fortunately this did not go unnoticed. The damn guard, who should have immediately shot that abomination, visually followed the line of sight of the zombie's finger.

"Talbot?" he turned and looked at me. "She's pointing at you, I think."

I stopped, frozen for a moment, hoping that she would drop that accusatory pointer. She didn't. The guard grabbed my arm and pulled me back to the fore. I was sweating and shivering at the same time. It was not a pleasant sensation.

"That's a zombie, isn't it?" he asked. I hadn't found my voice yet, it was locked away somewhere in shock and awe. "But how could it be, for chrissakes she's pointing, ain't no zombie can point. Right? But I can smell her from here. And the way she moves, she ain't human."

I don't know who he was talking to. I hadn't even acknowledged his existence yet. My concentration was centered on her, it. My attention became so focused, I don't know if it was a trick of the light or she was magic, to this day I still haven't figured it out. The only way I can describe what happened next was as if my consciousness was pulled to within a few feet of her. Her pointing became a gesture of 'come here,' something which I could tell was a difficult maneuver for her considering the rigor that had to have set in. That finger being able to curl and unfurl made her grimace in concentration. She mouthed the word 'come.' I was thankful that this was only my consciousness and not my true presence. I could see her breath and it had nothing to do with the cold. Every impulse screamed at me to flee, but I was even more compelled to go.

"Open the gate," I told the guard. The voice didn't sound like my own, it was distant and small, so much so he looked at me to see if I had even spoken. Or maybe he had heard me but thought I was out of my gourd.

"Open the gate," I said with a little more force, but still this wasn't much above a whisper. At least I knew he had heard me because he responded.

"No way, man."

Awesome, I thought. I guess I don't have to go and meet my waking nightmare. I wanted to kiss the guard, even though he wasn't my type.

"Dad, where are you going?" Travis asked in alarm.

I could no more respond to him than I could control my motor skills. Why was I climbing over the fence? What is wrong with me? Two decades of smoking pot did this to me. I should have listened more carefully to those reefer madness movies. They seemed much more relevant at this moment. Why wasn't this asshole guard trying to pull me off the fence? Dick wad! Fortuitously, or unfortuitously, the razor wire had not been in enough supply to cover the fenced gates, this was made up for with more armed personnel but that fact was not going to stop my ascent. I literally sat on the fence for a moment, semi-safe haven of normalcy on one side, crazy disastrous immoral face of all that is unholy on the other.

"I'm going to get mom!" Travis yelled, hoping that this inherent threat would awaken me from this possession. It didn't.

If it wasn't for the cold protrusions of the top threatening to pierce my favorite unmentionables I might have stayed there for a significant amount of time. I climbed down. As I began to walk away the guard thrust a small Smith and Wesson .38 caliber pistol through the gate.

"Take this," he pleaded.

"I don't think it would do any good," I answered him. My eyes locked on to his, still hoping that he would find a way to stop me.

Damn legs of betrayal, I had never been so let down by a body part, except for that one time in college (whole different story). I slowly trudged my way to her. She had finally dropped her arm. The smile that formed on her face made every hair on my body stand on end. I looked like I had been struck by lightning. Fear didn't creep up on me. It ran rampant through my soul. She was not of this earth, at least not from aboveground.

My limbs did not move of their own volition, how could they? What would MAKE me go willingly toward a zombie? My mind raced in circles while my legs plodded on. To the non-discerning eye I most likely had the gait of a zombie. 'Zombies in the night, exchanging eyeballs…'Zombies in the Night, sung to the tune of Frank

Sinatra's <u>Strangers in the Night</u>. I mean no disrespect to Frankie, it was just what was going through my mind. The ravages of the disease had not been good to her. As I approached, I could see all sorts of parasites had taken up residency. There was a caravan of maggots that trailed from her ripped open left cheek to the top of her semi-scalped head. The cold did little to prevent the waft of her presence. Her dark eyes were almost invisible, sunken into the black flesh that surrounded them. What I could see did not bode well for mercy. The depths in those eyes only led to one place, and it was a lot colder than where I was now. This was insane. Why was I doing this? Was I hypnotized? Was I curious? Did I have a death wish? I used every fiber of my being to make my steps stop their imminent treachery. It was not any easy process. The zombie girl's smile faltered. That more than anything made my sphincter slam shut. Hey listen, I'm about as proud to write that as you are happy to read it. What had previously seemed just the cold reptilian stare of predator to prey turned sinister. The fathoms of hell peered into my spirit. It was a good thing my ass puckered up because I might have rivaled her stink. Again I'm not proud of this.

I *could* stop my forward progress. The ability to turn around, however, was still being an elusive SOB. The zombie girl watched intently as I tried to impose my will on my own body. Her arm came back up. The pointing finger was back, but it was not directed at me. This time it was pointed towards the mountains. What the hell does that mean? Her arm slowly tracked over to me and then back towards the mountains.

"What, me?" I asked, being the brilliant conversationalist that I am. "You want me to go to the mountains?"

And then it happened, the soulless sound of the dead, a ghostly whispered keening issued forth from the fissure in her face. "Go." It hissed out, it was more an exhalation of air escaping from a tightly sealed crypt than anything resembling speech.

"You want me to go? Go where? Away?" I asked in rapid succession. I think I asked so many questions because I didn't want to hear the rasp of her response. The pulling of dry fingernails down a new chalkboard was infinitely more appealing than to hear one more utterance from this abomination.

"Can I get my family?" And still her arm pointed westward. "Can I get my friends?" Come on, even I knew this wasn't going to fly. She wasn't here for prime real estate. She was here for prime beef. For some reason I couldn't even begin to fathom, I was being given a free pass. Who knows, maybe she thought I'd be too stringy, no, more like gamey. Without a shadow of a doubt I knew this was a one-time offer and it was for me only. If I turned and walked back to the complex all deals were off.

"Why me?" I begged. Her silence only confounded my bewilderment. "I can't."

The thin wisp of what some may construe as a smile vanished. As her arm came back down, I could feel the reneging of the offer. She approached slowly. I was going from freedom to food. My brain screamed for flight, the fight portion was nonexistent. This was no battle of wills, I was helpless, like a fear-frozen marmot I waited for the screaming eagle to descend and sink its claws deep into my flesh. I did not even have enough control to close my eyes. I watched in increasing horror as she approached; death would not be swift. My bladder burned to be released. I was denied even that last suffrage of indignity. A fly crawled into her nose. She paid it no more intent than the lice that swung freely from her dirty matted hair. A beetle plowed its way through a small hole in her neck holding a small nugget of meat, a trophy garnered from who knows where. The only thing still working was my olfactory sensors. This had to have been done on purpose. Gorge tried in vain to roar up and out of my stomach. The fetid odor was so palpable, I could see it, I could taste it. Like Campbell's soup it was so thick I could eat it with a fork. Yeah, she hadn't cut off my sense of sarcasm either. Thin strips of flesh which used to be lips parted, revealing black cracked teeth from which strings of meat hung in decaying strands. Her charcoal gray tongue flicked over them, attempting to pull away some of the tastier morsels. She stood toe-to-toe with me, not six inches from my face. Sweat coursed down my body. I shook from impotence and then that stilled. I wouldn't die fighting, but at least I'd be standing, small consolation. It's like 'winning' a participation trophy in Little League baseball. Who gives a shit.

What would it feel like to have your face ripped open? Would she still my pain centers? Doubtful. I couldn't tell much from her near frozen features, but still I sensed that she was taking some form of perverse satisfaction from these events. She moved in closer; I would have offered her a mint if I had one. My eyes still were not allowed to close. My vision of her blurred as she moved in even closer. A fly landed on my eyeball. It was singularly up to this point in my life, the most disgusting thing that had ever happened to me. Then my zombie girl topped it, she kissed me. My innards roiled in protest, my guts churned like a washing machine on spin cycle. If I wasn't allowed output through my intake or outlet valves this was going to blow a hole through my midsection a la Ripley's Alien. The kiss was not so surprisingly, very cold, but very surprisingly tender. It was literally the kiss of death from the dead. It doesn't get much more ironic than that, does it? A Brillo pad wrapped around coarse grit sandpaper applied at 190 revolutions per minute under skin scalding hot water would never allow me to feel clean again. I was tainted, for fucks sake a zombie is kissing me. Didn't she get my bio? I'm a card-carrying germaphobe! As she slowly pulled away, a dark viscous fluid kept us tenuously connected. The fly finally descended from my eye to land on this small bridge. Her tongue shot out, incredibly long, and pulled the fly into her canines. I swear I could hear the small crunching of its delicate exoskeleton. The spin cycle was in full throttle. A whoosh of haunted air escaped her lips. She was laughing, she had known exactly what she had done and she found humor in her dark actions. She pulled back another foot and let loose her controls. I fell to the ground, afflicted with crippling cramps. I rolled into a protective fetal position hugging my midsection. Mount Vesuvius erupted. Hot refuse steamed on the cold ground; the whoosh of air which accompanied her amusement persisted. Glad I could be her entertainment. For long minutes I alternated between evacuating my stomach and pulling in long cold drags of air. How long this happened I'm not sure. The pain lessened minutely, small fractions of degrees is the best way I can explain it. Each breath was better than the previous but only in infinitesimally small measures. It might have been minutes or days, all reference to time was lost, although my cheek touching the ground was rapidly becoming cold and my refused refuse was not steaming anymore.

"Mike?" I heard a tenuously thin voice try to break through the paralyzing grip of insanity that was beginning to blanket my mind.

"Mike?" There it was again, a disassociated voice speaking an incoherent word. "Grab his legs, I'll get his head."

I felt myself being lifted and then mercifully blackness sheathed my capacity for thought. I was floating in a white void, but I was not afraid, I was free, free from burden, free from sin, free from responsibility and then I think I puked again. Not because I could 'feel' the sensation but because I heard the disgust from one of the people carrying me. I found it funny the same way an insane person finds humor in slinging shit at walls. How different was this from that? I was close to the edge, maybe I had even taken that first perilous step over and gravity had finally worked its magic. I was being pulled down into the abyss. There wasn't a drug invented that would raise this sinking ship. I spiraled down. Whiteness faded to black, cognitive thought became an illusion.

Mike's return 12/17 – CHAPTER 19

Tracy's Journal Entry - 1

'Hi reader, this is Tracy. Mike's journal has not been touched in three days, since he has finally come back to me, to us. I now have the strength and will to fill in the events as they have been unfolding since that thing did whatever it was she had done to Mike.

That fateful morning, Justin had finally arisen and seemed to be getting better. After the initial bliss had passed, the stress of everything came back two fold. I went out to the garage to try and calm my shattered nerves. Mike had caught me smoking once or twice, but I don't think it made a connection with him. He looked like he was trying to assimilate his own set of nightmares. At this point I went to the clubhouse to get some rum. It was that or suck down another pack of smokes to make my quaking hand stop its palsied movements. I ended up running into a bunch of other wives sitting near the fire drinking some Chablis. The talk was animated and at first I was reluctant to join in, but I found the conversing and the wine to be calming influences. Hours passed as we talked of all sorts of things, and thankfully none of them involved team sports. My head was swimming in a sea of bliss when I heard a huge commotion from outside the clubhouse. There were three men in the back of a pick-up truck applying ministrations to some poor soul laid down in the truck bed. I stood up as my glass shattered to the floor.

"Mike!" I screamed. How I knew I don't know. That I knew it was him was unquestionable. I darted for the front doors.

The women stared at my retreating back. "Talk about

drama queen," I heard one of them say. I think it was Cindy. She was a heavyset dirty blond. I hoped she was a smoker, I was going to make sure she paid double the going price. 'Bitch,' I thought viciously.

They kept talking but I was already through the doors and into the howling wind. All that mattered now was what had happened to Mike. As I expected, the truck pulled up to our front door. The three men jumped down. One of them undid the tailgate and the other two pulled the prone form of my husband from the bed. I nearly collapsed right there and then as I saw the pallor of his skin. I honestly thought he was dead. The cold air burned in my lungs as I struggled to keep black dots from growing in my vision. As I got closer though, my initial fear was relieved as I saw his mouth moving. It was, however, replaced with a different sense of dread. Mike was uttering the Lord's Prayer, which in itself would be scary considering he hadn't been to church in over thirty years. No, the real problem was that he was saying it BACKWARDS! IN LATIN! My soul was scared!

"What's he saying?" one of his bearers asked.

"I don't know, he must have hit his head hard when he collapsed. It's just gibberish," answered the second man. But I could tell he knew this wasn't gibberish. There was a cadence and a tone to the words that made them sound unholy and just because he didn't 'know' that didn't mean he couldn't 'feel' it. They wanted to unload this package as fast as they could; Mike had the greasy feel of evil all over him.

"What happened to him!" I screamed as I opened the front door. The men rushed past me, quickly depositing their load onto the couch. Both absently wiped their hands on their jackets as if they were wiping off some foul contaminant. They were both backing out of the house as they answered. I got the gist of the story before their eagerness to be done with this foul deed was completed.

I asked if he had been bitten, but his mere presence within the compound answered that question outright. I could find nothing physically wrong with him except for some tar like substance adhered to his lips. Vaseline, warm water, soap and a face towel finally removed the sticky substance but I couldn't help but feel that he had been poisoned. By whom or for what reason I didn't know. What kind of poison can make you speak in a language you've never spoken before? The only reason I recognized it was because of the six years I had spent in Catholic school. I had never told Mike about my time there and I had never let him know I could speak and read Latin. What was the point? It's a dead language, or the language of the dead? My thoughts reared up in one of those 'aha!' moments.

Some color had returned to his features, but that was more the flush of the fever setting in than anything healthy. For three days Mike ran to the edge of death and then slowly retreated. Each brush to the proximity of the other side seemed to drain more and more energy from him. The kids and I held constant vigil, each of us at one point or another saying our goodbyes.

Tommy remained silent throughout the entire ordeal. Apparently even Ryan Seacrest didn't know the outcome. Thankfully, Mike never broke out into prayer again, I honestly don't think I could have taken it. As close as Mike was to death, was as close as I was to insanity. Our kids were inches away from being orphans, where Mike would be leaving physically I would be leaving mentally. Three times during those three days Mike's fever spiked to 105 degrees and each time it broke he shouted a word. It wasn't until later that I thought to put it altogether, and even then I could make no sense of it, at least not until much later. 'She.' 'Is.' 'Death.'

Mike shouted the word "Death!" and sat up just as the first shot was fired in the fight for Little Turtle. His gaze crossed over the room as he tried to orient himself to his surroundings. How different a normal living room must look like compared with the gates of oblivion. Recognition didn't dawn on his features until his eyes rested on mine. It was long moments before the glaze peeled away from his visage. "Tracy?" he asked tentatively.

My chest heaved. A sob involuntarily forced its way through my lips.

"Tracy?" he asked again.

He was still a-sea and I had not yet thrown him a lifeline. My throat was clenched closed with emotion. I managed to choke out the words that it was indeed me. I saw a beacon of hope shoot through the fog of the war Mike was battling through. I watched in fascination as Mike clawed and inched his way back from the brink degree by degree. I hugged him fiercely. I kissed him tenderly. I willed him forward, talking softly in his ear, yelling when I thought he might be slipping. Hand over hand he pulled forward, as seemingly eons passed by. Invisibly summoned, all the kids came to bear witness to the unnatural scene unfolding before them. Mike shattered through the veil like a drowning man might come through a thin skein of ice from the depths of a winter lake. A ghost of cold breath issued forward from him, even though the house was at 70 degrees. His lungs were expanding and contracting with the force equivalent to a man who had just completed a 1500 meter sprint in world record time. Sweat seeped into and dampened the covers he was wearing. His teeth chattered for a few seconds. I thought the force would crack them. And then it was over, his eyes fixated on my own and he looked into the depths of my soul. It was Mike, thank God, and it wasn't. I couldn't put my finger on it. He had either lost or gained something in the internal war that had raged in him for three days. The pain of war cannot exceed the woe of aftermath, just ask Led Zeppelin.

"Thank you," he uttered and he kissed me softly on the lips. He stood up with not the slightest sign of vertigo or ill effects from his sickness.

"Boys, get your guns." And that was it. He went upstairs to get dressed.

It would be a longtime before we talked about what happened. He was reluctant to revisit it, that much was for sure. Even still, there were more pressing things happening and we did not find much time to sit down and idly chat about anything. Survival is an all-consuming event within its own right.

CHAPTER 20 - The slaughter begins

 **Journal Entry - 17**

Eventually, I will tell you what happened while I traveled the netherworlds, but that all hinges on what happens in the foreseeable future. I had come out from under my unnatural hibernation in remarkably good shape. There were no ill effects that I knew about; they would manifest later. I had lost weight and I was as thirsty as I had ever been, but after downing three huge glasses of water I felt right as rain, even more so. Now I know this sounds weird, but power is the word that comes foremost in my mind. Maybe healthy would be a better descriptive but not as accurate, or as powerful. I just don't know and I really don't have the time to dwell on it.

As I dressed, I peered out the window, appalled at what my vision took in. That alone should have frozen my bowels. Thousands upon thousands of zombies were shuffling their way to our haven. Gunshots that had moments before been sporadic and spread out were now continuous and unrelenting. Hundreds of zombies fell. It didn't matter. It was like burning ants with a magnifying glass, kill one there's a thousand more to take its place. It seemed more a waste of bullets. Most of the shot zombies were still moving. Headshots were for trained marksmen and most of these folks were anything but. If they were used to shooting at all it was at center mast on a 500-pound elk, a much easier shot than the 20-pound melon of a human head. Even if they were zombies, it was still unimaginably tough for these people to get over the aversion of shooting a human form. At least if they made a shot to the body it would be less noticeable and therefore more palatable.

The only thing we had going for us was that once the shot zombie hit the deck he was likely to become ground beef from the hordes that would pass over the unlucky soul. I had made my decision. I would stay and fight until it was a lost cause. Regarding the outcome to Little Turtle, I already knew the answer. What remained to be seen was if I could get my loved ones out of this mess intact. I was duty bound, and worse, honor bound to help the residents as best I could. I would not desert them. Justin had managed to get out of his bed although it had cost him nearly his entire reservoir of energy. I caught him as he was putting on his socks.

"Where are you planning on going?" I asked him sternly.

He looked up. I involuntarily stepped back. His features were starkly outlined from the darkness that rimmed his eyes. His skin was pulled tight in some places and slack in others. The effect was disconcerting.

"To help," he answered, taking a break after putting his right sock on.

"The only thing you'd be able to help with, is getting us in trouble." I didn't mean to be so callous, it just came out. If it came down to a footrace with a zombie and Justin, smart money went on the undead.

Justin's eyes welled up with hurt and rejection. "I just want to help, Dad. I want to make sure Mom and Nicole are going to be all right."

"That's what I want too, Justin. But I'm also concerned about you, Travis, Brendon, Tommy and everyone else. You get the point, right? I'm not sure you could shoot a gun without falling over." I hadn't appeased him at all. He still appeared dejected. "Justin, if you can carry this ammo can," which I was holding, "I'll think about letting you come." I wasn't going to anyway but I figured I'd give him a chance.

He eyed the can speculatively. Full of ammo they can top fifty pounds. He was having difficulty with an eight ounce sock.

"Dad?" he said with true remorse.

I felt his pain. "Justin, you need to stay here with Paul and defend the fort."

His eyes closed in defeat. I crossed the room and grabbed his chin, forcing his eyes to mine. "You've seen Paul shoot, right?" I asked him. He perked a little at that. "If everything goes to hell, Justin, I'm going to need you here with all of your strength, for your Mom, for Nicole."

He knew he was being manipulated, but he didn't feel useless any more, he had a purpose.

"Okay Dad," he said as he laid his body back down. "I'll go defend the house as soon as I get up."

"Good idea," I told him with a small laugh as I tousled his hair. His head still felt warm, not the dizzyingly burning heat it was before, but I didn't think he was out of the woods completely.

Paul was waiting in the hallway as I quietly exited the room and shut the door.

"How's he doing?" Paul asked.

"I wish we had more medicine and a highly skilled doctor," I said to him.

Paul's features furrowed in shame.

"Dude, I only have so much energy to pick people up. Listen, I don't think he's going to turn into a zombie, but he's got an infection of some sort. Who knows what kind of germs the undead carry, I'm sure they don't use Purell. Listen bud, I told you before, I'm not blaming you for what happened, so get over it."

Paul looked even more hurt at those words.

"But now it's time for payback," I told him.

He looked at me, trying to ascertain my meaning.

"If something happens to me, whether today, tomorrow or any other day for that matter, you" and I emphasized 'you,' "are to take control of this family, because that's what we are now. It's not just you and Erin anymore."

He looked at me, absorbing all that I was telling him. I could tell from the time it took him to process this information that he hadn't thought of it like this yet. Paul had always had an unnaturally high fear of commitment. I still sometimes wondered how Erin was able to get him to marry her. She'd probably had to resort to blackmail.

"Paul," I said trying to shake him out of whatever thought loop he was in. "Do you understand what I'm saying to you?"

He nodded ever so slightly. I wasn't overly thrilled with his response.

"Paul, YOU are the last line of defense here," I told him. Paul weakly motioned towards Justin's door. "Dude, I'm not sure he has enough strength to get out of bed if he needs to piss. If push comes to shove though, he will get up and do what he can when the time comes." What I left unsaid was that I didn't have that same faith in Paul. I think he got the underlying current of my meaning.

He looked hurt when he spoke. "You know I'd do anything for you, Mike, and the kids… and Tracy," he added hastily.

I eased up. "That's all I needed to know Paul. We'll be back."

Travis and Brendon were waiting impatiently by the door, rifles and ammunition cans by their sides. Tommy was on the couch doing a crossword puzzle. Not a lick of concern creased his features.

"Hey Mr. T," Tommy said from his seated position, looking up at me with a big smile across his face.

God I loved that kid, he knew what was going on and was in a great mood despite it. It was infectious. I smiled back. "Yeah, what's up Tommy?"

"What's a four-letter word for 'seven days?'"

At first I didn't grasp the question and then I noticed the puzzle book in his lap. My dim-watted bulb finally flickered on. "Week, Tommy, it's a week," I answered, happy to be able to help him.

His expression changed dramatically; he became extremely solemn when he replied. I would have almost thought he was a different person as he intoned, "Exactly."

I know my face ashened. I could *feel* the blood running out of it. Tommy had just told us how long we had. I opened the door and headed out before anyone could see my betraying visage. We had enough to be worried about. I was hoping that nobody else hearing Tommy's words had come to the same realization. If they did, nobody said anything. Brendon, Travis and I went to find the best vantage point to begin our beleaguered defense.

Before we climbed the guard tower, I got them into a small group huddle. "Listen to me boys." It was difficult to be heard over the cacophony of battle. I shouted again. "Boys! We do *not* separate. Do you understand?" I looked at each one in turn to get my confirmation nod. "If you need to take a piss or get something to eat or just take a rest, you go home and you go with each other, do you understand?" Again I looked for and received the confirmation nod. My words were having the desired effect. I wasn't sure that they were getting the seriousness of the situation we were about to become engaged in. Fear rimmed their eyes as much as their male bravado tried to suppress it. Scared was good though. Scared kept people, soldiers, alive. It was fucken heroics that got good people killed. I made it abundantly clear I didn't want any heroes.

"Once these walls are breached," I started.

Brendon's eyes snapped to mine. "Breached?" he asked incredulously.

"Dad?" Travis asked.

My heart dropped, his fear was palpable.

They both looked like they wanted to bolt for home right now. Trust me, I wanted to join them.

"Holy shit, Mike," Brendon said he looked back towards the house. I knew what he was thinking. He wanted to get Nicole and get the hell out of Dodge while the getting was good.

I grabbed his arm to focus his attention back on me. "Brendon, you've seen what's on the other side of that wall, right?" He nodded. "How far do you think you'd get?" He still wasn't convinced. "There's nowhere to go, yet." He looked back at me, all of his hope fixated on that one small word, 'yet.'

"Now listen," I said to them both. "I have a plan for when..." And I stressed 'when.' "… this wall is breached, but it depends on all of us making it back to the house. Once the zombies are in the compound it's going to be everyone for themselves. As hard as it might be, I don't give a shit what else is happening, when I tell you to get your asses back to the house, you'll do just that. Don't stop for anything or anybody. You two are my responsibility. If one of you decides to take matters into his own hands, I will have to go and find you. Now if something happens to one of you and to me, all of my plans go down the shitter." This is when I drove my point home. "Now if I'm gone, you've sealed Mom's, Nicole's Justin's and Tommy's fate, not to mention Henry. When I say home, we ALL go!"

For the moment the boys crowded so close to me we looked like some humanoid form of octopi. That was just fine with me. We climbed up the nearest tower. It was forty yards from the house. Even at a slow trot we should be able to make it home in under ten seconds. That was little solace as I turned my gaze away from my home and into the crevice of psychosis.

"Glad you could make it," Alex said as he clapped my shoulder.

"Wouldn't miss it for the world," I replied.

Alex looked at me, trying to decide if I were serious or not. I let him keep wondering as I shouldered my rifle.

Four hours later, my shoulder throbbed, my back ached, my trigger finger was having muscles spasms and still they plodded on. This wasn't a battle in the traditional sense. We shot firearms, they caught lead. There was no battle cry, no call to arms, no rallying, no retreating, no strategy. Just onward, relentless, implacable, obdurate, pitiless forward momentum. Those that fell weren't heroically pulled up and treated in the rear echelons. They didn't cry out in vain. They didn't scream for their mothers or a nonpartisan god, Buddha or Hare fucken Krishna. They fell like cordwood, hundreds upon hundreds of men, women and children. I couldn't convince myself, no matter how much I tried, to shoot a child. I knew instinctually that they weren't human and if given the chance they would eat me alive, but I could not bring myself to shoot anything under four feet tall. I made sure to always keep my aiming point higher than that. My nightmares were going to have nightmares already. I was not going to compound it any further.

So far the merciless gunfire had kept the zombies from reaching the walls, but that was going to change real soon. It had been a stalemate so far, our lead for their bodies. It had been light out, we had been well rested and still stocked with plenty of ammunition. All the pros in our corner were as rapidly retreating as the sun over the Rockies. Every able-bodied person with a gun had been manning these walls and we had done little more than delay the inevitable. With darkness came fatigue and hunger and hell, probably even shock and trauma. As people peeled away from their posts the zombies gained precious inches.

I had finally been able to stretch out my trigger finger although I was now suspecting it might always include a perceptible hook. Travis was leaning against the far side of the railing his head drooping ever so slightly and his eyes following suit. Brendon wasn't faring much better. When I had first been exposed to combat in Afghanistan I thought I wouldn't be able to sleep for a week. The rampaging fear and adrenaline rush commingled into one hell of a toxic stimulant, but it came at an extreme price to your system. The crash was a near catatonic state. I could sleep for almost forty-eight hours straight after a firefight. I knew what was coming. The boys would have to learn the hard way.

"Brendon, take Travis and head back to the house," I told him. He may have wanted to argue but he was already riding down the other side of the adrenalin slope. He clapped

Travis on the shoulder and motioned towards the house. Travis looked back at me and I nodded my approval. "I'll be there soon," I assured him.

The fifteen or so people that had started the day on this platform were now whittled down to three. Myself, Alex and a third guy I didn't remember ever seeing before.

"Some day, huh?" Alex said as he slid down to sit next to me.

"I've had better," I answered in a serious tone.

Again Alex just looked at me trying to ascertain my true meaning.

"I'm sorry," I laughed. "It's my New England sarcasm coming out in full force." Folks that don't come from that region have a difficult time truly understanding what is being said to them. Many will find it an abrasive form of communication. It is, without a doubt, an acquired mode of information dissemination.

Alex appreciated my honesty. "So how do you think it went?" he asked.

"About how I expected," I told him. He kept looking for more so I elaborated. It was much easier talking now that most of the gunfire had fell off to some sporadic shots. "You can do the math as well as I can, Alex. This is a lesson in futility. We'll be out of ammo in a few days, a week at most. Then, I don't know, the food might hold out for a month and then what, we can't go anywhere."

"What about the truck? Couldn't we fill it with as many people as possible and just run the smelly bastards over?" Alex asked with a glimmer of hope.

"You gonna pick who stays and who goes?" I asked with a raised eyebrow.

"We could do a lottery or something."

"Yeah that'll go over well, you better hope all the ammo is gone before you make that little proposition. Besides it won't work."

Alex looked to me to question the validity of my statement.

I obliged. "The truck will make it through the first few waves and then the bodies will start to mount. You'll end up high centering on them, and that's if the radiator isn't damaged from the excessive hits."

He wasn't done letting go of his idea. What was the harm, we only had time on our hands now. "What if we fixed it with a plow?" He was piquing my interest. "I could attach a grill that would protect the engine housing and we could put a skirt around the entire thing so no bodies would fit under it."

The more he talked the more convinced I became that his idea had some merit. The problem was that we had close to three hundred residents here and this wasn't going to be an alternative for about two hundred and fifty of them. But some was better than none. I started to head down the ladder.

"Where you going?" Alex asked.

"I'm going to talk to Jed and let him figure out how to choose who stays and who goes and then I'm going home to get my finger massaged."

Alex laughed, "Yeah, your 'finger.'" he said with air quotes. "Is that more of your New England sarcasm?"

I don't know if we were going to have enough time together for him to realize when I was kidding or not, but I honestly meant 'my finger.' Eh, let him think what he wants. Sex might not be the furthest thing from my mind but I could almost guarantee it wasn't even on Tracy's radar screen.

Finding Jed was not all that difficult. He had pretty much set up residence in the clubhouse since the beginning. He was sipping some hot coffee over by the fireplace. He had the look of a man who wasn't going to warm up anytime soon. He was a tough old bird, he probably only beat me here by a few minutes. He smiled a little when he saw me enter. He winced a bit as he raised his arm up to motion me over.

"Your shoulder hurting too?" I asked him.

"Why the hell I thought buying a twelve gauge shotgun was a good idea I'll never know. My arm's stiffer than a sailor's dick at a Village People reunion tour," he guffawed.

"What is it with all the sexual references?" I asked. Jed ignored me.

"So what do you want, Talbot?" Jed asked.

"Am I that easy to read?" I asked in surprise on my face.

"Just don't ever cheat on your wife. She'd be able to tell before you got out of your car."

"Yeah I don't play cards either just for that reason."

Jed arched an eyebrow at me, furiously rubbing his hands together for the meager generation of heat it created.

"Okay, Alex has an idea that I think might work."

"So at this point is it 'and' or 'but'?" he asked.

"Wow, it is a good thing I didn't mess around with Allison," I said with introspect. "But..."

"Wonderful, I was hoping for some 'but'"

"This isn't another sexual reference is it?"

"Look at me Talbot. When do you think is the last time I had sex, damn, even a hard on for that matter?"

There was another visual I was now going to be laden with until my dying days. "Thanks," I muttered.

'Go on' he signaled with his hands, clearly getting a little irritated.

"But," I said hastily, trying my best to erase an unabolishable image, "it'll work for about fifty or so people."

What little light had been in Jed's eyes quickly extinguished. I outlined Alex' plan and Jed nodded in agreement to most or offered some better alternatives.

"Women and children, right?" Jed asked, even if it was a statement.

"Without a doubt."

"What about Tracy and Nicole?"

"Oh I'll want them to go, but they won't."

"Can't you make them?" he asked seriously.

"That's funny, Jed, how long were you married?"

He nodded in acceptance of my unwritten truth. Women ruled the roost. Men were merely figureheads. 'Yes dear' was the accepted vernacular in any successful union.

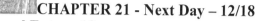

CHAPTER 21 - Next Day – 12/18
Journal Entry - 18

Different Day, Same Zombies. See how I substituted zombie for 'shit,' cause that's what it smelled like, one giant pile of fresh maggoty dog shit. If this were summer the sky would be thick with flies. It would be nearly impossible to breathe without swallowing some of the offending little beasts. Because of the fetor, intake of air was a nauseating task. Appetites had dropped off the charts. Last night, I had grossly underestimated how long our food supply would last. It might be indefinite. Nobody could work up any desire for food. Sometime during the night the zombies had made it all the way up to the gates of Babylon. Single digit amounts of feet kept us separated. Being this close and seeing the devastation the disease caused on these people was excruciating. Skin tone ranged from fax paper white to plum purple and everything between. There were your ashen grays and your burnt siennas. The thing that they had in common was that none of the pallors were healthy looking. Strips of torn skin hung like rags on more than most. Knees and hands were bloodied. Congealed gore splattered the masses like an all you can eat lobster fest gone bad.

For all the broken bones and shredded skin and clouded visages, there was no suffering. There was no self-pity or loathing or hate for that matter. There was only determination and hunger, wanton hunger. It was from this insanely close distance the morning's firing squads commenced. The stench began to liquefy in the air as the bullets tore through the rotting corpses.

I know I have gone on and on about the stench of the zombies, but unless you have lived through it you can't truly assess how disruptive the smell was. Just think when you've watched a movie about some snowbound people in say, Antarctica. So you're watching and these suffering fools teeth are chattering and they have frozen snot coming out of their noses and they can't feel their fingers or their toes. I mean they are just miserable, and you the viewer are sitting there trying to experience what they are feeling and you're like 'boy that sure looks cold' as you munch your buttered popcorn. That doesn't really grasp the full effect for you. Until one day you get some tickets to a football game and it's in Green Bay in December. You are outside for a maximum of three hours in the warmest gear created by mankind and you are still freezing your ass off. It takes a thermal nuclear reaction to get the circulation back in your feet and hands and that is just a taste of what those poor souls lost in the Antarctica are going through. So now back to my problem. If you, the reader really, REALLY, want to know what was going on in Little Turtle, go feed your dog or your neighbor's dog some chili, slathered in hot sauce and maybe throw in some chocolate cake. Okay wait for it, WAIT, now about a half hour later your dog's innards are pretty much going to rupture so make sure he's outside. Now while this steaming pile of shit is still warm and fetid, place it in a plastic shopping bag - DON'T TIE IT UP! Now place the carrying handles one on each ear and inhale deeply. You must walk around with this bag draped across your face continually, is this starting to punch through? Now, every time the dog crap begins to harden up and lose some of its edge, go grab yourself another refreshing pile of fresh dog offal. While you are breathing deeply of this savory concoction, try to eat some enchiladas or maybe some lasagna. Oh hell, just try to sleep with that thing affixed to your face. Yeah, not quite as much fun anymore. So that, my dear reader, is why I am going off the deep end to explain the stink. It's all pervading. There is no relief, no giant bottle of Febreze. There wasn't even a prevailing wind that could help relieve us. We were surrounded by the never-ending miasma of decomposition.

By noon that day of death layered upon death, I

noticed something strange. The zombies were getting taller. I jumped down from my tower and ran for the clubhouse. I voiced my concern to Jed after taking a few deep breathes which I instantly regretted. "Jed, you have to call a cease-fire!" I finally spit out.

"If it's about the bullets Talbot, I already feel your concern but we've got at least a week's worth," Jed replied.

I was still breathing heavily from my run over. I had been reluctant to take deep breaths and it was only partly because I had let my cardio routine lapse in the last few months. So I rushed out my words without explanation. I pretty much got the response I deserved.

"The zombies are getting taller..." next breath I finished with "...Jed."

"Booze is tougher to get than a fresh T-bone, so I know you haven't been drinking. Some of that wacky tobaccy then?" Jed asked with a raised eyebrow.

As much as it pained me, time was of the essence, two gulps of unsavory air, a brief respite and I started over again. "Jed, that wall out there is eight feet tall."

Jed nodded in agreement, looking a little perplexed with why I felt the need to run in here and let him know that.

I elaborated. "Jed, the zombies standing at the wall are sternum high with the top."

"Huh." The dawn of recognition had not lit yet.

"We've been shooting so many..."

Jed finished, "Oh shit. The live zombies are standing on the bodies of those that have fallen."

"Another couple of hours Jed, and they'll just start falling in. And once that happens we won't be able to stop them."

"What then, Talbot, we can't wait them out. They aren't just going to leave."

I could only shrug. "I don't know Jed, but we have to deal with this more immediate issue. We can think of something else later."

Jed gave me a look that said he believed that as much

as I did.

"It's over then," he said as he made his way over to the emergency P.A. system that had been rigged all around the complex. "Cease-fire!" he yelled. He was midway through his third call before the shots began to trail off. There were still one or two distant shots as if those person's trigger fingers were having a difficult time relaxing.

Jed laid it out over the speaker. The Little Turtle complex's bubble had just been burst. Whether anyone thought we could shoot our way out of this mess was irrelevant. They had all just been notified that this course of action would lead to our demise. Inaction meant the same thing, but there was a lot less satisfaction in it. Normally quiet means peace; this, however, was the quiet of the dead.

It was disturbing to say the least. As I walked home, the feeling of being in a fishbowl gave me the skeevies. Almost all the way across the wall, the zombies were peering in at us. I didn't want to look at them. I could feel hundreds of sets of eyes on me and it wasn't because I was the pope, more like a leg of lamb. Hands in pockets, head bowed, I entered the house. Tracy was peering out the window at the wall. She shivered involuntarily.

"What now Mike?" she asked without looking away from the scene she was fixated on.

Again with the shrugging, I was getting real sick of being asked questions I had no answer for. It was like being in 12th grade all over again. But at least then I was usually stoned and I didn't care. Now was the time I had to have answers, our lives depended on it. My shrug, at least, had a desired effect. Tracy pulled back from the window to look at me. Okay so maybe not so desired. I felt like an albino under the withering gaze of an Arizona sun, my cheeks flushed.

"You don't *know*?" she asked. It sounded accusatory to me, but it was intoned with defeat.

I walked over to her and wrapped her up in a big hug and then I lied. "We'll get out of here." And she believed it about as much as I did.

The preternatural silence was occasionally disrupted by the staccato sound of gunfire. Apparently there were still a few die hards on the walls that weren't willing to give up so easily. I was going stir-crazy sitting in the house. I couldn't find anything to do that even remotely kept my mind from thoughts of zombies. Crossword puzzles – zombies, model building – zombies, reading – zombies.

"This sucks!" I said as I stood up from the couch. No one argued. We had been sitting in near silence for over an hour. "I'm going to see how Alex is doing with the truck." This was not a source of easement either.

When I told Tracy about the idea her eyes had lit up like Christmas trees. It had warmed my heart to see the new life that had been breathed into her, even if it was only short-lived. She was a smart person and she could see that I wasn't nearly as enthusiastic about the plan as I should be.

"What's wrong? Don't you think the truck can get through?" She had asked.

"I'm having my doubts, but if the timing is right it'll have a good shot."

She searched my face for the answer she was seeking. Shit, I must have had the words emblazoned on my cheeks.

"You're not going," she stated flatly.

My eyes told the truth. "It's women and children and even then we won't be able to get them all out."

"Fuck that!" She screamed at me. I stepped back. At 5'2" and 110 pounds she scared the shit out of me like no drill instructor double her size could. Her vehemence was unmatched. "Well, I'm not going!" She yelled as she circled the room like a tiger waiting to pounce on its prey. And I was the one feeling like the goat. "What if the truck gets stuck, what then Mr. Bad Ass Marine? You'll be delivering canned goods to the zombies. All they'll need is a can opener and a fine Chianti and they can have a huge smorgasbord."

I put my hands up in a placating manner. I might as well have tossed the whole can of gasoline on the fire. "Calm down," I begged. Ooops, wrong tact, the spitting volcano erupted, Vesuvius incarnate.

She pushed past my arms and punched me full force in the stomach. Whoa, I hadn't been expecting that. I bowed over from the force of the blow, the wind knocked right out of me. Good thing she didn't follow up with an uppercut, that would have been real embarrassing. I was busy gasping for air as she retreated. It looked more like she was circling for another opening.

Finally being able to come up to a near stand, I was ready to answer her. Her pacing hadn't slowed. I was choosing my words carefully. "There aren't many alternatives, Tracy," I pleaded. "If some of us can get away that makes it worth it."

She huffed. "To what end?" came her question. "Where are they going to go? What are they going to do? Better to stand here and fight until the end."

"But they'll live to fight another day. We can't be the only holdouts." I hoped that was true, or truly what was the point. A truckload of women and children wasn't going to repopulate the planet.

"I'm not going," she stated. Her pacing stopped as she stood in front of me, daring me to disagree with her.

I thanked God she wasn't leaving and cursed the fates at the same time. She was forsaking the best chance of escape. I had to press further regardless of the threat to my stomach.

"What about Nicole, are you answering for her too?" I asked.

Tracy lurched forward, I at first thought it meant the start of round two and prepared for my defense. It turned out it was more of a swoon. I was reluctant to put my guard down as I stepped forward to keep her upright. She pushed me away.

"We live as a family," she gulped, "and we'll die as a family." She spun and left the room.

Ten minutes later, still standing there I couldn't tell if my stomach was more upset by her punch or her words.

CHAPTER 22
Journal Entry - 19

Alex was busy welding the front plow into place. I stood back and watched, uneasy in the feeling that the greenish yellow arc of light was burning my image into the brains of the hundreds of zombies that were watching.

I had turned around and was looking back at the drooling masses when Alex clapped me on the shoulder.

"You get used to it," he said. "Just pretend you're a famous celebrity and they are your adoring fans."

That didn't help. "Most fans don't want to eat their object of adoration," I said as I turned back around. Alex laughed.

A few minutes later he asked, "What do you think?" as he grabbed the plow.

"Looks impressive," I said as I finally wrested my vision away from my adoring fans.

"Once I get the skirt on, I'm going to put some handholds on top of the trailer for some gunmen."

I was still staring at the plow.

"Talbot, you all right?"

"Tracy and Nicole aren't going," I told him.

He nodded in solace. His wife and child were getting on the truck. Hispanic families were different from American. The males still had the final say so and Alex had exercised his right. Because the truck had been his idea, his wife and child were exempt from the selection process. They had earned a ride.

"Are you going too, Alex?" I asked

His eyes fell. "Jed said that I was eligible for the same exemption as my wife and kids, but I couldn't find it in myself to take the place of some other woman or kid. What kind of man would I be?" His eyes met mine. "I am going to put my name in for one of the gunners on top. If God deems it, I will go with my Marta." He kissed his hand and made the Holy sign of the Trinity on his chest.

"How much longer?" I asked, pointing to the truck. Alex seemed happy to move on from the subject we had reluctantly broached.

"Tomorrow at the latest. I'm working on a couple of ideas for the skirt. I want to make sure it doesn't cause the truck to hang up on anything."

We didn't touch that with a ten-foot stick. But as Alex' eyes briefly met mine, the point was made. He was entrusting his wife and child to this design. I jumped when a shot rang out no more than a hundred yards from our location. Alex had turned back to his task at hand. I was going to ask him if he needed any help, but this felt more like my cue to leave. I contemplated going into the clubhouse and talking to Jed, but the likelihood that he of all people would do anything to elevate my present mood was unlikely. I loved the old man, but he was a crotchety son-of-a-bitch. Then again so was I. I mean the part about being a son of a bitch, not crotchety. Ha, I could elevate my own damn mood, I said sourly as I began a slow walk around the perimeter of Little Turtle. I received the occasional greeting from some of the sentries but for the most part I was left alone. It was when I reached the far side of the complex that I 'felt' a difference. I couldn't at first tell what it was, but the change was thick in the air.

I looked around trying to figure it out. It was an absence that was causing the difference, an absence of prying eyes. There were no zombies watching my every move. No zombies debating on which part of me might be stringy, which parts succulent. My spirit nearly soared. It felt like a reprieve, a last minute call from the governor. Even the air smelled a little sweeter, marginally. On this side of the complex the wall was built on top of a small rise, maybe six feet or so. The other side of the wall had the same drop off, so that would explain a lot. There would have to be a lot more zombies killed on this side before their vision would peek over the top. But it was more than that, I hoped. The air was less heavy here, that's the best I can explain it. But I wasn't convinced. You don't grow up on the East Coast and not hold on to a certain measure of cynicism. I climbed up onto the nearest guard tower, startling the guard to no end. Not realizing how close I had just succumbed to friendly fire, the view was worth the chance. There were some zombies milling about but not anything near the volumes on the other three sides. I couldn't believe my eyes.

"How long has it been like this?" I asked the portly guard.

He was still recovering from his scare. (Must have been National Guard, I mused.)

"They started moving away around ten," he answered.

"So about the time they started to see over the wall on the other side," I stated more to myself than him. He half smiled and shrugged. He had no clue.

"They've just been leaving in streams pretty much since," he said, kind of like he was looking for some praise, friggen idiot.

"So you're telling me the zombies have been vacating this area for the past three hours, and you didn't feel the need to tell anyone?!" I yelled at him. He backed away.

"I...I...I um, Fritzy said," he stammered.

I was pissed, a potential escape route was staring us in the face and this fat fuck couldn't get up off his ass to let anyone know. I was closing in on the guard, for what I hadn't decided yet, but as he pulled back and covered his face with his hands I knew it was time to ease off a bit.

"What about Fritzy?" I barked.

"He... he...he..."

Great, I'm in the middle of a war and the only person with relevant information is a stuttering fool. The Gods must be crazy! I backed away some more; his speech impediment greatly improved.

He swallowed loudly. "He said he would let Jed know."

I hadn't gone in to talk to Jed but this wasn't a secret Jed would have kept to himself, he sure as hell didn't know.

"Where's this Fritzy guy staying?"

I got the information I was looking for with a little more yammering and headed off. I was fearful if I stayed any longer I might do something that guard would regret. Why I went looking for 'Fritzy' I couldn't say. I would have been better off minding my own damn business. As it was I was thoroughly pissed off and I was looking for a punching bag to vent on. I went to his front door and rang the bell. Well to be honest, I pushed the button and I didn't hear the familiar dingdong accompaniment. I banged my fist against the door hard enough to make the frame rattle. No luck, this stupid puke was probably passed out in front of his defunct TV with half a bottle of Jack in his lap. I tried the lock, no luck, most people in this neighborhood had always kept their doors locked and nothing that was happening now had made the place any safer. His two front windows had the shades drawn. LEAVE! My senses screamed. I paid them no heed. I walked around the back of his building. His gate was unhitched. LEAVE! That pesky voice said again. I'm not psychic in any capacity so I most likely had these feelings of foreboding after the fact, when I could sit down and write about it. But it would be nice to think I had a higher consciousness that was looking out for me, much more comforting that way. I walked into his small, unadorned backyard, minimalism at its best. He had one bleached out patio chair and an umbrella that hadn't stopped anything much smaller than a basketball in a couple of years, laid out on his concrete slab of a backyard. In the far corner stood a small bundle of bricks and two bags of cement from a project that didn't look like it would ever get completed. The cement in the bags had gotten wet and was set, he basically now had two 100-pound paperweights. My back ached just with the thought of moving those things. I was stalling. There was something wrong here and still I plodded on. His back sliding doors were also covered with long brown vertical shades. I pressed my face to the glass but was not rewarded for my effort. The murk from within was not yielding any secrets.

I knocked, but not nearly as loudly as I had at the front. I convinced myself that I was afraid of breaking the glass, but it was more than that. I felt like an intruder, I was now on his property uninvited, but why should that matter? I tried the door. It was locked. 'Whew, good thing,' I thought. My mind was saying 'Get the fuck out!' while my hands were popping the sliding door out of its tracks. I had pulled my gloves off and with the friction from my hands, I pushed up on the glass and as it came out of the bottom groove I then wrapped one of my hands around the side and pulled it towards me. The waft of warm, stink filled air that hit my face nearly made me drop the door. It smelled like he was cooking a zombie, or maybe it was just broccoli, I couldn't tell. Both of those smells skeeve me out. I pushed past the greasy shades and was greeted with the low deep growl of a large animal. I froze. Out from the gloom of the hallway approached a mid-sized bear. Its throat rumbled a warning, or maybe that was its stomach. What's worse: getting eaten by a zombie or a bear? Not much of a choice, pretty much like deciding if getting stabbed or shot is better, they both suck.

I was halfway in and out of the shades and was afraid the movement to reach and grab my rifle would cause the big animal to attack. I eased my hand back to my belt. I had the foresight to strap on my 9-millimeter but I wasn't feeling all that lucky. It would take three or four well-aimed rounds with that caliber to take down a bear and I had maybe one or two max before this thing would be on me. Well, at least I knew what the stink was. This bear must have eaten Fritzy. The next question, however, was a little unsettling. What the hell was a bear doing in here in the first place? My hand had finally reached upon the pistol and the bear must have realized I was up to no good, at least for him. He charged full tilt. Two shots my ass, I had barely got the pistol out of the holster when the creature slammed into my legs. I fell over, my hand slamming into a foot mat. I was tangled up in the shades and rolled around, finally pulling them free from their moorings. The rail gave me a glancing blow across the top of my head. That was the least of my worries. I was kicking my legs like a marathoner in the hopes that Smoky the Bear wouldn't be able to find purchase. Sometime during the fray I had lost the pistol. The rifle might have been in a safe for all the good it was going to do me. The bear would be digesting me by then. I was moving like an epileptic on crack, shitloads of movement with no purpose, but still no bone crunching rending. I paused for a moment, my trip-hammer heart making that a difficult process. I sat up expecting to be face-to-face with the beast. Nothing. Did I imagine it? I looked around my immediate vicinity. No, the thing had hit my legs hard enough to bruise them. A bruise was infinitely better than what I had been expecting. I sat up fully now, curiosity now beginning to overtake the ebbing fear. It wasn't a bear. It was Bear. Over by the gate was the biggest Rottweiler I had ever seen. Bear had been a resident of Little Turtle for at least as long as I had lived here. I had seen him around the complex on numerous occasions. His previous owner must have met an untimely demise. How he ended up at Fritzy's house I wasn't sure. Bear wasn't paying any attention to me in the least. All of his focus was at the back gate. As I stood up and slowly approached him, I could tell he was shaking, but not from the cold. When he heard me coming, he swiveled his massive head. His large eyes were rimmed with white and his mouth was pulled back in a perpetual grin, but there was no happiness here. This dog wanted out. Bear looked balefully at me, pleading for me to open the gate. I still wasn't convinced that this wasn't a bear or maybe at least a hybrid of bear and dog. He was easily 180 pounds, maybe more. I cautiously moved closer, doing my best to convey my harmless intentions to the animal.

"Hey, good boy. You're a good boy aren't you?

Right?" They say animals can sense fear. If so, we were both in trouble. My teeth were chattering and Bear's tail was wedged between his legs. "What's the matter boy? Is it the zombies?"

Well, that doesn't make any sense, now does it. He would have been better off staying in the house. I dared a glimpse back to try to ascertain what in that now harshly uninviting house had scared this brute to his core. His head lowered imperceptibly as I inched closer. My hand was inches from its massive skull. One bite and he could have half my arm. I undid the latch and he pushed the gate open with his nose. Bear looked back once as if to say 'Thanks' or 'Are you coming?' Either way, he didn't wait long to find out. He galloped off, long strings of saliva dragging on the ground doing little to stop his momentum.

I should have left. I wanted to leave. I also wanted my Glock back. I had paid a lot for the gun and I loved it. Stupid gun. I walked back to the door. Even with the shades off, the place seemed darker than it should, almost as if there were anti-lights in there. Some device designed to remove light and replace it with darkness. 'That's crazy talk, are you hearing yourself? Yeah, and you are also having dialogue with yourself. True, true, but still anti-lights, that sounds like something out of a scary movie. Yeah well so do zombies.' I stopped in my tracks, I hate it when I'm right.

"I just have to get my gun," I said aloud, maybe to make it sound more convincing.

I wouldn't have to go in more than a foot or two. I stuck my head back in the blackness, fearful that if I went in too far I would be sucked into a portal of the damned, forever lost in a land of the insane. How close to right I was I could not have known. I felt around the tangled fallen shades, convinced that I would find my prize momentarily and be able to get out of there unscathed. That is of course, unless someone was videotaping my escape from the shades. All dignity had been lost at that point. I was on all fours patting around the floor, not liking how vulnerable I was feeling, nothing. I even pulled the shades out the door to make sure the gun wasn't hung up in the slats somehow and I had missed it.

'Damn it!' I muttered as I stood up and took my first full step across the threshold. I didn't feel the rush of teleportation but that didn't make me feel any better. I took another step and then another into the gloom; the smell worsened. I wasn't going to be caught off guard again. I brought my rifle to the ready. Another step, still no Glock. I was halfway across the living room when I spotted a reflective glint of metal. It was partly down the hallway where my new dearly departed friend had first showed himself. I could not even begin to understand how it could have made that distance. I was feeling like a baited rabbit being led to slaughter, but I couldn't help myself, I inched forward. I was smart enough to see the design of the trap but not smart enough to get out before it was sprung. If the design for this model town home held true, then the gun was positioned directly in front of a small bathroom, easily big enough to hide four or five zombies. Sweat beaded up on my brow. My hands were getting clammy. My exhausted heart once again began its furious beating. I stopped, waiting for some small scuffling sound, or a cough or a sneeze. But near as I can tell zombies don't sneeze or cough or lay traps for that matter. Something sinister was happening, I knew without any doubt. If I didn't hurry this along I was going to need to use that bathroom before I went ahead and wet myself. No noise issued from the impossibly blacker entrance to the bathroom.

I was leaning forward stretching my arm as far as it would go, wishing I would become one of my favorite childhood toys, Stretch Armstrong. If I remember correctly it didn't end well for him either, green goo everywhere. I shuddered. I had my left arm straight out in front of me, my right arm gripping the rifle like a vise, and my head swiveling like a top between the entryway and the floor. When I looked away, I felt my neck was dangerously exposed, not that it mattered to these zombies. They would just as soon chew into my smelly feet. That was not a comforting thought. My hand scraped against the edge of the gun barrel. Heartbeat after heartbeat I desperately tried to grip the gun. I turned my head to better locate my quarry and all hell broke loose. A loud sound came from the bathroom. I pushed myself off to the left, falling over and hitting the far wall. Hands gripped around my neck. The rifle was useless, the barrel sticking out farther than my assailant. I pulled the trigger anyway hoping the noise would scare it away. Nothing! The safety was on! My fingers frantically scrambled for the selector lever. The grip around my neck was making starbursts in my eyes.

"I'm sick of passing out!" I screamed.

My hand came off my useless weapon at the same time the pressure on my carotid artery loosened. I reached my hands up to my neck, and felt nothing except the nylon of my rifle sling. In my panic I had cinched it tight. The noise whooshed again from the bathroom. This time my rationality took over and I knew the sound for what it was. The toilet bowl was leaky and would periodically have to refill itself. "What is wrong with me? I could make a whole 'America's Funniest Home Fuck-Ups' episode," I laughed a little to ease my inner tension. A few more jolts to the heart like this and I was bound to spring a leak somewhere. I sat on the floor and readjusted my rifle. With pistol in right hand I placed my left on the floor to assist in my ascent. It was then that I felt the slow heavy vibrations emanating up through the floor. I have to be a sadist. Why I didn't think I had had enough I'll never know. I knew the sound for what it was, club music. I had a neighbor that loved that techno crap. He played it morning, noon and night until I had a long talk with him. It was actually a short talk but it was a long barrel. I told him I was going skeet shooting, but that my wife was sleeping and if he could keep it down I'd appreciate it. His head nodded at all the right times but his eyes never left the steely black barrel. Never did have to go over there again. In fact, he moved out the next month. Hope it wasn't anything I said.

What do I care if there is some other yahoo in this world that likes techno music, I need to get out of here. I knew all about 'The Make My Day Law.' I voted for it. So far I had broken into his house, damaged his property and let his dog go. I'm sure he wasn't going to invite me in to his party. I opened the door to the basement. All of my senses were assaulted. Now I knew why there was no light on the main floor. Everything he owned was in the basement. Light flooded like a supernova. The music (if you want to call it that) was eardrum shatteringly loud. In the worst of my Heavy Metal loving days I had never turned Iron Maiden on half as loud, and to top it off I had found the origins of the stench that pervaded this abode. Every cell in my body protested forward motion and yet into the light I went. I checked and rechecked that I had a bullet in the chamber and the safety was off, even though I knew Glocks don't have an external safety. I instinctively knew I was going to need bullets, again with the psychic crap. I had no clue but this felt wrong, and for good or bad I was going to find out.

The basement was finished, for that I was thankful. It meant that my descent down would go unnoticed. Otherwise, there would be that time of exposure where only my legs would be visible from below as I went down the stairs. Then like a cheap horror flick, there would always be the potential of a hand coming up through the openings in the stairs to grab my ankles. This should have made me feel better but it didn't. My eyes were having a difficult time adjusting from soul sucking black to radiant dawn white. I found myself excessively squinting. Then I began to ponder why there wasn't some form of 'squinting' for ears, the better to shield me from the crap coming over his speaker system. As I neared the bottom step I saw tiny moving reflections of light somehow brighter than the ambient lighting. I had seen this before. It was from a disco ball. Well, out of the frying pan and into the fire. I stepped onto the landing at the bottom of the stairs and then cautiously peered into the main room of the basement. At one time this was a playroom for kids. Video games, board games, and a rocking horse were carefully stacked in the far corner of the room, but that was not the case anymore. It was a playroom allright, but one with far more sinister games and only the highly deranged played in here anymore.

Attached to the floor with five large chains was a naked female zombie. There was one chain on each wrist, one around its neck and one each wrapped around its knees. These were then bolted to the floor with large screws. It was chained in the classic doggy position, but the situation was about to get stranger. On the opposite side of the room a man came out of a bathroom fully dressed in a form-fitting cat costume, face make-up and all. He had yet to notice me, so intent was he on his impending conquest. He walked around the zombie alternating between stroking her and slapping her. She moved her head as best she could to get at him but he had placed the chains with strategic precision. I didn't think this was the first time he'd used this set-up. After his third or fourth time around he stopped behind her. I didn't need to be the Amazing Kreskin to figure out what was going to happen next.

I fired a round into the ceiling. That got his attention. He spun around almost as fast as the animal he was portraying. He was preparing to pounce on his intruder but the cold black muzzle of a 9-millimeter made him reconsider. He walked over to his stereo system and lowered it somewhat. I tracked him all the way expecting a ruse.

He turned to face me, nervously licking his lips. I wouldn't have thought it strange if he began to lick the backs of his hands next, this was one twisted person.

"Want some?" he said invitingly, pointing to the zombie.

At first I was too astounded to even consider his request. "What the fuck is wrong with you?"

"What? I'm just having a little fun. I'm not breaking any laws," he smiled.

"How about rape, false imprisonment, assault, fucken necrophilia." I'm sure there were half a dozen others but I made my point.

"She's a fucken zombie, shithead!" he yelled.

"There's that too. You have to immediately let someone know when a zombie gets in. What if she had bit you?"

"Not a problem." His grin widened as he went back over to the zombie. He grabbed her head and bent it further back than seemed naturally possible. Her mouth was snapping, trying to get a hold of one or any of his fingers that were cradling her head. She had no teeth. They weren't just broken out with the butt of a gun or a hammer, they were gone.

"How?" I mouthed. I was feeling sicker by the second.

"I knocked her out," he said proudly. He saw my incredulous look. "Yeah, I didn't think I'd be able to do it either. I tried ether first, that almost ended badly for me. Then I just whacked the hell out of the back of her head with a crowbar."

I wanted to ask why he had ether, but I already knew the answer.

"As soon as I got my little pretty all chained up I took out all her teeth with a pair of pliers." The sick shit was smiling, realizing the effect this was having on me. "It's a good thing I got them all out too. There's been a couple of times when we've really been going at it that I kind of lose control, and she'll get a hold of a forearm or something. She tries like hell to break the surface, she's a wild one alright," he said as he affectionately stroked her hair. All the while she kept trying to bite that hand. "So we come back to the original question, want some?"

I was revolted. My mouth hung open and I had let my gun hand fall to my side. Cat man, Fritzy, sick fuck, saw his opening. He sprang like a coiled snake. He was fast, almost unnaturally so, but he had to cover ten feet. All I had to do was raise my hand. I fired two rounds into his stomach just as his hands brushed up against mine. That contact repulsed me. I shuddered from the feel as his hands slid away from mine. The bullets had punched through, gut shot. I should have felt sorry for him. There was no more painful way to die. The zombie started pulling frenetically against her restraints. The smell of his spilling innards was driving her crazy.

"Your suffering is over," I said as I walked up to her and placed the muzzle of the barrel directly on her forehead. Her head snapped back as I delivered a round deep into her gray matter.

Fritzy was laughing, it was a blood filled sound but it was a laugh nonetheless. "Oh you liked her huh?" he said laughing. "She was *so* good." He was fighting through the pain, trying to hold his insides in place. "Umm, that cold pussy. She was so special. The others always lost the will to live after a little while but she was already dead." He laughed again, and blood spilled from his mouth.

I had to get out of here. My head was starting to spin from the smell of the zombie, the discharges, and the insanity issuing forward from Fritzy. The music, the lights, it was all too much. Vertigo was making my head swim. I fought to find a wall to lean against. My breath was coming out in raggedy gasps and still he laughed. I had my head and shoulder leaning against the wall as I pushed to the stairs and potential freedom from this 'house of horrors.'

Panic began to well up in Fritzy as he realized I was heading out. "You're going to get help right?" he pleaded. "You can't leave me like this," he cried. Now the idiot was seeing the light. I don't know if he was repenting or fearful his secret would be exposed. "Fuck you!" he shouted, spittle and blood flying forward. "Talbot!" he yelled. I stopped halfway on the landing, thankful that I had got this far. "Yeah I know who you are, the mighty Talbot. I'm only sad I never got a chance to get a hold of your lovely wife or maybe your dau..."

I shot him in the head. Gouts of bile dispensed forth

from my overworked stomach, so much for not leaving any DNA evidence. I staggered up and out of the house. The sun still shone brightly, the weather still felt cold, but I felt so different. This was another stain on my soul. I hope they have some version of soul Tide when you die. I walked through the gate and out onto the back alleyway, my thoughts running rampant. I was trying in vain to steer them anywhere but back to that denizen of death. But like trying not to think of a pink elephant, you get the point. I'm not exactly sure when Bear fell in next to me, probably the moment I left the small carport at the back of Fritzy's house. All I knew was that my hand on his back was the most comforting feeling I had felt in a longtime. After the nightmare we'd both been through I think we were going to be co-dependent on each other for a while.

CHAPTER 23
Journal Entry - 20

Tracy didn't say a word when I walked in, my face sheet white, my Glock still out and my hand shaking. But she about had a coronary when my new friend padded in behind me.

Tommy came running from the couch. "BEAR!" he yelled happily as he threw his arms around the dog. I don't know if he knew the dog, yelled out what he thought it was or was expecting it ala Ryan Seacrest. When the dog started licking Tommy's face, Tracy visibly relaxed.

I walked upstairs, put my gun away, burned my hands clean under scalding water and laid down on my bed, boots and all. The knock on the door came a lot sooner than I had expected. I got up from the bed and stood at the top of the stairs as Tracy answered the door.

"Hi Jed, want some coffee?" I heard her ask.

"Is Mike here, Tracy?" Jed asked.

"Jed, what's going on? You look upset... and why are these two guards with you?"

"I told them it wasn't necessary but they insisted," Jed answered.

"Who insisted? What's going on, Jed?" Tracy's pitch began to elevate.

I walked down the stairs. "Jed," I said as I nodded. He nodded in reply. "He had it coming."

"Maybe so, Mike, but that wasn't your call."

"Who had what coming? Mike, what is this all about?" Tracy was nervous, the situation was becoming volatile.

"Mike, can you step outside?" Jed asked. I had never seen him so downtrodden. The guards tensed for action. Bear had padded up beside me and was bristling. A low menacing growl issued from him. One of the guards began to move his hands towards his sidearm; he was nervous. Couldn't say I blamed him.

I laid my hand on Bear's neck, "It's all right, boy." The growling stopped, but the menacing posture didn't. I brushed by Tracy, giving her arm a small squeeze. "I'll be back," I said to her.

I opened the door, and was facing my small escort party. "Turn around, please," one of the guards demanded. I was going to protest. I have a thing about authority but Tracy was rattled enough, I didn't figure she needed to see me get beat down too.

I felt the cold steel of the handcuffs close around my wrists, not for the first time, but it was the worst time.

"Where are you taking him, Jed?" Tracy nearly sobbed.

"The holding cell down at the clubhouse." From his demeanor, Jed must have witnessed firsthand the scene at Fritz' house. I could tell he fundamentally agreed with my handling of the situation, but laws were laws.

The walk to the clubhouse was silent. I waited until I was in my 'cell' and the guards had gone before I talked with Jed.

"He was a piece of shit, Jed!"

"I know Talbot, I went over there. But you killed him, you broke into his house and killed the man."

"But he had kidnapped and was raping…" I stopped. What did it matter what he was doing to a zombie? If it had been a human girl I would be paraded around as a hero. "How bad is it Jed?"

Jed's head bowed, "A council was being set up to deal with Durgan and now they'll be hearing your case too. Talbot, they're talking about Capital Punishment."

My head snapped up. I wanted to scream to the heavens. "Oh that's fair, my life for that piece of shit. I saw his set-up, this wasn't the first time."

"No, it wasn't," Jed solemnly answered. "We checked out the whole basement. He had a 'trophy room' full of pictures and other things," Jed shuddered, "of all his other victims."

"They weren't all zombies, right?" I grasped.

"Not by a long shot." Jed looked a little green around the gills.

"But that's not going to help me?" I asked downcast. Jed just shook his head.

"I'll be back in a little bit with some food."

"Don't sweat it, it'll be a long time before I'm ready to eat again."

"Me too," Jed said as he retreated out of the holding area.

"Welcome to Shangri-La," Durgan said, as he sat up on his makeshift bed, then stood up with the assistance of a crutch.

"Oh this day just keeps getting better and better," I answered sarcastically. When I turned around I was face to belly button with one of the biggest men I had ever seen in my life. Even with only one leg he outweighed me by a hundred pounds, easily.

"It looks like I'm going to make good on that promise I made," his voice boomed from above.

"What's that? Not wearing white after Labor Day?"

"No, you little fuck, killing you!"

Did he think it was necessary to clarify himself? I saw no choice. My Marine Corps training clicked on. I pivoted sideways and struck out with my right foot as hard as was humanly possible and was rewarded with the audible pop of Durgan's only knee being crushed backward. He fell in a heap. The only thing worse than Fritz' thumping techno music were the shrieking wails of Durgan in blind blistering pain.

The expletives he issued forth, while colorful, are too long and complicated for this narrative. Suffice it to say he left nothing to the imagination. He even had the audacity to include my grandmother in some of the more long-winded diatribes. If Durgan was going to kill me now, he was going to have to start at my ankles. I hopped up onto the now empty bunk and watched detachedly as a medical team came in and took him away. I rolled over and immediately went to sleep. It had been a long day and I was bushed.

Who ordered the Molotov cocktails, nobody knows. This is a small fact that will be forever lost in the annals of human history, should there be any humans to bear witness. Was it the result of some bored guards or the initiative of a defense tribunal? It doesn't matter, the result would have been the same no matter who pulled the trigger. It was common knowledge the brain of the infected had to be destroyed in order to stop the zombie, what was not known was what effect fire would have. Could a zombie be cooked to the point where they would be inoperative? Somebody decided to find out. The result was disastrous.

The first cocktail was served three hours after I was incarcerated. The guard had the presence of mind to realize that a bottle lofted into the air would have great difficulty finding open ground upon which to shatter and spread its fuel. At one time in his life, the guard had been a pitcher and a Triple A prospect for a minor league team. A drinking problem had nipped any chances of a pro career in the bud. He called upon all his skills to deliver an old Budweiser bottle at ninety-three miles per hour into the unsuspecting skull of a zombie. Ironically, had it been measured it would have been discovered the zombie was sixty feet six inches away. The zombie fell hard, its skull crushed beyond repair, but it had held together long enough to shatter the bottle and let the accelerant spread to seven or eight of his best zombie friends. The effect was immediate. The zombies burned quietly, the crackling of skin and hair reminiscent of a cold winter night and reading a good book curled up on the couch by the roaring hearth. Because of the crowded conditions, the fire rapidly spread among the besiegers, but the desired outcome of disbursement was not what happened. Again, maybe history would have the luxury of discerning the truth, but the immediate was not concerned with the future. Instead of tucking tail and running away, the milling zombies coalesced and began pushing, into the barrier that kept them away from their desired prize. The guards could only watch on with increasing alarm as the first couple of rows of zombies were quite literally pressed into nonexistence from the pressures being exerted on them. Zombies were erupting like eggs left too long in a microwave. Sheets of viscous bodily fluids flew high in the air. Nearby personnel were covered in the gore; more than one lost their respective lunches.

Between the crushing force of the zombies and the retaining wall, something had to give. Reinforcement two by fours creaked and groaned under the added pressure, and cracks began to manifest near knotholes. Boards began to pop with the sound as loud as rifle shots, first one and then a cacophony of explosions. Guns fired wildly trying to stem the tide of the onslaught, but like trying to bale water out of a sinking ship with a thimble, it was too late. Many realizing the end was near took off for their homes. Some stood in shock watching as hairline fissures began to form in the seemingly indestructible wall before them. Some of the residents rallied together, the air trembled with the cumulative shots being fired. The effect was like one continuous clap of thunder.

CHAPTER 24
Journal Entry - 21

I had been dreaming a particularly vivid dream before I was so rudely interrupted. The sound of booming thunder had cut through all semblances of sleep. I had no sooner come to full consciousness when the klaxon of alarm erupted. All hell was breaking loose, although at the time I had no idea how close to reality I was. I was trying my best to look out the window and find the source of the clamor, but the angle wasn't right. Unless the problem was in the pool I wasn't going to find out much information this way.

"Talbot, get your ass over here!" Jed was yelling from the locked door, fumbling frantically with the keys trying to find the right one.

Flashbacks of every horror movie I had ever seen ran through my mind. You know the part where the person that is about to die fumbles with his or her keys, giving the monster in the flick the needed time to catch up with and dispatch the lowest paid actor in the movie. As I neared the door I could see the tremors in Jed's hands, and this wasn't the advancing age palsy either; this was the full-blown San Andreas type.

"Jed, take a deep breath, breathe for a sec," I said to him, trying to instill a calm in him that I wasn't even feeling, and I wasn't even sure what was going on. Jed looked up at me, and my heart sank. His face couldn't even be considered ashen, transparent was a better descriptive, I could see every blue vein perfectly etched in his features.

"Jed, what's going on?" I asked in alarm.

"The end Talbot, the end," he answered sadly.

I had never seen him so resigned. I wasn't so sure now that I wanted him to open that door, maybe I could just ride it out right here. That was an option I didn't have the luxury of exploring. The lock rattled open, and Jed jerked the door open.

"Get home Talbot," Jed said without much inflection. Jed might not be a zombie, but he was dying inside.

"What about the trial?" I had to ask. I didn't want attempted escape added to my offenses.

"I don't think there'll be enough people left in a couple of hours to worry about that," Jed said, his shoulders slumping even further.

"Oh shit, Jed, it's that bad?" I asked as I felt my heart drop.

"The wall has been breached in at least a dozen places. If you don't get out of here and home now you'll spend your last time on earth with him," Jed said as he pointed to the far corner of the rec room slash converted cell where a drugged Durgan was recovering from the ad hoc surgery done on his shattered knee.

Sometime while I had been sleeping, Durgan had been wheeled in on a gurney. It was clear that he was not getting anywhere soon under his own volition. It was also clear, to me at least, that I couldn't leave him. Yes, he was a murdering scumbag who had personally threatened to kill me and would have carried out his plan if given the opportunity, but even then I couldn't just leave him. I looked longingly over Jed's shoulder and the way out and back towards Durgan and the Christian-like thing to do. Who was I kidding, I wasn't even a practicing worshipper. I was more like a pretend worshipper. I couldn't even do what the vast majority of other pretenders did and go to church on Christmas Eve. Despite all that, I still went back to get Durgan. He jerked awake as I disengaged the foot brake on his gurney. His murderous black eyes quickly lost their postoperative haze and locked onto mine.

"What the fuck are you doing?" he mumbled. Even half asleep he was an asshole.

"Getting you out of here, the zombies have gotten into the complex," I hastily explained.

A small smile curved across his lips. He was pulling out of his stupor by leaps and bounds. I was halfway across the room pushing the gurney when Durgan spoke.

"You know I'll kill you the first chance I get right?"

"We've already been through this, why don't you give it a rest."

That seemed to piss him off to no end. Durgan's body had been reduced to a shell of its previous self, but this was something that his mind had not yet grasped. He was a bully in the truest nature of the word and was ALWAYS used to getting what he wanted, how he wanted it, when he wanted it. Physical intimidation wasn't just a means to an end for him, it was a lifestyle, so what issued forth next was pretty much par for the course for him.

"And then when I'm done with you, I'll kill every one you're close too," he said as he croaked out a laugh, his throat unnaturally dry from the anesthesia.

I didn't even respond, I took my hands off the gurney, walked past Durgan and out the door.

"Wait, where you going?" Durgan yelled. "I was kidding, you can't leave me here. Wait!" he screamed in fear for maybe the first time in his life.

"You're an idiot," Jed said to Durgan as he pulled the door shut and locked it.

"Old man, you can't leave me here."

"Son, if I were so inclined to help you, which I'm not, I don't have the strength to push what's left of you out of here. Your best chance of survival just walked through this door. And to be honest, I'm glad you opened that big mouth of yours because if you hadn't, and Talbot had tried to save your worthless life, he might've lost his in the effort. There would have been no justice in that." Jed walked away, not feeling bad in the least as Durgan's insults faded away into blubbering incoherence.

"Fuck me," was all I could think to say as I walked out of the clubhouse.

Zombies were everywhere. Some of the townhomes

were on fire. I would later learn it was from the zombies that had been firebombed. The few residents of Little Turtle that weren't hunkered up in their homes were running for their lives, most without much success. Ravenous zombies were making short work of their unlucky catches. More than one victim would be busy looking over his or her shoulder at their pursuer only to run headlong into the loving arms of another zombie. I stared in fascinated horror as I watched what was once a guard (I could only tell by the uniform) literally have his face peeled off. The zombie had grabbed a piece of the guard's chin in its teeth and pulled straight up. By some sheer witless luck his entire face had come off as neatly as a banana peel. The muscles underneath contorted into a scream but were cut short as another zombie ripped out his Adam's apple. The ragged hole in the man's neck leeched off what would have been an earsplitting shriek. Blood flowed freely from the faceless man's eyes. My mind was in denial. It looked more like special effects in a low budget movie. I could not recognize what was happening as truth. This was an impossibility. People don't get their faces ripped off. This wasn't Silence of the Lambs. The guard's eyes locked on mine, which brought me back to the here and now. I would later convince myself that in that state, the man was not capable of higher cerebral thought; he had to be in shock. But in that moment I was sure that he knew who he was, what was happening and what was about to transpire. The moment was broken when another zombie stepped between our line of sight and honed in on its after dinner parfait, me.

'Run!' my mind screamed. I obliged. I had to pull out all of my high school football running back moves. At 43 years old I was lucky not to pull anything else. For every zombie I dodged, two took its place. I figured at this geometric rate I would have to get by 64,000 of them by the time I got to my front door. This was not going to be easy. To my right the remnants of the wall were being pushed over as the main body of zombies fought to get their fair share of fresh meat. None of them wanted to be late for the party. I was twenty-five or so yards from the front of my house when I realized I would never have enough time to knock and convince who was ever on the other side to open the door before I was swarmed over. And my moments of having enough maneuverability were rapidly diminishing.

"Mom!" I heard a familiar voice yelling. "Dad's coming!" Justin had been watching the front of the house and Travis had been watching the back just in case something like this happened.

Within seconds gunfire erupted from the upstairs windows as Justin, Travis and Brendon opened fire, widening a hole for me that I could have driven a truck through. I would have liked to have sauntered up to the front door like I was John Wayne, but I was scared shitless. Tracy had opened the front door and the security door and was yelling at me to hurry up.

"Are you kidding me?" I yelled back with what breath I had left. "What makes you think I need any incentive?"

Paul had stepped onto the front stoop and was covering my entrance. I dove through the front door like the hounds of hell were on my heels. The move was unnecessary; there wasn't a zombie within fifteen feet of me. I stood up, dusted myself off and tried to act as nonchalant as possible. Tracy calmly locked the security door, not having any of the jitters she had experienced the last time she faced zombies in her yard.

The front door slammed shut just as the boys finished their barrage from above. In the ensuing quiet I heard the roar of the semi as the engine turned over. Someone was making a run for it. I silently wished them good luck and was despondent that I wouldn't have the chance to get my family on that rig.

"Dude, it's good to see you," Paul said enthusiastically.

"You and me both, brother," I said as I hugged him.

The boys made their way noisily down the stairs to

greet me.

"Thank you boys," I said as I grabbed Tracy and gave her a hug. She uncharacteristically hugged me back.

"Did you escape?" Travis asked.

I disengaged from Tracy, happy to be home. "No, Jed let me out." I caught them up quickly about what I had been doing, although there wasn't much to say. I had been sleeping for most of it. Travis told me about the Molotov cocktails.

"Yeah that didn't work out so well," I said. Tracy looked at me quizzically. "That must be why some of the townhomes are on fire."

Now her expression turned to one of alarm.

"Boys, go back upstairs, make sure that no burning zombies get within fifty feet of our row of houses."

Tommy came up from the basement. "Hey Mrs. T, all the water is upstairs now." He grinned one of his signature smiles and waved enthusiastically at me. "Hey Mr. T," and then followed the other boys upstairs.

"Well that wasn't much of greeting," I mused.

"He knew you were coming," Tracy said matter-of-factly. "He's the reason I had the boys at the windows looking for you. I don't know if I would have thought to do that. I was pretty much in panic mode."

"Ryan?" I asked, wondering if it had been Tommy's spiritual guide that wrapped itself in the guise of television celebrity Ryan Seacrest.

"No," Tracy said shaking her head. "Bear."

I looked at her confused.

She shrugged. "Don't look at me, Tommy said Bear could smell you coming."

I knew I reeked a little bit, but there was no way that dog could pick my mellow funk out over all the odiferous odors that were pervading our atmosphere at the moment. I was going to let sleeping dogs lie, so to speak. With Tommy there was a good chance I'd never understand what was happening. All I knew was the big lovable kid was a

Godsend to have around.

"What now, Talbot?" Tracy asked me. She was starting to get that look of defeatism that I had last seen Jed wearing.

"It's not over yet, Hon," I countered to her gloomy outlook. "We're all safe, we have enough food and water to last three months or so." I hoped that was enough to raise her attitude. She gave a dispirited nod of the head, apparently not.

"And then? You saw them Mike. They won't leave. They have all the time in the world.

"I have a plan," I said. That noticeably improved her outlook.

Unfortunately that was lie, not an out and out lie, more like a stretching of the truth. I had the outline of a plan, more of a plan per se. And it wasn't so much a plan as an unformulated idea. In reality it was a last ditch effort which I put our odds of pulling off at a 1 in 3 chance and by 3, I mean 99.

"I don't believe you," Tracy said, but she hugged me fiercely. "But I love you for that lie."

That was a first. I had never had a woman ever, EVER thank me for lying to her. Chalk one up for the good guys!

It snowed that night, if not for our locale I would have called it a Nor'easter like back home in Boston. The snow thankfully blanketed out the few remaining zombies who were still human roman candles, and it also had the added benefit of muffling the screams of the few remaining Little Turtle inhabitants. There were still some holdouts yelling out of their windows looking for anyone else that might be alive, but I didn't see the advantage in yelling back to them. They couldn't get to us and we couldn't get to them. All it could possibly do was bring further attention to us. Once the fire danger had ebbed, I had everyone in the house help with covering the doors and windows with plastic. Mostly it was trash bags but I also had some of that shrink-wrap film that is supposed to help with energy costs. The power had stopped about an hour after the zombies had broke through. I wanted to be able to preserve as much heat in our house as possible and I also was hoping the plastic would keep the smell of us away from the zombies. Did it work? I don't know, that had mixed results, they weren't rushing the house but they weren't leaving either. My thought was that they still had the memory of us being here. I know it sounds crazy, but these also weren't the mindless zombies we'd watched in the movies either, they had rudimentary skills.

We spent most of the next day in my office, which had been converted into Nicole and Brendon's sleeping quarters. The window had been covered with a green trash bag and no light seeped in. This also had the added benefit of not letting any light seep out. So between me, Tracy, Nicole, Brendon, Justin, Travis, Tommy, Paul, Erin, Henry, Bear and half a dozen candles the room was toasty and downright stinky. Henry was ripping farts like there was no tomorrow. Maybe he knew something we didn't. Even Bear was doing his best to keep his nose under the covers and away from the odoriferousness that emanated from Henry. Henry seemed blissfully ignorant of the whole affair as he slumbered through our protests. A couple of times I was fearful the natural gas would blaze and we'd have a blue fireball spiraling through the room. I was considering sleep, there wasn't much else to do, when Erin started to talk.

"Do you think they can starve?" she asked out loud, to nobody in particular and anyone who might be willing to answer.

I had been thinking about this but hadn't had enough time to just sit and contemplate until now, at least. Nearly everyone in the room had been either dozing or in the process of doing so, but when I answered Erin, eyes began to open. I had a captive audience. What can I say.

"I think, now this is just my *opinion*," I clarified. Erin nodded. "I think they are alive, they are not the living dead like we think they are. Whatever has these people acting the way they are, whether it's a virus or a germ, a parasite or a damn alien, they are alive. I haven't seen any zombies that looked like they clawed their way up through a grave. And judging by the stains in most of the zombies' pants they still have their digestive processes going on." Nobody, and I mean nobody wanted clarification on what was being digested, that was to remain unspoken.

"Dad, what about the wounds some of them have?" Nicole asked. "I mean I've seen some of them with their chests blown open and half their faces missing." She shuddered.

"I'm not gonna B.S. you, Nicole, I don't have all the answers, but the human brain is a powerful thing. Somehow it is rerouting all function up to it. I mean, how it can keep circulating blood with a damaged heart or keep someone from bleeding out with a blown off leg, no clue. It might be that these zombies are using way more brain function than we can even understand." This comment got me more than one upraised eyebrow. "Okay, okay, tough room. I'm obviously not saying smarter, except for maybe Paul." That got some laughs, which I was happy for, those had been scarce. Paul flipped me the finger. "I guess this brings me back to Erin's original question, can they starve? Yeah, I think they can." I finished the rest of my thought quickly before anyone could have their hopes raised too high. "But I also think it would take months for them to show any ill effects." I thought they could go for years but I had already run over everyone's hopes. I didn't see the need to back up and finish the job.

"Dad, we don't have that much food," Nicole had only said out loud what was on every one's mind.

"The zombies should be gone long before our food is gone," I said confidently, hoping it was true.

What I was leaving unsaid was much more potent than what I had said. Before the zombies left they would have to completely deplete their food source. Now, this wasn't some wild grass in the savannah, these were our neighbors and friends. It was not a bright moment in the Talbot household. I feigned sleep so I could turn my head. I didn't want anyone to see my face as I wept silently for those I would never see again. For my mom and dad, my three brothers and sister, for the friends I loved, and even the ones I had fallen out of touch with hoping one day to reconnect. Hell, if given the time, I'd weep for the Barista who made my coffee every morning. I was so tired of this shit. My stress level was through the roof. I couldn't even conceive of how I was going to keep everyone in this room safe, but the responsibility rested on my shoulders. I had fallen asleep sometime during my moments of doubt and shame. As I stirred awake, I had not a clue what time it was. Someone had blown out the majority of candles and the room was nearly coal black. I surveyed the jumbles and bunches of bodies that lay in every conceivable position. My gaze came to rest on two eyes that shone with a light of their own. I thought that possibly I hadn't fully awaken and I was in the midst of lucid dreaming, but Henry's flatulence erased any of that notion, unless of course I had received the special ability to smell in my dreams now. The eyes bore into mine. Searching through my mind, they found that worm of doubt that was wriggling around dementedly, and like a boot to a cockroach squashed it out. Tommy laid his head back down. I was released from my trance. I wanted to thank him for what he'd done but I wasn't sure if he even knew.

I had always been a spiritual person and believed in the Yin and the Yang. There must always be a balance in the world. Love balances out hate, peace balances out war and in my mind, Tommy balanced out the zombies. Had he been this gifted before this shit storm began raining down on us? Probably not. Thank God for Wal-Mart and their affirmative action hiring processes. I disengaged myself from my sleeping bag, doing my best not to disturb the four or five people that were between me and the exit. This was worse than having a window seat on a jumbo jet. After stepping on a few body parts and receiving some rather colorful protests I made it to the door and to my ultimate goal of the bathroom.

There were times, especially recently, where I missed my youth. My carefree days in my late teens and early twenties, when the world was maybe not my oyster but definitely was my playground, when I didn't yet know the next girl I was going to kiss. Responsibilities were someone else's concerns. Then I would come back to the life and love I shared with my wife and kids, the unconditional love I felt for all of them, even stinky Henry. And I remembered that getting older was not necessarily a bad thing. I am telling you this because I just want to give you a glimpse of how my brain works. I wasn't really reminiscing on the past so much as reveling in the present. My actual happy thought came from the fact that I was not a couple of years older with an enlarged prostate. All I could keep thinking was how much of a pain in the ass it would be to have to get out of that room four or five times a night to piss. Yeah, welcome to my world.

CHAPTER 25
Journal Entry - 22

The air temperature in the hallway dropped a good twenty degrees. I had almost forgotten why I was even out here when my bladder gave me a refresher. I finished my business and was reluctant to head back into the sauna. Between Tommy and the chilled air I was feeling invigorated, maybe not enough to go on an early morning jog but enough to do a circuit around the house. I had made it downstairs and into relative safety, or so I had thought. I let one rip that Henry would be proud of, then laughed to myself.

"God, I've been holding that beauty for two hours."

"Hey Dad."

Busted, dammit! "Hey Trav," I said. My first inclination was to go on the offensive, ask him why he was down here. It would have all been a ruse to hide my embarrassment at getting nailed. Eh, what was the point. The smell alone should be punishment enough. I was quick to leave the room, so was Travis.

I went to the fridge and poured a glass of milk. I wanted to go through the perishables before they went bad. "Want some?" I asked Travis before I put it away.

He shook his head no, that was of course until he saw my secret stash of white fudge covered Oreos. We sat in silence for a few moments, relishing in the moment. Cold milk and Oreos, father and son, it could have been a commercial except for maybe the darkness and the threat of being eaten alive. Yeah, Nabisco probably wouldn't be knocking on our door anytime soon. I sat back, my stomach content, hands on my belly. Travis looked over at me in alarm.

"You're not gonna rip again are you?" he asked genuine concern across his face.

I laughed. I couldn't help myself. The last time I had been that busted, my mother had walked in on me just after the newest National Geographic had arrived. There was no such thing as the Internet back then! I was 13. Stop being judgmental.

"No, I'm good now," I said patting my belly. "I'd been working on that one for a while. Should be good to go now, although I think I blew a hole in the back of my pants." Travis laughed. It was good to see him do that.

"Dad."

I stopped smiling. I knew there was something on his mind but I was going to let him get to it when he was good and ready.

He continued. "I miss school. Stop giving me that look, I don't miss geometry, I miss my friends. I might even miss a teacher or two."

I knew how he felt. He missed the routine of a normal life, something that I didn't think we would ever find again. I couldn't assure him that his friends would be all right or that things would eventually return to normal. Those would be empty promises, and he'd know it for what it was. I could promise him that we'd be okay. I would pass on the hope that Tommy had given to me. I reached over and hugged my youngest son for all I was worth. As I released him I spoke in his ear.

"If you tell your mother what I did down here, I will disown you."

"Yeah if I'd known you were going to do that I wouldn't have helped you make the house airtight," he said as he pointed to the plastic covering the kitchen window.

Some early morning light was diffused through the opaque bag, but most of the ambient lighting came through the upper right hand corner where the bag had become detached. It was something about that little patch of light that warmed my heart, the dawning of a new day, it just felt good, new hope and all that. Believe me when I say Tommy was the only one blessed in this house with the gift of foresight. If I had known how the rest of this day was going to turn out I wouldn't have gotten up to take that damn leak.

"Hey Bear!" I heard Travis say behind me.

Sometime while I was zoning out the giant dog had made its way downstairs. Travis was busy giving the big guy an ear scratch as Bear happily finished off an Oreo that he had given him. No sooner had Bear finished the Oreo than he pivoted his head towards me. The train-like rumbling that emanated from his throat would have evacuated my bladder had I not taken care of that earlier.

"Whoa, Bear," I said as I put my hands up. If he had turned, I was screwed. I hadn't even thought to take a gun with me and my son was right next to him. "Take it easy, boy." The hair on Bear's back was standing straight up. His posture changed as he went from happy-go-lucky, to on the verge of attack, and he was looking at *me*. Trying to erase any signs of fear from my voice, not wanting to give the dog any ammunition, so to speak, I spoke to Travis. "Get up and out of here as slowly as you can. When you get to the stairs, haul ass and get help and guns." I wasn't thrilled about alerting the zombies to our presence with gunfire but that couldn't be helped at the moment. That prospect was a whole lot more appealing than having to fight off a miniature grizzly bear. Who was going to win the fight was a foregone conclusion. How long I was going to last was open to debate.

"Bear's not going to hurt you, Dad," Travis said without much conviction in his voice.

'Yeah, he's gonna kill me.' I thought sourly.

"Get out of here Trav," I said through gritted teeth. I wanted my son out of harm's way and I didn't want him to see me get ripped apart either. Bear didn't so much as blink when Travis loudly squealed his chair as he pushed away from the table. "That's a good boy, Bear."

His uncropped tail didn't move, it was pointed straight back, the slight curve gave it the appearance of a furry sword. Everything about this dog pointed to menace. Its lips pulled back to reveal inch long canines, drool flowed from its maw. Hair bristled, its haunches coiled low, ready to pounce. I needed my son to get out of here before my legs gave way. They were shaking that much. Travis had made it to the entryway in the kitchen and glanced back once to look at me. I hoped it wasn't the last time he saw me alive. As Travis rounded the corner, I heard him run up the stairs, I was guesstimating that help was ten or fifteen seconds away, Bear was positioned to strike, now. I moved slightly to my left hoping to get within range of the knife stand. Either the damn dog had extrasensory powers and knew what I was about to do or my number had finally come up. He lunged. I pushed over all the way to the left, my hand grasping wildly for anything that could be used for defense, my hand gripped tightly on a dishtowel. My brain had no true higher function. I was on the lowest plain of thought, SURVIVAL. I whipped that towel out in front of me, ready to deliver one hell of a bullwhip crack. I braced for an impact that never came. Bear had jumped up and put his large fore paws on the counter by the kitchen sink. His gaze riveted to the kitchen window. I was praising any deity that would listen for sparing my life. Help was bounding down the stairs. I looked to my hands and my ineffectual weapon and dropped it lest I got caught with it. Justin was first around the corner, .357 waving wildly, his fever-racked body barely able to hold the weapon.

"Hold on!" I said putting my hands up as I stood up and stepped in front of Bear.

I was as much in danger from that wildly swinging muzzle as Bear was. Justin looked confused. He had been sleeping soundly when the call for help had come. He wasn't even clear about where the help was to be directed. He was moving quickly from the sleeping world into the waking one but not at a speed quick enough to avert a potential disaster.

"Justin!" I yelled, "It's all right, put the gun down!" He wasn't convinced. "You sure?"

"No," I answered. "I mean, in the immediate yes, but

something is going on."

I moved slowly away from my blocking position of Bear's back. He still had not moved, his gaze fixated on the window, his muzzle pulled back in a wicked snarl. I knew what I had to do. I just didn't want to look through that window. It was an omen of bad things to come, a window into the unfathomable, a gaping wound in the fabric of humanity. Use whatever adjectives you want, it was all of those things. I climbed onto the kitchen counter. Bear managed a sidelong glance at me as I brushed past his enormously large teeth. The big bad wolf had nothing on this dog. I took a deep breath as I began to move closer to the gap caused by the bad tape job. I became enraged for a moment at who had put this bag up and their shoddy workmanship. I wanted to get down off this counter and 'give it' to whoever had not been able to tape a bag up correctly, as if this was the cause of all our ills, as if this small hole had manifested whatever demons were lying in wait outside. But I knew that was ridiculous, it was just a stalling tactic. I didn't want to see what had to be out there. It was Fritzy and he was going to exact his own revenge. I moved closer to the triangular shaped opening, convinced that a cold flat black eye would be staring back at me.

Or it could be even worse than Fritzy. The zombie girl was standing alone in my backyard signaling me to open the back door, and she wanted me to one by one send out my family and friends. She wanted me to watch as each person I loved and cherished in this world was torn asunder. She would laugh as she tore each of their throats open, drinking greedily of their lives. I shook, and Bear whined.

"What is it Mike?" Tracy asked as she came up to the counter and began absently stroking Bear's raised mane.

I shook my head trying to clear away the malignant thoughts. "Uh, I don't know." I didn't want to tell her what I imagined was out there or that I hadn't built up enough courage to look.

And in her typical pragmatic way she said. "Well

don't you think you should find out?"

I wanted to yell, 'Why don't you fucken climb up here and find out for yourself! Because I think it's either the fucken crazy guy I murdered yesterday coming back to take me with him into the seventh circle of hell or it's my zombie girlfriend come to give everyone I love the kiss of death!' But instead of the histrionics I merely answered with "Yes dear." It seemed more appropriate.

For the fourth, fifth…tenth time I took a calming deep breath. Whoever tells you that works wonders is full of crap. It did nothing but more fully oxygenate my overactive imagination, like putting gasoline on a tire fire. By now the entire population of the house was in the kitchen, armed to the gills, and all eyes were on me. I put my right eye to the hole. What I saw perplexed the hell out of me. I saw…nothing. Well I mean not exactly nothing, there was the grill, the bench swing, Henry's sunbathing couch, a snow shovel leaning up against the garage. I guess what I meant to say was there was nothing out of the ordinary. I pulled more of the bag down so I could survey the ground. The snow was as fresh as when it had fallen. There were no foreboding footsteps leading up to the backdoor, no drops of blood from a vengeful specter.

The gate had not been opened or it would have left the telltale signs in the snow. There was no valid reason as to why Bear had behaved the way he had. I was about to re-adhere the bag when I noticed a bit of snow falling. That doesn't mean too much in the middle of winter in Colorado, but the day was sunny, with not a cloud in the sky. The snow had fallen off the fence that separated my yard from Techno Neighbor's. Something had bumped up against it and in turn had knocked off some of the snow that had accumulated on the pickets and supports. I still had no reason to be overly alarmed, but Bear had already set the precedent. No sooner had the unsettled snow landed softly in my yard than the fence came crashing down into my grill, knocking it over. The noise was phenomenally loud. I hopped off the counter, not taking my eyes off the developing scene in the backyard.

"Mike, what the hell is going on?" Tracy asked. She couldn't see what was happening from her vantage point.

"Uh, zombies," I said flatly.

Zombies were pouring into my yard through the busted fence. I was half tempted to go out there and yell at them for messing up my grill. I loved that thing, the Char-Broil Master Smoker. I had paid good money for that when I was still earning a decent paycheck and to see it just get trampled like that pissed me off.

"Uh, Mike are the back doors locked?" Paul asked.

My eyes went to the back door. That was the weak link in all of this. I swore at myself for having not gotten around to fixing that. I just always assumed the gate would hold, and technically it did. It was the freaken fence that had let me down.

"Mike?" Paul asked again.

"Yeah they're locked, but they wouldn't hold back a determined woodchuck if he wanted to get in," I answered. It was time for action, not reflection. "All right everybody, grab whatever you can out of the fridge and under the cupboards and head upstairs."

Luckily not everyone gets as lost in their thoughts like I do. The kitchen was bustling with activity. Nobody stopped for more than a second or two to realize just how close the zombies were. Bear and I went into the living area to keep an eye on the back door and to also get out of the way while the kitchen was quickly emptied of food. Everyone stopped when the first body impacted with the door, their heads jerking up, their backs ramrod stiff. It looked like a pack of meercats when a threat is detected. I flipped off my safety; Bear got into his pouncing pose that I had just recently learned. "No, Bear," I admonished him. "You go with the boys." I was happy when he didn't abandon his post, but I still didn't want him here.

"Tommy!" I yelled without pulling my eyes away from the creaking door.

"Yeaf?" he asked, standing up from under the cupboards. I had to look, his arms were full of boxes of Pop-Tarts and to lighten his load he was halfway through one.

"Take Bear and yourself and go upstairs," I told him.

His face fell a little as he began to put down the Pop-Tart boxes.

"And the Pop-Tarts too," I told him.

His strawberry-laced teeth smiled brightly. "Come onf Bearf," he said.

Bear looked once at me, back at the door and headed upstairs with Tommy.

The whole doorframe shook from the next hit.

"Tracy, how much longer?" I asked, backing a step or two away from the doors.

"Couple of minutes at the most, I'm boxing up the rest of it and waiting for some help to get it upstairs."

"Don't have a couple of minutes, carry what you can now and get going."

"But..." she started.

"Hon, we won't live or die if the ramen doesn't make it up. On the other hand..." I motioned towards the door.

I received a withering look worthy of a much larger offense. I took it in stride. Zombies at the door trumped pissed off wife. Tracy had left the kitchen and I was planning on being right behind her. I had no sooner entered the kitchen when the French doors gave, typical French, must have been the same makers as the Maginot Line, 'strategically ineffective.' The doors crashed into the wall with enough force to break the drywall. Honest to God, my first thought was how much drywall repair mud did I have in the basement, again with the resale value. Zombies were coming through like Holiday shoppers on Black Friday at a Best Buy with 50 inch plasma televisions on sale. It was pandemonium. More were getting crushed than making any forward progress. I didn't help matters as the world's worst doorman. I opened fire. The .357 that I had snagged from Justin earlier was deafening in the crowded space. Four out of my five shots were kills. The fifth did more drywall damage, dammit. No bullets, no time, I was out of the kitchen, down the hallway and making the turn to go upstairs when I caught a glimpse of light brown. I halted in my tracks, one foot on the landing, one on the back hallway. Tracy was looking down from the top of the stairs.

"What are you doing Talbot?" she screamed.

"It's Henry!" I shouted back up.

Tracy loved Henry, no doubt about it. She loved him like any good dog owner should, but that's the difference between us. To her, Henry is a warm lovable, cuter than all get out, DOG. To me though, Henry was my fourth kid, well fifth now, I'm counting Tommy too. I couldn't leave him behind. No bullets, check. Zombies coming down the hallway, check. Henry under the coffee table, check. Crappy checklist, all in all. I tucked the gun in my waistband, thankful there were no more rounds in it. I'm not the smallest endowed man in the world but I still didn't feel like I had enough to spare. I ran to the coffee table and dove down. The first of the zombies had made it to the end of the hallway and was now turning into my living room. I know up to this point I have labeled Henry as this big fat mush bag. To be honest he is lazy and he does have a lot of extra skin, which makes him look fat. But he is 65 pounds of pure stubborn muscle. If he doesn't want to do something, that's pretty much the end of the discussion. I tried to pull him out from under the table. He dug his paws in. Wonderful! I had lost enough battles with him trying to trim his nails or give him a bath. It was time the home team won. I booted over the coffee table; Henry was momentarily surprised as his cover was exposed. I picked him up and threw him over my shoulder like a sack of flour. I was going to need a good chiropractor after this. Too late, three zombies were closing in, the room was only 12 by 15 and it had furniture. There weren't a lot of options for evasion. I'd like to say there was a 'face off' but the zombies take that stuff way too literally. I had to try to get out while there was still the possibility of success. I stiff armed the first one, and was about to duck under the second one's outstretched arms when the Benelli shot gun made its triumphant roar. It was the 'whoomp' and thud afterwards that had me confused. The zombie I had previously stiff-armed was crumpled in a corner. It was still moving but having a difficult time standing back up with a ruined spine, which I could see because the 12 gauge had ripped a hole through its side.

More zombies were making their way into the living room and I was only halfway across. I was waiting for the Benelli to speak up again. I looked over to the landing and saw Nicole in the process of getting back up. The shotgun had literally put her on her ass. 'Really!?'was all I could think to myself. Nicole with a shotgun was akin to a 6-year old with a lighter and gasoline, no good could come from it. I watched in fascinated horror as Nicole this time propped her back up against the wall, I wanted to shout 'don't do it' to her but it was too late. The shotgun reverberated and the only noise that could possibly be louder was Nicole's screams of pain as she dropped the shotgun with her now battered shoulder. It was over, I had five or six zombies between me and the stairs and a few were now peeling off towards Nicole. I had barred windows to my right and a knee-high wall to my left, but that room was now home to at least twenty of the foul creatures. Henry was panting like he had walked one hundred yards, which for him was a lot of exercise. I thought at one point I was bleeding but it was Henry's drool running down my back. Not a pleasant sensation. Through the crowd I saw Nicole get physically wrenched from her spot, pretty sure it was Paul or maybe Brendon, didn't matter, the only thing that registered was that my baby girl was safe. Then out of the gloom from the stairs came the familiar sound of the M-16, rounds were flying wildly. More than once I felt the heat of a shot pass by my head. I dropped down to a crouch, duck walking my way towards freedom. Justin with the M-16 was almost as scary as Nicole with the shotgun. The noise did have one bonus, the zombies forgot about me and were converging on Justin. The problem, however, was that they were going exactly where I needed to be.

Justin had gone through the 30-round magazine in as much time as it took to pull the trigger that many times. Of his thirty shots, maybe five had been kills and that was more from blind luck, nice going Rambo. But unlike Rambo he didn't have an unlimited ammo supply, he was one and done.

"Dad I'm out," Justin said with a whisper because of his flagging reserves.

Yeah I figured that when the shots went from sixty to zero in faster time than a pitcher of beer lasts at a bowling tournament. I didn't want to answer him. The zombies were fixated on him and I saw no reason to alter that. I had made my way near the front and was only one row away from getting there. Justin had headed back upstairs. I hoped he would make it all the way before I made my try for freedom. There would be no further cavalry charges. This was on me and me alone. I muscled my way past the lead two zombies. I don't know if they were more pissed off that another zombie was trying to cut in front of them or surprised to see food. The two zombies head butted each other in their excitement to get to me. No real damage was sustained but it bought me a few valuable seconds. I made it up the first third of the stairs and was looking at a quandary. Do I dare to attempt my zombie trap laden down with a squirming Henry on my shoulder? Nope. I pulled Henry off my shoulder and with my adrenaline fueled muscles, I looked up at Tracy's anxious face and heaved him at her. She went over like a bowling pin. Any other time and I would have been howling with laughter. The gambit had cost me time; I felt first one and then two hands circle my left ankle. I figured I had about two seconds until the ensuing bite. I grabbed on to the handrail for all I was worth and was simultaneously trying to pull myself away and kicking out blindly with my right foot, occasionally being rewarded with a nose crunching connection.

"Come on Mike!" Paul shouted urgently. He was

leaning over the banister with his outstretched hand. There was a good eighteen inches of distance between our connection.

"Dad, behind you!" Nicole screamed in pure panic.

Now was not the time for sarcasm, but REALLY!? Tracy had recovered from her bowling accident and had my Ka-Bar knife out. She looked me in the eyes as she placed the sharp edge against my pinion ropes. A swift pull of the knife would send me and the zombies plunging into the basement. She was going to give me the benefit of the doubt but only if it was soon. My foot lashed out again and suddenly I was free. I felt fingernails tear as they tried in vain to re-obtain purchase on my pants. I was one step above the trap when Tracy cut the ropes. Vertigo, adrenaline and fear made me sway. Paul quickly grabbed my shoulder, preventing me from joining the two zombies that had made the Nestea plunge. The zombies weren't dead, not even seriously injured as they looked back up at the hole from where they had come, but they weren't upstairs and obviously that was the most important part.

"Holy crap, that was close!" I said as I regained my composure and got to the top of the stairs.

"For Christ's sake Mike, it's only a dog. You risked your life and your kids for a damn dog!" she yelled.

My triumph was short-lived as I sat down on the top stoop and realized how close to disaster this situation had come. As any good ally should, Henry came over and licked my face. Inwardly I smiled. It had all been worth it.

CHAPTER 26
Journal Entry - 23

The constant 'thudding' of zombies falling into my trap was unnerving. We were all on edge. The only thing that broke the monotony of the 'thud' was the bubble wrapping 'snap' of the occasional limb being broken. A guard had to be posted but I made sure everyone was clear on the use of bullets: 'Only when necessary.' I had seen what the rampant discharge of bullets had done at the wall. Before we knew it our stair hole would be filled with zombies and the dead would bridge the gap to us. As it was, the fallen zombies were having a hard enough time clearing out of the way before their brethren fell on them. I relieved Erin after only an hour into her two hour shift, just to get out of my office. The mood was not good. What I thought the zombies were going to do to change that was beyond me. Henry had come with me. He hadn't left my side since his rescue. I'm sure he knew just how close he had been to becoming a meal. And I'm not sure, but I think that he was getting a bad feeling from Tracy. If I had saved him from the zombies then I would surely save him from the mad boss woman, little did *he* know.

It was comical to watch the exaltation on the zombies' faces as they thought they were nearing their prize, and then the shock as they fell through the stairs. With nothing else to do, I kept track of a couple of the zombies as they made their circuitous route from falling, to recovery, to climbing back up the basement stairs, to attempting the second flight of stairs once more. One was in his early thirties, wearing what was at one time a nice Armani suit and now wouldn't fetch a dollar fifty at Savers. He wore one wing tipped shoe, a red argyle sock, and his other foot was bare. His tie was off and the first two top buttons of his shirt were undone. The guy had probably been unwinding at Hooters after a hard day at work when he had ceased to care about stocks and bonds or accounting or selling insurance. No, the suit was too nice for that. He was probably a lawyer when he checked out from the human race. He seemed one of the more determined of the bunch to get at me and registered the biggest surprise when he 'fell' short of his goal. I dubbed him 'Go-getter Gilbert'. He was averaging eight minutes from fall, to recovery, to fall. Another zombie I had been keeping an eye on, 'Dumpy Dorothy,' was maybe in her late forties, early fifties. She was dressed in an undersized moo-moo, pink slippers, and in what remained of her hair were curlers. She was taking noticeably longer to make the circuitous route. She was right around twenty-two minutes. Maybe she was stopping to snack or check out the new book of the day by Oprah. Gilbert was making his sixth trip, almost lapping Dorothy again, when he changed his routine. He stood at the bottom of the landing, looked up at me, looked at the hole, all the while being jostled by zombies who were passing him up. I was intrigued. I stood up to get a better view of him. He followed me with his eyes; the dim light of intelligence was unnerving.

"Fuck this," I muttered. I shouldered my rifle and took aim but suddenly he was gone.

Nothing else stopped. The zombies kept climbing, the zombies kept falling, but Gilbert never came back. He had unnerved me. I wasn't expecting him to come back with a homemade ladder, but he had recognized the futility of this avenue. My sincerest hope was that he had gone on in search of easier prey and not away around my defenses. Dumpy Dorothy had made one more trip around, this time with a noticeable limp, before my shift was over. I was thankful to get back to the office, the inside of the house was easily as cold as the outside given the back doors were not even attached anymore. The office wasn't a whole bunch warmer. My thoughts of us holding out for three months or so seemed overly optimistic at this point. Nobody was talking, even the ever jovial Tommy was pressed into the corner of the room, face towards the wall with Bear in his arms. I could tell that his chest was heaving and I thought he might be crying. I left him alone. If he wanted to be consoled he wouldn't have been facing away.

I grabbed a book off my bookshelf that I had been reading before this mess had started. It was called After Twilight, I laughed out loud. That got me some annoyed looks from those around me. It was a zombie book. I hummed the book across the room, the noise blending in with the latest pitfall victim. I was stewing, wallowing in my own self-pity I guess, when Nicole called out to me.

"Hey Dad, you should probably come see this," she said. "I was in your bathroom and I was coming out and I noticed something strange."

'Stranger than zombies in our house?' I wanted to shout. It's not her fault, Talbot, relax!

It was go see what was 'strange' or stay here and be miserable. I got up.

Coley grabbed my hand, something she hadn't done since she was 12 and went from being Daddy's little girl to some hormone-infused alien. That made me even more concerned. She led me into the bedroom, so far so good. On the left was our king-size bed, on the right was a dresser with a 25" television. The dresser and the television were against the wall we shared with dearly departed Techno Guy. She led me around to the other side of the television and then just pointed. In the gloom I still didn't see anything. She pulled the shades open and peeled back the plastic covering, I saw a dark, blackish-red stain about the size of a bowling ball about three feet up on the wall. Even as I was watching, it was expanding. Unease descended on me like a heavy rain. I didn't know what it meant or what it was but that it wasn't good was clear enough to me.

I kept looking at the expanding stain. "Everyone up!" I yelled. I didn't hear any signs of sound other than our tripping guests. "I said, EVERYONE UP!" I bellowed this part like I hadn't bellowed since I had been in the Marine Corps. This time I heard the satisfactory sound of shifting people, live people that is.

"What is it?" Tracy asked from the doorway, wiping the sleep from her eyes.

Bear and Tommy were behind her. Tommy was clearly trying to rub the tears out of his eyes, fruitlessly I might add. It looked like he had been pouring it on.

"I'm not sure," I answered Tracy, keeping my eyes on Tommy.

He knew something, and he wasn't telling. That couldn't be good by any stretch of the imagination. His eyes trailed to the stain, even though from his vantage point he couldn't see it.

"The attic," I said.

"What?" Came Tracy's reply.

"Get everyone in the attic!" my concern raising my voice.

Nobody was moving with a speed I felt the moment warranted. There were moans and groans of protest about being uprooted. Paul had managed to get the stepladder out of the hall closet that was used primarily for getting into the attic. When he had put the ladder in place and pushed the hatch open he was greeted with a blast of super cold infused air.

"Mike, are you sure about this?" Paul shouted from the hallway. "The attic makes the rest of the house seem like the Bahamas."

As if in reply a loud cracking noise ensued from the bedroom. A two-by-four had just been broken. The drywall on my side bulged dangerously outward. The zombies were using the only tactic they knew, overwhelming by sheer numbers. There must have been dozens of zombies on the other side of this wall just pressing with all their weight. The liquid on my wall was the seepage of the zombies that were being pressed hard enough to be juiced like an orange; a blood orange. I backed away. When the wall finally went it wasn't going to be subtle. It would be like someone had opened the floodgates.

"Paul there had better be three people up there already!" I shouted.

I jumped when I realized he was behind me. "What's going on?" he asked. "I heard the crack."

"It's the wall! Get everyone up in the attic."

He looked at me for a moment longer. His cold-addled brain was working overtime to grasp the situation. A white dust covered hand broke through. Paul didn't need any more evidence. He was off like a shot. I could hear the commotion behind me as Tracy, Paul and Erin were debating the merits of what should go up in the attic.

"No time, guys!" I shouted as I fired my first round into the forehead of the interloper. It did little to stop the tidal surge of zombies as the one foot gap in the wall quickly became three feet.

The dresser and the TV came crashing down; never did like that TV. Bought it on Craigslist for $100, should have talked them down to $50, oh well now I could get a flat screen. You think I'm kidding, right? My mind was having such an unbelievably difficult time reasoning with the fact that zombies were busting through my bedroom wall it became much easier to regale in the mundane. Thankfully though, my reflexes weren't hampered by the same problems. My Marine Corps honed combat skills were in full effect, aim, breathe, squeeze, reacquire target, aim, breath, squeeze, reacquire.

Between shots I was inching my way backwards, yielding as little ground as possible, but the sheer press of numbers had me constantly moving.

"Paul, I need an update!" I yelled, as I dropped a zombie no further than two feet away.

"All the kids are up, Tracy's getting water!" was the reply.

I had been pushed out of the bedroom and was two

feet away from the top of the stairs. I lost valuable time as I reloaded the M-16. My first shot struck the ground as a zombie batted the barrel away in an attempt to get to me. I collapsed my tactical stock, making the M-16 much more easy to wield in the increasingly tight space.

"Tracy, you're about to make orphans, GET UP THERE NOW!" I shredded my throat trying to get my point across.

I backed up some more, making short work of the zombie that had the audacity to block my shot, but the ground given was my last. The heel of my right foot rested on nothing, I was at the edge of the stairs. There would be no further retreat. Zombies in front, zombies behind, and many bullets to shoot before I died.

"Bear, come on!" Paul yelled from the ladder. "Mike, everyone's up except for Bear, me and you."

I heard Bear come up beside me, his menacing bulk and deep growl made for a welcome ally. I moved to my left to get to the ladder before all means of retreat were cut off. Too late! In my haste to watch my precarious footing, a zombie had ensnared himself in my sling. I would have given him the damn thing if I wasn't so tangled myself. I couldn't even bring it up to shoot. So this is how it ends. I had always expected something a little more dignified, but in those last few seconds the revelation hit me. What could be more dignified then dying in defense of one's own family and friends? Bear felt the same way. He launched himself at my assailant, bringing all three of us down into a Twister Game Gone Bad pile. The barrel of my gun was all that kept the zombie from tearing into my face. I kept it between us like a fat guy would keep a box of Twinkies between him and a personal trainer. Bear was ripping and rending the zombie from the back, pulling his head further and further away from me. I pushed up with the gun to give the massive dog some help. I began to squirm out from the pile when Bear placed his colossal jaws around the zombie's head and crushed it easier than I would have been able to crush a Coke can with

294

my hands. The zombie's eyes flew out, striking me in the chest. Diseased gray black brain matter leaked out of its mouth and nose. I was already in overdrive to get out from under him; I now found another gear.

I had finally freed myself when I felt another hand on my shoulder. I couldn't catch a break. I jerked my arm trying to break free.

"It's me, dude," Paul said reassuringly. "Come on man, let's go!"

I was at the foot of the ladder. Bear was the only thing that stood between us and death. Paul pulled me up to my feet.

"Bear, come on!" I yelled raggedly.

I knew it was futile and somehow so did Bear. If he retreated now, most likely all three of us would die. There was more going on here than just a zombie attack. What it was I hoped to live long enough to find out.

Tommy poked his head through the opening. "Bye, Bear," he sobbed, his tears striking me in the face.

Bear turned around and looked at Tommy and then me. I will swear to this day that he was smiling as he gave me a slight nod of his head. And then this thought was implanted into my head: 'Don't make me die for nothing.'

Paul must have received the same broadcast. He jumped up and grabbed the lip of the opening and hauled himself up, turning around and thrusting his hand down to help. Didn't need it. With all the adrenaline I had flowing, I could have jumped from the first floor and made it. I closed the lid, not wanting to see Bear's final stand. Tommy had pushed as far away from all of us as he could, grieving in his own way. Bear never whined, yelped or barked, for that I am thankful. That would have been too much; no matter the consequences I would have descended into the maelstrom to help.

CHAPTER 27
Journal Entry - 24

The loud crack from below, which I could only conceive of as Bear's demise, was immediately followed by a debilitating piercing through my skull. I rolled onto my side, hands thrust up to cover my ears, as if that was going to do anything. That gesture was about as useful as giving the finger to a blind man. The feeling was tantamount to drinking the world's largest Slurpee in world record time on the hottest day of summer. It was a brain freeze delivered on a heated ice pick. White flashes arced across my vision. It was long tense moments before I realized that I hadn't had a stroke and that I wasn't blind. As the effects agonizingly wore away I slowly sat up, rubbing my temples and looking around. Everyone in our small group was in some state of recuperation from this attack.

"What…what was that?" Brendon said holding his hand to his forehead, trying to find the entry hole the ice pick had made.

As the last shadows of the electrical storm in my brain petered out, I shifted my gaze to Tommy. He wore a grim expression on his face, but it wasn't from pain, at least not the same pain that had afflicted the rest of us. A few ideas about what could have caused this were bantered around, including the change in temperature, but I knew the answer. Well not exactly, I knew who had caused it, I just didn't know why.

A few hours later our small band of survivors were huddled in the center of the attic, trying in vain to conserve our body heat. It was quiet except for the constant chattering of teeth and floorboards creaking below us. This was to be our final resting place, enshrouded in pink r-16 fiberglass. It seemed fitting given the circumstances. The only thing I hated more than fiberglass was sticking forks in my eyes, you get the point. I was slipping in and out of sleep. The soft light of dawn began to trickle in through the eaves. The tinny sound of Jingle Bells heralded in the new day. I must be slipping into a coma, I mused, well what better place than the North Pole.

"Wha...what is that?" Travis gabbled.

I had been under the impression the noise was only in my head I was too fogged out from the cold to realize that it was external. I lured myself back from the abyss, my hands shaking as I reached into my pocket. It was my Blackberry, I had set the alarm after Thanksgiving to alert me to get up and make Christmas breakfast.

"Everyone get up," I said shaking those who didn't stir. If I had been that close to perpetual sleep than so were the rest. I kept shaking them. "Get up, it's Christmas."

I don't know why I felt so jubilant, the last Christmas miracle I had heard of happened two thousand and ten years ago. Everyone had finally stirred and was looking at me with mixed results. Some irked that I had awoken them, others thankful, but all were wondering why I wore that idiotic grin. Tommy was still mourning Bear but apparently my grin was infectious because he began to don one himself.

"What's going on here Talbot?" Paul asked.

"Yeah," Erin piped in. "Do you know something we don't?" she asked as she breathed warm air into her cold hands. Her movements were restricted from the bear hug she was enclosed in from Paul.

"Nothing's going on," I intoned, much to the chagrin of the crowd. "It's just that it's Christmas, we're alive."

"For how long?" Tracy threw in. I ignored the comment.

"I could go for some bacon," Travis said.

"Oh yeah, and some of those cream cheese stuffed rolls Mom makes," Nicole added.

"I could go for a beer," Justin said, pulling his head

off the floor. I looked at him sternly but secretly that sounded good. Lord knows that we were living in a refrigerator. We should get the benefit of its contents.

We passed a good portion of the day relating some of our fondest Christmas stories, even some of the worst, which elicited a lot of laughs. Tommy heard the noise first and pointed over to the eaves. I was about to ask him what he was pointing at and then the rest of us started picking it up, faint at first.

"Does that sound like bells to anyone?" I asked incredulously.

"Yeah it's Santa," Tracy said sarcastically. She was having the toughest time throwing off her cloak of pessimism.

"That's not bells," Brendon said, "I lived long enough up in the mountains to tell that sound. It's chains, tire chains," he clarified excitedly.

The tire chain sound was immediately followed by the incessantly strong thrum of a large diesel engine and then a blaring horn. Whoever it was, wasn't trying to hide their presence.

"Everyone, cover your ears," I said as I grabbed the Benelli. It took three ear-blasting shots, from which I would lose a fair measure of hearing, before sunlight streamed in from above.

The hole was big enough for me to fit my head through, even with my inflated ego. I could see the giant semi heading up here from the direction of the clubhouse. It was slow going as it pushed zombies away with its giant plow. The truck body herked and jerked, whether from the contact with the zombies or an inexperienced driver I couldn't tell. I didn't care how Santa got here, just as long as he was on the way.

"What is it?" came the consensus questions from the attic.

"It's Alex' beautiful modified truck," I shouted down triumphantly.

"Is it coming here?" Tracy asked hopefully.

I had just assumed it was, but there was no real reason to believe that. It was time to give it one.

"All right everyone, cover your ears again." Two more blasts later and I had managed to get half my body through the hole. I felt like a cork in a wine bottle.

Paul had come up behind me. "Ever hear of Atkins, fat boy?" he asked sarcastically.

"Wonderful, everyone needs a smart ass, now push me through," I said sourly.

Paul and Brendon each grabbed one of my legs and pushed. I popped out like a Mentos in Diet Coke. For one fateful second I thought I was going to tumble off the roof and into the gaggle of zombies below. Paul poked his head through just in time to see me come to a stop a mere foot away from the edge of the roof. The six inches of snow more than likely saved my life. If I had hit a clean roof, I would have bounced once and gone over the edge.

"Whoo, that was close," Paul said, color coming back to his features.

I gingerly crawled back up to the hole. "You're telling me."

The horn blared again and the lights flashed on. No need to worry about being seen. The truck ambled up on to the lawn and stopped directly in front of our house. The window rolled down a few inches. Because of the way the light reflected off the glass, I still couldn't make out who it was.

"Hey Gringo!" Alex shouted. "I knew your white ass was too tough for the zombies to eat."

"Good to see you, my friend," I said in vast relief. I felt like I had been holding it together fairly well, but the safety of my kids had my stress meter pegged. I finally felt like I could let the meter drop a notch or two. Although we were still far from safety at least now we had an option. "What are you doing here, I heard you pulling out when this thing started."

"Damnedest thing!" Alex shouted. "I got this piercing pain in my head and then a message. I figured it was an angel telling me to save your Gringo ass. I just want you to know when you get down here and into the truck don't expect a welcome wagon from my wife. She hasn't spoken to me since I turned this thing around."

Tommy had stuck his head through the makeshift exit hole, smiling, strawberry Pop-Tart smeared across his face.

"How, Tommy?" I said too softly for even my own ears to pick up. He was still smiling. I don't know if I was asking how he summoned help or how he found a Pop-Tart.

"Happy Christmas, Mr. T," Tommy waved. He was chagrined as a piece of his prized possession flung off his hand and into the snow. Again I had enough questions to flood Wikipedia for a month, but Alex's next words brought my attention back around.

"How many of you are there?" Alex asked as tactfully as he could.

"Nine, my friend. Nine," I said jubilantly. "And you?" I asked hopefully.

I received the universal thumbs up sign. "And thirteen more. I have handholds on the top, can you jump down?" Alex asked.

The truck trailer came up to just about the level of the second floor. Hanging down from the gutters, provided they held, would make the drop about two feet from shoe to roof. I couldn't get the image of bouncing off the truck like rice on a drum out of my head. Vertigo had set in. I plopped on my butt. It seemed a safer bet than pitching over headfirst. The ladders would have been perfect right about now; unfortunately they were safely stowed away in the master bedroom.

"I'll go first," Paul said.

He inched down to the edge of the roof and then placed his right foot on the gutter and planted it. This allowed him to turn his body over. He slid feet first on his stomach, ever closer to the edge. I had a momentary irrational fear that I would never see him again. He was now just hands and a face, Kilroy with a beard. Then came the solid thud of contact.

"I'm good, bud. Start sending everyone else, and have them bring the rope," Paul shouted.

My vertigo had eased but I was not yet ready to stand. Justin came through first, swaying to a beat almost matching my dizziness. Brendon passed Henry to him, nearly toppling him over. I scrambled to help Justin sit down on the roof in a controlled manner. Brendon apologized for his lack of foresight. Travis was next bringing some rope, followed by Tommy.

"Okay that's enough for now," I said through my circling haze, my fear being that if everyone was on the roof and someone lost their balance it would look like a bowling alley, and a strike would not be good right now.

"Justin, get yourself onto the truck. I'll hand the rope down, you two get secured, and then I'll send Tommy and then Henry." I wanted Justin tied to something. His ashen features were not inspiring comfort.

Alex was watching over our egress off the roof and onto the truck with apprehension. Zombies had encircled the truck and were making a concerted effort to get into the rear where the survivors were. His wife Marta was sitting next to him and was gazing up at the roof, impatience radiating from her. It was when she spotted someone familiar that all other feelings were erased.

"Tommy?" she shouted.

"Hi Aunt Marta," Tommy waved enthusiastically. "Want a Pop-Tart?"

I don't know whose jaw dropped more, mine, Marta's or Alex'. I just wished I had five full minutes to think this out, but our zombie hosts were not being overly gracious. If we didn't leave now we might never get out. Within fifteen minutes we were all secured onto the top of the semi, the only close call coming when I tossed Henry down. He did not appreciate the gesture whatsoever and was squirming like a five-year-old in a dentist's chair when Paul and Brendon caught him. Paul's left foot briefly hovered in midair. The only thing keeping him from becoming Gravy Train for the zombies was the ½ inch mountaineer rope around his waist.

"See, Talbot!" Paul yelled. "This is just one more reason I hate dogs!"

I looked longingly back at the house I knew without a shadow of a doubt I would never see again. It wasn't my dream home but it was home. We had shared a lot of laughter and love here. The past was laid to rest, good memories tucked in with bad. From the known to the unknown we would travel. Only God knew the outcome and He was on hiatus.

So ends the first Journal in the Zombie Fallout Trilogy. Look soon for excerpts from the second Journal and the further alternate realities of Michael Talbot.

Epilogue

The Canadian Incident

Just a moment's preface on this, I'm going to include the actual story as reported in the Denver Post, page 23. (By the way, who reads that far into the newspaper?) I'm going to follow it up with what REALLY happened.

Local Man Accused of Smuggling Booze – Feb 23, 2000
As Reported by Aria Manuel

In what can only be described as an international incident harkening back to the days of moonshine runners and gun toting mobsters, local man Michael Talbot was arrested early Sunday morning on the Canadian – Vermont border. Michael, who was traveling with his wife and three small children, apparently used as cover, was pulled over by the border patrol on the Canadian side for a routine inspection before entering back into the United States.

Eyewitness Captain MacIntosh of the Royal Mounted Police had this to say. "So I motioned the accused to pull over so we could check his vehicle for any undeclared and illegal substances. We periodically choose cars at random to look for contraband. I noticed straight away the accused was extremely agitated and was becoming more hostile by the moment. When Mr. Talbot refused to get out of the car I had two of my deputies assist him. At this point Mr. Talbot became belligerent and punched one of the deputies in the nose, next thing I know he has PM Leonard in a choke hold."

The Captain is referring to Prime Minister Charles C. Leonard the Third who was returning from New York City after attending a conference to improve trade relations between our two proud nations. The Prime Minister had stopped into the barracks on the Canadian side to see how his troops were holding up in the harsh weather the region had been experiencing recently.

"Somehow in the confusion, Mr. Talbot had obtained one of my deputy's tasers and repeatedly pressed it into the PM's side, I guess to keep him from getting away. Eventually some concerned citizens tackled Mr. Talbot from the back. The PM only suffered some minor injuries including a broken nose. Mr. Talbot was detained and his car searched. We found a trailer full of beer and a bag of marijuana. Mr. Talbot is being charged with smuggling, possession of drugs, kidnapping, resisting arrest, and assault. All of these penalties combined could mean a term of 25 years to life in our prison colonies."

This incident sparked anger and outrage all across Canada as residents wanted to shut all borders to their rude and hostile southern neighbors. After further questioning and removal of the 'evidence,' Michael Talbot's family was free to return to Colorado where they will await a trial date for their head of household who will remain in Canadian custody indefinitely.

Now for the 'true' version. Oh and by the way the retraction the Denver Post said they were going to print got bumped for a JC Penney ad, women's shoes I think, way more important than my exoneration. (They lost my subscription FOREVER, and the Internet is much more up-to-date than that aging newspaper)

Okay, calm down Talbot. I'll start from the beginning. Ever been in the car with three small children? If so, enough said. If not, just wait your turn, it's coming. So the ride from Montreal to the border is somewhere in the hour and a half range and the kids in the backseat are going at it like there's a championship trophy on the line. We're still a couple of hours drive away from this awesome little bed and breakfast in Vermont where I had made reservations. We were on a family vacation that included stops in North Dakota (don't ask, relatives on her side. I wouldn't have stopped there if the car was on fire), Montreal, Vermont and then on to New Orleans before heading home. Tracy and I thought it would be a great experience to have the kids see the country by car ride, dumb asses that we were. So we were approaching the Canadian Border and there is a line easily a quarter mile long. The CRMP weren't 'randomly' checking cars like their illustrious Captain said. They were checking every last one of them. I swear to this day it was a ploy for us to spend our money at their crappy little gift store before we hit the good old US of A. Yeah, couldn't wait to buy a stupid stuffed moose that cost $22 and is made in China to put on my knick-knack shelf. So we're sitting in the car for another hour and a half, easy. The kids have ratcheted up their squabbling to new and unusual heights. I'm a half-inch, or if you use the Canadian conversion, 1.25 centimeters away from blowing my stack. I had turned over my right shoulder to tell the kids for the four hundredth and seventy sixth time to SHUT UP. Okay, 'be quiet' for you non-capital punishment types. Suddenly Captain Custard comes knocking on my window with a flashlight. It was 10:00 in the morning. The sun was out for Fuck's sake.

"What!" I yelled at him as I rolled the window down.

"Farkin Yankees, think they own the world! Step out of the car!" he shouted back.

Being from Boston I take serious offense to anyone accusing me of being a Yankee. Now deep down I know he didn't mean it in the sports sense, but I was already irked to my limit and I let my mouth slip.

"Go Fark yourself!" I said back, borrowing his accent. He wasn't amused. He motioned over to two deputies who came over and pulled me out through the window. They mashed my shoulder and then more importantly my 'junk' into the car door, and then unceremoniously deposited me on the ground. They laughed as they saw the damage the frozen dirty slush water did to my expensive jacket. I was indignant. Without even thinking I grabbed two handfuls of this dirty slush water and heaved it into the face of the unsuspecting deputy on the left; he also was not amused. I scrambled to get up as I saw him reaching for his Taser. I had been hit with one of those once, on a dare in college, and I was not going to let it happen again. I had regained my feet and was heading for the only cover I could think of, the crappy little gift store.

I could hear the deputy behind me wrestling with his Taser and ordering me to halt. I had just passed some man who, I was able to notice even in this awkward moment, had on a more expensive jacket than I did. I would have liked to ask him where he had gotten it but it didn't seem prudent, given the circumstances. I had no sooner passed by this man, when out of the corner of my eye he started to collapse. I could see the two Taser leads hanging out from the front of his jacket. Maybe just a little higher than his stomach. I knew that shot was meant for me and felt guilty this man had 'taken one' for me. I stopped and got behind him, holding him up before he had fully dropped. His body was spasming from the current being forced into him from the bad aiming, forgetful deputy. The idiot was still holding down the discharge button even though he had the wrong person. By the time he had finally registered his error, the man in my arms was near to passing out.

In the meantime his partner, Deputy Dumber, had let fly his Taser prongs. They caught the man I would later learn was the prime minister in the cheek, and not the round curvy kind but the one on the side of his face. His teeth chattered from the shock. Before he fully slipped out of my arms and onto the ground, I smelled the telltale sign of a man who had unwillingly lost consciousness. His bowels released like a torrent. I almost threw up over his expensive cashmere jacket. As I gently laid the man down, realizing there was nothing more I could do for him, I stumbled over a small child exiting the bathroom and fell over. Deputy Dipshit and his partner were on me in a heartbeat. Even while I was being wrestled into handcuffs, I noticed the leggy blond administering to the man on the ground. I would have had to be in *his* condition not to notice her. She was smoking hot and half his age. As for the 'trailer full of beer,' well that would have been some neat trick considering I didn't have a trailer; it was three cases of Molson Canadian. So you're saying to yourself, why bother, you can get that in the States. Well, the answer to that is yes and no. You can get Molson Canadian, but number one it's not as fresh, and number two, Canada brews its beers under different regulations. It has a stronger alcohol content and it just tastes better. If you've never had beer in Canada then that is something you should put on your 'bucket list,' that is if they are still making beer since the zombpocalypse. As for the 'bag of weed,' their version of CSI or The Anal Retentive Squad as I like to call them, had to use tweezers and a magnifying glass to pull out this minuscule piece of a roach embedded in my carpet from who knows when. If there were two shreds of marijuana leaf in that thing I would have been amazed. So the deputies couldn't back down; the idiots had twice tased their leader and that wasn't going to look good on their permanent records. Better to fry an innocent than lose your pension. I sat in jail for over forty-eight hours before all charges against me were dropped. The reason? Well you know how I had been telling you that my kids were fighting? Well it seems they were fighting over using the video camera. Who knew? Justin caught the whole thing on tape: First the cops overreacting and pulling me out of the car, the whole taser fiasco and the coup de grace, the leggy blonde (who by the way was not the Prime Minister's wife). Everyone felt it was in everyone else's best interest if the whole case was dismissed. I, however, was still pissed about losing the three cases of beer. The trip was over when I got released from jail. Tracy was furious that I had put on that kind of display in front of the kids. They, on the other hand, thought it was cool. The ride back to Colorado was monotonous. The kids didn't even fight. They were too scared. Tracy was melting the car seats with the anger that exuded from her. I broke a ton of land speed records getting back home, the quicker to be out of arms length and harm's way. It all worked out in the end, and Tracy eventually forgave me, but she never did forget. I bought Justin a Nintendo GameCube for his excellent film work.

"Eliza's coming and death trembles in her wake!"
As recorded by Mike Talbot's wife as he lay tossing and turning in a semi-state of sleep.

Check out these other titles by Mark Tufo

Zombie Fallout 2: A Plague Upon Your Family

Zombies have destroyed Little Turtle, the Talbot's find themselves on the run from a ruthless enemy that will stop at nothing to end their lineage. Here are the journal entries of Michael Talbot, his wife Tracy, their three kids Nicole, Justin and Travis. With them are Brendon, Nicole's fiancée and Tommy previously a Wal-Mart door greeter who may be more than he seems. Together they struggle against a relentless enemy that has singled them out above all others. As they travel across the war-torn country side they soon learn that there are more than just zombies to be fearful of, with law and order a long distant memory some humans have decided to take any and all matters into their own hands. Can the Talbots come through unscathed or will they suffer the fate of so many countless millions before them. It's not just brains versus brain-eaters anymore. And the stakes may be higher than merely life and death with eternal souls on the line.

Zombie Fallout 3: The End...

Continues Michael Talbot's quest to be rid of the evil named Eliza that hunts him and his family across the country. As the world spirals even further down into the abyss of apocalypse one man struggles to keep those around him safe. Side by side Michael stands with his wife, their children, his friends and the wonder Bulldog Henry along with the Wal-Mart greeter Tommy who is infinitely more than he appears and whether he is leading them to salvation or death is only a measure of degrees.

As Justin continues to slip further into the abyss he receives help from an unexpected ally all of which leads up to the biggest battle thus far.

Dr. Hugh Mann – A Zombie Fallout Prequel 3.5

Dr Hugh Mann delves deeper into what caused the zombie invasion. Early in the 1900's Dr. Mann discovers a parasite that brings man to the brink of an early extinction. Come along on the journey with Jonathan Talbot is bride to be Marissa and the occasional visitations from the boy with the incredible baklava. Could there be a cure somewhere here and what part does the blood locket play?

Zombie Fallout IV: The End...Has Come and Gone

The End...has come and gone. This is the new beginning, the new world order and it sucks. The end for humanity came the moment the U.S. government sent out the infected flu shots. My name is Michael Talbot and this is my journal. I'm writing this because no one's tomorrow is guaranteed, and I have to leave something behind to those who may follow.

So continues Mike's journey, will he give up all that he is in a desperate bid to save his family and friends? Eliza is coming, can anyone be prepared?

Indian Hill

This first story is about an ordinary boy, who grows up in relatively normal times to find himself thrust into an extra-ordinary position. Growing up in suburban Boston he enjoys the trials and tribulations that all adolescents go through. From the seemingly tyrannical mother, to girl problems to run-ins with the law. From there he escapes to college out in Colorado with his best friend, Paul, where they begin to forge new relationships with those around them. It is one girl in particular that has caught the eye of Michael and he alternately pines for her and then laments ever meeting her.

It is on their true 'first' date that things go strangely askew. Mike soon finds himself captive aboard an alien vessel, fighting for his very survival. The aliens have devised gladiator type games. The games are of two-fold importance for the aliens. One reason, being for the entertainment value, the other reason being that they want to see how combative humans are, what our weaknesses and strengths are.

Follow Mike as he battles for his life and Paul as he battles to try and keep main stream US safe.

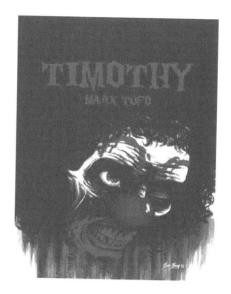

Timothy was not a good man in life being undead did little to improve his disposition. Find out what a man trapped in his own mind will do to survive when he wakes up to find himself a zombie controlled by a self-aware virus.

Please look also for:
the story '**My Name is Riley**' published in the
Undead Tales Anthology by Rymfire books!

Follow Riley an American Bulldog as she struggles to
keep what remains of her pack/family safe from a zombie
invasion.